The reader might choose to consider "Judith Beheading Holofernes," the title Kevin Kilroy selects for one of the two novellas in his new novel, to best appreciate the architecture that is *The Chicago Window*. Kilroy, himself the sacker of Collage Novel grids, He portrays Holofernes, the notorious threat to Judith's city, as a powerful "urban planner." Is Kilroy calling attention to the incongruity of his own vision of architectural beauty and the Chicago grid—he is, after all, the sacker of the planned Collage Novel—when he writes, as if seduced by a Judith of his own creation: "But their juxtaposition—I do love how they look next to each other, this elsewhere…and this here, what we occupy now"? A walk along The Fortress of Bethulia clears the narrator's head before he loses it: "[T]here are more ways than one to exit a building…It was as if the map had initially been accurate, and then corroded into this carnival of deformed imagination which I stared at now." In Metcalf's *Genoa*, in the time before the corrosion, the apogee for the great Collage Novel is on record along with Judith's biblical addresses. For decades, writers inspired by the monumental architecture of Cortázar and Perec have worked at making a cultural industry of drawing up architectonic blueprint novels with trap doors and no windows. Alas, after Cortázar and Perec, most of the writers tear down the structures of collage only to erect their own elaborate puzzles (mirroring *Hopscotch*) or tricks (retro-Life: *A User's Manual*); some of the newest high-rises are built to fall apart, fractal by fractal, style by style (Mallo's *Nocillo Trilogy*, Mitchell's *Cloud Atlas*). Vines, graphic novels, digital humanities, and flash fiction—like a working Gutenberg printing machine created by a 3D printer—are not revolutionary. Kilroy can make his contemporaries sound like the humorless instructor who cannot see Zeno's paradoxes for exacting parodies of logic taken to the extreme. I realize reading *Chicago Window* gave me a sensation I'd felt before, always aware of the unseen ocean, on first encountering Sebald's *Vertigo*—here is a writer who has never abandoned the ambition to write the novel.

RICHARD BLEVINS, AUTHOR OF *PLANTING THE HOUSE*

THE Chicago Window

KEVIN KILROY

In the Penal Colony,
Moby Grape,
&

Judith Beheading Holofernes

SPUYTEN DUYVIL
NEW YORK CITY

ACKNOWLEDGEMENTS

In admiration of Gentileschi's and Caravaggio's *Judith Beheading Holofernes*, Kafka's *In the Penal Colony*, Moby Grape and their albums, *The Bible*, Walter Benjamin's *The Arcades Project*, Werner Herzog's *Conquest of the* Useless, and Michel Foucault's *The History of Madness*. To Richard Nickel for the cover photo, for Chicago, for folding then upon now. Loving thanks to Michael Ciapciak for showing me refinement, the woman in The Yellow Book for alluring me so, Leesaw Andaloro for the room where much of this was written one cold January at Tigermen Den in New Orleans. To Atomix Café, where *In the Penal Colony* began. To Jonata Vineyards, where *Moby Grape* began. To Sue Dinko for your $150 office at the Northwest Tower where *Judith Beheading Holofernes* began. To Charlotte Street Foundation where this work was completed during my Studio Residency. To Tod Thilleman and Spuyten Duyvil Press—thank you for seeing the value of my work. To Alyssa—thank you for loving me. For Matt Dees, a genius and a friend, for everything you turned me on to.

ISBN 978-1-949966-90-9

Library of Congress Cataloging-in-Publication Data

Names: Kilroy, Kevin, author.
Title: The Chicago window : In the penal colony, Moby grape & Judith
   beheading Holofernes / Kevin Kilroy.
Description: New York City : Spuyten Duyvil, [2020] |
Identifiers: LCCN 2020031161 | ISBN 9781949966909 (paperback)
Subjects: LCSH: Chicago (Ill.)--Fiction. | Gentrification--Fiction. |
   LCGFT: Novellas. | Novels.
Classification: LCC PS3611.I45284 C48 2020 | DDC 813/.6--dc23
LC record available at https://lccn.loc.gov/2020031161

The Chicago Window is structured similar to the eponymous architectural phenomenon: two double-hung sash novellas flanking a fixed center novel. The three panes include: *Moby Grape, In the Penal Colony,* and *Judith Beheading Holofernes.*

In the Penal Colony

On September 1st, 2001, as if god had pulled a bottle of La Sangre from Humboldt Park Lagoon, fourteen residents escaped from The Fortress of Bethulia. On the corner of Pierce and Leavitt of Chicago's near northwest side, The Fortress was originally built to serve as a hospital for those injured in the Great Chicago Fire of 1871. This halfway house had come to serve the crazed and delirious, the drug fiends and the perverts, the blasphemous and the desperate. The proper city officials set to work. No one wanted madness where it did not belong. This magnum of fermented grapes, god's hands grabbing in the scummy waters, city officials searching in gangways and garden apartments, in dumpsters and diners, at bus stops and behind the bushes in the park.

Yet ten days after, the case was quickly abandoned with the assault on the Twin Towers. Local agents prepared for what many cities second to New York City feared— that the next strike would be directed their way. And the search for the escapees ceased—everyone watching each passenger jet roar through the sky, fearing it would fall, fearing that we, too, were doomed. It was over for us. Each plane which flew too low triggered this hysteria again and again; all the while, fourteen escapees reintegrated into a society which had abandoned them long ago.

Given what I am about to tell, I fascinate in the immediacy of my wreckage. Not to confuse you with incapacitating uncertainties—only the wonders of what revealed itself once the eyes no longer watched.

2: IN THE PENAL COLONY

On September 1st, 2011, ten years later to the day I heard a voice. Sounding as if it were spoken from the bottom of a caisson which held up one of the mid-rises along our lake shore. I had often been caught thinking of such infrastructures, the underground systems which prop up our built environment. Those despicable cement columns, buried wires, those pipes, the steel. It outraged me. The voice as well, speaking from down there, among all that. It asked me cordially how work had been going. To this I could not answer.

"Your detecting, sir—have you no recent cases?" it said.

"I cannot hear you at all—you either asked me about detection and cases, or the dead thing and caissons. Which is it?"

"Cases."

This did not help but I switched tacks and I answered, as I have learned to do, in a way that did not betray my confusion. "There have been many, but their qualities elude me at the time being."

"I read about you in the papers."

"What papers?"

"The morning ones."

"I would imagine myself to be very popular in the morning. The evening crowd does not have the same taste for my authorities."

"Incorrigible."

"These jurisdictions of the mind we all learned to abhor."

"Either way, my name is Charles Darwin. To hire you—that is my wish."

I took a seat at my kitchen table and began staring out the window. My roommate, when he had lived here years ago, and I used to sit across from each other at this weathered wooden table we were told once resided on a farm. Somehow it escaped and we purchased it down the street, or what was once down the street, at a junk shop with men who had splinters in their hands, cigarettes in their teeth, exotic snarls and chiseled glances. The window overlooked the backside of a row of rundown houses and two-flats across from the park. Staring at these reminded me that Chicago began with its backside, and if you learned to like that view than the city would offer you its face. The trees and electric poles, draping wires—above all this loomed the elderly Section 8 and the Northwest Tower, a decrepit art deco office building. Clouds. The mind's ether. An occasional star, or mortar shot, exploding. But it was dark outside, very little to see besides my reflection, so I carried on the conversation.

"You know my name, but tell me how does one come to call upon my alleged services?"

"Meticulous planning. The evolution of cunning."

"A cunning evolution."

"You are following all this nicely. Have you the interest to find out more?"

"These details bore me."

"As caissons bore the earth."

"You should see me make my way through a crowd. Call me once more in the morning. As I said, my spirits do not lift very high at night and one needs self-confidence for a conversation such as the one you are proposing."

"The moor of the morning it is." And in mentioning my predilection for the uncultivated tracts of time, the voice responded with silence. A silence which barred my entry yet kept me whole. A silence so heavy it broke under its own weight. A vacuuming suck. A whoosh—a fanboat—a whip's crack. Beginning a tide pool of my senses. My blue suit—gone. A Moby Grape at Fillmore East poster pulled off the wall and then the canary's cage—gone. Two forks, the spoon, the bowl. My Baltic record collection. Gone. The Old Testament I kept in my utensils drawer—gone. The red curtain dividing the kitchen and the bedroom, my favorite, the one I had found for three dollars on sale at the Dollar Store on Chicago Avenue—rings and all—pulled and gone. My schematics for the Metropolitan Correctional Center laid out across my guest bed, the cabinets, the linoleum, the light fixtures—into the swirl and gone.

Me at the kitchen table sharply against the void, and I wondered: given the void's lackings, how might I or a table contrast that which is not? Surely I went with it. Gone from the night.

I looked outside to find the morning. Whether the next in succession or the previous, or out of order altogether, I did not bother to wonder. Who does? Stop to wonder when one is in the middle of a case, or at the beginning of a caisson, or as the casing is just about to be tied off. Only that it was morning. And the voice spoke: "There are not many who do work of your kind," it said, slightly parched, sounding so close, as if standing behind the wall I leaned against. Or within it. A consideration I interrupted immediately upon its arrival, not wanting to begin an inventory of the structures and mechanisms placed within walls, as I had foolishly done wondering about what lies beneath the city. What I can say about this wall is that it is the same wall I always leaned against in the mornings, next to the toaster, near enough to the faucet, the glasses, the butter always out and locatable, a knife in my hand.

"The work of my kind is not everyone's kind of my work."

"Is that so?"

"Do you appreciate the details of life? The small things, as a wise man once said?"

"What is small to me might be what is me to might be small."

"There are lives at stake. You play, others suffer. Stop. Before we proceed, you must know my name."

"What is it?"

"Sir Isaac Newton."

"Being for the time."

"Have it your way. Are you preoccupied?"

"Depends on who is asking?"

"Sir Isaac Newton."

"I have little patience, but I happen to have time. Bunches of it."

"I like you. You scrub my language as if it were a feral dog deemed worthy to show. Please. I have become involved in a complex assignment, running a course of many years, and I need the assistance of a composer such as you. My orchestra is deep in a pit and they need a guiding wand."

"You need a sheriff, is what you are saying, for your bad boy town?"

"A lewd metaphor, but understandable given the course of our conversation."

"I've had a few hands on my balls after the smoke cleared."

"A smoking gun would give it an easier go."

"Answer me: is that *Peter and The Wolf* you are listening to?"

"It is."

"A coincidence no doubt that I, too, am listening to *Peter and The Wolf.*"

"I should hope that a coincidence such as this should be acted upon. Especially by one so practiced in synchronicity."

"Agreed. Where should I meet you?"

"At the Laundromat on Damen Avenue, south of Augusta. I will be playing our favorite game: Ms. Pac Man."

"Never regular Pac Man."

"Never."

"Too slow for the quick witted."

"Too languid for the laughing heart."

"Too hairy for the horrid who."

"Exactly. See you in one hour."

"One hour in you'll see."

MOBY GRAPE

I arrived in Santa Barbara on a Friday, my head as foggy as the coastal morning, and hurried, as if being dragged forward. I carried a hanging bag with suit and hailed a cab outside of the airport. Though Levi's wedding was to take place deep in the hills of Santa Ynez valley, a room downtown at El Prado Inn had been booked for me.

Driving along Highway 1, I stared out the backseat window. As uncertain as existence itself, Santa Barbara wavered between its drive to live and its drive to die. Ocean, rock, brown sandy hills. The clouds build—rain never falling. A desert, but still it flowers. Orange poppies and purple lupine. Indian paintbrush. Five spot. Fairy Lanterns. Larkspur. Coral trees. Angel's Trumpet. Off the highway and through town, the neighborhood yards filled up with lemon trees, orange trees, avocados, kumquats. The dry parcels of land were like blotting tabs hiding hallucinogens. Beautiful nothingness bouncing across the taxi windows. It does not make sense to my Midwestern mind where the soil is black, the grass is green, and the winter produce ships in on a truck. I no longer wondered why Levi Seeds chose this location for his vineyard. For his epicurean fantasy, his wedding. For these delusional games that took control of my life, smashing it like a vandal bricks a car window, a pile of dizzying fragments left on the curb.

In the trip from the airport to El Prado Inn, the cab driver said nothing but words to advance the transaction. Upon dropping me of, as he rolled around the circle drive, I watched him wipe the sweat off his forehead, catch his breath and make the sign of the cross. The attendant at the front desk was nice enough to walk me to my room.

She was young, tan, wearing flip-flops and a sleeveless company dress, El Prado stitched in script, like finding a stewardess on a beach. "Welcome back, Mr. Yeager. It took a little shuffling, but we are happy to provide you with your favorite room."

Not only had I never been to Santa Barbara before, I had never told no one nothing about no favorite room. I didn't even have a favorite pair of socks. That's not true, my green ones with the race horses, but I knew immediately Levi had a taken a personal interest in my arrival.

"Everything has been taken care of."

Accept for the tip no doubt. "As I tell everyone who asks, it's not just the atmosphere of El Prado, it's the customer service." I palmed her a twenty, held her little hand a little too long, gave a wink, and smiled in that lecherous way I had learned long ago stirred fear and lust in girls her age, contempt and regret in older women. She would keep her distance.

I put my stuff down, took a shower, turned on the tv— it was ice hockey—shuttered, turned it off and stepped outside my door. The second floor balcony overlooking the pool. A white plastic chair sat next to a side table only big enough to fit an ashtray and a drink. I went back in and put on a pair of shorts, grabbed my cigarettes, and returned to take a seat. Nothing makes me more pleased than a perfect place to smoke.

My thoughts circled on the questions I had not been able to fathom: What had become of Levi Seeds? Who was his bride-to-be Miriam dos Santos? Why had he invited me when it had been ten years since we'd spoken? Was he in trouble—maybe this was his way of employing my services? I had a specialty. Cleaning up the wreckage of communes and cults. Fathers would grow tired of their child's journey towards self-discovery or nonsense phase or vision quest or however they dismissed it, each one a different name for the same thing: their child had left, minimized contact with them, until one day a letter or phone call or spur of the moment visit would come letting them know they had a group of friends and they were planning something amazing, something beautiful, and there would be no means for communication there, so do not worry about them, everything was fine. Most often a request for a little money, sometimes a lot, and very little else to go off of as they would begin to wonder where had they gone. To what place had they vanished. I knew these circles of tribes, these leaders with perfunctory visions, these traditions of building one's own world hidden from the dominant culture, folded into the wilderness or the deep city, doing the work that millions of other youth and jettisoned elders only schemed about. Communes and cults—my specialty, and when fathers came with their last letters, their recounting of last conversations, more often than not all they could say was "she seemed manic, she seemed momentary" or "he almost acted like he was doing this begrudgingly" or "last I knew, she was in the Pacific Northwest, but nothing sense," and this would be enough for me to begin my investigation.

As the afternoon sun burnt away the clouds and the ocean breeze grabbed my open hotel window, I remember smiling at the thought that California would cure me. How fortunate, I mused, to be set forward on a trip to paradise. And I had not seen nor spoken to the groom in ten long years. Nothing but violence and remorse had come my way since the day I received the invitation in the mail. My fortune, I realized, was a hazard running through my crumpled body. When the afternoon sun fell to evenings' long shadows, I got off my plastic seat overlooking the Motel pool, emptied the overflowing ashtray, and got dressed.

A shirt I hadn't worn in nine years but which called to me when I was packing—a swanky blue number which I had purchased in Florence with Levi, something to wear to the lavish dinners his brother Gil had bestowed upon us in the form of an American Express Gold Card—swankier than I would have liked to admit—the buttons about to pop when I sat, but stylishly trim when I walked. And walk I did. Down State Street to the beach. I walked slowly, feeling the frustration of being in a place which moved at a different pace and with different intentions than I was used to. These people were lost in a leisurely glamour. Resident or tourist, you couldn't tell, everyone moving to forget, escaping from realities they never even knew—just melodramatic stories they told themselves over and over again about their lives. There I was: the janitor awkwardly costumed and stumbling out in the middle of the Soap Opera set. I was ruining the shot in a world where there's never a take 2. But there was a time in my life when I fit right in with this crowd, and performed a high class air better than the rest of them. A time in my life which I had since sworn out of my memory, but came flooding back in with the mention of Levi Seeds. I needed to think long and hard about hidden stories from my past, and I wished I was surrounded by the bulk of blunt Chicagoans to do it. Instead of these dangerous territories. I arrived at the boardwalk, skate park to my left, beach to my right, and a long pier ahead. I walked out on the pier and bought a bowl of chowder. Strange how they were selling me Nantucket when all I wanted was something near, something graspable. California—so mythically drenched. So nonexistent. Like a series of trapdoors beneath one's feet.

3: IN THE PENAL COLONY

I assumed the voice had left, and if not, well, let it listen because I had my favorite sitcom to watch. I turned on the television and I waited for Holofernes, or as the others called him, Dr. Holofernes. DDS, make no mistake. A syndication, they ran two or more in a row at that time in the morning—I often watched it for hours. Each day the episodes seemed to have no end in sight, in-between the thirteenth and the fourteenth episode, there would be Holofernes, regular as reception, at my door with the mail. He knew I did not like to go out-of-doors. My most earnest friend, Holofernes had a regular job, a steady world, sunglasses, a consistent haircut, headphones, fashionable tennis shoes, a wallet. We told stories to each other about back-in-the-day, growing up, our time together in preschool, old sports teams we used to worship. It was always as normal between us as I could imagine a conversation to be. Friendly neighbors like him make life palatable.

Full House made me laugh because it rang so true to my life and my childhood. Almost as if I shared a body with DJ, Stephanie, and Kimmie. And maybe it was why I liked Holofernes so much because in *Full House* there was the character Bernard who was a San Francisco Postman and always talked for awhile with Danny, helping him through the trial of being a single father. Bernard could sympathize, because he had left his wife and family in Detroit years ago, and he heard all about it from his baby's mother. Though the writers never fully explained this, it was an enigmatic doubling mirrored between Danny and Bernard; many race and gender issues being at stake as well. But my favorite was how Michel, once she was old enough to talk, always tugged on Bernard's navy pant leg and said, "You're nuts," or "Big Daddy, give me my mail." Sitting there that morning, I became struck by how strange that the character Michel was played by a set of twins, Mary Kate and Ashley, and we never knew who we were looking at on the screen. Though twins look the same, that they are different people is something I think we can all agree.

But that morning, the television did not turn on; nevertheless, I sat on my comfortable chair, not that rigid one at my kitchen table, but an upholstered, soft, swivel chair I had picked up in the alleys one time or another, and I waited for Holofernes' arrival. Staring at the walls, I was treated to the beautiful light show which noontime sun casts through the stained glass adorning the front window of my apartment. A spectrum of color streaked and bubbled, beginning on my west wall. Similar to days spent lying on the grass in the park watching the movement of clouds, cozy yet eager for flights of whimsy I watched the streaks and amorphous bubbles of color slide inch by inch across the west wall towards the pocket doors, which slid to shut off the north wall leading to the rest of the apartment, then the east wall where my bookshelf, a large built-in, showed the titles of a decade of research. I watched a streak of violet, yellow, and pink grow and then bend to let in blue, green, and orange and then swirl inch by inch and push into the next wall and across the pocket doors, then speckle into constellations of violet dots and orange dashes that kaleidoscoped into blues yellows greens pinks, jumping chaotically from dot to dash to wave to streak. Knowing that each day the migration of prismed light traveled differently—according to the different angle of refraction— I reveled in the fact that unlike Full House, this spectacle of light was singular, never to be repeated, and seen by no one other than me. The blue dots, yellow dashes, pink swirls transmigrated between forms—yellow dots, blue streaks, pink dashes, converged closer and closer, and I swiveled centimeter by centimeter following it until whack! The spectrum of colorful shapes converged into these unforgettable words across my pocket doors:

Brick by brick. Morning each morning. All the unbuilt buildings are built anew. But one.

As quickly as I could reread it, the letters began to dissolve. Inch by inch returning to the constellations of colorful shapes, shifting and sliding towards the east wall covered with books. I did not move to write this down and I did not need to. I had seen this riddle before, although never translated out of its mother tongue. A bastard form of Yiddish spoken deep in the countryside of endless Russia. Funny it should make its way back in my life. This, the riddle with two answers, two logical and legitimate solutions. Commonly referred to in Yiddish as God's Riddle: as paradigmatic as one's view on the predicament of God's existence, one's answer to this revealed whether or not one's past lives were still available to them—in tune with the dynamic multiplicity of dimensions chaotically in flux on this earth. Or one lived solidified, like a statue, by only one perspective.

This was the very riddle which led me to break from

the secret sect of RARAR—Riddle Anonymous Riddle Anonymous Riddle—formerly located in the lower swamps of Louisiana's amorphous coastline. Notice of its disbanding had reached me years ago, but I never thought they would come looking for me.

At that very moment, my thoughts were interrupted by the flapping of the squeaky hinged mail slot. Holofernes had arrived. Befuddled, I went out to greet him.

"Holofernes, I need to talk with you."

The moment I saw him standing at my door, a gentle run from a finger-plucked piccolo sounded and what was previously silence was replaced with Brahms concerto in D. My nerves began to recoil, taut with a secret knowledge that my conscious thoughts were not privy to, and I stared at Holofernes, wondering whether I would ever know if it was Mary Kate or Ashley who played Michel in my favorite episode of *Full House* when Michel's older sister Stephanie mistakenly got on a flight to Auckland, thinking she had heard them say Oakland.

"Charlie. Hi. Why don't you take this?"

"What is this Charlie nonsense—it's like you don't even know me."

"Read the envelope."

"The previous tenant, no doubt. Look at the next one, or the one after that—you'll find my correct name somewhere in there."

"Chuck?"

"Nope."

"Charles."

"Not it."

"Yeager."

"Who are you trying to fool?"

"Manasses?"

"Come in."

He handed me my mail, only it was so small and dense in my hands, like a little bean rattling around in a plastic cup.

"I'm right on time, Manasses. Two o'clock sharp."

"Yes. But must you say sharp?"

"My apologies."

My shirt was unbuttoned to my naval and I made no gesture to excuse myself or remedy such a social faux-paw. Across my chest, I knew Holofernes had seen it before, I rubbed the feathers of a bald peacock, unconsciously stewing over my recent encounter with the terrible RARAR.

"A glass of water? It must be hot out there."

"No need, Manasses. Here, would you like a sip of this?"

"Thank you. I really like that blue you are wearing. Is that Federal-issued?"

"State-issued. I am happy that you like it."

"Very stately, you are right, soothing." My fingers rubbing across my chest.

"That's the idea. How has your morning been?"

"Morning, each morning, splendid. No. Taxing. Revelatory but strenuous. Did you know it's been them all along? Have I ever told you about them? Oh, Jesus, Holofernes. Sit down. Down here, sit."

"I have a few more rounds to get to."

"Where should I begin?"

"Towards the end would be preferable."

"Your humor, Holofernes, really you have the best sense. I am sure everyone you meet feels that way. That's what I tell others about you, Holofernes —my most normal friend but he is such a kidder."

"You said you like the blue uniforms."

"I do. A calm blue. The blue of eyes. It was just such a blue which we cloaked ourselves in before I broke from the sect. A funny color to wear in those swamps— did nothing for us in terms of camouflage. You've seen Mountain Spring Water written on a bottled water you like?"

"Yes."

"Well, quite similar to us, however, we believed in swamp water. The bloated floating trunks, bark disintegrating, the moss, the oils of the alligator's leathery skin, tree's roots gnarled beneath water's shimmer, the true muck of decomposing organic bodies, all of it absorbed by the waters and the waters we would drink in the deep dark of night on our search for the answer to God's Riddle."

"And it is these people you met in the swamps who are keeping you here?"

"Keeping me here? No sir—no one is keeping me here. I am free to come and go as I like, that is why Aleph invented doors."

"Aleph —you've told me about him, haven't you? Is he a member of this secret group, what is its name?"

"RARAR!"

"Shhh, Manasses. The others might be sleeping."

"RARAR. The Riddle Anonymous Riddle Anonymous Riddle—so we were called. But, Aleph has given me many great gifts, including the power to locate trapdoors and utilize them to enter and exit rooms."

"So what?"

"Don't be naive, Holofernes. It is only in this room that you see me, but this room isn't the only one I exist in."

"I see."

"You're writing that down? Go ahead, make note of it—it is probably a good thing to remember to tell others. Write it on the neighbor's mail. Do that. Let them know, too."

"Why did they turn against you?"

"It was fated. I was always the one who was meant to find the other answer. Although it felt so accidental at the time. You see, besides the spirits bubbling in the Louisiana swamp waters, another integral component to our search existed there: a crease in space which folded back and forth between the swamp waters we inhabited and the rural pastures of Russia. The very lands where the Yiddish outlined God's Riddles to begin with. An utter necessity of our contemplation."

"So, at one moment you'd be in the swamps and the next on a Russian Farm?"

"Nonsense. Rumor had reached us of such a space crease and we went forth to discover. Shrimp boat fishermen let us in on it, one night in a backwater bar, drinking their homebrew. I won't say any more. That led us to the gator-trappers. Around a fire we danced through the night, offering them sickening laughter, the type of nonsensical jibber-jabber that, like too much sugar, balls up and croons the stomach. In the midst of this laughter and pain, they drew us a map to the space crease. In fact, most gator-trappers in the Louisiana swamps are Yiddish refugees."

"Seems like wild times."

"Yes. Do not tell too many others. Really, it would be sad if they were found and deported. Immigration laws, naturalism—your politics not mine, right?"

"And the map led you to the portal?"

"Not a portal. Not. A space crease—where two distinct places fold on top of the other. Like, for example, Subway."

"A subway or the Subway?"

"Imagine Subway, and then imagine Burger King. Now, a space-crease between the two would create a situation where you stand in line at Subway and when it comes your turn to order, you understand yourself to be ordering a five-dollar tuna salad footlong, but not only are you doing that, also you are ordering a Quarter Pounder Meal Deal at the McDonald's register. Simultaneously."

"What about Burger King?"

"Same thing."

"Really, I prefer the Whopper."

"So the Cajuns showed us that, drew it on a map. And that kept us entertained for quite some time. Devilishly existing in two places, carrying on two conversations, dancing and drinking twice as much as our fill. All simultaneously. Until, in our explorations of the space, I disappeared."

"How so?"

"You ask the best questions, Holofernes. This is what I always say to the others— Holofernes, he is so inquisitive. Really, the space-crease existed within the confines of a ring of monkey-bat trees. That's what the Cajuns called them. You might know them better as Echinacea trees. We built a barge-like walkway, where we could walk and dance and sing, and strung a net from the monkey-bat trees which we could sleep in. All to keep us safe from the horrendous waters below, filled with man-eating carp, gators, snakes, psychotic otters and insects you would never know existed. Each of us took our turns investigating below the water's shimmer, which continued to result in some strange dual-existences—one member found himself in a bathtub with a large Yiddish woman, another in the pisspot of an eccentric aesthete—but nothing more. When that day of my disappearance arrived, it was my third voyage into the waters. Each time prior, a soft murmur could be heard as soon as my head was dunked below, but I had been unable to locate its source. The thick gnarled roots of the surrounding monkey-bat trees created the most confounding of obstacles. That is, until I realized that one could swim beneath them, that their arching roots formed a tunnel. It was traveling through that tunnel, moments away from aspirating, which led me to a false bottom. I pushed and I pushed at the pile of swamp-weeds, thinking I would die, and then I rotated and began to kick. Crash! From that underwater tunnel I fell and landed in a rustic barn which I later found out to be deep in the heart of pastoral Russia."

"And this was your disappearance?"

"One might be more correct in saying that this was my reappearance. The question at hand is: did I drown? I believed I did—simultaneously existing in the barn and bloating to a float in the swamp. The cow that I landed next to was not, as one would expect, alarmed by my face, and the farmer who rushed in soon after welcomed me back with a sheepish grin. I spent the following weeks deep in study with the Yids. A romantic time period of my life that I often grow nostalgic for, but return to the swamp, I must, and return to the swamp I did."

"How long had you been gone?"

"Silly question, Holofernes. It was a space-crease not a time-crease. Time is equivalent on both sides of the field."

"Of course."

"The members of RARAR were not pleased with the news I had to share upon my return. While studying with the Yids, they had revealed to me, against my obstinate duress, another answer to God's Riddle. One I felt which rang with a more harmonious truth and which did not include duping poor shrimp fishermen and gator-hunters, nor living in a vast field of muck and things that bite. I informed them of my discovery and they tied me to the trunk of the monkey-bat tree. They tortured me until I was a wrecked bag of lumps, but still I did not renounce the Yiddish perspective of the other. There could be two perspectives I cried, but no, they would not have it. They left me tied up there, bleeding, bruised, and deformed as a sacrifice to the gators and the otters and the carp, all gods simultaneously elsewhere, whichever claimed me first for their lunch."

"How did you escape?"

"You've seen my foot, right? My left foot? All the toes are missing. Here, look."

"Your awkward walk—that explains it."

"It does. The carp came first, and nibbled away my toes. But, in doing so, gnawed the rope which strung me up. It broke and unleashed me. I fell to the waters with the thud of a dead man's chest, and smack! I reappeared in Chicago, having landed in the fountain around the corner from here in the center of Wicker Park, right next to a naked baby who was playing in the shallow water. Going pee-pee. I don't get too hussy about those things."

"Manasses. What are the two answers to the riddle?"

"Did I say two answers? I meant two riddles—there are two riddles with the same answer."

"You asked earlier, long before this story began, to speak to someone. Someone special. I will see to it that you find him. He has been asking about you."

"As you like."

I had some thinking to do. And an appointment to make.

2: MOBY GRAPE

When the evening came, I ponied up to a bar. A Chinese joint named Jimmy's. Detroit Tigers pennants hanging above the oak bar. A series of four tops with vinyl tablecloths along the wainscoting, an oak veneer. Drop panel ceilings. A dive with an aristocratic air—I felt just enough at home to actually talk to someone. My favorite someone. The bartender.

"Jimmy, show me the wine menu."

"Jimmy is the owner, sir. My name is Stephen."

"Chris, Kevin, Stephen—how about a menu?" You have to get a little rough with these types. He took himself seriously, as if service was his calling. All that said to a guy like me is he knew how to serve because he had been served—that he was from affluence. Affable my ass, I had every intention to drill him about Levi and see what he knew about Las Sangres Vineyard.

I didn't think I'd be so lucky to find his wines on the menu.

"Funky place like this and you got all these expensive bottles. What gives?"

"The region is blossoming. We like to open up with it."

"Nothing like a big, viscous, tannic wine and an order of General Pao's chicken, right? I'm interested in having a glass of this wine by Mister Levi Seeds."

"You mean Kung Pao."

"Do I?"

"As you can see, we carry La Sangre de María Elena—a Sangiovese if you care. Scored an impressive 97 with *Wine Advocate*."

"By the glass?"

"No, sir."

"How much for the bottle?"

"Two seventy-five."

"Fuck me. How much for the dim sum?"

"I believe three dollars and ninety-five cents a piece, sir."

"Right."

"It's worth it to those who want it, but for those who don't—it's a rub."

"I have a joke for you. How do you make an egg roll?"

"You push it."

"Heard that one."

"Right."

"Does the winemaker come in here?"

"Many winemakers do. I rarely see Mister Seeds. However, well, there are some things one acquires with sophistication and experience. An appreciation of wine is one of them."

"However, what? However he's your lover?"

"Your jokes reek of somewhere else. Please, make yourself at home. I'll give you a minute to decide." He had something to say. Something that wanted to be said but he felt the weight of it and stopped. We all want to speak that which weighs heaviest upon our current sense of self worth. He knew he was valuable. I like value, and can read it on someone's face a mile away. When he came back, I decided to let him be valuable.

"Not too many come to this part of the country with so much disdain."

"I've got too many interests. I'm looking for a reason not to get another."

"You must be here against your will. In-laws often bother Midwesterners, correct?"

"Every other city I know is caked over with salt—I figured I try this sweet cream you all have layered atop Santa Barbara."

"That's the spirit. I've come to believe it's the palette not the ingredients which creates good taste."

"My palette's more suited to meat than manners. When's the last time you had a glass of that María Elena, Jimmy?"

"It's been some time."

"I don't want to drink it all myself. What do you say you have a glass with me?"

"You want to purchase some of the icing you've heard so much about?"

"I do. And I want your palette to explain to me why it is so good." Though I could tell he was an aficionado, like all barmen, he was already calculating his $50 tip. I'd leave him $40 and wondering why.

"Of course, sir. I will return shortly."

The restaurant was full and the bar was getting packed with those waiting for a table. The life of the leisure class, you can't beat it. Friday lunch stretches into the evening. A school of fish swimming gently against the tide of honest work. There's nowhere to be but near the crowd. Though I got the feeling that half of these people were born elsewhere—aren't we all from somewhere else, from some other life which we promise ourselves we'll return to soon enough—they assimilated to the leisure class nicely. Here to experience something they have heard of or dreamt, something they desire. More than wine, of course, these people desired glamour. Salubrious postures, salivating eyes. Their faces like the Pacific blue waters basking in the sunset—a deep glow of warmth for something they could never be near themselves.

"First, a sip."

"To see if it is corked?"

"More importantly if it suits you."

"Fine enough."

"I will pour two glasses, that is correct, sir?"

"Please do, Jimmy. And my name is Chuck."

"Very nice, Chuck. This will round you out just fine." As if rehearsed for years, he dipped his nose into the glass, inhaled, swirled, sipped and shut his eyes. I just poured it in my mouth, and watched him, waiting for his knowledge to burst in his desire to spill it. "Very quick to pepper, and so smoothly the bold blackberry hits your throat."

"That hard to do?"

"Very."

"It's delicious, no doubt. Tastes inky. It rises in my mouth like a circus muscleman jerking weights."

"If you must. Notice the legs along the glass. Shows the high alcohol content. A big wine. It could walk right out of here."

"Then it falls—the dumbbell at the back of my throat. Say, this big-legged mama is worth every penny for the visions alone. I've paid more for similar in the French Quarter."

He let me be and carried his wine with him. But soon enough he was back with an empty glass.

"María Elena is very good, but for me, his best is La Sangre de Josefina. A Cabernet Franc, Merlot blend. 1994."

"Pour another," I said.

"Very generous."

"María Elena, Josefina. These Seeds' Mexicali muses?"

"The story goes that he names each blend for the best worker's wife. As a humble acknowledgement of the families who work these lands. This year they bottled La Sangre de Miriam."

I gagged, spitting a little blood down my chin. "How generous of him. A glass of water if you could."

"Levi Seeds is known in Santa Barbara as a righteous man, eccentric and lavish, but fair to his workers and a magician with his grapes. He's quite loved."

"Who's behind this vineyard. I bet a lot of the Hollywood types buy a plot of land, throw some vines in it and call it a chateau."

"You might be right about that, but this wine is owned by a Frenchman. An impressive family from what I hear—one as tied to the land as they are the French government."

"Corruption—now that's a world I know. I'm here from Chicago."

"I couldn't put my finger on it, but that explains everything."

"Say, Jimmy—we're friends but not friendly, see?"

"Corruption, if you must, is the very tip of it from what I hear."

"And I'm sure you hear a lot."

"I do."

"Drugs? Women? Real estate?"

"It would be foolish to think that one could separate such businesses."

"Cartel, then."

"Well, maybe, but not all Cartels begin and end in Mexico."

"Transnational politics—say, that was my major in college."

"I skipped college for the military. Most Israelites do."

"Jimmy—I would have never guessed. You, a uniform and a gun? Well, I'm glad to know you."

"Not all things fit your model, Chuck. Sorry to be so friendly."

"Had I known, we could've been friends from the very start. Say, why is it that Levi Seeds doesn't drink here, do you think?"

"Do you know Mr. Seeds?"

"Once I did, but that was long ago."

"Well then you're aware of his devotion. My guess is that he spends his weekend nights engaged in Kabbalistic practices."

"All I know about Kabbalah I learned from Madonna so please fill me in."

"Torah study, meditation. The rule in Kabbalah is that the more a person has, the more they need to work on themselves, in every area. With that power of having so much comes a greater challenge, a greater amount of work to become humble about it."

"Sounds like Seeds is putting in the extra hours."

"People in our community know Seeds for his devotion and his work for women's rights. He emphasizes the Kabbalistic notion that women are higher beings. Women, as it turns out, don't need to be on Earth—their reincarnation is assured, and they're here only to help men achieve their purpose."

"And I always thought women were the devil. Come for the wine, stay for the wisdom, Jim."

He took a big gulp from the glass and I could feel it coming. "However his wife, well you might say she has not taken to it with the same fervor. While he's observing Shabbat, she's frequenting this bar. In fact, the very seat you're in."

"He's married, you say?"

"Yes, but her suitors might tell you otherwise."

"So, it's like that?"

"It's very much like that. The other weekend it was a woman. The weekend before that a man half her age— and half her height. A jockey by the name of Benoit up from Santa Anita."

"French-Canadian? Seeds can't be happy about that."

"Don't get me wrong, she carries herself with class."

"How could she not? Money shines all shoes."

"Don't mistake winemakers for wine purchasers. You'd be hard pressed to find a winemaker anywhere as wealthy as the company he keeps."

"Whatever he's got, I'm sure she makes it look good."

"See for yourself."

I turned around. Walking directly towards me was a vivacious platinum blonde, lit up from head to toe. A sky-blue top, sheer and cut low in the back. A cream scarf around her neck, soft and debonair. Red sunglasses matching her red lipstick. Her tan skirt clung to her thighs, outlining legs worth every disaster and dispute. She held me in her eyes, or at least I thought she did— every man nearby no doubt felt the same. So much fantasy in her curves, her presence triggered deja-vu in all the men she past, toppling them like dominos. California was looking less and less like Chicago every moment I sat there. To hell with my Third Coast snobbery. She made Santa Barbara make sense. Her gaze receded from me and moved towards Jimmy the bartender, who grinned devilishly at the timing and sting of her entrance.

"You gave up my seat. Patience, Stephen, is the only virtue I require in a barman." As soon as she spoke, the slur of her face showed through. I could smell that gin-smell like I could hear my heart thump.

"It's Friday night, and you, my dear, are a Saturday type of girl."

"If only I was still a girl, then you'd really know trouble."

"Tell me more."

"Besides, tomorrow has been planned."

With a woman like this, who needs an illicit thought. Dazed by her charms, I told her she could take my seat, forgetting that I was standing next to the present wife of a man who's wedding I was to attend that next night.

"Very kind of you—I never drink while standing. Something about it weakens the knees."

"Your wit no doubt loses its wind?"

"More like my grin begins to drag through the gutter."

"Sounds delightful."

"I see you've met Stephen."

"Can I buy you a drink to make up for any inconvenience?"

"What are you having?" I began to say a bottle of María Elena from Las Sangres, when the piece of information I had just been given came back to me like an omen. It hit hard, and I stumbled a second, looking at Jimmy the Bartender I regained my composure, as his face showed traces of the same thought. Funny how quickly accomplices mount. With a wink in his direction, I said, "Something horrible—a red which I would not repeat. You know the infantry, what do you suggest?"

"I suggest retreat."

"Then make it two." I've always wanted what I've been told I can't have.

"Two Negroni it is," said the barman.

"Muddle mine a little extra; sometimes that gin bites back."

"A muddled man, are you? Got something on your mind?"

She kept up quick, which I liked. But I had been there before: sharp wit, devastating looks, an insatiable aquarium on the other end of her mouth—she was one and the same all across the country, one or two in every neighborhood. Only she out-shined them all in the California sun. The kind of trouble you teach yourself not to repeat, as hard as that may be. Still, I was happy to bite back.

"It's just that you're the third woman to come up to me tonight saying this seat was yours."

"Guess I'm just another face in your crowd."

"A face without a name, something none of the others did anything about." She smiled and turned directly towards me.

"You poor thing. Is that how you got conned into buying a three-hundred dollar bottle of shit wine?"

"Something like that."

"The third time can be a charm, but some charms wear

off when the whiskey runs dry. My name is Ursulines."
And she took off her sunglasses.

I stumbled again. I get like that—so caught up in the chase that my tail is all I can bite. This tail, however, was of a long ago past. Ursulines Lis, the last woman I knew who Levi Seeds was in love with. The one who his parents had told me left him for his wine-making friend, Jacob Growler, up in Napa. Now she was the infamous Ursulines Seeds. I had a lot to catch up on, and the weekend away had just begun.

Something shifted in her eyes, too. Assuming she could see straight.

"Ursulines, I do not mean to be so rude, but standing here all the other men keep bumping me in the back, trying to shake me from your side—a hint like a hammer on the head that it is my time to say, adieu."

"Adieu."

She said it like it was her natural tongue, and with this quick exchange in French, a long forgotten game returned to our eyes. Terse yet lyrical, we each knew our tongues had spoken French once before. Jimmy the Bartender had neglected serving drinks so he could stand near enough to hear every last word of our conversation, and thankfully was right there with the bill. I signed, said goodnight, and headed out to State Street where crowds of thin, glamorous, extravagant Santa Barbarians passed up and down the stretch of restaurants, boutiques and clubs searching dutifully for the mysteries of night. Hoping when they found it, if they did, that it took credit.

How Ursulines had not recognized me I could only chalk up to the abuses time and terror had etched into my face—the sunken eyes, the crow's feet, the mustache, the balding, the drowsiness which had overcome my being—yes, I thought at the time, I look less like myself than I realized. All it took was a chance mirror from my past to let me know. That, or she was skunked and every man was the same man, every night the same arousal. How quickly I dismissed the possibility that she could have played as coy as I did, not letting on that we had known each other once, and the reason for our initial friendship again was the same reason for this night's encounter: a winemaker whose life was becoming more intriguing by the minute.

3: MOBY GRAPE

The day I received the invitation to Levi Seeds' wedding in the mail, I had been three days away from my apartment, tracking down a thirty-three year-old named Greg in the Pacific Northwest. He had risen in the ranks of an intimate group proclaiming opium, if done at the right dose, neared humans to *god's divide*: one foot in the physical and one foot in the spiritual. I referred to them as the Dividends, a pun twice spun, but historically they had branched off from a group of San Francisco artists centered around Philip Lamantia. Greg didn't write poems, like Lamantia had, he didn't make art or produce anything of value from his tip-toeing across the divide. He just cooked opium tea, drank, and divined. Talking with the locals of Ashland, Oregon, I came to understand a deeper concern of this group: they believed that their occupation of god's divide served as a bridge for godliness to pour into his realm. As they sat there, a proper nod, never too much, they served as radio antennae transmitting the waves of godliness. When Greg's mother had realized her stocks had been sold and her savings emptied, she knew it must be him and that is why she contacted me. My plan for that day was to got through the mail and then write a letter to Nancy, informing her of Greg and the Dividends intent with her money—they were researching and experimenting on how to invent a "radio" for their transmissions. Some way to symbolically order, communicate, and broadcast God's vibes as they flowed through them. They were pushing themselves, their bodies and their minds to decode the messages they now believed were divined within them. And I had gotten there too late.

To ease the grieving process it was my philosophy to overnight the loved-one a letter, before I called to talk over the phone. Some chose to meet with me, some did not. Some derided me as an imbecile, incapable of my work and giving them misinformation. I did not blame them, and some days I agreed.

The stash of mail neatly arranged by my upstairs neighbor, Alice, in front of my door included a check from an old client, an issue of *Harpers* with a feature article on Alberto Vargas, coupons for Pizza Metro, Jewel Grocery, and a fancy envelope with a California return address. Geographically, Southern California is a planet away from Northern Illinois, and Santa Barbara was the farthest thing away from my Chicago mind. My first thought was that California was god and Chicago was human and I did not want to be the go-between. I stuffed all of it but the *Harper's* into the kitchen drawer where I kept the fast food coupons, and I went into the front room and lied down on the couch. I fell asleep with visions of pin-up girls and Vargas' days in Paris.

About an hour into sleeping, I awoke to a bang on my gangway window. Tom Hanks' *Big* was on the tv, the scene where his friend, still a child, visits his New York City loft, enjoying the trampoline, toys and pinball machine. I always liked how he spent his money; how he impressed his best friend with his toys. Another bang brought me back from my reverie, a sound like something slapping the glass, and I got up from the couch pulling my gun from my holster hanging on the coat rack. I get paranoid, to say the least, trembling and delirious when I return from my occult trips. I could've kept drinking and committed myself to alcoholism, but I have always been masochistic enough to find value in the pain the withdrawals brought on. I clicked the safety and slid to the window's side, peeking out to see who was there. *Smash*—a brick through the glass and past my face. I looked to see if I had been cut, and a book flew through the window, landing on the dining table. *In the Penal Colony*, a book I did not know. Hesitating, just enough confusion, my mind blank and stuck in pause, but then a reaction took hold and I jumped in front of the window firing two shots at a shadow that rounded the neighboring building. I ran out the front door and down the stoop where I fired again at the figure, this time sticking him in the calf. He immediately fell but got up again, stumbling forward around the corner until stopped by my neighbor Holofernes.

Holofernes spent his days leaning on his cane against one corner or another. In the summer, he wore his shirt island-style: unbuttoned to flaunt the riches of his belly, covered by a thin a-frame ribbed tee. In the winter, he wore an oversized parka with a faux fur-lined hood. Always patting his belly. I tucked my gun between my pants and back, forgoing a coat, and I walked towards the struggle.

Holofernes threw back his hood and yelled at me, "You fuck—that bullet could've missed and hit me."

"I knew I had him."

"I heard three shots, Chuck—you sure every time you shoot or just every other?"

"Next time you hear a shot, consider heading inside."

"Fuck you. Should I take my cane off his throat, or choke his larynx to a pulp?"

"That's not your style, Holofernes. I'll drag him down to your garage, you go down the alley and open it up."

"Alright, but hurry."

Holofernes was quick to help without hesitation. Why get messed up in any of this? He was an old-timer, so I didn't give it much thought at the time. We were friends, but only as friendly as two neighbors from different sides of the border can be, no more. I took off my button-down shirt and wrapped it around the guy's leg, hit him in the head to shut him up and dragged him down the alley where Holofernes was waiting for me, smoking, leaning on his cane next to the open garage door.

"Watch out for the books. Worth more than a year's pay."

"About time we had a reading room on the block."

"Good money in books."

"Only good money in books is a hundred-dollar bookmark, Holofernes. Now help me get this flea jumping."

I threw him in the corner and shut the garage door. A young punk who Holofernes recognized from Humboldt Park around the way. "What the fuck you want from me?" I screamed.

"Fuck you, *puto. Pinche jota*, Fuck you." He spoke in Spanish which I had long ago picked up from living in this neighborhood.

I dug my knuckles into his wound, he screamed.

"Cut that—someone will hear him across the alley," Holofernes said.

I heard sirens in the distance. "Tell me who the fuck you are."

"*Pinche jota, yo no digo nada.* Chuck Yeager *muerte. Muerte!*"

So I asked Holofernes to translate.

"He said you're a dead man, Chuck."

I pulled out my gun. The sirens were getting too close. I only had a few minutes. I bashed his forehead with the blunt grip. "Tell me or I'll refry your beans—would you like that?"

He spit blood across my chest so I cocked the hammer and put it at his hand. Blood and saliva hung from his lip and he did not take his eyes off me. Possessed. The police had pulled up to the corner store and it was only a matter of minutes before Holofernes threw me out of the garage. So I put the gun at this zombie's hand, lifted it towards the sky and shot off his thumb. The bullet through the finger-splattered roof.

Holofernes yelled, "I just laid new shingles. Stop with the shots."

Then quickly I moved it to his right foot, his soccer playing foot, and cocked the hammer. "That wake you up, Frankenstein?"

"Rorick! Ruben Rorick!"

With that I threw him at the garage door, which Holofernes was there to open, rolled him into the alley and kicked him in the chest. He screamed and the cops came around the corner. I passed inside through Holofernes' house, out through his front door, and was approached from behind while entering my apartment. Quickly in hand cuffs and thrown in the squad car. An ambulance pulled up. I knew the kid would be okay, besides not being able to grip a Corona or stroke his cock with his left hand. I kept my mouth shut and could only hear repeated again and again him saying, "Rorick. Ruben Rorick." A name like a piston that punched out and turned me in a different direction along a conveyor belt I didn't know I was on. All of it leading me to him.

4: IN THE PENAL COLONY

Tucked into a wall of beautiful, ragged, three-flat buildings, one could not miss the Ms. Pac Man machine standing in the window of the Laundromat. Five minutes late, not bad for me back then, or even now, when I arrived, the arcade game stood unchaperoned. I walked past the rickety machines, a long row of washers to one side, dryers to the other—a folding-table in between. A Technicolor television on a shelf in the corner watching over all of this, playing *General Hospital*, the same soap my father watched while he'd iron our clothes and straw sip a Pepsi can in the family room. Beyond, a change machine which had been out-of-order for the decade I had been coming here. A little deeper in, tucked in the back, was a counter with a bullet-proof partition, where Gil attended to the needs and maintenance of the shop. As well as sold candy bars and made change. I asked Gil to break my dollar. He agreed. Though I always prepared myself for his refusal.

When I returned to the Ms. Pac Man machine, there stood a man. Lost in his game.

He was dressed pleasantly: gray slacks and black shoes. Crisply. His sports coat folded across a seat-back shoved between the video game and a large fan spinning loudly. His button down shirt was a light cream, threadbare with small horses patterned everywhere. He wore a brimmed hat and a thin mustache.

"May I call you Peter?"

"May I call you Wolf?"

"For the sake of appearances."

"Delightful."

"Did you receive my call?"

"I saw your signal in the sky, Batman."

"We have met here before. Quite coincidentally. But that is not a history I subscribe to."

"*Outdoorsmen, Gentleman Quarterly*—surely your dentist brings you those."

"Do you wish to play a turn? While we speak?"

"I'd like that. One player or two?" Which was a leading question, I admit that now.

"One player is fine. I will do most the talking."

"My quarters or yours?"

"This is not a paying job."

"Carry on then."

"I have been hard at work, and am missing one piece to the puzzle. One large piece. A piece shaped very much like you."

He sized me up and down. Quite queer. Nonetheless, I was confident. For I, too, dressed to impress. My color choice tended towards green and though I could not find a clean shirt worthy of this meeting, I did dress in my hunter's green suit, satisfied with simply a white undershirt. Though my brown shoes were scuffed by years of salt and missed steps, they were a fine, soft leather which, to me, was enough. I wore no hat, but decided immediately that one was in order. He looked terribly handsome. My beard, I knew as well, would soon be shaved down and sculpted into a fine stretch of hair above my lip.

"Puzzles," I finally said. "I do love puzzles. Almost as much as I love a game of chase."

"That is what you are known for: chase."

"Oh is it? One never knows. How one is known."

"Public opinion is the finickiest of beasts."

"I don't believe that is a word, finickiest?"

"Pay attention, absorb all you can—there is no room for foolishness such as doubt, such as convention. The details of all I have in mind might astound you, but no worries, let them lie however they might."

More than intriguing, even though a few words had been lost in the loudness of the spinning fan at our side, my memory aids in filling gaps such as these. To show my professionalism I shuffled to his other side so I could hear him better. When we first met, he and I chomped across the screen in opposite directions, Pinky chasing me; Inky, him. We disappeared off screen, returning on a crash course. Seeing each other, we dashed up simultaneously, leaving the ghosts to crash. Though in love now, he will chase me through the next intermission. My eyes still on the screen; my hand still on the joystick. His face grew stern, perplexed, and then he began to explain.

"I have been anxious as of late that a certain case gone cold demands solving. Do you know of The Fortress?"

"I walk by it often."

"Are you familiar with the events ten years past which culminated in the escape of fourteen of its most insane?"

I erupted in laughter. I did not know then and I do not know now, but a sickening laughter overcame me in response to this question. A triumphant succession of fresh deep sincere scoffs and giggles. The Wolf did not respond in kind.

"They were never apprehended. I have more than enough reasons to believe that they have taken shelter in the very neighborhood which we are surrounded by. And I am certain that they are still in contact."

A question arose in my mind and so I asked it: "What of this concerns me?"

"As I said, all conundrums must be cracked. Splayed out and studied. Mechanized and dated. Tagged and reported upon. I need your assistance; I need you to track them down."

Thinking back now, this was less of an explanation than something to entice my hunger and seat me firmly in a five-star chair at a zero star establishment. Exactly the type of trickery I am obsessed by. I made quick work of the blue stages, the layout of the maze suits me, intuitively. Avoiding a Pinky and Blinky sandwich in the left corner by dashing towards Sue, a bull charge, reversing and then back to have Blinky reverse as I followed closely out of the dead end. I recalled the Mystery of Shallow Pools, a riddle designed by Trük Maki in the 14th century which involves taking one's thoughts to the furthest outpost away from one's purpose, waiting for death to begin its crumble of the senses, and then high-timing a logical discourse which in it's occurrence shakes loose the answer to the riddle; one has to grab it—immediate apprehension—han act of spontaneous attention, which when I mastered, opened up a network of energy nodes I could travel between after the proper amount of intoxication, meditation, or laughing gas.

"So, you *are* familiar with my work."

"Your Möbius Stripper riddle had me racked for weeks. Were you at a burlesque when you thought of it?"

"I was."

"Listening to your Walkman, I'm sure."

"You have it reversed—I was in the Walkman, listening to the strippers."

"Ha!" He laughed. No one but those who solved the Möbius Stripper laughed at that joke.

"You are aware that your puzzle therapy was employed by good Dr. Holofernes at The Fortress of Bethulia?"

"I have not thought of it for years, but yes, I do recall this fact."

"The complexity of the pieces, the contraptions, the theoretical framework—my god, Peter, it continues to astound us all. Tell me, did you concern yourself with the solutions, or did you only aim to raise the riddles' stakes?"

"One and the same, my informant. To know what you are asking and to know with what materials you are working is to know what the answer is—that is riddle logic 101."

"So the true task is to understand the question—to understand what is being asked."

"What is being asked is what is being answered."

During the banana stage, Clyde came directly after me from the start. After stringing him along for awhile, I decided to run him though the warp tunnel on the upper right. Clyde did not come out on the other end. I completed the stage, easily with one less ghost on my trail; however, distracted and wondering, I worried that he would reappear at an inopportune moment, spinning me to my death.

"I made it my duty to not contact you before I knew every inch of your past."

Every inch. I had never considered my past in terms of length, width, or depth.

"Besides The Fortress' utilization of my puzzle therapy, in what ways does my presence assist you?"

"The inmates, they lived for your deft twists, your perversions of logic were their pornography. How they loved you. It is rumored that you were the inspiration, their muse in creating an escape."

"Rumors are more roux than stock."

At this point, all the fruit eaten, all the mazes visited—the meet, the chase, the progeny—only Blinky remained, also known as Shadow. The level began and neither or us moved. Content to wait, until I had it: conscious of me, the ghost considered my existence.

"They sought out your Level 2 puzzles after they had worked through the standard issues, and they spent years studying them. One in particular."

"The Dogma Change of the Walled Nightingales."

"Funny you should know."

"Did they solve it?"

"Don't play dumb, Peter. I have spent quite some time with the Walled Nightingale myself. It drove me out of my tree and it wasn't until I tried one last effort of committing myself to The Fortress that I too was able to solve it—it is devised, I realized, in accordance with its context. Its solution is the very escape plan the Mad Fourteen utilized!"

His acquisitions were aggressive, and though their truth was suspect, they were fair. Better than that, they were exactly what I wanted to hear.

"Don't act surprised."

I didn't know that I did.

"It is by solving your puzzle that I learned my method

of escape. I did not go to all this trouble simply in pursuit of fun and games. I want those Mad Fourteen returned to their rightful place in society: locked up and realigned with god."

"Did you say 'society'? Because I thought I heard you say 'what has podiatry got to do with it.'"

"I do not wish to debate with you. The spiritual reintegration of the mad is my missionary task."

"Plum fancy tap dancing."

"It is only through social exclusion that they will ever be welcome back into the folds of god."

"'Moldy sod?' Well lawn maintenance always tickled my toes."

"Whether or not you believe, your riddle begins here. These fourteen have left it for you, waiting all these years. It is their homage to your work and I have come to realize that I am only the first pawn. Solve it and all fourteen will be located. Do not worry about apprehending them— leave that to me."

"I am honored. What material have they left me to work with?"

"They have left you everything."

"Excelsior Springs?"

"Your entire existence. Only limited by Western on the west, Fullerton on the north, Edens on the east, and the railroad on the south."

"Contraptions!" I stared at the screen and saw my map transposed across the maze of Ms. Pacman, and imagined my own ragged hunt through Chicago's streets. I wondered—would I be chasing them or they me? Ghost or pellet-popping yellow puck with a bow in my hair?

"Your entire being and everything that occurs to you, as well. Including every word that I say. Have said."

"What about the words of our friend Gil here?"

"Yes. Starting now."

"The words of the cashier at the bakery?"

"Yes."

"The cute girl behind the counter at the cafe?"

"Yes."

"The pizza delivery man?"

"He is only a boy, but yes. Everything."

Blinking walls—red, blue, peach—flashing circles— all done up, I had my fill, and with one pellet to go, stopped to stare at the warp tunnel, and even though I had no evidence that Clyde resided beyond, I tended to this as if for certain, communicating telepathically with Clyde or the hallucination of Clyde, I'd rather not know the difference.

I turned to him, "Well, Sir Charles Isaac Newton Darwin the Wolf, your clues stick out like thumb's sorest pulse. I'll have it figured out by dawn of next week."

My next player was beginning but I did not grab the joystick, listening intently as the ghosts scrambled furiously, foolishly predicting which ways I would bolt.

"Monday's dawn—I'll hold you to it. The stakes, my friend, are unutterable. I leave you with the riddle. They titled it The Maze of the Minotaur's Ornamentation. Listen close:

Who escapes the escapees
once the escapee is fed
to the Minotaur's maze
is where what's purple, huge and lives

in the ocean looms a thread
bare of luxuries and walls
at the edge of what you hear
who escapes the escapees."

I blushed at its complexity. My jaw open as the orange one moved through me.

"Solve it and you will find me again. Fail to do so and I will eat away at your sanity like a beetle buried in your brow."

But I could not except that threat as real for the game had already begun. And only one player remained.

Everyone knows the story of King Minos and the Minotaur. To aid in the battles his kingdom was wrought with, the King had called upon Poseidon. Up from the seas, sensitive to such peril and playfully amused with such a request, the God lent a helping hand, but on one condition: at the end of the war, he would send up a bull from the lowest depths of the sea, and King Minos would be called upon to slay it. But when that day came, beholding the mysterious and magical bull of the sea, the King tried to trick Poseidon, killing one of his stock instead, and keeping the prize as testament to his kingdom's majesty and dominance. Poseidon did little but watch, and soon enough the King was away and Queen Pasipahë, lonely, grew mesmerized by Poseidon's bull. She ordered artist-architect, Daedalus, always at the mercy of his court's extravagant whims, to build a mechanical bull which the Queen could enter and present herself. The perversion! It thrills me. One cannot imagine her pleasures, her pains, locked inside a bull costume and mounted.

As I think about it, maybe this story is told wrong.

Maybe Daedalus is to blame—he locked her in this contraption, the filthy old man, knowing the Queen was ripe for a child. And with the birth of that child—half man-half bull—famine, terror, and disease spread throughout the kingdom. All according to Daedalus' eccentric desires to build a labyrinth worthy of history—a labyrinth which held the mystery and meaning of life. Knowing not what else to do, King Minos agreed to Daedalus' idea: the kingdom would build a maze, a wicked maze, from which that child, the Minotaur, could not escape. And to keep all evil at bay, the kingdom fed the beast fourteen virgins from Athens. Every ten years, King Minos made King Aegeus pick seven young boys and seven young girls to be sent to Daedalus' creation, to be eaten by the Minotaur.

Daedalus patient in his plan, hiding within the walls, watching.

Until one day, when the warrior Theseus landed on the shores of the kingdom, and beautiful Ariadne seduced him, for she was next to be sacrificed, and led him directly to the Minotaur's maze. With a kiss and squeeze of his loins—one wonders why she did not save herself and just fuck him, striking her name from the virgin list—Ariadne pulled a ball of string from her sack and said, "Tie this here at the beginning and you will not lose your way, as all the others have. If you can slay the beast, this will allow you to find your way back." Theseus did so, plunging into the maze with the memory of the grasp of his crotch and its promise of what awaited him when, if, he returned. Having slain this product of immorality, indiscretion, bestiality and betrayal, Perseus made his way back along the string. He heard whispers, read rumors across the walls, messages from those before him that the Minotaur had already been killed. In fact it had been killed multiple times—and the one who slays the beast became the beast. A bull head carved out and worn by each new monster.

A rumor of Daedalus' making?

What my riddle concerns is not the hero's tale but the tale of those before him, the tales of the horrors, intensities, and exhaustion of those trapped by the corridor in their escape from the beast. And the tale of their transformation—Daedalus, the architect, sick with his designs.

Before I left the Laundromat, ignoring Gil's pleads, I too tied a string: one end on the threshold, the other around my waist.

Gil finally acquiesced and asked me: "But, sir. Why is corn so hard to escape from?"

Shocked. I turned to him. "My how you've grown, Gil. I didn't expect it."

That is how it began.

I had a few blocks to go and, looking back on it now, I am surprised that I arrived anywhere, let alone my intended destination. If someone were to tell me they were watching me and on that day I never reached where I intended to go, instead fell to the ground in an alley and slept with my eyes open, I would not second guess them. I became lost by this heightened attention to the world.

Every riddle thrives by its cunning turn of phrase, and I was obliged by this truth to free my neighborhood from its surface-level order. The profusion of diverse meanings lurking beneath the surface of the buildings, storefronts, faces and words made what was visible ever more enigmatic. The overwhelming power of fascination.

Women passed me on the sidewalk and my stare must have welled a despicable distance in their bodies. As I studied the details of their passing faces, several men began to greet me as if they knew me but they couldn't quite place me, only upon a closer view of my derangement did they stop short of a friendly word or wave. The exquisite buildings of Wicker Park peeked a brilliance which I will never forget. Each ornate etching, caketop cornice, molding, window trim, overhang, and ledge began to vibrate, buzz with a supreme existence and grow, yes extend and expand, swirling near and enrapturing me in the purity of decoration. Each brick, each stone, each stoop and iron fire escape popped through the wonderful mess of ornamentation, demanding my attention, whispering to me secrets hidden deep in these minerals churned and charred a thousand and one times throughout history, metamorphoses from nova to ocean floor to flatlands to rockbeds to mountains to gargoyle to turret to sidewalk to road to home to city. No longer buried underground, I awoke to the outward push.

Spinning and running and crawling through the streets and parks, examining each contraption which only my delirium could perceive. I felt as if a team of men dressed in ragged suits, organized throughout the alleys, designed this stage which I acted upon, coordinating my folly with the positioning of every prop. And they held strong as I threw my body against it all.

I knew the answer to Gil's little riddle. Simply put: because a corn is maize. A play on maze, something hard to escape from. I had encountered this riddle, as so many had, in a comic book. Used by Batman's nemesis, the Riddler. Batman figured it out quickly, then tracked Edward Nashton, the Riddler's real name, to a maze which he had designed to be the ultimate death-trap, challenging Bruce Wayne to escape before a bomb, hidden in one of the many passageways, went off.

The answer to this riddle was not the end of it—it is how it relates to the playing field which the Wolf had defined: this neighborhood. This riddle came from a comic and to Quimby's Comic's I would go.

Fascinated.

4: MOBY GRAPE

Chicago is people. People on the sidewalks, people in their courtyard building, people in their car. People outside the liquor store, inside the corner store, on their bike riding through. People maneuvering tossed garbage cans, walking their dog sipping coffee, on their cell phone at the busstop. People dead and written up in the *Tribune*, people talking talking talking written up in the *Sun-times*, *La Raza*, *The Reader*, people glancing at this talk and turning towards their thoughts. People commenting on other people to someone nearby, people looking at other people wondering what they are doing here, people applying for jobs behind counters on the floor of retail with the city with the corporations with the grocery. People in office buildings, people buzzing below on the sidewalks, people considering moving to some suburb, people taking the lines drawn across their apartment buildings across their school districts across their neighborhood their parking permits their paychecks and just taking it and taking it and bitching. People complaining about being a loser being a fan of a losing team about coaches about players, people complaining about who you are and who you aren't, people drinking beers and loving them and complaining about the beer the other guy is drinking. People worrying about cell phone plans, people worrying about the men in the park, the women who bring their children there, the mothers, the worrying the drugs gang immigrants breakfast at schools the race of the school the traffic and how it limits their livelihood. People at risk, under fire escapes, at intersections waiting to cross. People smoking cigarettes in alleys outside of sandwich shops, people attending free concerts in the park, nostalgic for free ice skating at the parks, driving moving trucks at the end of the month. People walking with other people, people online while walking, people online while home thinking about events and food and music and do-it-yourself projects. People buying *Streetwise*, people taking English as a second language at the community center, people complaining that there needs to be more community centers. People leaving the old neighborhood, people wondering where the city stops, people visiting people in prisons, people wondering how different he will be she will be when she gets home he returns. People watching television, on their couch, a window somewhere nearby. People on their front stoops watching children, watching newcomers, watching their friends never stop talking. People at city colleges, people dressed in nurse gowns, people on the bus falling asleep, reading books, wondering who will get on next. People gun-shy, gun-weary, government prone. People with their Link cards, with their fur coats, with their two hats on in February. People taking time off unpaid to visit their neighbors in the hospital, people relegated to coachhouses, top floors of high rises, garden units. People cooking, flames beneath pots, beneath meat, people pouring food from boxes onto dishware. People surrounded by tourists, surrounded by newspapers dispensers, coffeeshops, people surrounded by a noise that drops to the background of their existence. People drunk and alone, drunk and sober, drunk and at a club at a bar at a restaurant at their home on the couch, people drunk through the night through the weekend through the week. People coldly now there is just people. And one person in some strange chain of people who are thinking of me, wanting me to know they are out there, wanting me to look into a book by an author I did not know.

These were my thoughts the entire time I spent in the holding cell, questioned and harassed, staring at cops faces, staring at the cement blocks, the bars. The next day to be set free. I felt complicit in the hatred. I felt the racism which Chicago had stirred into my blood.

In no way did I intend to kill the kid who did it. I couldn't remember making the decision to open fire, it felt far more reckless than my typical wall slide in the shadows. But I had done it and now my hope was that the Chicago Police Department would want him behind bars, or that they could squeeze him for a bigger bite. I had guessed right— Holofernes DeMarco, son of an Italian fighter and a Mexican country woman—tough road ahead from the moment he was born. He had a rap sheet longer than a sawed-off shotgun and though quickly hospitalized, was monitored and locked up until he squealed just the way the CPD can make a man squeal. They didn't give a shit about me, though we had had our run-ins before, and they let me go with disdain and a smirk when they realized what line of work I was in.

When I returned home, I should have gotten into bed and slept for days. Instead I put on a pot of coffee, took a hot shower, cooked up some eggs, and wore my fatigue like Joseph wore his dreamcoat. So dire I was splendid.

It was freezing in my apartment, and I remembered that the window was broken. I took out the roll of plastic and taped it up for a temporary fix. Then I unrolled another layer and I taped it up for good measure. I decided that tomorrow I'd check in with Holofernes—but for now, all I could think about was Ruben Rorick: who was he and what case was it that got me on his bad side? Splendid question. I pulled my journal from my desk drawer where I kept notes on all my misgivings and mishaps which I call a living, and I sat down at my kitchen table, began reading and skimming for that name, eating my eggs, and battling my shifty mind with coffee. Splendid coffee.

The west side was the wild, wild west and I loved it. Each year in the 90s brought me more work. In 1997 I turned down more cases than I took. There had always been middle-aged artists living on the cheap, weirdos you might mistake as eccentric geniuses but were dick in a mustard jar weirdos, simple as that, addicts who had an air of wisdom but no way of articulating it, the sexually adventurous, and the violent rebellious bar-fighting types mixed in with the background lives of Hispanic immigrants and section 8 blacks. But when the art students flooded into the neighborhood, so did their alternate realities. So many variations of cults and communes began at the Inner Town Pub, Artful Dodger, over lunch at Leo's, The Rainbo Club, eating Shirley's muffins at Tuman's Alcohol Abuse Center. Stoned and reeling with charisma, a cult leader is born every night in this town. Neighborhoods like Wicker Park are what I call incubators. People get a taste for how great life could be, how alluring and feasible Utopia seems when you find like-minded people, when you get inebriated, when your sexuality bonds you to anyone who shines stunningly through the shadows. I left my cards around, so friends of friends who had disappeared could call me, or pass it on to the adults who swarmed the scene as soon as three weeks went by of no response from their loved-one. I know these neighborhoods, I know these desires, these fantasies, I know society, I know charisma, drugs, sex, I know manipulation and trust, the vulnerabilities of spiritual journeys, the ecstasies of new friends, the psychologies of power, how to dish it out and how to real it in. I woke most days with a mind to start my own cult, fuck everything that walked, live off their money, and make them raise my kids. But I could never stomach the needy, deleterious souls that black holes attract, so I got my fix by dipping my toes in as I investigated the missing person in question, sometimes going as far as to allow myself to be recruited, though I learned the hard way again and again not to get in too far with the sheep, for wolves are hidden within all of us.

I opened the cabinet above the sink and pulled out a bottle of whiskey, one I saved scrupulously for special occasions. A fine Irish whiskey my good friend McLiney brings back from Ireland: Writer's Tears. I was through holding back the good stuff. I sat down, poured a glass neat, lit a cigarette and began to write. Who had I crossed? Who would waste their time with me, want me dead? Which cases had involved more than I had realized?

Maybe Ruben Rorick led a cult. Maybe he had grown interested in cults, and maybe he had an interest in keeping me away from what interested him.

But *In the Penal Colony* was no hockey stick to the knees. It felt more like an invitation. A way in to a building which most sane people would trample others to get out.

My time in this city has not been filled with friends. However, there are many of us who survive on acquaintances, never getting to know another past the interactions we have on the sidewalks, at the registers, on the bus, in the park. Do not be fooled by Chicago's past— we have many leftovers, but today I am surrounded by swarming minds, listless styles, men and women who are not concerned with the narratives of American happiness, of farm and field and bible, who are willing to sacrifice the possessions and luxuries of materialism for the romp across the midnight, the mystery buried in the gutter, the early morning crack of nothing, the ringing of music through one's dreams, the madness and temptation of any given moment—we see each other in the streets and we know we have not forsaken our souls for a job, for a company, for a shoe that does not stomach. Though often we pass each other as if ghosts. Disappearance, a virtue of this city. This spectacle, this Chicago is real, this the brilliance beneath the Polish brick which has weighed these streets down for a century and a half.

The mustache you see on the streets is not genuine. It is a disguise. The bravado has crumbled into piles of teeth. The dive bar, no longer serves as a safe-haven from a working stiff's wife, but a pooling of filthy pearls, indolent illustrious men and women drinking not wanting to be hidden away ever in the pockets of day-to-day living. We have burned through, and the singed holes pocked across this city are now the homes of birds, nests built and songs sung within these buildings and across these streets. This city's grid has been deconstructed into its million pieces and individually put back together into deformations of character, bountiful structures of thinking, boulevards, avenues, streets—all winding towards intersections of personal ethics.

This word, ethics, has great significance to this city. We are not without are rules, are faults, and surely we will be paved over ourselves.

I look out my office window and see the trains full heading downtown.

I wanted to know which one of them interrupted my sleep to throw a book through my window. I wanted to talk to an acquaintance about a slim book where the first pages concerned the future of the very neighborhood I lived in. Where the narrator lived in the same building as I: 1958 Evergreen, there was no mistaking it. I grabbed my coat and alpaca hat, then headed out to see Michel over at Quimby's. I love saying the word alpaca.

5: In the Penal Colony

Quimby's Comics on North Avenue held an eccentric selection of publications and ephemera. On the magazine racks one could find titles like *Cheesecake, Subterranean Psychonaut Hygiene, Daytrades from the Cuddle Puddle,* as well as endless shelves of xeroxed pages folded in half and stapled together filled with drawings and words, seemingly created by other residents in the vicinity, things that discussed their anecdotes about avoiding capitalism, or their tastes in perverse sadistic narcoleptic teachings on taking over insomniac minds, or simply a sparse gathering of words coupled with copious images. I never knew if I were holding the work of a train-jumping, knife-wielding troubadour or a mystical noon-charged madame. Michel Comté, an old accomplice of mine and source for the strange, charged underground buzz, worked here sporadically and lethargically, leaving me reason to believe he owned it but no evidence to support this besides assumptions and a legacy of confirmation bias. We were close friends and had known each other long enough, but it was what we had been through, not how long we had been through it, that solidified our bond. I knew however, that searching for answers from him could never be a direct exposition. Tall, lanky, a dirt grey beard to his chest, a tank top in any season, he greeted me in his typical manner:

"How old benevolent hours have horse hairs near their houfs not growing in haste."

Always a game.

"Solidifying rates of long queer history over Japanese boardrooms breaks every half hour."

"Brooms suck ballerinas off as dusts discover twilight twice twinkled houndstooth suits."

"Why cruel jack hammers after claws forget me not to assuage."

"She asks and I ask and they know Peter Miller."

"Almonds lack what I can generate through meditation routines."

"Plum fact we forgot to fruit the loom."

"Hazards to borrow: stamps, olives and dice."

"Steak water, they bought a cow."

"Love my gun and twinkies."

"Skip made a face."

"Thou angst angry."

"Solidified hood."

"Stick."

"Saddle."

We were not alone; a teenage boy watched us in shock; the mania we tapped into has been reported to be infectious. Who knows how that boy changed in our midst. Surely he has grown less satisfied with the prosaic discourses that besiege us outside the comic store.

Our ritual always begun with fourteen and proceeded towards one word. Often to others' enjoyment and cheer. Once, taking stage at a concert during a set break, in front of the Empty Bottle hip, our exchange caused such a stir that all drinking ceased, the band came on the stage, and twenty minutes later at its conclusion we were given cigarettes by a group of art students and asked questions for the duration of the smoke.

"Anything new to share, Michel," I asked, hoping he would provide the next lock for my foolish ship.

"Always, my friend. My friend, have you encountered *Moby Grape*? It has a frenetic propensity. Unrequited freedom. Unhindered consequences that will never be comprehended beyond the first moment of beholding. Consider that! It might not be true. *Moby Grape*. Reborn in the breath of another tongue by an artist named Ruben Rorick." He always referred to comic book people as artists. "Lost for centuries, friend, he dug it up at a Pei Mai estate sale in Beijing. The deceased was the last of an esoteric Buddhist lineage specializing in the creation of dream objects. Not what you would assume! Their meditations were performed collectively, actively composing the landscapes, the houses, the little knick-knacks, all the household and civic items of the most irregular type you could or could not imagine. They forged them and then, my friend, they cast their creations into the worlds of those who happened to be dreaming at that very moment. At random. Consider that! Pei Mai's collection of books include a series of comics named simply by the Aleph א which Ruben Rorick has translated as *Moby Grape*, yet I would translate as *His Labyrinthine Story*, wouldn't you agree, friend, that is more suiting? Ruben took it upon himself to continue this lineage of dream meditations, and the comic, well, there it is. No, here it is, don't just consider the idea—be it. See it, my friend."

The cover was a brilliant spectrum of colors which at the center formed a square building which had no top, no bottom, a cornice on every side, square windows and a square door at the center. The title across the top in an oriental font, which I criticized to be foolish and mocking. The pages were sparse of strips at the beginning and the end, but gathered into an exquisite density in the middle.

I said as much to Michel. Then I asked, "How should I read this?"

"Notice the progression. The placement of the strips on the page. Follow them—they are in the design of the sacred maze of the Chinese scholar Pei Mai."

"I should like to take it with me."

"The price suggests extravagance, but friend, considering the story behind it, someone like you should understand."

"Ring me up."

"Around and around again!" He turned to the teenage customer, "And you, boy, would you like to taste a madness far greater than LSD? Speak up! Well, I'll take your silent acquiescence as a yes. Come with me in the backroom, there we keep our most curious editions, the knowledge within them shall diversify your perspective into a stunning crest of intuitive epiphanies."

In the shadow of Michel's debauchery, I snuck out leaving a quarter on the counter, and headed up Winchester, or was it Wolcott.

5: MOBY GRAPE

Quimby's Comics on North Avenue held an eccentric selection of publications and trinkets. On the magazine racks one could find titles like *Terryworld, Entheogen Cult Babies, Hypnotism for Realtors,* as well as endless shelves of xeroxed pages folded in half and stapled together filled with drawings and words, seemingly created by other residents in the vicinity, things that discussed their anecdotes about working menial jobs, or their tastes in lucid-dreaming fantasies, or simply a rant about something that could be hated. I never knew if I were holding the work of a wizard or a pre-pubescent girl touting the regality of her dolls. Michel Comté, an old accomplice of mine and source for the strange, charged underground buzz, worked here sporadically and lethargically, leaving me reason to believe he owned it but no evidence to support this besides assumptions and a legacy of confirmation bias. We were close friends and had known each other long enough, but it was what we had been through, not how long we had been through it, that solidified our bond. I knew however, that searching for answers from him could never be a direct exposition. Tall, lanky, a dirt grey beard to his chest, a tank top in any season, he greeted me in his typical manner:

"What would we wear were we werewolves where wearing what we wear were wolves?"

Always a game.

"Extracurricular essence activates that which circularly adorns the bodies free time to play."

"Lapping milk from untapped faucets while we wait out the monster within."

"Three plays played backwards returns us to the night we fled."

"He who does not scare himself to sleep races eternity."

"Rattles beneath the asphalt of the city's wallpapered daydream."

"A horse to be shot through a gun."

"The park planted over the dark key."

"Four steps to the harmony door."

"Grumbling in the collection hat."

"Denounce thy banana habits."

"Sell your trip."

"Tourniquet insurance."

"Oatmeal."

"Plaque."

We were not alone; a teenage boy watched us in shock; the mania we tapped into has been reported to be infectious. Who knows how that boy changed in our midst. Surely he has grown less satisfied with the prosaic discourses that besiege us outside the comic store.

Often to others' chagrin, or even protestation, our ritual always begun with fourteen and proceeded towards one word. Once, at a Gala in our youth, in front of the height of Chicago society, upon running into each other in the middle of the dance floor of the Grand Ballroom, our exchange caused such a stir that all dancing ceased, the band came off the stage, and twenty minutes later at its conclusion we were escorted to the street by men in tuxes. We were not wearing tuxes. Our reputations forged but our invitations out dwindled.

"Anything new to share, Chuck," he asked, docile with my ulterior motives.

"Always, my friend. My friend, have you encountered *In the Penal Colony*?"

"Slim book? Fourteen fire escapes on the cover, right?"

"I have it here."

"Well, there are several customers I have who would be interested in this, to know of it, to hold it."

"Why is that?"

"Some say it has prophetic properties. Others that it shape shifts. All I know is what I have read within the pages, whether it changes for another or whether it predicts our neighborhoods unfoldings, we'd need more data to understand."

"Occult stuff?"

"Not exactly, but yes. How the very moment we are living shifts based on our perceiving. Right up your alley. How did you come about it?"

"A gift."

"Let me guess, The North Coast Video guy—is his name Jason, I always forget?"

"No."

"Maybe you should talk to him, though, he has traced the contours of this text, even created a few companion maps. Word is they are making it into a tour—you remember Stan, right? He'll be the guide."

"This all seems cryptic, Michel. What do you think this book has to do with me—I don't even read. I stopped reading books when I was twenty-four, stopped watching movies a few years before that. Who is the publisher?"

"It says here Las Sangres. The bloods. This is the only book that I know they have put out. Your reality is unmediated, I like that, you know I do. But, anyways, here you are, brought by a book. You can't escape *In the Penal Colony*. Look, it came with a bookmark."

Michel handed me a business card. Ruben Rorick. His title was listed as Vineyard Manager for Las Sangres. The address seemed eerily familiar to me.

"Michel, I received mail from this same address yesterday. In California."

"What was in it?"

"I didn't open it."

"You don't need a bookseller to read you the newspaper."

"Las Sangres isn't a book publisher; it's a vineyard."

"A bottle of wine would have broken your window much easier."

"You're sharp today."

"Would you rather I say, you know, like, you know, something seems weird, man. You know."

"Maybe it's not their wine that they want me to drink."

"*Via con Dios, Senior.* Follow the blood."

"Time for you to go back to sneering at your customers."

"See you on the tour."

"Right. Tell Stan to mention me by name."

Returning home, I pulled the mail out from the pizza coupon drawer and opened up the California letter. An invitation to celebrate the marriage of Levi Seeds and Miriam Dos Santos. My childhood friend Levi would be married in 10 days on Las Sangre Vineyards.

There beneath the location and details of the celebration was what I believed to be a prayer:

Your eyes, they watch over us.

Your temperature is our blood.

We walk with you. Never alone.

We walk with you. You return us home.

Your blessings. Your riches. In your honor.

Ruben Rorick

In the RSVP envelope, a plane ticket and confirmation for a room at El Prado Inn. Ruben Rorick. Who was this man? And what did he want from me? I knew then and there I would be attending a wedding at week's end.

Ten years ago, Levi would have asked me to stand up with him as a groomsman second to his brother, Gil. But ten years ago he was with a different woman, and we were both different men. It's funny how the most innocent aspects of childhood can return to you later in life filled with vengeance. It's sad how past offenses can fester, grudges can grow into hits. Levi Seeds, as I said, was a dear friend, I'd go as far as to say my best friend; he grew up in the building directly across from mine on Surf Street. An odd name for a Chicago street but Lake Michigan has its waves too, and our neighborhood of Lincoln Park butted up against the beaches and harbors. In those days, most of the beachgoers were junkies, the closest thing to a surfer was a homeless man riding the waves of Wild Irish Rose. The neighborhood was a wreck, but we felt proud to be so close to the Gold Coast and Old Town neighborhoods to our south with respectable types. We knew they were coming our way, but neither Levi's nor my parents saved for it, and while we were away at college, they were going broke by rent hikes, losing hope watching the erasure of the place they knew, mom and pop store owners packing up while chain stores took over the multi-thousand dollar leases. Instead of finding a new neighborhood, they moved to the suburbs and withered away until their early deaths. I was at both of Levi's parents' funerals in Palen-tine, while Levi sent flowers in his place.

Though we went to our share of funerals growing up, one I remember vividly connected to Levi. A classmate of ours, Dontae Williams was shot coming out of Carousel Foods, a little grocer on Lincoln Avenue with circus neon signs dancing above the entrance. It was dark, right before close, and the car sped away as his body dropped across the lit-up cement. Everyone said he was in a gang, that is why he was shot, as if that was a reason that we should not worry, as if that was a legitimate excuse for one to be killed. Those of us who knew him knew that he was in a gang as much as I was on the Cubs—he wore their gear, tried to talk to them when he saw them, told stories of the things he heard them do, but Dontae was twelve years old. Gang-related, the reporters wrote and no one knew what to make of this phrase, but Levi, even at that age, he had another point-of-view: "A sacrifice," he said to me—"Dontae was a sacrifice the gangs had to make. Our neighborhood had to make—there was too much tension building up, didn't you feel it, Chuck, tension with all the robberies and all the complaints by our parents. He was sacrificed, and now there will be a calm in our streets."

Strange thinking for a twelve year-old, and his logic, I even felt then, was skewed. But the passion with which he discussed this—you couldn't argue with. He knew what he knew and did not budge from all it compelled him to do.

At the funeral, Levi brought with him a doll that he had hand-stitched. "This is Dontae," he said as he opened up his jacket and pulled it from the pocket. "I performed a few rituals I read about at the library, to heal him. Rituals which need to accompany the sacrifice."

He said all these things to me and I was in too much shock to register the severity of the waters he was wading in, so I just listened. Attended the funeral dumbstruck. No burial because there are no more burial grounds left in Chicago, so he was cremated, and placed I do not know where. After the funeral we all planned to meet me at the park with our friends to throw around the frisbee, there was talk of a six-pack of Milwaukee's Best, and when Levi did not show, I searched for him, finding him with that doll, setting it to flames on the sand of Oak Street Beach.

Levi's convictions were scary at times, but our friendship never stilted. After graduation we traveled together, wrote letters, spilled our lives out in front of each other. Each of us eager to confess something that the other one was not quite able to hear, not quite capable of being distracted enough with our own obsessions to process another's. It's easy to blame it on him because as an aspiring winemaker, he sought the kind of fame which changes a man. But something had begun to change in me over the years as well. Something that was always there but took its time in coming out. The cases I handled more atrocious, the clients I accepted more despicable, the thoughts that crossed my skull more forlorn. Hope, I could barely persuade my clients I had the guts to take on their problems—hope was a youthful sin I had long ago forgiven myself. Life has a way of dismantling our relationship with the past and the person we thought ourselves to be.

6: In the Penal Colony

In his backyard, my neighbor Hector did not see me when I returned home. I walked inside, up the stairs, and made myself comfortable in my kitchen, brewing a pot of tea which seemed fitting for my indulgence into this strange, allegedly Buddhist, comic. I sat in my favorite chair, let the heat escape from my ceramic cup, and stared out my window. I could see Hector, hanging out in his garage, rolling a joint as he listened to the weather on his transistor radio. In the alley, a scavenger collected cellophane and foil in his shopping cart, along with pizza boxes, which I presumed, he would cut the coupons off, and upon reaching twenty be rewarded with a free pizza. That's what I would have done. If I were him.

I opened the *Moby Grape* and as I did so, a piece of paper the size of a fortune fell to the table. Michel must have understood my code.

It read:

"I dig out tiny caves and store gold and silver in them. Bridges of silver, crowns of gold—they are the smallest you could imagine. Sooner or later, everyone comes to me, though the sound of my work terrifies them. Who am I?"

So much in so little time, I took a deep breath and walked into my office. There, among the scraps and pieces of my life's work, I pulled out the boxes marked: Mentor, Nightingale, The Loom, and Luxury. I slid the desk drawer open and pulled out an empty notebook and a pen. I had received this notebook as a gift some years ago. Though I could not remember from whom, I knew I had been saving it for an unforeseen task, and there was no doubt in my mind that this was that time.

I would write myself out of this maze.

Common riddle knowledge states that clues build upon each other and should not be looked at in isolation. They delineate a world, a logic of their own and this must be traced.

Seated in my rolling chair at my desk, I wrote and swiveled, swiveled and wrote. Back and forth, slowly in a circle, glancing around my office, gathering clues and insights as they came to me. My past crammed into this little room: colorful playbills and posters overlapping one another, my prized piece of art by Neo Rausch—I knew him as a child, consulted his coming of age—an archive of puzzles in boxes stacked to the ceiling, masks from the parades during my time in the 7th Ward, big insects pinned to the wall—thorax shells like oil puddles splayed with light—phone numbers written on the wall, easily one hundred phone numbers were visible to me, and psychedelic posters, Bill Graham's finest—I took pride in organizational feats such as this, though over the years I have always relied upon speed to accomplish such things, as if it wasn't me at all who did this, instead the motor-machine which each new day flips the on switch—and on the floor an intricate, thin, hand-woven oriental for which I traded my first royalty check, a puzzle splayed out in geometric and floral patterns. I rested my eyes on this, activating my riddled mind. And I began transcribing into my notebook.

Like a tongue sliced by heaven, my mind forked. Then folded, as Michel would say, like a loving crepe. The pages of the comic butterflied before me. My consciousness spread through the expanses. But in the middle of a frame, I would return to this real world we share, like a yo-yo finished with its tricks spinning back to its master's hand, and find that I had not been transcribing the pages before me, but staring out the window to my left.

I have no recollection of how this transaction took place or at what exact moment, but my attention shifted from image to window in the slyest manner. It took me longer than I desired to get through this great book, and I wondered what transpired outside that window.

I saw a long granite platform with train tracks on each side. A blue and white mosaic of tiles caught my eye across the ceiling of the tunnel. There were others, but none would turn to me to show their face.

I admired the pattern of the tiles, turning the pages at a slow pace staring up. I made out the geometry of fourteen Native American faces over seven paces, fourteen magicians over the next seven, then fourteen sunken slaves, then fourteen homeless men slouched into the corners of fourteen extraordinary intricate and ornate buildings.

Between the magicians and the slaves I passed an accordion player busking for change. He did not smile in return to my bow, intent in his haggard squeeze, a song I had heard many times before: "Strangers in the Night."

He sang the lyrics in Polish and I noticed a mistranslation in his words: "Strangers in the night/ I hear them calling/ wondering what a sight/ will be their falling/ how to realign/ a row of pearly whites."

The answer to Michel's riddle felt near.

This song, I knew it well, but I could not remember from when in my life. I recalled a cold building where

I once spent many hours staring at my thoughts as the speakers built into the walls cycled through Barry Manilow songs, along with other soft rock of that era. This memory gathered so strong throughout my body, but it was as if a dream, unlocatable in the real world. A soft rock. A rock soft. A lite melody. A tune dripping with lovely sentiments. A gooey mid-afternoon snack. I could not help but be fascinated by soft sincerity.

The dentist.

A loud thunderous rumble interrupted my reverie. I pulled the change from my pocket and dropped it in the hat. The train pulled up and I got on.

A con, no doubt. The age-old sleight-of-hand played out across me. The quickness, the dexterity of the hand which concealed the nut within the cup impressed me, yes, but it hurt much worse to know that for one thing, I was on the losing end, and for another, as everybody knows, that nut is only present at the beginning of the game, and mid-shuffle, the con man removes it. One gets lost in the show of this game and does not have the strength to admit that it is an illusion.

There's more to train rides than the initial consideration reveals. An onslaught of bodies underground. Traveling through a world of Rats and steel and caissons and bums and garbage endlessly and workers in yellow vests always huddled in repair or tight squeezed to the wall as the train zooms by. Bedrock. The feeling. The possibility to arrive elsewhere is often taken for granted. But its true mystery is not lost on me. I bathe in this gesture until I reek of destination. An incongruity. There exists a willingness and a capability to believe in something else, something other than what is right here and now which often goes overlooked.

I did not know which train I was on. Alone in the car, I felt there was no way of finding out.

This worry lied at the center of my confusion, paralyzing me at my kitchen table, unable to make my morning coffee or pour my bowl of Trix. Simply staring at my thoughts, all my attention displaced from my open eyes. And in transcribing א, traveling off and back again, I realized: if it is all just a game, then I would be as much a game as the game I played.

With this decision, I began to discover an immense energy, ever-present, malleable. Every detail, every situation, every person, even history itself manifests and behaves according to the logic which organizes it. And equally, my perceptions were welded by a similar stone and cutter. I dislodged myself from the logic inherent to the riddle and I multiplied my perspectives, projected my field, swelled my being so as to define that which once defined me, surrounded me, chewed me into its name brand pulp.

I looked at my calendar: *2pm Dentist*. I did not know many things, like whether this calendar had been kept current or remained on my walls from years past. But it was something to go on, so I laced my shoes and grabbed at the space where my hat would be had I already gotten one like previously planned. And I walked down the stairwell and out my front door.

6: MOBY GRAPE

Not long before Levi and I fell out, we traveled Europe together. He, excited to drink European wine, visit vineyards and tout his expertise, and I, at the time, had given up reading, the books which had formed the backbone of my being. I wanted to live, I wanted to read my experiences as I used to read the pages of Genet, Celine, Gide. Ursulines Lis met up with us on that trip. It was in Biarritz, a quaint affluent surfing town on the Northern Coast of France. Indeed, very much like Santa Barbara. I, of course, was as struck by her stunning beauty then as I was that Friday night in Santa Barbara. I could not keep my eyes off her. And to make matters worse, she spoke French fluently, whereas Levi announced time and again that he could only hold his own in Spanish, the language of farmers, cooks, the silent peoples with whom he aligned his soul.

It was only a few days, but excited to have a companion to converse with in a foreign language, Ursulines and I talked incessantly, annoyingly back and forth about life, our dreams and philosophies, our desires and passions, our sufferings—just as we imagined the French would, just as we had seen in Godard's films. Yet all of it, I see now, cut with the suspense of Clouzot. It all felt heightened; as it should, pouring forth in that language seeped with romance. We were young. Worlds away from our hidden selves. Levi became upset by our chemistry, and one night in particular he let it be known.

Though we were able to cough up the money for flights, neither of us had worked for long nor had any wealth to speak of. However, Levi's older brother had climbed the ladders at Younger Cole, a high-powered real estate investment trust based in Manhattan. Gil Seeds, none more smoother, suave or witty than he. Eight years our elder, growing up we admired him from afar—his stories of fantastic nights, crazy friends, drugs, sex, the debauchery all teenagers long for. Successful in everything he did—painting, sports and girls in high school; straight A's, fraternities and girls at Princeton; high-paying job, fast famous friends, and women—the type of women every man wishes this life was filled with—as soon as he arrived in New York. The spectacle of his life was all we knew. The pressure Levi felt to be like his brother was something that constantly made him suffer yet pushed him to excel. Gil had sayings, which Levi made famous among our groups of friends. One of them was: "Make it nice." Another: "Spend it all tonight; we'll make more tomorrow." These were his philosophies of life. And in this vein he had given Levi an American Express Gold card for "whenever the occasion called for it." And in every city or town we passed through on our travels, we would choose a night to celebrate life and youth, and we would inquire about the sexiest restaurant in town. We performed well in our high society roles, until the booze set in and we would nudge laughter out of each other's ribs. Cause a minor scene and stumble out the already opened door.

Gil met up with us in Paris. He had been working on land transactions for certain European companies which I knew little about, but when he spoke of them, they seemed to be the premiere, the eldest, the most respected in their field. I remember our night, its gluttony and debauchery. The way Gil laughed at every sin, from deep inside, and how it ended, our night, passing prostitutes back and forth between us, each in a different room separated from the hallway by a curtain. We did not leave till sun-up, awash with sex and tobacco, I think only I was high but who knew what each of us had ingested in our separate dens. I told them I was in love, Monique, I said, she is my heart and soul. Gil tensed up, and said, No, my friend, she is mine. Well, you may love her body, but I, good Gil, love her *entirety*. He ran back in the nondescript door we had only minutes ago exited. Levi and I lit a cigarette and waited, smiling and shaking our head in shame at the same time, when suddenly Gil burst back out dragging Monique behind him, barely dressed. Let's go, he said. Monique, mi amor, take my hand, I said. She was scared I could see it in her eyes, and Gil pulled her further from us, rushing up the street to who knows where, to do the devil knows what. We didn't see him again that trip.

Levi dismissed the events, never bringing up the night, but his mood had noticeably soured. He was embarrassed, possibly ashamed that our night together with Gil did not go down into the book of stories to be told for years to come.

After ten or so gluttonous nights such as this, the thrill had dried up, the event and the quality taken for granted. But in Biarritz, with Ursulines there, we had someone new to share in this spectacle. Like fat French kings bored with our filth, we were excited to show off the decadent tastes we had acquired over those past few weeks. Whereas in Madrid and Lisbon we had gone out dressed like slobs in tight t-shirts and tight pants—Euro-trash style as

Gil had called us—that night with Ursulines we revisited our dark suits and stylish shirts which we had tailored for us at the beginning of our trip in Florence. Ursulines as well knew the thrill of glamor and glitz, and Levi had taken her shopping that day where she purchased an exquisite red dress; a color, as she would say, that might make my man want to drink me more than his precious grapes.The dynamic of three is always difficult to manage, and on that night we each were feeling at the center of the world's attentions—sexy, rich, and powerful. All a charade made possible by a piece of plastic with a Manhattan billing address and our individual desire to live a story worth telling. I knew exactly what I was doing: I just didn't yet know how fragile love between two people can be, and how seriously I could damage it. I was playing my part—acting suavely with a put-on charm, wit, and style. Just as Gil Seeds would do, I thought—and, though I would not find out for years later, just as he would have wanted.

I remember clearly the view of the bay from our seat at the restaurant. The pink and orange sky fading to indigo. The stars blinking through this world's veil, constellations we had never seen before, allowing us to feel we had stepped into an alternate reality. The sunset surfers hanging around on the beach, laughing in the easy seat of life. The white cap waves evenly and rhythmically building with the tide, crashing an exhilaration as old as dreams; the undercurrent inhaling all it met beneath the surface. The cliffs, pedestals for romantic villas built in solitude and grandeur upon the most remote and dangerous overlooks. There were only five or so other tables on the terrace where we sat, and their eyes were on us, watching our evening unfold. A dazzling sight of youth—they surely knew that the girl's attentions were our gold. As if they were pushing us further, deeper into the drama that was between us—three souls excited to be so near such a vulnerable edge. An extraordinary feat of balance and poise which the most fantastic moments of life require. A topic we continually returned to during our days in Biarritz was life's potential to be extraordinary. We questioned our experience of life—could one revel in the spectacular while experiencing it. Or was this impossible, and experiences only became extraordinary in hindsight, in history—in the retelling. A dangerous subject which was more like a dare than a discourse. The stakes were high, pushed to mythic proportions by our words. We ordered our first bottle of champagne, and drank to our night, together, in the only place any of us wanted to be. The fictions of our mood socked us in. And the unraveling began.

"To Ursulines," I toasted. "Your arrival is right on time."

"Yes! To Ursulines. Thank you joining us, my love," Levi said.

"No need to thank me. This is France," Ursulines said. "Better, I admit, than nights spent at Harvey's. I'll have to work a few extra shifts to pay it off, but then again, maybe I'll meet a French winemaker who'll make good on all my debts."

"Maybe you will," Levi winked.

"Who's Harvey?" I asked.

"A dive around the corner from my house."

"Does the wine taste differently?" I asked. "Here rather than there."

"I mostly drink PBR there, Charlie, so yes, it does."

"You're the only woman besides my mom who calls me Charlie. She hated that my dad chose Chuck."

"It is a little déclassé. Are you from Ohio, maybe, or is it more rural Maine?"

"Ask Levi, growing up in Chicago has its déclassé moments. Sounds big city, but really, a bunch or derelicts licking their head traumas."

"Wine is not just what's in the bottle," Levi picked back up. "I wish it was simply a matter of making the best wine, but the French will always have the States beat based on the ambiance alone. It's like a word, Chuck, or should I call you Charlie, too—when you use it in the best sentence the word comes alive in an entirely different way."

"I'm done with words in sentences. I told you, no more books—only life. Only *this*: tonight, this glass filled between three friends. The stars. Our eyes, our minds, the cooks sweating it out over fish."

"Harvey's is more of a phrase, I would say, than an entire sentence," Ursulines rounded the two of us out nicely.

"A dependent clause maybe."

"What about the hangovers," I asked. "I'm interested to know if they are any different here than back in your bed around the corner from Harvey's."

Levi Responded, "Why already be thinking about this night from the perspective of tomorrow's hangover?"

"All devious men premeditate their actions by contemplating the experience of digesting them, don't you think?" Ursulines said, "That Charlie is devious?"

"I know all too well how Chuck works. I am only trying to re-engineer his make-up."

"Never too late to be saved," I said.

Levi continued, "See, I believe it is possible to feel more in the moment than one could ever feel for the past." Levi, as always, took the romantic position.

"Surely you've covered that ground before I arrived," Ursulines said. We had arrived to the scene we always hoped for: philosophers in France, filled with sex and wine, not a care for money, or tomorrow.

I reveled in this cynicism. "The problem is that in these most romantic of times are the times we are closest to death."

"But once you become trusting of death, isn't a nearness to death a true proximity to life?"

"Yes," Levi agreed. "Though many despair in these more passionate moments of living, it is the realization of how desperate one is to live, and an acceptance of this that allows one to empty oneself and clear way for life, pure energy of being, to enter."

Ursulines went on, "This shift in perspective is only possible in these beat, emphatic moments, invigorating the soul at a deeper register than possible as rememberer, onlooker, storyteller, whatever."

"And it is the shift which upends us—we are tumbled along with its grit and petals alike."

"But," I argued, "one becomes blinded by this moment of pure energy—is utterly crashed against the rocks by it, unable to find some understanding to fit it into. And so all that you speak fails in that true moment—is so separate from what you speak. Is only true now, once you have past it, regained your senses and chronology of being— once you begin to philosophize."

"Your favorite pasttime."

"It's just I do it so well." We had begun to cut.

Ursulines agreed, and then carried on in that forbidden tongue. *"La durée de vie est dans le sang, et non la veine. Dans le baiser, pas les lèvres."* (The life is in the blood, not the vein. In the kiss, not the lips.)

"Oui, la joi de vivre est une folie pour la danse, pas le partenaire." (Yes, the joi de vivre is a madness for the dance, not the partner.) In saying this, half of me recoiled, while the other half—the part of me which exists in my eyes—hissed. Our conversation was overheard and enjoyed until the waiter interrupted to the crowd's dismay with our dinners.

"You speak with a madness," Levi said. "I love you for it. However, your French might be the death of me. Nothing more boring than to be on the other side of understanding."

"Look at these plates," Ursulines said. "I've never seen such artistry with food."

"Fish caught in the waters which we watch. Here's a toast. To love, philosophy, and to the allure of life."

"Yes."

"And to living the life we imagine," added Ursulines.

"The one our souls yearn for," I said. Looking back now, I become disgusted with the intellectual idealism and pretension I carried myself with when I was young. And, of course, the way I flirted with my best friend's lover, behind his back yet before his eyes. Despicable. But what else is expected of youth? The urge to gather all of life, all the magic of existence into one night is to say yes to every impulse, every temptation. With age I have begun to understand that such a risk cannot be sustained, and it is what we can carry on, what we can beckon and be met with day in and day out that is the only available merit of life. Less a feast but less a fool.

Ursulines brought us back to contemplation of life lived versus life relived. "What about the more inane moments? Less crashing against the shores, more automatic and boring. Take for example some perfectly insignificant daily experience. I don't know, like."

"Like the chance encounter of two people in the lobby of an apartment building."

"Good, exactly. And I find my neighbor unlocking his mailbox."

"You have never seen each other before, you glance at each other briefly."

"And his back is turned as he struggles with the large magazines inside. These fragmentary instances of life express a profound truth."

"There's no truth in stained carpets, sand-filled cigarette spittoons, poorly shutting glass doors."

"Of course there is, that's exactly it as you're saying it—all these ordinary details of life lived testify to the shabby anonymity of a meeting place between the luxurious private lives that stand side-by-side behind the doors of the private apartments like individuals closed off from the others' subjective reality."

"The dreariness of waiting rooms, public bus stations—all these neglected places of collective living."

"But the essence of all those moments of living is to be inessential. Only the storyteller can inject an epiphany or any sort of symbolic meaning to these moments of life."

"These moments are what they are based on perception. Put such experiences in the eyes of a detective." Oh, I loved Ursulines. "I learn that the man I saw does not even live in my building, that he was in reality opening a murdered woman's mailbox."

"Your shift again. This shift in perception."

"Yes."

"With a detective you have a tireless appreciation of daily life, of lived routine and continuity, in which possessions are counted up and evaluated."

"And you find an uncharted wilderness in which the very notion of perception is called into question and revised."

"You two and your secret destines. Do you truly believe there is a kind of nemesis lurking beneath the surface the city? Or is this all a contemplative spectacle which gives not so much the illusion of life as the illusion that life has already been lived?"

"Proust, can I still speak of Proust even though I no longer read?"

"What's stopping you."

"Proust felt this keenly, this whole antagonism between spontaneity and self-consciousness. For Proust we can only be sure we have lived, we have perceived, after the fact of the experience itself; for him the deliberate, willful project to meet experience face-to-face in the present is always doomed to failure."

"All good conversations in France end with Proust."

"Agreed. I had a dream last night about lobsters," Levi said.

"You know my rule," Ursulines said. "Don't tell me

about your dreams and I won't sigh out of boredom."

"What?" I exclaimed. "Not hearing about Levi's strange dreams is like growing up without *The Muppets*—those weirdos just make life more fun."

"But he's no Jim Henson. Hearing someone trying to recall their dreams—it's silly."

"I know your rule, Ursulines, but Chuck anticipates hearing my dreams more than he anticipates his morning espresso, his romps with the women of Montmartre."

"They're often satanic, you know this Ursulines? What was that one, Levi, about the goat on the roof of your house being slain?"

"Right, and the fire bursting in the fireplace."

"Don't forget all the dolls coming to life in your child-hood room."

"But that was Paris and we don't want to bore Ursulines with Paris."

"Ursulines, we don't have to analyze them, just hear the story."

"One cannot help but take dream imagery and occurrence as symbol—it is a plague of our culture. Not the French."

"Cut it about the French, okay. My new rule is no more conjecture about French Culture. No more pretentious elitism which results in stereotypes. And no more speaking in Paris-talk."

"Paris-talk? Whoa."

"That's three rules."

"Three tenets to one law: no more French."

"Alright," we both agreed. Awkwardly turning our attention to our plates.

"So, the lobsters. Tell us before you are done eating."

"Is this why you ordered lobster—because of your dream?"

"The dream didn't come back to me until I saw they had lobster on the menu. But for me, dreams reach back from the future just as often as they extend from the past. So I would say that I dreamt about lobster last night because I had eaten it for dinner tonight."

"So, a question of causality, I like this."

"Yes, not a before and after type of thing—time moves forward, but some causes we cannot see, we cannot know—they reach back from the future and affect us in the now."

"Will you order another bottle of those Languedoc grapes when the waiter comes back by?"

"That bottle was brilliant, wasn't it? So in my dream, Chuck, you remember that Italian tailor in Florence where we bought those shirts, the one you are wearing tonight, so I was back there, making love to the Italian woman behind the counter. Well, not making love, but pleasuring her," he said a little embarrassed, "I was between her legs."

"I thought you said this dream was about lobsters," Ursulines said.

"I like to tell as much as I can remember. I guess there was really no pleasure involved because the whole time I was going down on her all I could think to do was to speak to her in Spanish. Being Italian, she replied in Italian, not understanding me and vice versa, until she finally became too upset and snapped her legs shut."

"Lobster-time," I said.

"Not quite. Something about the Spanish maybe, I'm not sure, but I found myself driving away from a big fat man. His eyes were turquoise. I had no idea what I did wrong but I began climbing all around in the car, which had transformed into a convertible, searching for what I possessed, which he wanted. I finally looked up, scared by the thought that I was no longer behind the wheel, and there, driving a car, was a lobster."

"Yes!"

"Quite a sight. Immediately I realized another lobster, this one more true-to-life sized, had pinched onto my sleeve. Then another on my back and another and each one I pulled off was suddenly replaced by another."

"Sounds like first course with Chef Pierre Gagnaire."

"Funny."

"Who's Pierre Gagnaire?"

"I began rolling around, noticed I was on the greenest of grasses, and looked up to see a beautiful villa shimmering before my eyes. Tucked into the hills of a small Mexican town along the coast."

"What was going on in the villa," Ursulines asked, admitting how attentively she had been listening, but her extreme impatience as well.

"I do not know. But I heard a gunshot, and I did not die, but found the walls of an insane asylum melting before me, as all the maniacs escaped across the land and jumped into the waters. That's when I woke up."

"Do you think the lobster symbolizes—"

"Don't start with it. Let's just appreciate it for the story."

"Fine."

"Are you eating that?" Levi asked as his fork pulled away from Ursulines' plate having nabbed a bite of her *poisson*, spiced with lavender and coriander.

"Guess not."

Levi's innocent charm and delivery had won the night back over to a lighthearted affair. We finished two bottles more of red, and with dessert a bottle of Sauternes, we did everything we could to make each other laugh. We were drunk and we were excited about how funny each of us could be.

After such a late and large dinner, strolling through town was a boring disappointment—the little life left were shadowed creatures, fixtures of the stone, dark eyes as only the French can see with. The three of us were arm-in-arm, trying hard to deny that the world around us would open up no more oysters, offer up no more pearls. We began gagging about the lobster dream again, moving away from the French's love for Jerry Lewis as our target of humor towards Levi.

"Wish we had a lobster to drive us into Spain."

"Wait. Levi has one hanging from his face!"

"That's just his mustache."

"Smells more like Italian pussy to me."

"*Oui, oui madame.*"

"*Aimez-vous déguster Italien?*" (Do you like to taste Italian?)

"*Oui, mais je sais que la langue bon.*" (Yes, however I know the proper tongue.)

We should have but we did not see Levi's fury coming.

"You know what, fuck this. You're nothing but a sloppy pimp. You really need another whore at your call to make you feel better about yourself? Do you?"

We were stunned. And he carried on. "First with Monique, now this? I've seen you flirt with everything that walks—this is the way you treat me, my brother? Fucking low-life who can't do anything on his own. *Comme un chien que vous mangez du sol.* (Like a dog you eat from the floor.) You think a man can make wine without knowing French?"

Drunk, Ursulines played up the betrayal. "Fuck you! You hide so much from me, and now I find out you've been playing spy? I can't believe it. You lie in waiting for an ambush."

"I knew you two would break my heart. Here's to life! Your precious moment of living. I hope you one day know how very close this moment has brought you to your death."

I said nothing. And he cut down an alley.

For a man who has been in the entirety of my life, I could not have imagined such a sudden disappearance. We were left there, disgusted with ourselves, yet angry and drunk. I had nothing to say, so as Ursulines pulled out a cigarette from her purse, I moved towards her and embraced her, passionately engaging her in a French kiss. As if to confirm all that Levi foresaw. As my hand slid up her thigh, I imagined the love we would make on the beach. I tasted it, yearned for it. The oblivion it promised. But then she was gone—out from my arms as suddenly as she had entered them, taking off her heels as she ran down the cobbled road.

I stood there exhausted by life, raggedly postured, stumbling in my thoughts. I tried to laugh a little, but it didn't hold—a vain attempt at mastering that which sucked me undertow. I could not return to the hotel, though later I would understand that is not where Levi fled to. Several figures, town urchins sneering about the night, slumped in the shadows of the stone streets witnessed this spectacle, and I could feel their eyes watching my collapse. I moved towards the beach, their eyes following me down. I could not comprehend all that I should have been ashamed of, only that I was ashamed to be alive. To be alive and to be so desirous of life. More, always something more, whatever the cost. And then I felt it in my pocket: Gil Seeds' credit card. We took turns signing the bill each night, and I had grabbed it from the table.

The stars did not receive me, the tides soiled the sand beneath my body, the cliffs stood as dark shoulders impeding my escape. Sleep took me, and the next day I began to make preparations to return to Paris—too lost in this self-contempt to let it play out upon my home. Too foolishly fortunate to not buy myself a week of whatever I wanted in the city that had always been the setting of my fantasies.

7: In the Penal Colony

Dr. Holofernes had held court at the six corners of Milwaukee, North, and Damen for as long as I could remember. The shabbiest of waiting rooms, it was once an Off-Track Betting facility for horse gamblers before the Doctor took it over. Hard-cracked, maroon vinyl seats staring at deep-tube televisions perched in corners, a betting window where now a receptionist resided, linoleum floors peeling up at the edges and pocked by cigarettes stamped out, the walls yellowed from the thousand cigarettes smoked daily, except for large rectangular absences where posters of horses once hung.

Years ago there was nothing out of place about it, but on that day of my appointment I couldn't help but laugh at its incongruous setting: next to it a Sushi restaurant, then a chef-driven Sports Bar, a French restaurant with a secret alley entrance, and on the corner a 5 AM bar infamous as a destination for young drunks to get laid; across the street a bank, a florist, a cigar shop, a brew pub serving Connecticut-style pizza, a fashion boutique. How did Dr. Holofernes remain?

Laughing gas. A small market, but lucrative. I often procured some before setting to work on a riddle book. Something to ease the ennui.

The sign on his glass door read, "Doctor Holofernes: By Only Appointment." I was fine in that regard, and always happy to unscramble syntax, though nervous about the dental work which awaited me. The problem teeth that I had were in fact due to the shoddy dentistry of the doctor—he had widened a space between two molars to fix a cavity yet never could figure out how to push them back in contact. Many warned me that I should seek a new dentist, but I had an affinity for the man, not to mention I lacked insurance and funds to pay in full, plus enjoyed his techniques, seldom practiced by others in those days.

I arrived a mere ten minutes early, though the receptionist had insisted it be fifteen, in order to fill out forms. They were the same forms I had filled out every time I had an appointment. I stopped complaining long ago. Though I admit, often I neglected returning them to him, excited by the array of magazines and the mystery of hiding said forms within their pages.

Anxious as I was about receiving more information than necessary in my attempt to interpret everything according to the riddle I was lost in, I chose neither to fill out said forms nor peruse the magazines. Instead I stared at the man next to me—a beige, gray, and green plaid polyester suit, a light yellow button-up covered by a thickly double windsor purple and green paisley tie, a long face when he stared, yet exuberant when he smiled, diminutive metal-rimmed glasses, cordovan shoes and paisley socks matching his tie.—wondering whether or not he was a ghost. A vestibule of the OTB.

I asked him a few leading questions.

"Which horse you on?"

To which he wittily replied, "The winning horse, guy. It's always the winning horse."

"Been to that Sushi restaurant next door?"

"Sushi? Find me a date and I'll take her anywhere."

"I hear ya. What about Kaleidoscope?"

"Is he running in the third?"

"You remember Frank's don't you?"

"Remember it—listen to this, when my son orders his hot dog, the kid says, 'make it right, ya hear.' Like he's some sort of shyster. I don't know what's gotten into him."

"Probably his mother."

"You said it."

Frank's had been out of business for at least two decades. Before I could begin rattling within the ghost's metaphysics to search for some answers to several of the menacing secrets of death, the man at the desk called my name:

"Manasses. Manasses?"

As if I wasn't the only person in the room.

"That's me."

"You can enter through that door to my left."

"Thank you."

"The doctor will arrive shortly. I will take you to your room."

Sitting in the dentist's chair, a panic bloomed across my every nerve. I looked out the storefront window to see a view of the alley behind the building and staring back at me a grim face pushing a shopping cart piled with broken furniture and pallets. I did not see the alley scavenger I had always known him to be, but instead, an instrument of this deceit which had suddenly blanketed my every moment of being.

Turtledoves gathered overhead. I do not know what it is about the electric wires which extend from this building across the alley, but this is the place the turtledoves want to be. The place they return to. At first they arrived as couples, calm in their companionship. And as the afternoon slipped towards evening, they gathered en masse. An accurate count eluded me, with all the cooing and nudging, but at most I counted fourteen. More flirtatious than confused, playful games erupted between them as I sat and stared. As the scavenger stared towards me, or at least towards the spot on the glass which had me directly behind it but I do not know whether he had his sights set on another vision, some reflection or some far off feeling fantasized again and again.

I came to understand the hustle playing out between us. Long stretches of eye contact, no matter who it's with, and wherever you look, there he is. But this understanding does little to ease the disquiet which ensued when I found it was I who was cooing and not the turtledoves which I watched through my window

Dr. Holofernes broke my contemplation. Wrestling his stainless-steel drill from the mouth of a taxidermy beaver, I felt threatened. The vertiginous unreason of the world derided the shallow ridiculousness of men like the scavenger and I. My hands atremble.

The stature of a bulldog, Holofernes wore a thin graybeard, bald head and sneakers. In the summer, a sleeveless undershirt revealing his hairy back, carrying around a towel which he used to wipe the beads of forehead sweat before they descended on his patients. In winter, he donned a parka lined with fur, his stocking cap folded up like a cat burglar. Recently, he had lost his vision and wore large, round, tortoise-shell frames—his friend Marcus had a connection at an eye-ware boutique a block down. When not above the swivel chair, he can be found at his desk down the hallway, smoking cigarettes, listening to the news on his transistor radio.

"Holofernes, you know the neighborhood, right?"

"This nuthouse? What a mess. Fucking beaver."

"How messed up was it?"

"Winston, look it. All this birdshit—it was all over the papers—I ought to pop each dove down one by one. People talk. You could have never known so much was going on here. Let go of the goddamned drill! Come on."

"Someone in your waiting room reminded me of the old days—you remember the old days?"

"You remember, too, like I told you get-the-fuck, ugh! There were seven of them, I don't know, at least. Another experiment on the crazies. Sack of beaver! From the inside. It was those seven who escaped, and they brought seven more with them. Hey, why don't you give me a hand? Aw fuck!"

"Did they ever catch them?"

"Everybody said it wasn't as easy as seeing a loon on the street when you caught one. God! Don't ask. Alright, who's my next patient?"

"I am."

"Was that your friend watching us?"

"I don't think so."

"Open up, let's take a look. Winston, you read, don't you?"

It is questions such as these that always leave me befuddled and hating mankind.

"I do, Holofernes. Yes."

"Just making chit chat. Here, hold this mask and breath in."

"Some other time, Holofernes."

"Five bucks a breath. You like that?"

"Is the weather going to stay warm?"

"That's what the weather man's saying. Feels like a few spots to drill. On number 7 upper, and number 7 bottom. Where's Carlton?"

"Is that his name?"

"Who? Your friend? Too much candy, Winston. You're not a kid, give that crap up. Let me just plug this in—that beaver took the charge out if it. Speaking of the neighborhood, you hear about Candyland? The fella had been camped out in his apartment for years—jars of piss, stacks of weird magazines, broken furniture, rolled up rugs—mess. He called his apartment Candyland. You didn't hear about this? He had thousands of them."

"The table top game?"

"The board game. It's a board game."

"I don't eat candy, Doctor."

"You saw this guy around. You had to. He was obsessed with a character in the game; guy called Lord Licorice. He dressed like him—kinda pirate-like, greased up mustache and villainous. And he invited kids over to play with him."

"You can stop there."

"None of the kids claim he did anything weird. Just that they played the game, Candyland, and he would get into it, dancing around, talking in a funny voice, all that. Kids said they had a good time."

I knew I should be going before the drill had a full charge, but this news was stunning. "So why did they capture him?"

"Turns out he harassed principals of the local grade schools. Write them letters. Prank call them in a weird villainous voice. Strange threats about pulling up the floors to reveal swamps, and popping the lightbulbs like piñatas with pencils. He wanted the principals to stop screwing up the children—he wrote this long manifesto about children being shackled by the structure of grammar school; that they needed imagination. He'd even got in their offices and stole objects from their desk drawers—staplers, rulers, quizzes—and filled them with candy. Wait, you hear that—it's ready."

"Alright, Holofernes. I need to hit the bricks."

I stood up, noticing hundreds of turtledoves had flocked above the scavenger.

"Here! One more before you go," and he shoved my head into the mask as the Carlton, the receptionist, handed me a complimentary sack of the usual: floss, travel-sized toothpaste, and toothbrush.

Walking along North Avenue, the bouncing pixelated lights of the Currency Exchange's mascot, Penny the Penny, caught my eye. Dancing and cheering between the words: *Checks Cashed! Sameday Service! Short-term Loans! All Welcome!* Absentmindedly, I opened up the sack and threw the hygiene devices to the ground. I sat down on the curb, transfixed. The #56 bus rolled by honking, a close-call I admit, and I picked up the toothbrush, examining the bristles, Dr. Holofernes' name and information printed in gold on the handle, all normal. The toothpaste I squeezed onto the cement and smeared, nothing there. The floss I opened and pulled the plastic until I felt a click. And resistance. I pulled harder, my head bouncing poofs of pleasure and wobble with the strain—tied to the floss out came a strip of paper the size of a Chinese fortune. On it read: *Two girls, who were born on the same day, of the same week, of the same month, of the same year, to the same mom, but are not twins. How so?*

Just then the crack of glass smashing on the sidewalk startled me. I looked and saw a tidal wave of coins spill in my direction. Payday—I filled my pockets fast and got up, running through the nearest alley before drowning in the silver.

7: MOBY GRAPE

After lying in bed for an extra hour, recounting every detail I could recall of my friendship with Levi, I finally worked my body out of bed, got dressed and headed out to talk to Holofernes. It was Sunday morning and I knew where to find him.

It was late February in Chicago, a time when nothing goes right for those who pass their time in the streets. While the professionals are curled up on their over-stuffed couches watching their flat screens and the exec-utives drive warmly to and fro in SUVs, the Vienna Beef bus-riders are encased in long underwear. The hustlers stay warm by the dopamine cook of their scheming. The good decent people are worried at their tables stiffened by wooden chairs eating end-of-the-week soup and sign-ing their paychecks over to People's Gas. Those teetering towards insanity, like I was, sit on the steps of Mission Christiana waiting for mass to be over and Holofernes to walk out. By no means was he a Christian man, and most in our neighborhood understood this, but Holofernes knew there was no better way to drum up business than to sing the salvation of *Jesús*, smile at the congregation and greet them with a handshake, *dios te bendiga*. And no group more willing to put up with an ingrate than Chris-tians—one never knows when a sheep will hear his shep-herd's call. It was an age-old practice which Holofernes executed flawlessly.

We used to keep a regular card game on Saturday nights, where he would drink a little or a lot too much and brag about his cons. I try to never judge another man's misdeeds because I believe we all run cons of different emotional or financial varieties. There is not a truthful one among us because we firstly always con ourselves and do not even know the truth to tell it. And I appreciate those like Holofernes who among friends openly admitted and discussed his exploits. However, as often as one boasts, one backfires, and word spreads like the flu among the fifth grade in a neighborhood like ours. It wasn't long before El Padre sat down with Holofernes and the others, no concern for a *guero's* soul like mine, and convinced them of the sin of cards, smoke, drink. It was the ill-repute, not the sin, which scared him away. And our card game folded one week after Holofernes won his last big pot. Conniving as he was, he could make a refrigerator out of a stove, turn a window unit into a hot plate, hang drywall faster than most can hang a painting, and fix a window stoned to kingdom come.

I waited until there were no more neighbors for him to converse with and didn't hesitate to interrupt his exchange with El Padre. "Holofernes, good morning. Come on over this afternoon? I've got a job for you." El Padre's brown eyes vacantly retreated as I said this, then he turned away to go back inside.

"*Que paso, guey?* Why you gotta make me look bad in front of the priest?"

"I got a broken window. It's costing me by the minute."

"What the fuck kinda shit have you been messing around with?"

"Word's out?"

"You shoot a kid's thumb off. Put a hole in my roof. It's all people are talking about—not the sermon, not repairs they need—your bullshit is costing me *dinero, guey*."

"It's cold. Let's walk."

"And you're already out of the slammer. Who'd you finger? People are wondering—I am wondering. You didn't mention me, did you?"

"No. Nobody. The cops don't give a shit if a gangbanger Mexican gets shot—they prey on busting your all's balls. I don't have to tell you any of this. What do you know about that kid?"

"I know he's not going to live a week once he gets out—whether he squealed or not, the kind of people he runs around with don't take chances."

"Who's he mixed up with?"

"Just who you'd suspect—drugs, whores, guns, Kings, all that. When did you dirty yourself?"

"I'm not my own fucking grapevine, Holofernes. Can you come by this afternoon?"

"It's Sunday. What the fuck do you mean, grapevine?"

"It's a saying."

"Say whatever you want. My *mamacita's* cooking tamales for the Bears game. I'm not gonna make it over today."

"They're gonna lose."

"Fifty bucks and pay me today."

"Fuck off, fifty?"

"You fuck off."

"Alright but you got to do me a favor."

"What do I look like?"

"Like a man who people talk to. Find out what has been circling these streets, whether it has to do with me, the kid or not. Anything out of the ordinary."

"Yeah, I'll ask around."

"*Hasta luego.*"

"Don't talk that fucking Spanish. It doesn't suit you."

"Yeah well I ain't looking to be suited. You're not gonna invite me in for a cup of coffee, quick card game on the alter?"

"No chance, *amigo*. Inside are my real clients. Not fucking *pinche guero* bullshit fix it today bullshit."

"3pm."

"*Pinche*."

8: MOBY GRAPE

An inch of snow had fallen in Chicago before Holofernes arrived that evening to fix the window. I had spent the day at the library researching Levi Seeds' career as a winemaker, reading microfiche of old editions of the Santa Barbara News-Press, trying to piece together any connections.

After he returned from Europe, Levi landed a job in Napa Valley working for a high-powered wine family, the Bucklers. He did very well for himself there and by the time he was twenty-five, the head winemaker, Jacob Growler, had been fired for unknown reasons, moved to Santa Barbara to work for a start-up venture, now extremely famous, called Howling Vulture. The owner of Howling Vulture was none other than Sam Jankewski, a billionaire heir of JCPenny who had no apparent motive to get into winemaking than to simply have something to brag about. Turns out he wanted not one vineyard but two, and Jacob Growler quickly recruited Levi to found and run Las Sangres. At the age of 25, Levi Seeds was the youngest head winemaker in the recorded history of California grapes. Three years into it they released their 1994 to critical acclaim. After write-ups in *Food & Wine, Spectator, Wine Advocate*, and a strong score of high 90s from Robert Parker, Seeds was an instant celebrity, selling his bottles for over a hundred dollars while limiting customers' purchases to three. All this, of course, creates a buzz. Opposite to the public's expectation, after Howling Vulture shut down operations, Las Sangres Vineyards reached new heights of popularity and acclaim. The sister vineyards had been sold and there was a tension between Growler and Seeds that I noticed in the write-ups, but nobody was named as the new owner of Las Sangres. There was a Frenchman, Armand Richelieu, mentioned as consulting on the sale of the property. At the time of his wedding, Seeds was in his prime—an unprecedented prime and early in his life, the age of 32.

There it was. Information. So easily I had all this, knew this much, and still knew nothing at all of the reality woven together. Just enough information to make sense of what Holofernes was about to tell me, or at least at the time for me to believe I had something figured out. Too much information combined with imagination and a headstrong desire to know can lead you down a path that doesn't even exist. A path picked out of thin air just because it seems as though one plus one plus one equals three, so how could it be wrong. Just because it seems like a motive ought to be there, that surely this was all adding up to something.

"You might be real fucked."

"Who was that kid connected to?"

"The window, amigo—not so easy to fix. You got damage to the frame."

"I'm not paying you more than the fifty I promised."

"You like tacos?" Holofernes had a stupid smile on his face, his eyes were thin lines.

"I bet you like tacos."

"Yeah. I do."

"Your wife make tacos tonight?"

"No, man."

"She just roll you a joint and send you on your way?"

"No, man. She rolled the tamales. It's Sunday."

"You all and your days of the week—love them routines."

"Yeah."

"You got some tamales?"

"No. Tacos. Why, you like tacos?"

"Cut to it, Holofernes."

"There's a guy you should go see. Ask him for *conejo y chivo*."

"Shit. I don't want to get deep into all this Mexican shit."

"His name is Umberto—he is very short. Shorter than a woman. He used to ride horses. Don't talk to the tall one—that is his brother, Roberto. You do not want to talk to him. Ask Umberto, for *conejo y chivo*."

"A little jockey named Umberto serving tacos out of a truck—this is what you got for me?"

"And a window, *guey*. Watch it!"

"Is it in?"

"You should really consider getting triple-paned."

"Those rolls of plastic are growing on me. A nice touch—lets the ladies know they have a man of substance."

"*Oh ei mi papa, no!*" and he yelped and grinned like a fool.

"*Mota?*"

"A little. *Es Domingo, cabron.*"

"Sunday, right. What's so special about *conejo and chivo?*"

"Umberto is from Jalisco. Very different cooking in Jalisco—very *picoso*, you will like."

"I've heard it's beautiful there."

"No, *guey*—it's a desert. But the land—*ai mama!* You could plant a man and get a mango tree. *Oh ei ai Mama!*"

"Where am I going to find him?"

"In the park."

"Fuck the park."

"Just make sure to ask for *conejo y chivo. Nada mas, si?*"

9: MOBY GRAPE

Because of the incessant drumming on congas, radios blasting salsa or *narcocorridos*. Because flat bed trucks pull up and sell watermelon, cantaloupe, bananas, grapes off the back. Because there is nothing as nice as a nap in the grass while watching a woman walk past. Because plantains fry nice, pork's *sabor* when slow cooked in its own fat, rice and beans is enough in the stomach to drink all day. Because *lengua*, *sesos*, and *chicharrones* are a taste acquired by those nostalgic for elsewhere. Because life is glorious when there is so much on the line. Because it was winter. Because the blue-sky illusion of warmth persuaded me to go to Humboldt Park that day. To visit Umberto, as Holofernes tipped me to do, as he served breakfast tacos where North Avenue intersects with California.

The snow-covered park was crowded with workers waiting, hanger-oners, and youth. Even god fears the machismo youth. All of them looked like little children: bundled, shivering, worried—their eyes crying for sunshine. Don't let anybody fool you, Chicago's chill comes from the sorrow and suffering of the people. The wind off the lake is a bluff compared to the citizens who year-in year-out flop 8, 2 unsuited. It's not the snowfall nor the pot holes; it's bracing yourself for so many boxed faces of poverty, the shrill of hysterical souls scratching at past trauma shouting on the Red Line, the constant threat of gunshots when 3pm comes and the schools spill their discontent into the streets. If you can afford a car or a cab, you have a chance of enjoying yourself; otherwise, these streets will leave you frostbit because they don't make long underwear to withstand Chicago's human wind chill. My eyes cried too but my insides had a snake's appetite for winter: I knew how to anatomize the brunt of it and slowly digest.

I eyed Umberto from twenty yards away. He must have been a great jockey—so small, tiny like a baby on the back of that horse. There was no way the man standing next to him could be his brother—he towered twice his height. Umberto moved quickly and brightly pulling hot tacos wrapped in aluminum from the insulated container in the back of his truck. His little fingers nimbly with the brown bags and napkins, taking money and shoving it in his jeans pockets. As I approached I heard the all too common greeting of *"Guero, guero"* whispering among the crowd.

"Un conejo y un chivo, por favor."

"Guero no like the *chivo,"* his high-pitched voice almost comedic.

"Si, I like."

"I not so sure,"

"A friend of mine tells me I will."

"I see. I see. You have lots of trouble this week already, no? And you are still hungry, *si*?"

"My trouble is my own taste."

"I see. I see." Umberto wrapped two tacos up, and along with something he pulled from his coat pocket he placed them in a bag. "Two tacos—twenty dollars."

"Of course it is." I paid him and stepped aside, knowing that the crowd knew more than I did. Knowing no one would come to help.

I walked over to a nearby bench, brushed off the already melting snow and took a damp seat. I left the tacos in the bag and grabbed what was next to it. Never had a little card of paper held so heavy in my hands. I could feel Umberto's little eyes reading my reaction. How could the business card of my old friend Levi Seeds, the toast of California winemakers, make it into the hands of an ex-jockey slinging tacos in Humboldt Park?

I looked up, met with Umberto's eyes, gave as nonchalant a nod as I could muster and got up from the bench, walking south through the park. Away from the Mexicans, looking for the asylum of Division Street, of the Puerto Ricans.

Something must have gone wrong in the way I reacted, a piece of information Holofernes left out either because he did not know or because he was stoned or because there are no accidents and I had no one I could trust. Umberto's brother, Roberto, left the truck and followed me. I picked up my pace, hoping once I reached the Puerto Rican territory he would lay off. My mind raced through all I could piece together. Ursulines. Ruben Rorick. Las Sangres Vineyards. Levi Seeds, an invitation to his wedding after ten years of not speaking with him. Either Levi was deep into business with the cartel or somebody wanted me dead. Unless there was something running far deeper through all of this—something I had not considered for years, and before I could arrive at where my thoughts were leading me, my face hit the cold bite of snow. Roberto was standing above me. His foot into my ribs, the taste of blood. His foot across my throat as I struggled to keep breathing, to keep from going dark. As my eyes fought to stay open, I saw a mallard duck land on the pond not twenty feet away. Its beak hit the ice and the water poured through.

Judith Beheading Holofernes

1

What do you think of the glass? It's traditional for Kwak. Belgian. I know, now tell me what they wore. Their style of being, he would say. How are those cheese curds? Friends in Fond du Lac brought them to me. Foot of the Lake, I would say. Ontology, he would reply. Holofernes was turning me on. And my words, as if he had been shunned from a kingdom, he would drink my words, drunk, and ask for more: Really, mustaches west of Pulaski? There's no one in Edgewater, I don't believe you, Judith. Yes, I feel the same about bandit scarves. Plaid again, it's miserable, but telling. These tacos? They're heaven enough to rent a nearby apartment. Details rollicked eagerly through my synapses after having walked so many miles through so many neighborhoods that I would feel as if I had snorted a line of asphalt, a commuter train, an electric alley. High with the city. Naked with Holofernes.

The Mexican bakeries, then, the Mexican bakeries! A portal to another world at 4:30am.

Only if it pertains to our mission.

The Fortress.

The Fortress. I love it when you say it. Were there bikes locked up out front?

No, but I was following her there. She doesn't know she is leading the way.

Good, Judith. I feel drunk with words tonight.

Eagerly I spilled what I had seen, leaning into Holofernes's ears, a prodigal daughter so happy my father had taken an interest.

More fell from there, at first words and clothes. Later, the extra hacks it takes to sever.

2

He said he was an urban planner. All of us were loose with our identities, disinterested in taking our conversations seriously. Which for us was utter seriousness. And I responded in kind, I too am an urban planner. I planned Atlantis. I planned Nineveh, Harappa. I planned Cairo, Thebes. I planned Nanjing, New Orleans, Meroë. You are Oglethorpe; I am Haussmann. I planned this city, battled up against the forces of the great other which binds and pushes existence to our faces. I am the foundry, a hulk of molten shapelessness. Well, he said, do you smoke? I like to discuss such things when I smoke. Or when I'm eating. We should do that, or the other.

There was something serious about the way he said this. And that terrified me. I wanted to suggest that we were talking already and we should continue to do so now. Of course I smoked. But now. Now? Penelope interrupted us before I could say anything more.

"What do you think, Judith? Is he a real urban planner or is it just a farce to get me in bed?"

"Penelope, if being an urban planner was all it took to sleep with you, then I would have built a dozen cities by now." And I would have. She knew it.

"We were just making plans to get together this week—where should we meet, Judith?"

"I thought we were meeting right now," I said.

"You know Atomix, Holofernes," Penelope said. "We went there the other morning for coffee, when you stayed at my place. You'll find Judith there just about anyday."

"The Ratacheks sell their pickles there. Great people.

Overwhelming garlic—which is the thing nowadays. When is good for you?"

There was no time that was not good for me—I was not in the habit of making plans. "Well, Fridays I write there all morning. Come by around two?"

"Let's make it 4pm. Friday. I lunch on Fridays, and I never know how long they will run. I might be a tad drunk. Do you know Smoke Daddy?"

"I do."

"Skip the cafe, Judith. That's it. Join us for lunch. 1pm. You know where it is?"

I did not.

"Alright, Judith will find it. I'm going to show Holofernes the wreck wall."

"I've only heard about it."

"It's a palimpsest of layered filth, and crayon, and maps, and miniature paintings and oversized poems and wooden blocks, I think there are shingles, and—"

"Follow me." And she said it with sincerity. A flirtatious seriousness and I wanted it to be me she said it to.

I wanted to say to Holofernes that it was very much like a city, in so many ways. I wanted him to be amused by my intelligence and talk with me now, not at lunch, not on a Friday nor a Tuesday, now. My neurotic desire for a wellspring of joy. A fountainhead of blood. I wanted to kill him then and there.

Miriam's apartment was lit with faces talking excitedly, lost in talk, moved by talk—you did not have to hear the words to understand it through the bodies, the arms, the shaking, the wide eyes, and little dances happening everywhere. Our actor friends were out with us that night, we called them The Actors, and they performed their moods, their stories—extracting love and bright visions directly from the supernovas as they simultaneously drilled their bodies through the earth. I loved The Actors, I really did. And Miriam's apartment teetered with excitement, a perfect juncture of all I wanted my city life to be.

I had been there when she moved in. Helped carry her boxes and furniture up the four flights of stairs. Her building—a four flat, heft of red brick, carved and mortared a century ago by the Ukrainians. Minimal ornamentation on the exterior, but pure beauty of substance—simple parapet across the top, yellow bricks forming rectangles across each brick front deck. A simple entrance on the lower right side—solid dark oak door, framed by stained glass—leading directly into the staircase which led to each apartment. The interior a little more intricate, but like the exterior, craftsmanship more than spectacle. Dark trimwork contrasting with the white plaster walls. A boxcar layout—brick deck, living room, dining room, kitchen, with a wooden deck and staircase, added later, satisfying the code writ for a fire escape to be in place. We used it to smoke and grill out. Between the living room and the dining room, a large throughway adorned by waist high bookshelves and Corinthian pillars on each side. A built-in hutch in the dining room. The kitchen tiled head-high in pink with a black-lipped runner across the top. Dark oak floors throughout, the varnish worn through in many spots and long gaps running between the boards.

I had seen many the same as this throughout our neighborhoods.

Finishing my glass of whiskey, I announced "I am

Jean Baptiste! I designed your city!" and immediately from across the room Wes met my eyes, lit up, and responded, "I am Ponce de Leon!" then Miriam, coming out of the bathroom, "I am Emilia Earheart!" I proceeded to the kitchen to pour another—"I am Jean Baptiste! You live in my shadow!" The door between the deck and the apartment was open, most of the cigarettes were being smoked near there—"Your shadow is brilliant with Nightingales!"—The Actors picked up the game and stood up from where they were sitting on the chairs and couch in the living room framed by an exquisite green and black checkerboard plaid hand-painted by Miriam's new boyfriend, Michel Comté. They followed me and everyone joined in. "I've gathered all the sidewalks across my body—watch the buildings crumble back into the earth!" The dining room had no furniture except for several wooden chairs, its floors covered with at least a dozen small Oriental rugs—"Your city is havoc and fantasy, all pleasure and wood!"—all of them knock-offs except one which her grandmother had passed onto Miriam in her will. "Tongue my platform to taste my trains!" Miriam loved her grandmother and designed the room in memory of her, the rugs overlapping each other and climbing the walls almost as high as the dark oak base molding— "I am Harukatanhenah!" "Design my muscle chin!" "Spout more purple! Fountain more grace!"—the room took on a soft dark chaos, an excuse to roll on the floor, to get lost in the full performance of dream. "I am Jean Baptiste! And you are my Mayor! You are my Aldermen! Dear Citizenry!" Sitting on the countertops and leaning against the appliances in the kitchen— "I am Jehovah and you are my Witness!"—the pink and black tiles behind them and above an ethereal sea green painted across the top half of the walls and the ceiling. The walls were painted gray, and sconces with pillar candles adorned the side with the hutch—"I am Simone de Beauvoir—where is Nelson Algren?!"—the other wall was the Wreck Wall, which Penelope was showing Holofernes. Every inch of it some spontaneous act. "Eckhardt Park is a portal to Paris!" Some art. Some object taped. "The El train renamed my mother—St. Gertrude slid up my spine!" Some cut-outs tacked. "Buy more soda pop and stop listening to jazz!" Some paint. Some pencil. "I am Jane Addams licking the bootstraps of Irish muffuletta!" Everyone was free to add and add and add on. "I am Alabama Whorley—welcome to my comic book!" And even raze what they wanted. Destroy what they would. Only to build again and again atop this bulging mess of terrain.

I am Beatrice. I am Beyond Windows. I am Sara Winchester. Daniel Burnham. I am Napoleon. I am Chandragupta Maurya. I am Cairo. I am Jersey and I am Oglethorpe and I am Missoula. I am Hellish Delhi. Zapoteca. I am Amenhotep. I am Blah. I am Wudi. I am Bangladesh. Santiago. I am the Red Light. The Alleyway. Gangway. I am the Sewers. Catacombs. Adulis. The Trombone in the Night. The Handkerchief. The Blueprint. I am the Window Washer Descending the Facade. I am Natchez. I am Mohenjo Daro. Iron Ore. I am Buckley drowning in the River Styx while Memphis obliterates Time. I am Sullivan's Zombie haunting Graceland. I am Jelly Beans across the Asphalt. I am Total Night. Total Tax. Toledo Dream. I am Rome. Touch me before I go away.

3

How he fell in with my crowd, no one could understand. People conjectured that a woman like Penelope must have represented that aspect of life that Holofernes was missing and therefore transfixed by. She was truly beautiful in that soulful, deep way, with her brown curly hair that she wore up as often as down, her slight frame and soft olive skin. Brown mellow eyes holding an intelligence, a unique perspective on all that she saw. She had studied anthropology and was interested in people's performance of culture, but sometime in college she had veered towards painting portraits and figurative expressionist pieces, finding it more satisfying to recreate culture through color and faces and bodies than through words and ethnographic studies. She did not care about success, about money, she loved her friends and drunken conversation more than a career would allow her. She was youth, I see it now, and Holofernes was form. And no other substance more than youth does form yearn to hold.

I knew she would capture what was to come once the deed was done. And we would hang her painting in the den, the eternal heart of The Fortress. And maybe she would sleep with me, too, I did want that, to have Penelope join our ranks and be my lover.

She was falling in love with Holofernes, but for once, I didn't care. Only because the week before I had seen an arousing and terrible woman who I could not stop thinking about. At a bookstore, The Yellow Book. I was standing in the middle of the tiny storefront, looking at the books on the shelves, and she walked in. Took me in with her eyes. Immediately I was scared of her, and I said nothing, until after ten minutes of glancing and excusing ourselves past each other—tiny does not do it justice—it became awkward and I wondered if she would like to hear me speak, so I prepared something to say:

"What about Philip K. Dick?" I said.

"I like him. But I prefer Gertrude Stein."

Exactly what I needed to know. "Any of her books here?"

"I just finished *The Autobiography of Alice B. Toklas* and put it on the shelf over there. Wait, it's stacked on the floor beneath Kathy Acker—do you see it?"

"*Great Expectations*. Acker takes Dickens work and castrates it."

"We must do what we must do to win this war."

She was radicalized and this gave me an idea. "I agree. You work here?"

"I   do."

"I'll see you again then."

And there was very little else to say right then, so I left. Fantasizing on the sidewalk about looking for a book in the back room with her. The strength of her thighs. The threat of her eyes as they bit into my neck. She couldn't know what I felt for her. Or what I had planned.

It had been three years and six months since Manasses had disappeared. I loved him—everything about him—I didn't mind that he was ten years older, or that he was a man. His disappearance was so sudden, we all considered him dead, speculating this and that. Once he was gone, I knew more than before the ways that women drew me in. But I was awkward coming on to women—so much of what I did during this life was done awkwardly—and I often naively forgot that men were attracted to me. In my head, I promised her intimacy, moments of pleasure which would tamper with the fantasies of future cities.

The next week, I saw her again on Washtenaw, she looked back but I don't think she knew it was me. Her alluring presence demanded abasement, hers or mine we would see. Dismissible in her rigor, she could easily put you off. Her cocky punch stirred me and I began following her. Her figure, tall and slender, jutted from side to side—I found it impossible not to sway in her presence. Her hair was cut asymmetrical, gathered up here or there, lofting to one side, thick brown, unwashed and chaotic. She wore glasses, stylishly too-big frames, confusing even more whether she took her beauty seriously, and calling into question whether or not I should either. Because it was not her beauty that she was offering but her ferocity. Her dominating intelligence. The prison of her body. She was mean. She was sharp, and I realized how much I liked the cut.

I would spend weeks on end away from The Fortress, following people—she was not the first. I had the fantasy of living in every apartment of every building throughout the city, climbing through the walls and collecting every experience of every funky interior, a cigarette at every window. And when I saw someone who interested me I wanted to know where they lived, so I could live through them, and I would fall behind and in step. Step by step, escaping from The Fortress, forgetting our accord, lost in one or another of the city's selves.

She did not end her walk at her apartment but back at

The Yellow Book. I stepped inside behind her hoping to talk a little more only to find a meeting had just begun.

They looked at me, and I sat down.

"Is she?" the man at the front asked the crowd.

The six or seven others shook their head or shrugged their shoulders.

She whispered in his ears. I still don't know your name, I thought. Tonight we will talk.

The man began speaking again. He was the only clean-shaven one in the room. His skin dark and taut across his skull, his hair brown and disheveled, his clothes black shirts, black jeans, black sneakers.

Two guys held beards as long as arms—mustaches flourishing the lips of the other three. Their clothes were dirty, brown or green, cut to cool the arm pits. The two women held opposite poses. One's acidic and angular features, straight hair and homemade t-shirt, looked at me like she wanted me dead and dust. The other a wild mop and nebulous softness in cut-off overalls, though her eyes seemed to veil red giant bursting stars, minded me none.

I listened as if I knew something; I listened as if I knew nothing at all.

This was the war she had referred to.

They were describing a system of points and a vocabulary of postures, how necks should be shrugged, how arms could be used to let the non-initiated know they were not welcome. They discussed increasing the frequency of clothing changes to throw off the rapidly adapting first waves. They discussed trickles of water, abandoned systems of pipes, electricity, and I sat there lit up with the full of it: how I would deceive Holofernes' army.

These people, they are pretending to be us. This is who the director would cast in the movie they make about the devout, the unruly, the eternal children of delight, keepers of the humble grace. Surely, they will work as bait. I will feed them to Holofernes first and then severe his artery. But when she—the she I had followed—went into the backroom and did not come out for a half-hour, I got up and left, still not knowing her name.

I left self-conscious of my jorts, my huaraches, my tank top and how my arms hung off my shoulders. I could have been sculpted in more suitable form. My eyes on my shoes and the sidewalk, he had to call my name to get my attention: "Judith!"

To see Holofernes was to see the beginning of a new muscle developing across Chicago's back. With a history of practical shrewd men with conservative clan-like values, this city had never put on such a spectacle of artisanal whimsy. Are you from the east coast, Holofernes? No, I am from here. When he said here, it was not the here of our heirs.

Across the street, next to a couple of Puerto Rican boys kicking a soccer ball against the building, Holofernes stood by The Florists' door. The repetitive thud in the humid slow night. The boys did not smile, just kicked the ball again and again.

A dog tied to a fire hydrant stared at Holofernes and barked.

Green plain-front pants tailored to his hips. A yellow button-down contouring his slender frame, touched with horse brass at his wrist. Saddle shoes, he had a pair of every color combination, playfully next to orange socks.

His body was color, verdurous as rainforest; his hair thick light brown curls let loose atop his head. At six foot four, like an umbrella handle, his neck bent his head downwards us. His arms at times a bazaar of concerns, ideas, and points to be made. This was a marketing executive, a creative director, an eccentric playboy, a palisade, an Ottoman, a Corinthian, an Assyrian. His face had an olive hue, a tan which never quite left him in the winters. His complexion clean as if dusted with concealer. A strong chin balancing out the heft of his mustache. This mustache which was not our fathers' mustache. This mustache which was playfully aware of its habitat, poking fun at the all too serious men who came before. An omnipresent wink. And when he was not talking, which was rare, he was smiling. A lightheartedness. A whimsy which only a burly confidence can carry.

We did not know what to make of him. But we knew the extent of his reach.

We were dive bars, we were sideburns, we were unshaven legs and hallucinations. We were beating our souls into mush, we were walking our bones into dust, we were intentionally unmeaningful and joyous. We were bus passes, we were backpacks, we were joints and tacos and Mexican sugarbreads. We were isolated and spacious, thrift stores and transient, we were soundless in the daydreaming night. We believed ourselves unpurchaseable. We believed ourselves unscathed. We believed ourselves irreplicable. But Holofernes was watching, mirroring us, culling what did not fit in his curation.

"Come over here!"

I crossed the street so absentmindedly that I didn't see

the car coming until I saw its headlights brighten my step. I ran as the car braked, swerved, and honked.

"You fucking cocksucker!" the man's head jutting through the rolled-down window veins swelled with a torrential hatred, and I knew he would kill me in that moment if he could.

I picked up a rock and I threw that rock just missing the bulging vein across his forehead.

"Judith, do you know how close that was?"

My heart raced as I stepped up the curb. "Fuck me. What are you up to?"

"Are you okay? That was insane! I was just about to head in here for the best goddamned tamale in the city."

"Where?"

"Isabel. She runs The Florist. Makes them special for me in the back, when I am picking up flowers."

"For Penelope?"

"Of course for Penelope. Of course, of course."

"I'm good. There's a girl I followed across the street."

"You follow people? Which girl?"

"Tall, slender, severe—big glasses."

"Ursulines."

"You know her?"

"I'll put in a good word for you. Come in with me, let's get a tamale. You follow people?"

"*Sí, se puede.*"

"*Que Sabrosa.*"

Just as he said, we walked through the humble ten-by-ten store front, with a rickety stand-up cooler of flowers on one side and several shelves of celebratory vases, balloons, cards and a rack of Spanish-titled VHS tapes on the other, into a back room where Isabel smiled at us, a vase of flowers on the counter next to a paper plate with two tamales. Behind her, sat an old woman who stared at us the entire time we were there, yet never said a word.

Isabel smiled and said, "You brought a friend. Let me get more tamales."

"Your kindness is only out-matched by your cooking, Isabel. These flowers look beautiful."

"So many lucky ones out there."

"I wish they were all for your sweet grandmother, if only she would learn to love me."

"She works very hard, hard life, you know, she loves you, my family very much appreciates your business."

She put another plate next to the first one, and she disappeared into another back room behind this back room, what anyone would assume was already the furthest back this building went. In my head I saw the city as a system of back rooms, a maze of secrecy and clandestine encounters, forever mysterious yet inescapable. I began to mention this to Holofernes, when lost in his own thoughts, he spoke: "She won't move, does that bother you?"

"Grandmother? I don't think it bothers me."

"She sits there, stares, listens. Let her listen. A repository like her could never come back to harm me. Do you know my greatest fear, Judith?"

"Death? Mine is to fall out of God's grace."

"I will not die, that does not worry me, but information. To be found out. Look at me, I wear what I wear, knowing that others know that this is not who I am. It's a performance, but neither am I sweatpants, nor Tevas, not a t-shirt, so why be that, wear that? I am scared of what I might be, though, if I ever could know. My true information, and it is her who reminds me of this."

"Why don't you find another florist?"

"Why don't I find another florist, Judith, you have not taken a bite of the tamale."

I did. It was good. When I considered it later, after more meals and discussions with Holofernes, I remembered it as the best thing I ever ate. The soft melting texture giving way to juice and flavor of the tender stewed pork, behind it a kick of salsa.

"Do you like legends?"

"I do."

"Let me tell you one about her, she doesn't mind, that we speak of her—she'd hear us one way or another. It might make you love what you've stumbled upon across the street even more. How long were you in there, anyways?"

"Thirty minutes, maybe. How do you know so much?"

"There is a story, of which I have been hearing little pieces and allusions to, that hidden between the manufacturing and residential districts along the South Branch of the Chicago River a fortress has been built. I have spoke with people who say they've been there, others who know of friends who have been there, and I have overheard conversations at cafes and bars analyzing it or critiquing it, even directly discussing the events which take place behind its walls. I have tried to find it myself. Many nights. I have heard that at night the glow of the lanterns flicker distinctly from the streetlights. A buzz of generators can be heard leading one in the right direction—but I have failed. I've been given specific directions, had maps drawn for me, but never has someone offered to accompany me there, for, as I've heard said too many times, That is not the way to find The Fortress of Bethulia.

"I do not know if Fortress is used as a chosen name for this compound, or if it is called that because Fortress accurately describes the construction and intention of the place built and the lives lived. I do know the lore of its history and it intrigues me, pleases me to tell it to you now. How is your tamale?"

"Very good."

"In the last decade of the twentieth century, Chicago's neighborhoods underwent a considerable amount of re-construction. Buildings were demolished and buildings were gutted, leaving rubble everywhere in the alleys. Doors were unhinged and tossed aside, windows were yanked out and stacked, molding and trim peeled from the walls and clattered into piles, bathtubs, toilets and sinks were lifted and heaved, stoves and refrigerators dragged out the back door, radiators, duct work and wires; pipes and light fixtures and hardwood floors; tiles and outlets, and cabinets. All of these materials, and this is only an account of the residences—the warehouses, factories, and commercial buildings amassed stranger, more exotic loot—were left over night in the dumpsters, for weeks in the alleys, in piles near the construction sites. A group of teenagers, so hard to imagine such young minds height-ened to a feat such as this, began collecting the bricks and stones, hunks of concrete, flooring and old-growth beams, and storing them somewhere near where the site of The Fortress exists today.

"Often, in turn, their stash was looted by junkers and

addicts, but there was more than enough of the buildings reduced to scraps for them to replenish their materials and become more savvy and strategic in their quest to build a city within this city. A Fortress for them to live and create and make love and drink and experience the magic of living in their own way.

"People talk and who knows what of it is true and what is false, but there are legends which have gathered around the personages who began and built, envisioned and brought The Fortress into reality. As a group it is said that they were not unlike most teenagers. They attended high school, had parents who worked and raised them. They were not necessarily deviants, nor members of some rebellious underclass whose goal was to overthrow the status quo. They grew up in the city during the 1970s and came of age during the 1980s—times which our contemporaries remember to be impoverished, ghettoized, and turbulent in urban environments—and this certainly had an impact on their ideologies. You don't mind, do you, that I say ideology? When in every suburb and town other teenagers at that time were getting into cars and driving to friends' houses, malls, parties, sporting events—all the things that kids do to get out of their parents' house and explore the world—the group who envisioned The Fortress were walking. It is said that it all began on a walk. They were not going anywhere, there was no destination—simply one of them, it is uncertain who, suggested that they just walk. Away from their homes, but in no specific direction. It was not that first night, but soon after, that they encountered a woman who would alter the course of their fates." And he began to tell me a legend about myself.

"In an alley, these paths behind buildings which soon became the course of their paradise, somewhere near Western Avenue, I am not sure how far North or South, a woman, a *bruja*, who it is said was born in Mexico City, spoke to them as they passed by her. She lied there, crumpled and in rags, hiding between a dumpster and a building. They had seen many people like this and any fear or mistrust had been lessened by the frequency of exposure, but none had spoken to them. She said, *I want to show you the Poets*. And she stood up, smiling wide her mouth toothless at the front, brushed off the filth which had gathered across her indolent body, and grabbed one of their hands. These Poets, they will make a new life for you."

"Poets?"

"It all begins with poets, everything, the true conjurers."

"A slow-paced couple of blocks later and this woman, she is known as La Ciudad Mujer by some, Eve by others, pushed aside a dumpster revealing an upright sheet of plywood, which she removed and there, a hidden entrance to the building. It was night, as was most of their walks, and beyond the hole in the brick wall was pitch black. Still, the group entered, disregarding the fears they should have heeded of being robbed, beaten, raped or any other paranoid fantasy which has dominated the collective imagination of nightmares. Of course, they expected to find a group, similar to themselves, who had forged a deep bond, but who had taken it to another level and begun their own living quarters away from other familial and societal ties. As they entered, they did hear movement, rustling, fits of motion which they could almost make out in the near distance, but when Ciudad Mujer lit a match and then a candle, and then a dozen or more throughout the room, there was no one there but themselves. Instead, piles of rubbled brick, palettes stacked against the wall, doors and windows organized against one another, architectural ornaments and radiators, metal cabinetry, urban signage, metal chains and more, there was so much, spread out before their eyes, flickering and bobbing and wavering by the candle light. *Here are the Poets*, Eve cried out.

"This became their first depository for the wealth of materials they would begin to amass over the next several months. When the room was filled, another location had been scouted, which I previously mentioned, and the relocation of their treasures began, a furtive operation in the late hours of the night, involving grocery carts and wagon-dragging bikes. Oh the bikes, Judith! So many marvelous bikes."

I loved hearing all this, not for a second wondering if it was true, but basking in the extravagance of this legend. What if I could lie this well? I had to learn how.

"Three boys and two girls, not yet the age of eighteen, and Ciudad Mujer forever watching and supplying secrets, began construction in the year 1991 on what is now known among those city dwellers privileged by this legend as The Fortress. Hidden between the manufacturing and residential districts along the South Branch of the Chicago River, this system of buildings relies on generators, plumbing connected to the river, turbines and windmills, lanterns and secret passages, tunnels and underground rooms, and it is said that what began as seven grew to seventy and in time 700, including children and of course, Ciudad Mujer. What they do there has been speculated on by many—their level of involvement with the rest of us, the extent of their interaction with the city which we inhabit, the great energy which they generate and disperse throughout the city outside their own. I will not explain the debates and discussions which many lose themselves in trying to get to the bottom of, but I will say that I believe their artistry can be found in the alleys, pasted and scrawled in paint and words across the backs of buildings, and their practices and cultures are beginning to spread into the communities of Chicagoans who have begun to treasure the idea that an enriched substance of life, a bread and a heart, exists which surpasses the pleasures of surface that the majority of others have succumbed to."

"And her?"

"Yes. I believe she is."

"Have you asked her?"

"Do you not know any poets?"

"I am one. My friends and I are poets," I flirted with the truth.

"Then you know why I do not ask her. Listen, pretty groovy story, right? I don't know what it is about you, there is something special. In fact, I thought of the story right when we met, I wanted to tell you then, for some reason I thought you would have already heard it."

"That's a wallop. I mean, to register it—cha-ching. Entirely reality dousing."

"Help me, Judith."

"With your identity?"

"Please no. With The Fortress. Help me find it."

"Sounds fun." And it did. To search for a legend. It infected my imagination. When we left that night, I walked home seeing the bums, the decay, the dereliction not as horror and dismay but as magic, resonating in the chords of another universe. Of course, there are many problems in viewing the lives of others in this way, I would remember that often, momentarily, yet a belief in magic activates powers beyond one's control, whether or not one has located its accurate source. For a while, I admit, I was led astray. I forgot who I was, until Sue came and found me. My humble mission supplanted by his sumptuous design. Oh the story we tell ourselves—what power it has over our reality.

4

At the time I was living on the second floor of a two-flat on Erie. One of two row houses on the street, my landlord owned both of them and lived on the first floor of the other. I'd have to dig out an old checkbook to remember his last name, but Fred kept the rents low in favor of keeping tenants. Manasses had been living there before we met. They thought he had it in him, but he didn't succeed. I moved in when we married—it became our outpost—and I stayed after his death, paying the same $250 month-in and month-out and never complaining about the unevenness which had warped throughout the hardwood floors, the 50s baby blue appliances, the lights' occasional flicker emitting an electric fuzz, the mold growing across the bathroom just weeks after I would scrub and re-caulk. The caulk was as thick as my arm when I left.

Living alone, this was my office as well as my home. I wrote at the cafes several times a week in order to be seen, but there was no separation between my kitchen and my stories, my bedroom and my notebooks, my windows overlooking the vacant lot on the corner of Hoyne and my books tossed and stacked throughout. I woke up and usually had my pen in my hand before my toothbrush. Not that I wrote constantly, just that it was there, in my hand, guiding me through the interiors of my apartment as much as the flickering overhead.

I did not collect things. My walls were bare, but for the writing which I taped to them in order to organize and see the narrative from afar, as if a map. A mattress on the floor, I would drag it from room to room sleeping wherever intuitively felt richest. I had accumulated enough kitchen utensils and clothes, and I added a sweater here, a glass there, as needed. Occasionally, someone would move out from another of Fred's rentals, leaving possessions behind, and Fred would knock on my door, like a mother, persuading me to go through their stuff, find something nice, and furnish this apartment. This is your home, Judith, he would say. Make it comfortable, dress it up for god's sake. You don't even have a teevee. And because I rarely say no to anyone's request, because I don't want to be the source of neglect, I would grab a rug or a lamp or some extra spoons, only to shove them in a corner or a drawer or a closet. Then later discard in the alley a block over.

I knew that if this apartment grew too comfortable, then I would not write, I would not daydream. I would lounge and grow lazy. And I must write in order to gain my authenticity, in order to complete my task. There are so many lazy people. Soon enough, if I did not, my life would be like theirs—waking up in order to leave, to rush away, to get to work—and rushing home again, to get away, to crave the comforts I had been away from all day. That was not the point, I'd think, my work is no different than my rest. My life does not need compartments.

And the funny thing is others told me that I was indolent. I asked them what they meant. Gloria at the laundromat said that I didn't exert myself upon life. Leo at Leo's Lunchroom offered me a job. At the Post Office, Heywood told me I should go running—look at your potbelly, he said. Betty told me one day at Specimen Guitars—buy some things and see what it means to be responsible, you need to attach yourself to some responsibilities. Out there, Gus at Crazy Man Records always said, in the real world. As if the world here, right here, was not real. As if my apartment was not life. The cafes just clouds across a summer lake. I was no badger, burrowing away, only to peak my head out to take care of my territory. I was a gargoyle, at home in my stone, at work in my stone. At ease in my fixed posture and terrifying grin.

When I was twenty-two or so, Manasses taught me the beauty of breakfast. Growing up, my family poured cereal, ate millions of slices of toast, drank a glass of juice—that was morning. Both my parents were tenure-seeking professors always elsewhere in their minds, never here in the kitchen. I didn't know that you could take your time, get lost in bacon sizzling, flipping it back and forth, cooking it evenly and just how you craved it, whether crisp or juicy, each morning a difference. And in the bacon grease, one could fry eggs. Or scramble them or cut up fresh vegetables and cheeses and fold the eggs over into an omelet. All the while, potatoes sliced or cubed, whatever shape you wanted, frying in the skillet on the other burner— my stovetop consisted of only two, one behind the other. To get them just right, I poured the oil liberally into the skillet, the flame beneath as hot as it could go, until the oil vapors began to wisp into the room as I tossed on the cubed potato—it took Holofernes to teach me about Yukon golds, fingerlings, butterballs, russets—flipping and shoving them with my spatula until they were evenly coated by the hot oils, letting them rest only so long before another round, doing this about five times, the mellow white gold browning on multiple sides of the cube, and only then turning down the heat, letting them rest longer between flips. This took time, attention, a patience with the day—the way it moved on while I remained behind.

I did this most mornings with a pot of coffee, occasionally turning the heat down to the lowest flame to write a thought down or work on a poem, stare out the kitchen windows at the alley, turn on the record player. For the longest time I had nowhere to be.

I'd be lying if I said all my days went this smoothly. Many are not worth remembering. There are moods that water down the rosiest wines and I suffered them. I'd try to do what I knew to make me happy, but instead my thoughts simply ridiculed each action with cynicism— each small act, the very things that on other days brought me joy, symbolized the meaninglessness of existence. I'd ask myself—this is all that there is? This is what we carry on for? For bacon, for the smell of Swiss cheese frying in the skillet grease? There is no life in that alley, that is death. The vacant lot next door. The mold. The repetition. I could not stand it. All I did with my life was fill up pages with words. Pages which would be blurred by the endless number of other books in the libraries which surely would be lost. Dust. The ground which other ignorant and hopeless beings would walk on.

The type of mood which tarnishes. And I had nowhere to go. No Manasses to anchor me. As long as I was on this mission, my life was in that apartment, smoking cigarette after cigarette until night came and the bars and parties could not refuse me. And the beer and wine would not allow me my widowed misery.

Which is how I formed my friendships.

I was content to hang out as much as possible with whoever it was that was doing the same, drink beers, listen to music, read novels, take naps in the sun in the summer, watch films for hours in the winters. My first book was coming out that fall, and the advance I had received was enough to carry me for as long as I could foresee, which admittedly was only through the year or so, but I did not wish to foresee any further. What I am trying to say is that the immediacy of time was more than enough.

Until Holofernes' camp arrived.

We knew they would come once the neighborhood hit critical mass.

I had big ideas of my own back then, schemes, I did. But I fitted and folded them into pages, into prose. Verse if they were rare and indistinguishable enough, but mostly stories, and, as I said, a book. I had no idea whether or not these ideas did anything more than fill pages. I did not wish for them to do anything more than that, especially now that they had accepted my book and slid a lump sum under my door.

Which brings me back to Holofernes. The day after our accidental run-in outside the florist, he made his presence known one evening, sliding a note beneath my door, and a box just outside it. The box was about the size of a head and I opened it in a rush, pulling out the tissue paper and finding olives, cheese and pickled fish spread out across a beautiful olive tree cutting board, next to it a bottle of plum wine.

The note read: "This is just to say I have eaten the plums that were in the icebox and which you were probably saving for breakfast. Forgive me they were delicious so sweet and so cold. I offer you this nostalgic Mediterranean feast in lieu of your previous designs."

On the back, it read: "Tasting Notes: The Grand Cru Surchoix is an Alpine-styled cheese cured for more than nine months, which creates complex flavors with caramel and mushroom undertones.

"The pickled herring is from Kurowski's on Milwaukee.

"The plum wine, I grew and fermented myself.

"The olives—from Stanley's, who knew they would have the best?"

I opened the wine, drank it, and wished for more. I ate the fine spread and with each bite wondered how anything could taste as delicious. And it struck me then and there: past potatoes and eggs, there are foods and pleasures which satisfy every craving that comes upon us. And I have just met the man who knows this, who is offering to usher me in, and show me a seat at the table of the grand feast.

I was lonelier than I admit. Less content with this life. I dreamed of a life far away from here—maybe it was a by-product of writing fiction, but I would have taken any yellow brick road I encountered. Meeting Holofernes, like all magnetic meetings, birthed some other presence inside of me. I tried to write that night after eating this gift, but it brought me down. Every notion drained a little more of my satisfaction. To sit with yourself and not be satisfied delivers hell upon hell.

Ed the landlord knocked on my door, going on and on about Katrina. The whole world knew but I had no idea.

"They got people on the roofs shooting guns at the helicopters. Fucking animals. The whole city is a shitstorm. Literally, the sewers and the chemicals all that shit is in the water and it's up twenty feet. Imagine this street with water up to your window."

"I had no idea."

"Don't you watch the news?"

"No teevee."

"What do you do in there?"

"I read a lot, Ed. And I'm writer, you know I'm a writer."

"Can't write and read all day. You're not writing now."

I was surprised to hear myself say it, "I've been thinking about getting one, I guess. I don't know."

"Over at K-Mart, I saw an ad in the paper, one hundred and fifty maybe two hundred. Televisions are getting cheap, the nice ones even. They used to go for a thousand. You should go check it out."

"A grand, Ed, that can't be right."

"Shit, honey, I don't know many writers, but I bet most of them got couches. A goddamn teevee to watch the news on. Didn't you sell a book?"

"Yeah, I got the money, it's not that."

"Don't be a moron, honey"

"Alright, alright. You think they're closed now."

"Those fucking places don't close. They just sit there and wait for you to come."

"I'm going to check it out."

Ed's consistent harangue wore me down.

And a couple mornings later, instead of a long breakfast and words words words, I woke up and I got dressed, put my hair back, and I felt I needed to walk, needed to witness the action of the streets, so much, so many, and the secrets everywhere behind the doors, the secrets of lives lived, hauntings, histories seeping through porous bricks, bikes stolen while owners ordered hot dogs, cigarettes smoked under awnings in the rain, a street couple with pigeon feathers stuck in their hats cackling in love, listless in the alleys. Beneath it all, somewhere, Holofernes told me The Fortress of Bethulia. But I knew his legend as a layer, a sheet across the city's ghost. I walked and I talked with people. I went into stores solely for the sake of seeing what they sold, the details of it, the prices. I sat on the sidewalks against the walls and I began to make sense of the people who lived where I lived, and I began to come up with ideas about what type of people chose to live where, what subtle differences of poverty looked like, which shops were authentic and which had been brainstormed within a corporate boardroom.

And that night, out all day, I came home and I craved comfort. And I did not know what to do. My austerity ruined by an appetizer tray for one.

5

That next week night, Miriam let me have it. I headed to her place for dinner, something we tried to do regularly. She lived in a towering red stone four-flat on Iowa Street, just west of Western and north of Chicago Avenues. The night before I had stayed out late with Holofernes, watching the scene at The Lava Lounge. My education, like so many Chicagoans, wet with booze. Our conversation played in my head as I walked through the subject of our conversation. Old ladies sat on stoops, glumly noticing me. A window open and a man there in the shadows, wrist and cigarette resting on the sill. Fleece blankets blue with Nemo nailed above entranceways. Bikes hung high on black fences. Schlitz tall boys crushed along the red-brick ledge. Fake flowers in plastic pots on stoops. The streets rigid with buildings, dressed in the green leaves of summer trees, cicadas' jagged buzz cut the night air, and I blushed to think of the blade.

"Those four," I remembered Holofernes interrupting our lovers talk to point out a group of guys leaving the bar, laughing. "Realtor types."

"Douche bags."

"More than that. Do you ever spend any time west of Western, or south of Chicago?"

"I live south of Chicago. We hang in Humboldt."

"Judith, let me ask: what do those two phrases mean to you?"

"Cheap rents. Fucking *muchacho*-talking *gringo* shit."

"They mean way more than where something is located. Western is the red dividing line across realtors' maps.

'South of Chicago' signifies a limited amount of residential, the streets quickly swallowed up by the manufacturing remnants of Chicago's industrial youth. It's all realtor speak but by now, realtor speak has become most of these lounge kids' consciousness. If not these, then the ones new to the area—like those guys—have these borders up in their mind."

"Blue light intersections. Danger! Danger!"

"Exactly. For one: Public transportation—the Blue Line cuts diagonally through West Town, literally alongside Milwaukee Avenue from Grand Avenue to Logan Square. This has been a large factor in selling or renting a building located in neighborhoods like these, but west of Western, south of Chicago—forget about it, that's a half an hour walk to the bus."

"Get a bike!"

"Judith, you get this, that's why I like you. In the 1960s, new immigrants and poor families were displaced from lakeside Chicago and moved west of the river. Into the West Town neighborhoods, which begin where three manufacturing districts meet: The Fulton Markets, Kinsie, and Clyborn Corridors. These are the dividing lines, the topography of the city. And this is where the Eastern European workers have always lived. What the Germans and the Danes began as an outlying suburb in the late 1800s. What Nelson Algren celebrated to be Polish, degenerate, and lost."

"Where's the neon wilderness, Holofernes—let's get the fuck out of here and go to skid row."

"Back in the 1950s, Puerto Rican women came over to fill the service jobs—maids, cooks, nannies—"

"Don't look at me that way—I'm Jewish."

"US women turned their backs on menial jobs after getting the opportunity to work downtown during WWII. And my theory about the Mexicans is they came to this part of Chicago simply because of the success the Puerto Ricans were having establishing shops and businesses. Underclass African Americans up from the south were drawn here because of low rents, less tension, low profile, and then Urban Renewal public housing efforts."

"I can't hear you very well, but I think you're talking fucking talking serious serious stuff here. It's not right. None of it. Where do we get off? What is this? Who's on first?"

"Tough economic times run rampant throughout the city. A renaissance to some has occurred, but by no means for the majority. In the mid 70s, hundreds of fires broke out across West Town—an ungodly number—and one has to ask who or what was behind that? Arson, surely, in some cases. Insurance fraud, yes. Accidents? That as well. The effect was vacant lots and abandoned buildings, driving property values to the cellar."

"With the roots."

"And all this happened in a lending climate where banks did not welcome loan requests for buying homes in the city, encouraging homebuyers to move to the growing stock of houses in the suburbs. Couple this with the Alderman's rezoning of the neighborhood to allow for more residents per property to be built, equaling higher profits for the developer, and the story of the Near Northwest Side becomes one of fierce speculation and profit, compounding the race issues. And we cannot forget the mayor, Richard J. Daley."

"What a dick!"

"Who, elected in 1956 and served until 1975, enacted policies and ignored realities which devolved much of what made the city a hospitable and supportive place to live."

"Let's not forget endearing."

"His focus was on skyscrapers, bringing in business, building airports and freeways. Economically, this is the time when manufacturing jobs were lost and the service industry stepped forward. The businesses that were attracted and the jobs that were created demanded workers of a certain level of education—advertising, banking, investors, management, architecture, etcetera. And education has always been a dividing line between lower and upper classes. Sleeper communities were made possible by the building of freeways and Metra lines for their commute, and banks' hostility towards home buying in the city. And J. Daley forgot that the immediate neighborhoods of his metropolitan area, though not the face of the city for tourists and investors, was where Chicago's life blood pumped, slept, socialized, and grew. Neighborhood schools and commercial districts being a huge center of any urban community. However, the schools were all but forgotten, quickly devolving into daycares and breeding grounds for class and cultural resentment. Altogether real estate speculators and bohemian types—"

"Bohemian types suck it."

"They began to arrive to take advantage of the cheap land which meant cheap rents. Light manufacturing properties abandoned everywhere you looked were taken up by those who fantasized about another SoHo, those who knew cultural and commercial revolutions began at a secret party in an artist's hidden-away loft where every-one mused on and on about how this used to be a leather tannery, this used to be a parking meter manufacturer, this used to be a clothes hanger warehouse."

"Come to my rubber stamp, I'll make some fish bowls. No no, we got something at this aunt Jemimah bottling company, it's gonna be toast."

"And West Town, in the late 80s, began a steady gen-trification, pushing old-timers west of Western and south of Chicago, making room for the newcomers. The heart of this being, what is now called, Wicker Park. Here, the highest, most ornate mansions were rehabbed. The Blue Line stops right in the middle at Damen, where a six cor-ners intersection ideal for commercial activity thrived. A park, Wicker Park itself, one block away from this. Beautiful tall canopy of trees, cobblestone alleys, and a housing stock to convert into condominiums. But, West of Western and South of Chicago Avenue…"

"Poverty and violence. Dark silences. Rundown resi-dences. Eclectic stores of disparate items."

"Here is where you begin to navigate the outskirts, the furthest edges away from Wicker Park. Your friend Miri-am—we met at her apartment, west of Western. I wanted to kiss you then."

"Kiss me now before you say another word."

True, Holofernes, we did. Along Augusta, west of West-ern, where I was headed, remembering our conversation and considering all this. Looking for it in the buildings, in what was lit by the street lights, the occasional passerby who met me with no warmth, no generosity of spirit—

was it my villainous typecast or the tried and true big Chicago cold shoulder? And I knew you wanted to kiss me, but I did not think I would let you live after the plum tree had fallen in Bethulia.

That Wednesday night, I began to tell Miriam all of these things. She listened and acted glad to find out more about her neighborhood, but also complained. I had grown too serious, she said. She couldn't tell if I was being serious or ironic at first, but she decided outright that it was the former, and this, she told me, as we finished our second bottle of wine and opened another, was a problem.

"What do you mean, Miriam? This is all important work."

"See, there you go. Important. What's up with that?"

"My book, when it comes out next month, that won't be important? My writing wasn't serious?"

"Nope. Others might proclaim this or that. I don't know. Critics might sneer and shout: eat serious—drink Ovaltine. People might care about your book, and let them, that's fine, but you, you're faced with goon breath. You are a brazen little bug. An aloof coyote. A monkfish eating kismet peas. Not a scholar. *Professionàl.* Not a tiger serious about its stripes. Lick your stripes, tie them around a gummy gazelle and make love in tarpits!"

She zinged especially well with wine vesselling her synapses.

"Oh man I saw the wildest leopard print today."

"Tugawar of jungle feasts!"

"Upholstering everything."

"Leopard mind, leopard toboggan, leopard girl leopard drumsticks drumkicks growls of leopard!"

"I was picking out a microwave—did you know the dollar stores on Chicago Avenue have microwaves? Fred tried to convince me to go to K-Mart. But talking with Holofernes, I realized how local economy and idiosyncratic shops bolster the everyday experience and rarity of a neighborhood."

"You're fucking serious."

"Leopard print everywhere. A lot of Mexican families shop there—I don't know if they have better prices—but they're able to establish a relationship with the owners, buy things on credit if they need to, gather information which helps them to navigate their immigrant existence."

"You aren't supposed to be serious."

"That microwave helps. You should get one. I will cook up breakfast one day and reheat the leftovers the next couple of days. Think about how much quicker I will get out of the house in the mornings. And dinner, I don't feel like cooking after a long day. Have you seen *Malcolm in the Middle*? It's a fucking riot."

"Let's get out of here."

"Where do you want to go?"

"Some people are hanging out at Nudge. I'm getting tired just sitting around."

"Alright."

I immediately thought of her: the girl from The Yellow Book, located across the street from Nudge.

We grabbed a six pack from Nevada Liquors—I tried to grab Goose Island's Sofie and began an accompanying anecdote about their storefront location attached to their brewery in the Kinzie Industrial District, but she scoffed, shoved me and grabbed Schlitz instead—and cut back through the neighborhood over to Augusta and California. The looming presence of the buildings felt like crumbling castles in my mind. Towering above us, their tops hidden in the canopy of trees, reminding me of the Tower of Babel—a series of Towers, multiple attempts at building towards heaven. I planned Babylon. I planned Zarathustra. I planned Caramel. Zihuatenejo. I planned San Juan. Sebastian. Alexandria. Chengdu.

Miriam enjoyed this and so I went on.

I planned Dakar. I planned Harappa. I planned Raleigh. I planned Tegucigalpa. Mizzoula. I planned Tibet. And in Tibet I planned another Tibet, to house the idea of the original Tibet. I planned St. Petersberg and then I planned Moscow to rival the bridges with its caps, to stalemate the power of Russia, to free Poland, free Georgia, free Belarus, and then I named it Leningrad and then I planned Stalingrad and then I planned St. Petersberg in the pages of a book and then I hid that book from Russia, a treasure which told them the plan for Moscow's destruction. And so I destroyed London. I destroyed Wiemar. I destroyed Wichita, Pisa, El Paso. I destroyed Beijing. I destroyed Singapore only for it to rise and be destroyed again. I destroyed Demascus. I destroyed Medina. I destroyed Corinth, Harappa, Zapotec. I destroyed Chicago by fire and let it rise twice as high, only to hush it with my turretic breath. And I planned the route of the Phoenix, towards Hollywood, towards Paris, towards Baton Rouge, towards Pompeii, towards Negril, towards Uppsala, Sarajevo, Kitar, Quebec, Santiago, Guayaquil, towards hallelujah, I planned Nineveh. Babylon. You arrived and met me hanging gardens inside stolen apples, my arms tied into the parapets, my legs gridded by the rebar, as my mind fuses with the window panes, my heart beats through the cement mixer the HVAC generators the candle, my tongue speaks through the wick, the asphalt rolling, the squealing of steel gastrointestinal terra-cotta, the corridor aging, the molding falling down marble ripped by the pigeons feet, a river's burial for machinery barges and barges of bolts stokers hard hats pistons and urns of molten paychecks cancering foglights into barges of petroleum Guatemalan banana dolls each a chinchilla fur's beehives and barges of pig guts barges of barrels barges of barges carrying each piece of Babel to the far ends of the earth.

Miriam was right.

Our friends were hanging out on the mattresses still left on the floor from the "Rated Triple X" art event last week—pornographic paintings and dolls and cocktails. Amusing stuff. Mattresses on the floor for people to lounge on and everyone grew primed by these images, but that night, we were all so aloof—each of us thinking I am the only one teetering with sex. That night there was no event, just María Elena and Fred, Josefina, Penelope, and a guy who I did not know, a friend of someone's or all of them: Michel Comté. He told me he was bicurious. Aren't we all, Michel? The door was locked and Miriam knocked and we joined them on the mattresses, but I kept turning back, kept looking through the window, stepping out front to smoke a cigarette with anyone who was going, hoping to see her. Ursulines.

The talk got crazy. We went and got more beer. Michel Comté had opium and we smoked that. María Elena had Adderral and several of us swallowed that. And our energy grew befuddled yet manically we wanted to eat each other's souls and dream each other's faces and hide in our own gestations, gutturally we screamed. Until it was early, the sun cracking through and María Elena, Fred and Miriam had left, gone home to sleep, to masturbate, to write. Josefina and Michel Comté and I stepped outside to smoke and watch the day return across California Avenue, Penelope passing out on the mattress, and I could not help it, I could not let it bury inside any longer, I told them I am wild for the girl who works at that bookstore across the street.

Immediately I regretted saying this. But they enjoyed this. Something to do. And convinced me. That we should knock on the door and see if she was in.

We passed an old lady as we made our way across the street. Cats, she said. Cats, my cats, she said. My cats are killing the birds. The birds are bloodied, she said. In the gangway. In the alleys. Do not go near. The blood will spoil, but who will clean it up. She said, my cats. And we laughed, our realities collectively blurring this night, this morning, these people, these elderly immigrants, us crazed and desperate for fiction, this is fiction, I said. This is Humboldt Park, Michel Comté said. This is the bookstore, Josefina said. And we knocked. On the glass, on the door. They were not open. She might have lived inside, we thought that she could, but she did not answer our knocking and I yelled, "You are mine. You are my darling. Don't you want to know who I am?" Laughing. Coughing. Nevermind the drugs, the alcohol. Nevermind the leopard print microwave television shows electrifying the city's grid, nevermind the office policy of open doors and windows and pigeons perching, oodling, howling across the art deco facade. Nevermind that she did not know my name, that I did not know our future, that I did not want to build that I did not want to plan that I did not want to knock or be serious about my passionate voice rising to the canopies looking down on me roughing me into a pulp of holy tremors my god how I knocked.

"Well, you got to leave a note," Michel Comté said.

"A note."

I took the pen and back-pocket notebook out and penned a note:

I am an Urban Planner and I want you to live in my city. Signed, The Girl Next Door.

6

What a night. What a week. I couldn't remember what time we were set to meet at Smoke Daddy but I knew it was after a usual lunch would occur. I got that wrong and was late but I am not sure how late, only that Holofernes's table was seated and laughing loudly, barely noticing the waiter pull up a seat for me at the corner of an already tight table. I got to know a few those faces over the next weeks, but at the time, I thought to myself, even when they're laughing they're serious. Not serious, but anxious. Not anxious, but fearful. Not fearful, but bold. Holofernes smiled and waved, then motioned to the waiter, but said nothing as the man next to him, Ruben, was telling a story about the first time Holofernes came with him to the Pride Parade in Boystown. I took a sip from the mason jar the waiter put in front of me, and my face soured to the piney, bitter, grassy beer. Ruben saw this, and said, "Looks like the new girl doesn't discuss sex over lunch." The table looked to me, the new girl, and laughed. "I think it's her first hops," Holofernes interjected, which I didn't understand at the time, but was grateful for what seemed to be a defense. Then Gwynn said, "every bunny takes her first hop when I'm around," and everyone cackled. Someone said, "Skin the bunny!" I guessed I was at least two beers late, so took a gulp, a little of the beer spinning around the screw threads at the mouth of the jar and then dripping down my chin and shirt. Ruben continued, "Well, obviously all my friends thought he was gay, but remember Ralphy, big Ralphy, right—he loved your outfit, your shorts. What were you wearing, Holofernes?" "Camouflage." "That's it, camo shorts, and Big Ralphy, listen to this, he's up in Holofernes's face and says in his gruff voice, 'let's go to the alley and I will suck your cock.' Holofernes says no and Ralph drops to his knees and looks up at his face and says, 'You can't hide that piece of meat from me!'" Cackling, everyone cackling.

"And he grabbed it!" I yelled. "And he put his mouth on it through the camos."

Everyone ignored me.

Gwynn changed the subject. "Ruben that is why I do not come to your Pride parties. All this talk about dicks and this barbecue on the table, really fellas, we gotta get down to business: Milwaukee."

"Ghost town."

"Churches and bars."

"Any church-condo conversions?"

"We've taken the temperature on that and it seems the population is still too religious for that to go well."

"Who do we have up there?"

"Let's not talk in all this detail," Holofernes interjected. "Business. We have Red Hook on tap, ribs, Urban Dijn our favorite bartender and country balladeer, so we have enough right here, to enjoy ourselves, yes?"

"Gwynn, tell us what's happening at IDEO?"

"Fantastic culture. Fantastic. I think any month the recreational cubicles will be installed. Clients are gonna get a laugh when they see those."

"Did they choose the paraffin compound or the graphite?"

"Paraffin. Someone said they'll have dummies sitting in them. Ice luges next Thursday."

"Fridays it's like, why bother, everyone's already had lunch or are out of there. I love that they do their festivities on Thursdays."

"It's all an inside joke, that's what Ballister was saying, the ping pong tables are fully convertible into a dark room playground, and there are Legos. Just to build with."

"Legos really are an artistic medium—we have so many childhood hang-ups about the world."

"Oh god, you're making me miss my job at Yahoo. In the Bay."

"Bay area has lost touch, *amigo*."

"It's beautiful. I don't care."

"The prices, the technology—this is not what it's about."

"Holofernes's right—" I had to pipe in. "This is Chicago, this is Detroit, Milwaukee, this is St Louis, Memphis, Kansas City. This is New Orleans. And if we get bored, we'll do Tulsa. Legos, pork chops, the side yard—all of it."

They smiled, tight-lipped, and looked at Holofernes.

"Where's our first move going to be?"

"There's only a couple options really."

"Pilsen."

"My vote."

"Logan Square."

"Logan Square."

"Jinx. Owe me a Coke."

"Bitch."

"And Bridgeport."

"Five years ago Wicker Park wasn't too expensive."

"Yes, but five years ago those two towers in New York went kaput."

"What's the connection?"

"They blew up Tower 7 themselves?"

"Who's they?"

"Everybody, listen," I said. "Those neighborhoods are bullshit. We need to follow the Forts. And I've met one, her name is Ursulines."

"You have an earnest pupil here, Holofernes."

"Judith is very interested to learn more about what we're up to."

"Penelope's friend, right?"

"What do you mean by that?"

"She's a twit."

"Whoever believes in The Fortress is a dickhole. That's not business."

"It's just another distraction. While Connor, Jake, the Maramounts—they're all killing it. Absolutely killing it. Us? We're gathering more data, digging up jack-offs like this gal."

"Leave. If you don't like it, call Jake—leave."

"I've got a doctor's appointment anyway. This doesn't mean I'm done, but figure it out, Holofernes. Figure it out."

Thomas got up and left

"That bitch still owes me a Coke," Gwynn said and everybody but Holofernes smiled.

"Thomas is too rational for us," Holofernes pulled us back in. "We aren't looking for the next best thing, boys and girls. We want the *coup de gras*. That takes time. Intelligence."

"Gravy," I said.

"Certain practices which others have not gotten behind. Next week, I will introduce you to a woman named

Sue Dinko. A dark-arts specialist. She owns my office at the six corners."

"Occult?"

"Her specialty is hypnosis."

"I see," Gwynn said. "Information."

"Information."

Half the table took their last sips and the other half didn't break eye contact. I decided to let this awkward silence resolve itself, though the comedy of my mind feasted on this séance.

"Judith had the privilege of meeting Ciudad Mujer."

"How?"

"Right place, right time."

"You need to bring us all in the loop here, Holofernes—a little could go a lot here."

"We've learned that the Forts have formed an alliance with Rat Patrol."

"Are they still in good with Guardian Angels."

"You can't be underground without the protection of the Guardians."

"I asked one of those guys to wear their red beret and he told me it was red with his blood, sacred, and then he slapped me."

"We're following all this on the ground, but we're years behind. Vestiges. Amputated limbs. Not the host source."

"Your case studies are washed-up dads. All they know is the 90s, what it was, and what they hear from their friends who hear from their friends who hear from a fucking bathroom wall about where The Fortress has moved. Holofernes, five years ago, I'd be tickled just to be having this conversation. Today, I'm ready to make a move and the market is primed. I'm taking my investment back. Best of luck."

Without saying anything, everybody but Ruben and Gwynn stood up.

The magnitude. Investment. These were the money people and they had left—I looked to Holofernes, expecting him to be sunk. He had his hand in the air, four fingers up to the waiter. "Friday lunch is Friday lunch."

Gwynn smiled, "Holofernes, are you thinking what I am thinking? The nerve, you goat. Let's do it."

"Will you work for us, Judith?"

"There are many services you could provide us. Your language for one."

"Your dress, don't we think her style is perfect." I was wearing cut-off jeans and an oven mitt knitted tank top that Dom had sold me at US #1.

"But are you sunk? Those big wigs just left."

"We are venturing on without them. They brought nothing to the table but initial cash flow."

"We've been pushing them to the edge for months."

"Cheers! To the trio. Plus one."

"Cheers!"

"That shit about the Guardian Angels, wonderful—wonderful!"

They cackled. Ruben said, "I'm buying!"

"Good, because I don't have any money."

They laughed even harder.

7

To walk, to become skilled at walking and to see a street in terms of its want, to see in people's faces the way they have judged themselves for their lack of imagination, to see their professions hardening across their skin, their last meal, how posture conforms to architecture, to see the strings and the glue, the attainment desired, to feel the charge of the body passing you and how it shifts your own valence, the storefront organism and your cellular capacity to distribute power or recede, to watch the neighborhood bestially clean its windows and alleys with its tongue. To be the tongue, the paw, the whiskers. To walk and feel each street's dialect, the ever-shifting text disappearing as you turn around. To walk, I told them, into the streets where you have never been, the neighborhoods a far mile from your own, to get lost and terrified by the closed doors which shoot bullets, hide abuse, realities dissolving before you can begin to sense their coherence, lost and mocked by the designing eyes that enslave, the storefront rules of class, why you sit where you sit on each bus, why you pay no attention to what you pay no attention while walking, to walk, I repeated, to be captured and to capture.

After my lunch meeting with Holofernes, I knew I had responsibilities, that I had consented to do things, but it was not clear what immediate actions I should take. So I sat at the window staring out over the vacant lot next door. I wondered if Fred owned this, too. My thoughts set to developing, planning, designing space. Urban space. I considered what type of building would look good there, aesthetically, and then I calculated what I thought that building would be worth, how much Fred could make from constructing it. Math in my head I held onto. These sorts of thoughts were new to me, but by the end of the week, I had out my notepad and instead of words, I was sketching architectural facades—something akin to the French Quarter, I thought, we'll need a new one after that hurricane—wrought-iron balconies and painted brick. Or possibly Victorian Italianate, as these streets near downtown once were one hundred years before. I considered immigrants. I asked aloud, what is a city? And then I drew a fractal, which soon after I began to smudge and deform, bloat, erase and sicken. Rococo mansions. Slanty shanties. Eyeglasses, nose rings, no right turns. Mexican candies, scratch and wins, revolving doors, gangways, a hush of arctic cold, unlaced shoes. Intersections, population density. Skyline interstates carnage and alienation mocking success teeth-gnashed on brass doorknobs. No one graffities property taxes across billboards, only slang and grit to soak in and reconstitute into another life form. I considered contemporary styles—glass curtain homes striped with metal. I drew sketches of buildings dominated by outdoor living space, even though the climate would not allow it. I zoomed in on details and fixtures. I dug colored pencils out from a box beneath my bed, and I blended yellows and oranges for the paint, browns and blues for the natural materials, green doors, red doors, white casing, purple—I did not have many colors, but my mind was set to wonder what was possible visually upon this building I was lost in, already having decided I would move in once it was built, already having written and sold the books necessary to afford the $1200 I estimated the rents would be on a 2-bedroom, the second one I'd use as an office but have it set up for guests.

Like I had crawled too far into a foxhole and gotten comfortable enough to forget that I was not a Fox. Only to be startled when I sensed more than me

Out my window, I stared down at a man who was staring up at me. His black leather jacket cracked and greyed, too short to reach the waistline of his sludgy brown shorts. Ashen legs. Soot on his face. He looked away disinterested, as if neither of us had seen the other, as if I did not register on his instinctual radar, and he walked toward the street. I didn't know what was going to happen next, but I took a step back when I saw a two-story freakbike amble by. Slime green, swelled where soldered, the rider wore a black felt top hat, a wiry beard, and sunglasses. His torn-sleeved jean jacket layered with pinned-on black patches of skulls and rats. The Fox started to jog alongside it as a hobo hopping a train, and then with acrobatic ease he climbed up with the help of the rider's outstretched arm, finding a seat on a crossbar, his legs on one side, watching me as if I were a sunset, they the sundance kids riding off.

8

Hungover with embarrassment for leaving the note on the bookstore, it took me a week to pass back by. Warm, the florist stood in the door to catch a breeze, the mechanic slouched on the bench drinking a tallboy in a paper bag. A beat-up floral upholstered couch had been pulled out in front of The Yellow Book, and on the shut door a note, right where I had taped mine. I looked through the window, not seeing her, I took the note and sat down on the couch to read it.

"Me: an invisible city.

You: a sheet to drape and trace my form.

Come inside if we're open.

Signed,

Ursulines"

Holofernes was right about her name. Before I could get up to walk in, the door opened and she stepped out. Large brown sunglasses, serious and full lips, braless a white cotton tank top splattered with paint fell over her breasts, faded green cut-offs, her legs long pale, scraped, a big bruise on her thigh. She wore no shoes.

"You?" she said.

"Hi," I said.

"Comfortable?"

"I can see you plain as day."

"It's nighttime when I disappear."

She sat down.

"You run around with Penelope, right?"

"We were across the street the other night—or morning—when I introduced myself."

"What are you up to?"

"Walking around, seeing things. I've been inside this store once before."

"This is my bookstore."

"You own it?"

"It's not an owner type of thing. Come on, check it out."

We walked inside. Except for four book cases in each corner, the walls were lined with shelves of books faced cover out: Acker, Saterstorm, Durand, Thoreau, Rumi, Huxley, Augustine, Gladman, Sir Thomas Moore, Plato, Le Guin, Coultas, Diderot, Alice Waters pamphlets, Anne Waldman epics, the Gnostic Gospels, Rabelais, Al-Farabi, Burger, Steiner, Hesse, Rand, Jung, Kapil.

"I dig this."

"At two hundred a month, I don't need to sell many. It's a project—I gathered mine and a few friends' books and this is that. We have meetings here. You came to one."

"I've read a lot of these authors."

"You write, isn't that true?"

"I do. I did—or I am not sure what the next book will be. My mind is out there right now, but it's not bringing back the usual suspects."

"No good plots?"

"I met a guy."

"Is it serious?"

"Looks like it. He has me wrapped up in this mystery—it's better than a book. The world is hiding something from us."

"I don't know if metaphysics is allowed in polite intellectual company these days. Or are you talking buried treasure?"

"I'm talking about that cafe that you wish existed. That little bar that no one goes to who only serves steak frites and red wine."

"I'm freegan."

"You know those friends you have always known were out there, somewhere, if you could only be at the right time in the right place in the right mood. That apartment, cheap, furnished, a top-floor turret's view, tiled kitchen, wallpaper like acetate film."

"You're positive it's all out there?"

"I've never been so sure."

"Well, maybe you'll bring me with you, when you go."

"As we're talking, I'm seeing a treasure map unfold, a hand-drawn palm tree, you beneath it."

"I'm more a bookmark than an X-marked spot."

"There's something behind one of these walls, beneath a building, beyond that turn in the alley you always fear is the future location of your mugging, beat-down and death. Waiting. Radiating. It's why the birds sing at night."

"Words suit you."

"You should see me unsuited."

"I think you might like this book I finished a few weeks ago. *Conquest of the Useless*. Werner Herzog kept a journal when he was in South America, filming *Fitzcarraldo*."

"Sure, I know of him, but not the book."

"He is lost in the night among these brutal wilderness-es and nightmarish visions, trying to make an impossible film, feeling the horror of incomprehensible lives. Of not having the appropriate faculties for comprehension. He is set on finding the edge, like you in your search for these romances. I have a copy in the back."

"The edge of what? I'd love to read it."

"Come and see for yourself."

As she turned to head through the yellow curtain, I saw a telephone on the counter, one you would find in a business who handled multiple calls with multiple buttons on top to switch between each one. Curious, maybe a thrift-store find, however the receiver was off the hook and set near us, the cord fully extended. Wondering if it even worked I looked at the wall and saw the jack then at the base one red light lit indicating the speaker function. Then I saw the hole in her cut-offs, the tattoo beneath it—an antique book—and I followed her, hoping for tight quarters.

"It might be in one of those boxes."

"One of those boxes up there?"

She took off her sunglasses. "Yes, up there."

I kissed Ursulines. Her brown eyes passionately serious and she pulled me close to her, our lips tongue hips quickly her shorts down and my hands full with her hips my top off, skirt up, she pushed me against the wall as her hand rubbed my cunt I squeezed her ass until she slid down my breasts teasing my nipple and across my stomach her tongue wet with a lust which she alone on this earth was responsible. I came and immediately, ravenously fell atop her fumbling for her clit and with my tongue tasted what I will always remember as a velvet curtain dancing with candlelight, a wooden board of fruit, a window open to city summer night.

Like that, we were lovers.

9

Beyond the cafe neighborhoods, beyond the restaurants, the boutiques, the bedraggled storefronts with hand-painted signs selling coffee, bread. Beyond the neighborhoods where folks live and invite people into their apartments for baked bread, for art hung on their walls and a projector mounted to the ceiling playing odd, confounding films with no volume, beyond the basement shows and the live-work spaces, beyond the El stops, the bus lines, beyond the tattoo parlors, the Mexican pizza slices, the neat Ethiopian diner, beyond any display of food for sale, clothing, trinkets, furniture for sale, there lies a wasteland of evacuated structures, rubbled streets, unzoned nightmares, brown fields and train tracks lost in fully grown weeds like humans had never interfered, no one can remember why, no depot no switch and there only abandoned thoughts, abandoned bodies, abandoned families of non-related persons unnamed and sunken, breathing there is breathing, pulsing faintly and I hear it, I greet it when I close my eyes and drift to sleep, it flashes as if synapses bursting eye veins fanning alluvial lands rich in mineral deposits, sediment life and we must know these lands, they will teach us, enrich us, and I let the current take me around the bend arriving there, walking the first to walk, arriving the arrival of me and I do not ask who I am, only that I am in need of fertile lands, ancient wisdoms sculpted into bricks the dust I snort like snuff and return, awake, alive in an office. Have you ever watched your crystal ball dim in the florescence? Your spleen contract and your liver blacken by commercial toxin filled carpet conveying your innards not data and schedules and a kiss from the one you thought you loved in a suit with an ascot, an itinerary, a library full of manuals. The office had a balcony and Holofernes and I would talk there. "You need to understand where I am coming from, Judith. I love these same things you love, have you ever heard Sharon Zukin discuss *kairos*? The past as it remains in the built environment, Judith, I am an addict. No, don't laugh, really. Socrates' *algama*? We must go through with this."

"Holofernes, we have our thing, but I'm falling for Ursulines."

"Judith Judith Judith."

I did not at that time believe I comprehended what Holofernes meant when he said *this*. But being as I am my thoughts flooded with anxiety about my transformation, my rebirth, which is a story I was telling myself at that time. This immersion into the city, how would it change me. This is about me. And my energy to discover myself, express myself as the universe asks. Which star worries about the fate of the cosmos as it burns? Which planet orbits according to concern for the solar system? These are all gods in the garb of language.

Then we sat outside on the couch and talked and smoked.

"I've never moved so quickly," she said, "in the daylight."

"Books turn me on."

"More than my body?"

"Your body is the book I am talking about. That tattoo—I hate to judge a book by its cover."

"Is that a bullet wound above your hip?"

"So many stories on our bodies, aren't there?"

"Do you know anything about the origins of Mexico City? I mean, such a random question, sorry, but my tattoo is a book from those times. Ciudad Mujer. Originally three cities—Tenochtitlan, Texcoco, Tlacopan. As the Aztecs fell to the Spaniards, a group of high priestesses went underground, not knowing what they were heading for but believing the magic possessed between them would vanish if they were killed. It is said by some that they began to write a book, a text which would not only carry forth their traditions but embody their spells."

"That's the book?"

"Well, recently, archeologists have begun to argue that no, they did not write a book—there are several in existence but none have been authenticated—what these women did was build a city. A city of their own within the walls of the Spaniards' city, Ciudad de Mexico. Half hidden, half in plain sight, where they continued their practices. Their magic, I believe, is founded in the understanding that the city is a woman and the woman is a city. To be a city is to draw from the mysterious wellspring which empowered their ways of life. To be a city is to be the manifold dimensions of a mirror. Never do we see the real thing—never does the same thing happen twice—never is there not another way of seeing."

Just then, the Actors from the other night at Miriam's walked by.

"Judith!" they shouted. "Pull my headdress, I'm falling down a wall."

And they laughed and laughed. Glazed over by what

Ursulines was telling me, I smiled and then finally shouted "Lego addiction amputated his forefather."

Each of them hugged me lovingly before chasing their laughter down California Avenue.

"Who were they?"

"They're the Actors."

And I sensed that Ursulines hesitated. Wondered. Reconsidered her passion for me. But it was too late, I loved her. I smiled and she said, "You look really good naked."

"Crack. My muscles tense and constrict when I'm high, makes me strong where others are weak."

She smiled. She wondered about me and she smiled.

10

Holofernes hid his private life well. I knew he had an affair with Penelope, and that was why he was at Miriam's house the night I met him. But that ended quickly, and Penelope had little to say about it. Especially to me once his attentions turned in my direction. Close with Penelope, I felt guilty for my tête-à-tête with Holofernes. But for Holofernes, Penelope soon became not enough.

Holofernes and I decided on a regular meeting around the corner from my house at Atomix. One day I was there, working on my walking stories, the ones I had promised for Holofernes now that I was on the team. He walked in, a sharp tan button down shirt, sleeves rolled up as if he had been busting the bricks of city hall all morning, gray slacks which were not wrinkled as my own, and brown leather shoes. I commented on the shoes, Great shoes. He said Thanks and took a seat at my table.

I did not want another cup of coffee, but he offered to grab me a refill, and I was nervous enough to know that I needed something to fidget with, spin around slowly, lift and touch, and sip, otherwise who knew where those nervous energies might take me.

He came back with my coffee and a cup of tea for himself.

"You've never told me what got you interested in urban planning," I said.

"As an architecture student I fell into a couple of urban planning classes. When I got out of school and realized that the buildings which clients were demanding did not suit my tastes and since I had no patrons nor fortune, I needed to pursue a career which would give me power."

"Power, that's a dangerous word."

"I should say influence, but honestly, one chooses: money, power, or story. I did not want to work for others' ideas, jockeying away at buildings or whatever it might be that I did not believe in. I do believe in beauty but the beauty of my visions. That is the story I want to be told."

"Yes, visions." I wanted to answer the question I had asked obscurely so as not to have to deal with it head-on for him. Visions is what got me going as well.

"That magnificence we are allowed access to. It's enough to drive you mad when placed next to this world we share here."

"The incongruity."

"Yes, very incongruous."

"But their juxtaposition—I do love how they look next to each other, this elsewhere as you have called it and this here, what we occupy now."

"A fine cafe."

"I agree."

"But everyone is quite Catholic here."

"Now what do you mean by that?"

"No one is making any noise. No one is looking at each other. All well-behaved in the eyes of the nuns. Are we in an intercommunicating conference room or a meeting place in the neighborhood?"

"People, it seems to me, save their talk for the night."

"Do you want to know what I would do to shift all this?"

"Yes."

"Talk begins at the nucleus, the center. And it also begins at the circumference, the edge."

"Your reasoning sounds circular, but go on."

"So if there is talk at the center and at the edge, then talk will be the norm in between, or at least one is encouraged to talk or listen to others, which is fantastic as well."

"So you would shift the design?"

"The design of this space and the design of the entire neighborhood. The counter should be a counter, a place to encounter the baristas, cashiers whatever you want to call the shop owners. Hiring the right kind of friendliness is essential—they should live in the neighborhood, that is key—but economically one needs motivation to keep up the sort of chatter I am referring to, and I would propose that each employee be made a part-owner."

"Of the cafe?"

"Yes. They would be paid according to profits, a small percentage, but a percentage, not a flat rate. There would be good months and bad, but the motives of an owner are far different than of an hourly employee. An owner feels the room differently, is more perceptive to what's at stake and what is possible. They become immediately involved in the experience of their guests. Friendliness, conversation, attentive service, all that is activated. Many mistake such an idea as communism, but really, it is capitalism at its most democratic level."

"I wonder how much more or less they would be paid?"

"Probably the same, who knows—it's the perception of the reality that counts, not the reality itself. Next I would make room on this counter for customers to sit and drink their coffee. European and bar-style counter. None of this nonsense we see now. Then I would move to the edges."

"I think intimate booths of some sort would be neat."

"I like it, yes. The edge is for more discrete conversations and meetings. Those that do not wish to feel public though they are in a public space. The lighting sources would be in the center, at the counter, and only the leftovers of all that is not absorbed from the middle would hit the edges. Dark enough to discourage intense work—this should be done somewhere in the middle—but enough light to see the face before you romantically, in its shadowy beauty."

"And booths, right?"

"Banquets, yes. Circle booths as opposed to across the table kind. Similar to Rainbo."

"That reminds me: how is your search faring?"

"For wall-hangings?"

"I didn't know you were in the market. I have a few paintings by Chicago artists—do you know the Hairy Who?—I'll show you soon, but for now, my favorite topic. The Fortress."

"I told you about the freakbike episode."

"You did."

"And The Yellow Book."

"How are things with Ursulines?"

"She has a lot to say and I love every word of it."

"Have you been to her apartment?"

"Look at you poking around for details. It's far away, so we don't hang out there that often."

"Where does she live?"

"Do you know the abandoned viaduct that stretches west? I'm not sure what her address is, but we usually take that. To get there."

"The viaduct, really? How do you get up there?"

"There's holes in a few of the fences. The other day, we were walking—it was dark, maybe 11pm—and I stepped on someone."

"Did you trip?"

"No. I mean, I didn't fall. It was dark but the moon was out and we were a little on the edge of the track looking in the bushes. It was like they had just popped up out of the ground."

"Where were you when this happened?"

"I don't know."

"Near Ursulines' apartment?"

"Yeah, we got off soon after that. The guy didn't say anything, just flopped around a little. Had to be a junkie."

"Good work, Judith."

I never resisted Holofernes's condescending offers of congratulations.

"Wait, there's Gwynn and Ruben walking in—you don't mind do you?"

And they came in smiling, disrupting the cool mellow tone of Atomix with their luxurious clothes, airs, and talk.

"Judith," Gwynn greeted me, "you pick the coolest places to do your thing."

Loudly Ruben asked, "Where are their pickles, Holofernes?"

"You two get what you need and then we'll have our meeting with Judith."

"Another meeting?"

"We have the specifics you inquired about. Sorry we don't have an official Human Resource department."

"Looks like I'm coming on board."

They sat down and spelled it out: $1000 a week. I felt like a hooker.

Gwynn, Ruben, and Holofernes had asked me to do two things in exchange for my money—they called it a stipend which annoyed me but the least of my concerns in the end. Walk and write. Walk further than I regularly would, past the neighborhoods where I felt safe. "Walk towards the outposts," Ruben said. "What we've gathered so far, yes there are a few in the neighborhood where you live, and we have a line on those."

"Yes, like the lot next to your apartment, Judtih."

"I saw a freakbike pick up a hobo the other day."

"We're surprised they're still using that entrance," said Gwynn. "I had to sleep with a freakbiker named Rancid Ralph to confirm that one."

"Enough of that. Judith, do you feel safe walking past drunk old Polish men?"

"Sure, I don't judge."

"You don't mind the Latino fellas whistling at your *culo*?"

"Yes, I mind, but that machismo assault won't stop me. I will earn my stipend, *mis amgios*."

"Gang-bangers, dealers, punks—you'll need to be ready."

"Ready for the onslaught of degradation that only the lower classes can provide. You three are insane. I've gotten more awkward leers from Holofernes in a week than ten years of yelps on North Avenue. Do women get this talk before they take a corporate job downtown? Honey, are you ready to walk past your boss' office and be called in to chat? Are your ready to watch them steal looks down your co-workers' shirt? Are your ready for the suit-pitching boners? Come the fuck on."

"Here's the thing, Judith—The Fortress couldn't hire better bodyguards than the impoverished, violent, depraved populations who live above ground from where they hide. You might be woke but the masses are not. It is your clarity that we wish to employ."

"The symbiosis is remarkable."

"Alright, Judith. So you will walk, you will notice, you will write?"

"Notice everything, write it down—but let us make sense of it."

"Watch for anything out of the ordinary—people you wouldn't expect, storefronts which look rundown yet inside demonstrate intentional curation."

"Yes, notice anything curated. Look for energies as well."

"We have volumes of studies about how the psychogeographic energy shifts with Fortress activity."

"Farming is big—any signs of agriculture: worms, compost, large squashes."

"Nice paint colors. Brightness attracts the people we are interested in. Body posture—any wellness or health is also something our vampires like to suck."

"Vampires?"

"Industry lingo—we'll brief you on all of it."

"It impresses the investors."

"Here's the thinking: we cater to those who feel a lack, who are missing components in their life and are looking to find some vision of a life, a neighborhood which seems to be the solution to what they are missing. Where the grasses are green."

"Right, except we need you to notice not what is there but what could be projected on the blank canvas."

"Those neighborhoods are canvases," Holofernes said. "And I am the artist."

I loved how insane they were—these philosophies, understandings were like beautiful heat-seeking myths.

I knew I could play along. And I loved being lost in the prodigality that ensued—Holofernes's extravagance knew no bounds. His daily patterns were adorned by olives, boutique vodkas, handmade soaps, artisan cheeses, breads, and beers. Everything he purchased was locally sourced and everything he wore handknit. He knew no industrial revolution, he knew no franchise, no department store, no big box. He touched the living skins of the cattle and pigs he had butchered; his hand felt the warmth of the hen's ass which laid his eggs; his milk was straight from the bucket—nothing pasteurized, nothing pumped with hormones, nothing mass-produced or fortified with vitamins. He found restaurants and bars, purveyors and street peddlers which the rest of us did not know existed. All in the neighborhoods we had been hanging out in for years. And he'd invite us there, and he'd pay. For ten-ingredient cocktails, gentle piles of cured meat served on wood boards, pimento pickle hot sauce grit dishes served in tin camping dishes. All these purchases, his consumer choices, were a simple matter of ethics.

And for a while it felt as if he were paying for the privilege to hang out with me. And he would surprise me, too, always with food: specialty chocolates, craft beers yet to be released or only found in Wisconsin, pizzas from places outside of our neighborhood, which was amazing because the only pizza where we lived was made by Mexicans and though I learned to love it and it was so cheap, Mexicans don't know anything about pizza. But Holofernes would present me with what I perceived as luxury almost every time he came. And he would ask me: How do you like it? How does it taste? Is it what you expected? Does it surprise you, are you satisfied? Describe, he always insisted that I describe my experience of the soda pop, of the ice cream, of the pork belly. He would corner me at dinner parties, and insist that I describe.

I was hungry. He had sugar; he had salt. Interrupting my original intentions, I ate and smiled and drank and felt like I was receiving my due attention. My rewards for my ethics and artistry of living. I was tired of my famished existence. And in return I fed him Ursulines.

11

Ursulines would keep me up late into the night. The hours passed midnight were her sustenance, ravishing conversations, mesmerized by scenes beneath street lights, at wild peace with night's silence. We went out, and we went out often. But even at home, the nights we would spend in her apartment, she would put a record and coffee on around ten, and we would sit in her living room, me on the rug near her feet as she sat in her chair, a short table between us, staring into each other's words. Staring into the room and all we conjured across its surfaces. Then we'd transition into the kitchen, sitting on the counter with the back door open to funnel out the cigarette smoke, drinking red wine until three. I could tell by the way she stepped outside to smoke one last cigarette and stare at the night sky that she desired more, she wanted to see the morning, every night the green dawn of day.

We were two souls brightening by the darkness of night.

"How about that CocoRosie you've got."

"I was thinking Joanna Newsom."

"How about Devendra Banhart."

"That sounds good."

"Holofernes's been buying his coffee from a guy over off Fulton and Damen, Exploding Nova. Really good—I mean like a fantastic cup."

"You sure that's not a band—Exploding Star Orchestra. They're playing at Whistler next week."

"You might be right. A lot of new stuff with a similar vibe."

"More like a derivative hide."

"That's too cute—you're playing my word game."

"We should go to that—three nights they'll be there. Like Monk used to do, all those Manhattan jazz guys in the fifties."

"I'm not so sure about the Whistler. Just one of those scenes, you know."

"No, it's a scene, but it's not like that. You just have to avoid the weekend crowds, like anything."

"I stopped by Rainbo a couple Saturdays ago—I don't know what I was thinking."

"You stay long?"

"I got a beer, played a couple games of pinball, but nobody appreciates that, you know, on those nights. They sour face me and roll their eyes. Pinball? Who's that fucking girl playing pinball?"

"Right."

"Not what they expect. They show up here and they want something else. I don't know."

"Right, they want some magic sexuality. They want celebrity whisperings."

"In high school, the girls a couple grades older than me, I remember how they started saying *party like a rockstar.* That was their phrase. When they talked about what they did last night, *Shit, girl, I partied like a rockstar.*"

"Yeah yeah, I've heard people say that."

"Or like what's going on tonight? *We're partying like rockstars.*"

"That's what you think people coming to this neighborhood want?"

"Fuck yes. Some mythic night. Getting so lost and enraptured by partying that, like…"

"That it becomes legend."

"Legend enough to justify their bullshit lives."

"Yeah, legendary."

"People are amazed by it—that dude parties fucking hard."

"Fucking high school, right?"

"These neighborhoods are like high school hallways. Checking each other out."

"The Wicker Park checkout."

"What's that?"

"Like you're saying, it's when you walk by someone and make eye contact and then you see their eyes give you a full body scan—shoes, socks, pants, belt, shirt, jacket, jewelry, tattoos, scarf, glasses, hat—judging each and every part of you in two seconds."

"Right, yeah—that's exactly what I am talking about."

"It's the *are you cool enough for this neighborhood?* look."

"More than that. I think it's an insecurity. It's *if this person is cool than I am in the right place.*"

"Got you, yes."

"But if this person is not cool than *shit, where are the cool people and I am embarrassed for still being here when the circus has already left town.*"

"Not for me."

"You didn't act like that in high school?"

"Yeah, but no. I didn't party. I didn't get wrapped up in those worlds where you are validated by who you are hanging out with. That's not how it went for me. But you did?"

"Oh yeah. It was all about the party. And the music, the drugs. I was drinking bottles of Hennessy freshman year. Throwing up a ton, right, but finding out all those limits the hard way."

"The rockstar way."

"More gangster way for me."

"You were a sweet little *G*?"

"This ain't nothing *but* a G thing. Drugs and all that were a part of it—we'd go to house shows, mountain parties—fucking miss partying in the mountains. Somebody's parents were always out of work, drunker than we were, trying to sleep with our friends. Rowdy stuff."

"Guns gangster?"

"Guns. Blunts, baby—we were flush."

"What happened do that hard edge of yours?"

"I swallowed that up when I got to Chicago. Maybe when I moved in with my brother. He shut me up anytime I got stupid. You were studious?"

"I guess so. Not in that nerdy way. I mean I think I was a nerd in a lot of people's eyes, but I never felt like a nerd."

"I bet you didn't."

"What's that mean?"

"You're so confident and have, I mean, you know so much. And you're goddamn sexy."

"But this is ten years later."

"Even youth can't hide that type of thing."

"I didn't fit in with most of what was going on. But I look back and think about the theatre kids, or the all the kids wearing band t-shirts, and I bet I would've gotten along with them if I would've tried. Instead I was kicking it with Molly McGee."

"You used to sell Molly?"

"What?"

"Ecstasy?"

"No. Oh, Molly, 'no—you're stupid. Janis Joplin. 'Me and Molly McGee.'"

"What's that song all about?"

"It's about being alone. Kristofferson wrote it while he was working on an oil rig in the Gulf Coast. I listened to it all the time and for me, it was like my imaginary friend. Good enough for me and Molly McGee. I did all those things you do when you're alone a lot—read, write in my diary."

"I'd love to see that diary."

"Some weeks I drew, I got a camera when I was seventeen. I didn't watch too much teevee, but I'd listen to my parents' records."

"How'd you have those?"

"That's all I had. That's what my Uncle grabbed for me when they were cleaning up or selling their stuff already. I didn't know to grab stuff, things to remember, I was too young to realize that I would ever forget."

"How old were you when you moved in with your Uncle?"

"Twelve."

"He was really good to you though, right?"

"He was the best. I mean the coolest dad you could have. I love him, but he didn't know what to do with me, a teenager. He showed me things, turned me on to crazy stuff, right, like Dada, Beefheart. He was silly, and so many movies—or I should say films, he always said films. A lot of things that didn't make sense to me—Tarkovsky, right, or Chaplin."

"What?"

"Yeah, I mean Hitchcock and all of that, but also Melville, Godard—the first time I saw a woman naked was Anna Carina in, shit, in, well I don't remember."

"*Vivre sa vie?*"

"That's it, she's naked in that right?"

"I think so."

"God, I fell in love with her. So, my Uncle was great, but I felt distant from everybody else. I could've gotten away with partying every night, like a real fucking rockstar, but I didn't know that I wanted to, maybe I didn't want to, maybe I got enough romantic fantasy from those records and movies and books, all those stories and all that. And nobody else knew what I was talking about, I didn't even know, but I kept quiet."

"Did you used to cut your hair like Anna Carina?"

"I did! Bangs, even dyed it black."

"It's already black."

"I didn't think it was black enough."

"There's black and then there's noir."

"Right?"

"So you partied like a femme fatale."

"You're so funny. All the time. Like 24/7 funny."

"Another cup of coffee?"

"Yeah."

"We should do a day, a whole weekend, when we go to Odd Obsessions and rent a bunch of the movies your Uncle showed you when you were growing up. I'd love to watch those with you."

"That'd be great."

"Just sit around on the couch—this winter we should do that—and watch like ten movies in a row. Make love in between. You telling me stories about your youth, how you felt, your first girlfriend, everything."

And we always talked about this, especially when the nights became too crazy or my walking and talks with Holofernes began to eat up all my time, and we'd say to each other that next weekend we would do this, we would stay in her apartment all weekend, but then she began to demand that it be the weekdays, the days I was working, only weekdays, she would say, have the right tempo, enough mood and structure to fold into. Just like that, there was her new desire: I just want to fold into it, you know? If they were playing well, she'd say: the drummer folded into the guitar lines in a really interesting way. She worked this phrase into everything she admired. And no weekend day was good enough, it had to be a weekday that we folded ten hours of movie watching into, or however long it was, we always made it impossible, but I would agree and she would agree, both of us telling each other we wanted this, our great simple plan, but we never did it. Every time we would be making up after a fight we would say this to each other, we would promise this. As if this day of movies we had planned was sacred, a sanctuary to place our love and if our love didn't have this, it wouldn't last. We knew this. But we didn't say this.

"I love how you wear those nerd glasses, it's like they're a relic from your youth."

"What do you mean nerd?"

"I don't mean that, I love them, but like nerd-style, you know."

"I don't think they're nerdy."

"No, they're, I mean that's a fashion. They're totally fashionable."

"I'm not Wicker Park, Judith. I wear them because I like them."

"Don't get me wrong. They remind me of you when you were younger—you know, what you told me."

"My first girlfriend, right—you wanted to know about her."

"Molly McGee?"

"Sharon Witsburgh."

"I know Sharon. Sharon Witsburgh from Chicago's north side. She wears plaid. Lives in a brick building."

"What?"

"Was this in high school?"

"Senior year. I kissed a couple boys before then, but she was my first. I mean she turned out to be crazy—she was in college, and I didn't know how it was as you got older, the games, you know. I didn't know, but she fucked with me, a little bit."

"She cheat on you?"

"It wasn't like that. It's different sometimes, at least she said that, god, what a nightmare, that girls didn't commit sexually, so we both cheated, or whatever. She was great at first."

"This is what I like about Devendra Banhart. This song."

"This one?"

"The way he sings about children, about family. He's this freak folk guy and I'm sure is all wild in whatever ways, but he's always singing about having kids. I like that."

"It's kinda strange."

"Community, you know, but with kids. It'd be great if more rockstars looked at life that way."

"What's up with Holofernes these days?"

"Running around, same stuff. We had dinner at his place, you should've seen the crowd. Last Friday, or you remember, whatever night it was you were working at Yellow. I mean, the money—at least they're impressed by my being an author. They think that makes me cultured and so share the same love for *foie gras* as they do."

"Holofernes's crowd is absurd."

"They're fun though."

"They make me feel like an animal in their zoo."

"Really? I guess, yeah, I can see that."

"Like I'm a specimen of something they are studying. I always play up to it, though, like they make me want to say the weirdest thing I can think of. One time, you know Geoff, right?"

"Of course, yeah."

"We were talking about the recession, right, and he was asking me about how it affected my art. And you know how that shit pisses me off, everybody thinking I am an artist or something, so I told him, I said, 'Every step I take is in direct deviance to art.'"

"No art?"

"You need to come to our meetings. Art is the culprit. It's what people follow blindly."

"It's hypnotizing. Art, brains, condos—zombies eat it all up."

"We are anti-art."

"Tell me more about everyone. We never hang out with your corwd."

"They don't hang. It's a different thing."

"That's a pretentious thing to say."

"Who do you think you are talking to?"

I hated it when she said this, and she said it often. It made me feel so distant from her, from everyone, like thrown out of our book and the cover slammed in my face. I did not know who I was or who she was or why we were together when she asked this rhetorical left hook.

"I'm going to put on Bonnie Prince Billy. Tell me if you think he sings about family in that strange way, too. Like he's preaching to a small frontier town. Before all this subculture split everybody into sexless factions. Or before sex was an issue of style, when it used to breathe life into a community."

"The heritage of trauma, yes—so positive."

"That's sarcasm."

"Sometimes I forget you used to be married. Grab that bottle of wine while you're up."

"Glass or cup?"

"I don't care."

"I like how Holofernes serves wine in cups."

These nights we would talk and we would live and we would drink. And I would wish for the night to pause, for time to stop, so that none of this would eat into tomorrow. And Ursulines would crave the passing of time, desire every inch of every minute to be fully exhausted and spent. And then morning, she would wake up, I would wake up, and I would run, move as fast as I could to outrun time, to gain it back, and she would begin again, fluidly through the day exhausting every inch of every minute. Downplaying time as one who has always had a home downplays shelter.

12

My book came out and no one was very excited, not even me. A small box of copies arrived at my house on a Friday afternoon in late March. Ursulines was over and I had talked her into rearranging the furniture. Over the winter, my relationship with the layout had dulled, my nights on the couch or in the overstuffed chair felt monotonous, and so I had decided to make it new, as some poet once said, and reinvigorate my homespace. The couch had been shoved against the west wall across from the television which stood on the trunk against the east wall. When lying down, the windows were to my left and the comfortable chair to my right, between me and the entrance door. A coffee table in front of me. My rug tied it all together, the real jewel of my decor. Handwoven green, brown and lilac threads, hints of tangerine and robin's egg blue, patterned in circles and vase-like shapes with a rectangle border roused by floral swirls and vine-like lines—often it was more interesting to look at than what was showing on the television.

I had already pushed the couch below the windows, feeling that with spring it might be nice to nap and stare out the sunlit, fresh air of the open windows. And I'd dragged the rug so that their edges met. I understood the functionality of a coffee table but was tired of the messes it gathered and banging my knee on it to and from the couch. What else could I do with it, I didn't know. I sat down, considering other furnishings I could buy to add dimensions of interaction and ornamentation to this room. Tall lamps which stood on the floor, maybe. End tables. A bookcase—that made sense, I might even begin reading at home again, I thought. An entertainment system, I had seen a good deal on one at the Dollar Store around the corner, something like 79 dollars. But I remember Holofernes commenting on Michel's, saying they were a little tacky, and I thought maybe he was right. A bar, maybe I could build a bar where the teevee used to sit. An armoire? I wasn't sure what that was, but it excited me. A chifforobe? I had read about one in *To Kill a Mockingbird*, I think it played a central role in the development of the plot, but I never could picture what he busted up when he helped her bust up her chifforobe. Seemed laced with sexual undertones. Maybe, I thought, maybe I was getting it all wrong, and with spring coming, I should pull my bed into this room, sleep with the windows open, graced by the nightbirds. This couch and teevee could go in my bedroom, or even the kitchen. I grew up with a teevee in the kitchen and it was always nice, somehow, to have that on while my mom cooked or we ate a snack. But then the breakfast table in my bedroom? The couch in the kitchen—I don't know if it would even fit and how would I get it down the hallway. There was madness to this and I liked it but also these thoughts worried me, like I was playing with something larger and wiser than I—a house's layout and interior design was a well-honed practice, surely others made these similar mistakes before and learned better from them. I did not know, but I thought it was something I should try.

We listened to The Handsome Family's *Odessa* album on repeat, so every 37 minutes we heard the song, "Moving Furniture Around."

"They don't live here anymore," I said.

"Who?" asked Ursulines.

"The Handsome Family. They used to live in these neighborhoods."

"Why did they leave?"

"They're in Albuquerque now. Alt-country, it used to be all plaid snap button-downs and Hulu girl tattoos. Schlitz. The Empty Bottle."

"You're still gonna find people drinking Schlitz at the Empty Bottle."

"Not like they used to. Now they do it because they saw these other people doing it and they don't know why they are doing it, they are just playing it cool."

"Why does someone drink Schlitz?"

"Chicago once had a scene. People lived on the fringes and came together. Now it's like a warfare and no one feels genuine—everybody's fighting to be seen as authentic."

"It's a neurosis."

"The Handsome Family knew the poetry of the great lakes urban hillbilly. Now they're gone and we got a roomful of real estate agents drinking $12 speakeasy cocktails."

"Not everywhere. You should get out of these neighborhoods a little more."

"I saw these two guys the other day. One was riding a bike as tall as a house. They looked like they had been born out of the Mississippi River's diesel undertow, clothes made out of river weeds, skin soaked in powerboat fuel, eyes like fireflies."

"Do you want to meet those guys?"

"Hang out with them?—I don't know if that's my deal."

"Did I tell you about the bus?"

"No."

"I've got a bus, or someone found one and said I could have it, an old yellow school bus."

"You love yellow. What are you going to do with it?"

"Live in it. There's a little spot of land out some ways that I have been watching and it's just a brown lot—whoever owns it has got to be dead. I'll park it there, it barely runs, and live there on my own spot of the city."

"Where is this going to be?"

"I'll show you, tomorrow, let's go check it out. You might meet some other types of people, too."

"Here it is: *'Whenever I feel I'm on my way down. I get up and move the furniture around.'*"

"I like that other song: *Listen to me, Butterfly. There's only so much wine you can drink in one life. But it will never save you from the bottom of your glass.*"

"Somehow you have a secret answer to a question the rest of us don't even know to ask."

"Follow me to the country, I said I got a piece of land. Follow me to the outskirts, I said give this lady your good hand. I got a bus and a feeling that we could make our stand."

"That's beautiful."

"I just wrote it for you."

And I leaned in and kissed her. There is nothing more potent in young love than a shared vision of a perfect life.

But before we could get our clothes off, the doorbell buzzed, and would not stop buzzing. I saw the FedEx truck outside and went downstairs. I opened the door and yelled, "What's the deal, man?"

"Last delivery of the week. I didn't want to come back tomorrow."

I signed for the box, took it upstairs, and set it on the ground.

"Aren't you going to open it?"

"It's probably my book."

"Well, let's see!"

I opened the box. I took out a copy, one of twenty—a generous amount, I thought—and stared at the cover, unable to remember what words hid inside.

Did I stop and read it then? Maybe, yes, I did—I stopped making out with Ursulines, moving my furniture around, and I read. I read the book that was my first book, the one which paid for all this stuff, the one I toiled over, but whimsically, as if work was something you did when whistling. And the first line, the first paragraph felt odd. Ursulines grew impatient and grabbed her stuff and told me she would come by tomorrow. Fine. The first few pages made my nerves light afire. I had not thought of this story for so long; it had been several years since I began it. I did not know that I could be so bold, so idiotic, so happy to twist a character's life into a mess of absurd behavior and conversation—this character must hate me, I thought. And so might many of her real life counterparts. She was working as an architect when the economy collapsed. Fired, she spent her nights drinking, laughing, flirting with men—taking her suffering seriously—and the bartenders thought she was a lush, the men thought she was a lunatic, though not in a sexy way. She made many plans, all of them backfiring. I read until the end. When she had checked herself out of the voluntary mental institution, and she entered a park, pathetically, and I could not finish. But I remember now, and many have asked me about it since—no not many, but a few—it was a Tuesday, and she left with a warm baguette in her hand. Entering the park, there were no crowds there, no one sunning in the grass, no one throwing frisbees to their dogs, no one lost in a book on the bench, no picnics—the parks had become horrible places once the architects had all lost their jobs. Only the filth and foul, the warted and hideous, the lunatics with sadness gathered there. Regularly; constantly. There leaned against a tree, a man larger than the trunk, a pile of being piled atop of itself, drooling, a sewer of drip from his lips—she could not tell if he was awake or asleep. His voice startled her. More an excretion of phlegm than a phrase, as his body tightened a bit, his neck gathering what strength to lift the bulbous head which enslaved it. Bread I need some bread. Of course, she said, here. And she tore off a chunk, walked closer to him, the tree above them catching the winds and shaking—she extended her hand and when inches from his face, staring into the strong yellow tint of his eyeballs and his pupils were about to break through his irises. A leering nose, a hissing, perverted and orgasmic, she could see his large hands the size of dumpsters coming to life. His entire body jerked, grabbing her arm and pulling her in.

I did not know what it meant. I was surprised that Genevieve, my editor in New York, never asked me to change it. I fear, now I am certain, that it meant everything. The stakes this city raises.

13

It wasn't my idea, but one night after dinner at Soul Kitchen, I brought Gwynn and Holofernes to Ursulines' apartment. She was expecting me, we were in the middle of figuring out her relocation of the bus. I had been telling Gwynn and Holofernes and others about this over dinner, and they were riveted, they had to know more, they had to talk with her. I have always wanted to really talk with Ursulines, Gwynn said, to really understand her mind, Judith—can you take us there? I loved talking about Ursulines with Holofernes' people, I felt animated and heard, that what I was saying was unique and real. Their attentions flattered me.

We left Soul Kitchen and I said, "Great, I can show you the streets on our way, a little tour du jour, wait what's night in French, okay, *tour du noir*."

"That's black," Gwynn said.

"Okay, let's walk."

"How far is it?"

"I don't know but its 70 degrees and there is so much to see."

"Taxi!"

"Judith, we don't want to walk three miles—there's one, Gwynn. Let's cab it over to her apartment."

To me, taking a cab was skirting the map in search of the treasure.

"This ruins the night," I said as we got in.

"Where to?"

"Dickens and—what's her cross street, Judith?"

"Penelope lives on Dickens— Ursulines is on Shakespeare."

"I have a friend who lives on Shakespeare, by the Charleston bar—near there?"

"That's in Bucktown. Cabbie, she's at Shakespeare and Avers."

"Way west."

"That's far."

"Judith, walk? Really?"

"Cabs suck. This denies the potential of the city to unfold its substance. There's no mystery at 25 miles per hour, no resonance."

"Tell us more about the bus."

"Where is she going to park it?"

"Does she need help buying it?"

"All of this you can ask her in no time."

I rang the bell and she buzzed without asking who was there. This always made me mad—what if it wasn't me? What if it was someone who had followed her home? Violence flares in this part of town and one might not even know they had it in them to do the acts which so brutally wreck the lives of others. Shut up—she'd say—I knew it was you. And she'd walk away into the apartment for me to follow. She knew it was me but did she know what I was capable of?

Ursulines was already talking before she opened the door. "Judith, I think this is figured out. I talked with Crimson, she has something in the works with—who'd you bring with you?"

"We brought good news—Judith is pregnant with your child. You remember Gwynn."

"Good to see you again, Ursulines."

"Sorry not funny—I just thought to myself, what would Judith say right now."

"I don't know, Judith, what would you say?"

"Huzzah! You are an apartment of sex!"

"We're plenty drunk, but maybe beer?"

"There's some in the refrigerator."

"Holofernes and I are making a move on the space."

"Still thinking Pilsen?"

"It's quite a world down there, really not many streets like 18th in Chicago—dense with patina."

"There's a curve to that street, an ocular illusion, I become lost in a thousand American cities all at once, in multitudes, but I enjoy it in the singular, meaning it's a pleasure, to walk down it."

"It is cool. What's that place, the bar with the seat belts, I went there one night. Very cool."

"Okay, but what about the Mexican community? How are you going to serve them?"

"That's a serious concern." I handed everybody a beer and we leaned against the counters.

"We're not thinking about any of that necessarily, are we Judith?"

"Did you hear PBR is putting out an IPA?"

"Right, they found that recipe which they used to brew in the 1800s."

"No, wait, they couldn't find the Old 47 recipe so they sent it to one of those chemical analysts who sent it through their machines and isolated all the ingredients, proportions, all that."

"It's a good point. But how will our little buy-up affect the Mexicans?"

"Let me tell you, our client just last week brought up something similar. It takes a level of interdisciplinary inquiry, the right questions, to see it all, but we concluded, really it came down to our principal, she said communities inherently converge and it is our job to facilitate this."

"What about this bus idea, Ursulines?"

"This bus idea?"

"Fascinating."

"It's not any of that. It's me, it's for me."

"Don't you think you could attract a little buzz?"

"Buzz Bus!"

"Here's where I get mad: I don't want to discuss this."

"We're discussing everything, Ursulines, everything—the next wave of our minds, we're riding this."

"You and I, Judith. They need to go."

"What about setting up something, Ursulines, I would love to have a little time with you."

"What for, Gwynn?"

"To talk, have coffee. Network."

"I have an idea. Everyone. There is a *paletas* spot, not far from here. I'll buy."

"Can we walk?"

"I absolutely love *paletas*, are you kidding? They're real fruit."

"Ursulines will you join us."

"Sounds pretty cool. But I'm all set. Judith?"

And I told them good-bye, seeing her eyes aflame, and I danced in circles moth-like as if I had never known what burns.

14

The week before we split up I began walking beyond the logical next neighborhoods. I had always made my way around the city, but never went this far out and with the intention to absorb the city and carry it back to my sessions with Holofernes.

I spent my days in the streets. Writing still, at night, when I got to my office—that is, on the nights that I went to sleep. Between the time I spent at Ursulines' and the time I spent wandering beneath the black sky, I began to know my office less and less. My gut began to tighten back up with all the walking that I did. All the hours of hunger that I sat on the sidewalks and ignored. I had been eating my meals in the cafes, a croissant or doughnut or sugar-glazed buttery fruit scone from one of the many bakeries which I passed in my travels for breakfast. A meager lunch consisting of one taco or a slice of pizza—always less than two dollars—maybe a baguette and block of cheese or several slices of meat if a delicatessen or fromagerie—there were no fromageries, but this is what I called places which sold Wisconsin cheese ever since I had begun reading works surrounding Haussmann's Paris. And for dinner, well, I relied on my friends often, or simply bit my thrift and sat down someplace for a meal. Living so variously across this city, there was rarely any overlap in the places I dined at night. Cork and Kerry in Bridgeport. Moody's in Edgewater. Johnny's Grill in Logan Square. Carnitas Don Pedro in East Pilsen. Each a meal before the push beyond.

Much has been written by poets about crowds and alleys and dark buildings suffering from demented tenants, but this never did take away from the curious allure these phenomena held for me. I tried to be practical in my perceptions, tried not to romanticize the shadowed corners, distempering moods which surge through the buildings' spirits, or the ecstatic lightheadedness which accompanies being surrounded by bodies everywhere in movement, approval and leer. As much as I enjoyed my walks, I tried to keep in mind that I was collecting data—I was reading chapters, I was deciphering text and if skewed, I could come to the wrong conclusions and be swept away in a fiction of horror and spit, much like the faces of the bums and delinquent souls propelled by city cough and covered in city phlegm.

There was much at stake and anything cliché would deliver me to monotonous jaws of abstraction, inaccuracy, common knowledge, which I knew by then was never perceptive and never based on experience from the field. Common knowledge was passed on from mouth to mouth, assumed truth viral in its dispersal and just as contagious. I could see how meaning had its sources, whether a horse or a fly, and I sought the source. I lifted the sheet of the ghost, as much weight of it as I could bare, and each time learned something new.

15

We moved our regular meetings to Holofernes' office on Tuesday and Thursday mornings. Up early and done with breakfast, I got dressed, packed my bag and set out. I had seen it, more so smelled it when locking the door to my apartment on Erie—a purple and black darkness was descending from the north. This storm in middle August which carried the crispness of the north, of fall, winds and waters which had gathered above glaciers and would take away the stagnant perch of summer. And I had gone back inside, back up those rickety yet warmly souled stairs, to grab an umbrella. It was not hard to find, lying on the floor of the front room where I had left it, though everywhere my furniture and possessions left in disarray, having not finished what I had started days before with Ursulines. I knew I should hurry—it was a thirteen-block walk up Damen Avenue—but for some reason I lingered, walked into my kitchen as if I were forgetting something else, into my bedroom, checked that the lights were off, wondering if seeing something would spark the memory I was looking for: the thing I was forgetting to carry with me out into the world. But nothing was jarred free. And I sat. Not on a chair, not on the counter, but my legs crossed Indian-style on the floor. A funny and mocking phrase, Indian-style, but that is what I thought, how maybe not since I was a child had I sat Indian-style on the floor of my home. A nostalgic reverie overturned me, caught me up in a sentimentality for what I was not sure. A weeping yet pleasurable structure built across my body and I admired it, I stroked it with my attention and I nursed it with my thoughts. But what it was I yearned for did not appear across my consciousness—as if my present being was the playground for a future I did not know was coming, or a past I did not know existed. All I knew was I had forgotten something.

As it faded, I began to feel stupid. Sitting there, nothing I could explain, no sane excuse for my running late. Anyone well-adjusted would dismiss such a bout of perplexing emotions and carry on towards their destination. But I stopped and let them conjure what they wished across my mind. I stood up and immediately my thoughts gathered around the city. Some might know it as a spark of inspiration. I had an idea. I saw something clear, which I had not seen before and which surely I would forget if I did not get to work at capturing it. I hustled back down my staircase, back out the apartment building door, umbrella under my arm, eying the line of darkness which bulged the blue out of the sky. And I made my way up Damen Avenue, intent on not losing this thrilled understanding of urban spirituality which had come to me.

I could see the Northwest Tower six blocks away, a 1930s flat-iron art-deco of minimal architectural décor, towering ten stories higher than the surrounding buildings, a triangle office building cut into the sky. I rode with Viktor, the elevator operator, to the third floor, walked down the musty hallway, and I turned the brass knob of the pebbled glass door to enter the waiting room. Holofernes kept the door between the waiting room and the work room shut so as not to let the dozens of cigarettes he smoked each day drift their stench into the hallway and neighboring offices. Even before opening the door I could hear that the window was open. It was a small enough room, only two windows wide, and standing there, shaking my umbrella and wiping the rain off my head with a towel, I heard the sounds of the street and rainfall, the train rumbling past, the brakes and tires spinning across the asphalt, the shouts and recorded announcement of the North Avenue's bus arrival. I am certain the window was open that day because when I passed through the second doorway, that was the first thing I noticed. Second: that Holofernes was not there.

I waited for a moment, leaned out the window appreciating the rain's blur of activity across the neighborhood, thinking that he must be in the restroom and would soon return. Ten minutes passed, and I had transitioned from the window to writing down my new understanding which had come to me less than an hour before. I was not worried, and I settled deeper into exploring and explaining my thoughts. And I remember them clearly today. As individuals and as a collective—the city inexplicably designs our story, and we relate to it in such a way that we concede to its power, its purpose, its vulgarity or grace. We blame it for our ills, and we praise it for our success. We butt up against its meaning, how it limits and propels our day-to-day existence, in the very same way as we butt up against the meaning of god. We have no access to *it*— that which is its center, its source of power. Its source of authority is invisible. Its presence traceable only across the surfaces. Though I lived in god's world, I could never know god personally. Though I lived in Chicago, it's veritablility was cast throughout its far-reaching corners, and no matter where I went, Chicago would elude me as much as possess me.

And an hour passed—I could not believe it was an hour, surely I arrived later than I remember the clock telling me. Still, no Holofernes. Maybe my lateness caused him to depart. There was something he needed to study in person out in the city, or a meeting downtown with developers, and so he left. But the door was open. The window open. The cloud of smoke still present to my nostrils.

I did not worry. I pondered this, but I was not concerned. There is always an explanation. And I was focused. My powers of attention were reaching new heights. I did not feel worn down by my writing, the energy of what would come next still fresh in my spirit. The rains pelting the sidewalk. Another hour passed. Another. I have no memory of how long I remained in Holofernes' office that day, but I know it was long enough that the storm had dispersed, the streets glistened with the setting sun. Vapors rising from the sidewalk. Puddles of mercury in the pocks and holes of the streets. Stones darkened by wet. Subtle drippings from trees. Lines of droplets across rails and power lines. Soon the streetlamps would buzz and flicker and their light would define the ways of night.

Before leaving the Northwest Tower—I was hungry and felt the urge to drink, needing an anchor to descend from my thinking—I rode the elevator up to the thirteenth floor to see the landlord to sign a lease for a vacant office on the same floor as Holofernes'. I was astounded at the quality and quantity of work which had just passed through me. It felt like transmission—something which my writing at home and in the cafes never felt like. Nothing preoccupied my mind but the matter at hand. An office, I realized, was essential to organizing one's life. Home, I told myself, or Holofernes told me through myself, was for comfort. For relaxing. The office was for work.

The view from the top floor knocked me back: as far north, as far south, southwest as the city stretched with downtown booming in the center. The lights lit and dancing in the purple hush of dark. Did the sunset drape its light across the buildings, or were the buildings draped over a sinister form bulging and growing below. I wondered if this city always exists and we slowly watch it revel itself, its nightmare, its body. People were no longer people from up here. Doors were too small to enter. Windows too miniscule to look through. A far different version of the city, a far vaster selection of delights and curiosities were sought from this height—records or charcuterie or freak bikes or shoulder bags ceased to matter—though I did not know it well enough to define them. There Ciudad Mujer sat smoking her cigarettes, drinking gin from a styrofoam cup, a lime and knife next to a bottle of tonic and Seagrams on her desk. Her back to the door and her body above the city as if an angel there floating, watching in the night.

"An office? I've got one available. There are forms you need to fill out, have you prepared for that? First month's when I give you the keys. Your name?"

"It's me, Judith."

"Judith. What will you need it for?"

"My work with Holofernes."

"Guys like him, do you know about that?"

"My girlfriend and I are happy."

"Playing innocent, good—well, what do you see, out there, in the lights?"

"I was looking for my apartment. And my old office where I edited textbooks up north."

"And do you find yourself?"

"I'm not sure if I can make it out that far?"

"About half the people I know have gotten mugged over the years in various locations out there, while I watched though not knowing, from up above. Let me tell you a story. Perhaps you will find what you are looking to steal."

"I am hungry, Abuela, but please, I will come back if you will have me."

"Look how dark it is outside. See those bodies fleeing. There, you see, and there. Rats, Foxes, you do not know the moment we have come upon. The time is now."

She began, and though I wished she would, she did not ask me to sit. I stood at the windows seeing the newly built glass high-rises pushing across West Loop, the manufacturing corridors south of my apartment, the last two standing towers of Cabrini-Green, the mid-rises guarding the lakeshores, the brown line tack its way towards the Indians, Koreans, Hassidic Jews, Milwaukee Avenue beneath us lined with traffic and bikes leading towards Sears Tower, the behemoth described by its architects as nine buildings built into one. And I listened. A story which held me captive. Her voice enraptured. Chain-smoking. Sips of Seagram's at any pause. Never taking her eyes off the city, her wrinkled hands jutting out from her bony elbows, casting towards the system of lights as if altering what was lit beneath:

"Now in the twelfth year of his reign, Nebuchadnezzar, king of the Assyrians fought against Arphaxad and overcame him. In the great plain near the Euphrates and the Tigris, he built a very strong city, which he called Nineveh. Of stones squared and hewed: he made the walls thereof seventy cubits broad, and thirty cubits high, and the towers thereof he made a hundred cubits high. But on the square of them, each side was extended the space of twenty feet. And he made the gates thereof according to the height of the towers: and he gloried as a mighty one in the force of his army and in the glory of his chariots. Smoke, please, take a cigarette, Judith."

"Yes, I do. Are there matches?"

"Then was the kingdom of Nebuchadnezzar exalted, and his heart was elevated: and he sent to all that dwelt in Cilicia and Damascus, and Libanus, and to the nations that are in Carmelus, and Cedar, and to the inhabitants of Galilee in the great plain of Asdrelon, and to all that were in Samaria, and beyond the river Jordan even to Jerusalem, and all the land of Jesse till you come to the borders of Ethiopia. To all these Nebuchadnezzar king of the Assyrians, sent messengers: but they all with one mind refused, and sent them back empty, and rejected them without honor. Then king Nebuchadnezzar being angry against all that land, swore by his throne and kingdom that he would revenge himself of all those countries.

"In the fourteenth year of the reign of Nebuchadnezzar, the two and twentieth day of the first month, the word was given out in the house of Nebuchadnezzar king of the Assyrians, that he would revenge himself. And he called all the ancients, and all the governors, and his officers of war, and communicated to them the secret of his counsel: he said that his thoughts were to bring all the earth under his empire.

"When this saying pleased them all, Nebuchadnezzar, the king, called Holofernes the general of his armies, and said to him: Go out against all the kingdoms of the west, and against them especially that despised my commandment. Thy eye shall not spare any kingdom, and all the strong cities thou shalt bring under my yoke. "You said Holofernes."

"Your innocent act need not last any longer. Do you remember from where you began?"

"No. I mean, I began in Denver."

"You did not. Holofernes called the captains and officers of the power of the Assyrians: and he mustered men for the expedition, as the king commanded him, a hundred and twenty thousand fighting men on foot, and twelve thousand archers, horsemen. And he made all his warlike preparations to go before with a multitude of innumerable camels, with all provisions sufficient for the armies in abundance, and herds of oxen, and flocks of sheep, without number. He appointed corn to be prepared out of all Syria in his passage. But gold and silver he took out of the king's house in great abundance. And he went forth, he and all the army, with the chariots, and horsemen, and archers, who covered the face of the earth, like locusts.

"And when he had passed through the borders of the Assyrians, he came to the great mountains of Ange, which are on the left of Cilicia: and he went up to all their castles and took all the strong places. And he took by assault the renowned city of Melothus, and pillaged all the children of Tharsis, and the children of Ismahel, who were over against the face of the desert, and on the south of the land of Cellon. And he passed over the Euphrates and came into Mesopotamia: and he forced all the stately cities that were there, from the torrent of Mambre, till one comes to the sea. And he took the borders thereof from Cilicia to the coasts of Japheth, which are towards the south. And he carried away all the children of Madian, and stripped them of all their riches, and all that resisted him he slew with the edge of the sword.

"And after these things he went down into the plains of Damascus in the days of the harvest, and he set all the corn on fire, and he caused all the trees and vineyards to be cut down. And the fear of them alit the inhabitants of the land.

"Then the kings and the princes of all the cities and provinces, of Syria, Mesopotamia, Libya, and Cilicia sent their ambassadors, who coming to Holofernes, said: Let thy indignation towards us cease: for it is better for us to live and serve Nebuchadnezzar the great king, and be subject to thee, than to die and to perish, or suffer the miseries of slavery. All our cities and our possessions, all mountains and hills, and fields, and herds of oxen, and flocks of sheep, and goats, and horses, and camels, and all our goods, and families are in thy sight: Let all we have be subject to thy law. Both we and our children are thy servants. Come to us a peaceable lord and use our service as it shall please thee. Then he came down from the mountains with horsemen, in great power, and made himself master of every city, and all the inhabitants of the land. And from all the cities he took valiant men chosen for war. Have you served in war, Judith?"

"Friends of mine enlisted. But not war. I've killed. Where I grew up, killing came with it."

"I can't tell if you're kidding."

I lifted my shirt to show where the bullet entered.

"Then you know fear. And so great a fear lay upon all those provinces, that the inhabitants of all the cities, both princes and nobles, as well as the people, went out to meet Holofernes at his coming. And received him with garlands, and lights, and dances, and tumbrels, and flutes. And though they did these things, they could not for all that mitigate the fierceness of his heart: For he both destroyed their cities and cut down their groves. For Nebuchadnezzar the king had commanded him to destroy all the gods of the earth, that he only might be called God by those nations which could be brought under him by the power of Holofernes.

"Then the children of Israel, who dwelt in the land of Juda, hearing these things, were exceedingly afraid of him. Dread and horror seized upon their minds, lest he should do the same to Jerusalem and to the temple of the Lord, that he had done to other cities and their temples. And it was told Holofernes the general of the army of the Assyrians, that the children of Israel prepared themselves to resist, and had shut up the ways of the mountains.

"Resistance."

"Yes. But Holofernes on the next day gave orders to his army, to go up against Bethulia. The war general found that the fountains which supplied them with water, ran through an aqueduct without the city on the south side: and he commanded their aqueduct to be cut off.

"Now it came to pass, when Judith a widow had heard these words, who was the daughter of Merari, the son of Idox, the son of Joseph, the son of Emmanuel, the son of

Elai, the son of Jamnor, the son of Gedeon, the son of Raphaim, the son of Achitob, the son of Melehias, the son of Enan, the son of Nathanias, the son of Salathiel, the son of Simeon, the son of Ruben: And her husband was Manasses, who died in the time of the barley harvest: For he was standing over them that bound sheaves in the field; and the heat came upon his head, and he died in Bethulia his own city, and was buried there with his fathers."

"Manasses was my husband."

"And Judith his relict was a widow now three years and six months. And she made herself a private chamber in the upper part of her house, in which she abode shut up with her maids. And she wore haircloth upon her loins, and fasted all the days of her life, except the sabbaths, and new moons, and the feasts of the house of Israel. And she was exceedingly beautiful, and her husband left her great riches, and very many servants, and large possessions of herds of oxen, and flocks of sheep. And she was greatly renowned among all, because she feared the Lord very much, neither was there any one that spoke an ill word of her.

"When therefore she had heard that Emmanuel had promised that he would deliver up the city after the fifth day, she sent to the ancients Chabri and Charmi. And they came to her, and Judith said to them: Bring to pass that Holofernes' pride may be cut off with his own sword. Let him be caught in the net of his own eyes in my regard, and do thou strike him by the graces of the words of my lips. Give me constancy in my mind, that I may despise him: and fortitude that I may overthrow him. For this will be a glorious monument for thy name, when he shall fall by the hand of a woman. For thy power is not in a multitude, nor is thy pleasure in the strength of horses, nor from the beginning have the proud been acceptable to thee: but the prayer of the humble and the meek hath always pleased thee."

"She's bringing the battle to Holoferenes?"

"And it came to pass, when she had ceased to cry, that she rose from the place wherein she lay prostrate, and she called her maid, and going down into her house she took off her haircloth, and put away the garments of her widowhood, and she washed her body, and anointed herself with the best ointment, and plaited the hair of her head, and put a bonnet upon her head, and clothed herself with the garments of her gladness, and put sandals on her feet, and took her bracelets, and lilies, and earlets, and rings, and adorned herself with all her ornaments, so that she appeared to all men's eyes incomparably lovely. And she gave to her maid a bottle of wine to carry, and a vessel of oil, and parched corn, and dry figs, and bread and cheese, and went out. "And when they came to the gate of the city, they found Emmanuel, and the ancients of the city waiting. And when they saw her they were astonished and admired her beauty exceedingly. But they asked her no question. And it came to pass, when she went down the hill, about break of day, that the watchmen of the Assyrians met her and stopped her, saying: Whence comest thou? or whither goest thou?

"And she answered: I am a daughter of the Hebrews, and I am fled from them, because I knew they would be made a prey to you, because they despised you, and would not of their own accord yield themselves, that they might find mercy in your sight. For this reason I thought with myself, saying: I will go to the presence of the prince Holofernes, that I may tell him their secrets, and show him by what way he may take them, without the loss of one man of his army. "And when the men had heard her words, they beheld her face, and their eyes were amazed, for they wondered exceedingly at her beauty. And they said to her: Thou hast saved thy life by taking this resolution, to come down to our lord. And be assured of this, that when thou shalt stand before him, he will treat thee well, and thou wilt be most acceptable to his heart. And they brought her to the tent of Holofernes, telling him of her. And when she was come into his presence, forthwith Holofernes was caught by his eyes. And his officers said to him: Who can despise the people of the Hebrews who have such beautiful women, that we should not think it worth our while for their sakes to fight against them? And Judith seeing Holofernes sitting under a canopy, which was woven of purple and gold, with emeralds and precious stones: After she had looked on his face bowed down to him, prostrating herself to the ground. And the servants of Holofernes lifted her up, by the command of their master.

"Then Holofernes said to her: Be of good comfort, and fear not in thy heart: for I have never hurt a man that was willing to serve Nebuchadnezzar the king. And if thy people had not despised me, I would never have lifted up my spear against them. But now tell me, for what cause hast thou left them, and why it hath pleased thee to come to us? And Judith said to him: Receive the words of thy handmaid, for if thou wilt follow the words of thy handmaid, the Lord will do with thee a perfect thing. For as Nebuchadnezzar the king of the earth liveth, and his power liveth which is in thee for chastising of all straying souls: not only men serve him through thee, but also the beasts of the field obey him. For the industry of thy mind is spoken of among all nations, and it is told through the whole world, that thou only art excellent, and mighty in all his kingdom, and thy discipline is cried up in all provinces. Moreover, also a famine hath come upon them, and for drought of water they are already to be counted among the dead. And they have a design even to kill their cattle, and to drink the blood of them. And I thy handmaid knowing this, am fled from them, and the Lord hath sent me to tell thee these very things. For I thy handmaid worship God even now that I am with thee, and thy handmaid will go out, and I will pray to God, and he will tell me when he will repay them for their sins, and I will come and tell thee, so that I may bring thee through the midst of Jerusalem, and thou shalt have all the people of Israel, as sheep that have no shepherd, and there shall not so much as one dog bark against thee: Because these things are told me by the providence of God. And because God is angry with them, I am sent to tell these very things to thee."

"Judith is selling out the Jews?"

"Listen. All these words pleased Holofernes, and his servants, and they admired her wisdom, and they said one to another: There is not such another woman upon earth in look, in beauty, and in sense of words. And Holofernes said to her: God hath done well who sent thee before the people, that thou mightest give them into our hands: And because thy promise is good, if thy God shall do this for me, he shall also be my God, and thou shalt be great in the house of Nebuchadnezzar, and thy name shall be renowned through all the earth.

"Then he ordered that she should go in where his treasures were laid up, and bade her tarry there, and he appointed what should be given her from his own table. And Judith answered him and said: Now I cannot eat of these things which thou commandest to be given me, lest sin come upon me: but I will eat of the things which I have brought.

"And Holofernes said to her: If these things which thou hast brought with thee fail thee, what shall we do for thee? And Judith said: As thy soul liveth, my lord, thy handmaid shall not spend all these things till God do by my hand that which I have purposed. And his servants brought her into the tent which he had commanded. And when she was going in, she desired that she might have liberty to go out at night and before day to prayer, and to beseech the Lord. And he commanded his chamberlains, that she might go out and in, to adore her God as she pleased, for three days. And she went out in the nights into the valley of Bethulia and washed herself in a fountain of water.

"And it came to pass on the fourth day, that Holofernes made a supper for his servants, and said to Vagao his eunuch: so, and persuade that Hebrew woman, to consent of her own accord to dwell with me. For it is looked upon as shameful among the Assyrians, if a woman mock a man, by doing so as to pass free from him.

"Then Vagao went in to Judith and said: Let not my good maid be afraid to go in to my lord, that she may be honored before his face, that she may eat with him and drink wine and be merry. And Judith answered him: Who am I, that I should gainsay my lord? All that shall be good and best before his eyes, I will do. And whatsoever shall please him, that shall be best to me all the days of my life. And she arose and dressed herself out with her garments and going in she stood before his face. And the heart of Holofernes was smitten, for he was burning with the desire of her. And Holofernes said to her: Drink now and sit down and be merry for thou hast found favor before me. And Judith said: I will drink my lord, because my life is magnified this day above all my days.

"And she took and ate and drank before him what her maid had prepared for her. And Holofernes was made merry on her occasion, and drank exceeding much wine, so much as he had never drunk in his life. And when it was grown late, his servants made haste to their lodgings, and Vagao shut the chamber doors, and went his way.

"And they were all overcharged with wine."

"And Judith was alone in the chamber."

"But Holofernes lay on his bed, fast asleep, being exceedingly drunk."

"You remember, my girl. And You spoke to your maid to stand without before the chamber, and to watch: And you stood before the bed praying with tears, and the motion of your lips in silence, saying: Strengthen me, O Lord God of Israel, and in this hour look on the works of my hands, that as thou hast promised, thou mayst raise up Jerusalem thy city: and that I may bring to pass that which I have purposed, having a belief that it might be done by thee.

"And when you had said this, you went to the pillar that was at his bed's head, and loosed his sword that hung tied upon it. And when you had drawn it out, you took him by the hair of his head, and said: Strengthen me, O Lord God, at this hour, striking twice upon his neck to cut off his head, then taking off his canopy from the pillars, to roll away his headless body."

"After a while I went out, and delivered the head of Holofernes to my maid, and bade her put it into her wallet. And we two went out according to our custom, as it were to prayer, and we passed the camp, and having compassed the valley, we came to the gate of the city. And I from afar off cried to the watchmen upon the walls: Open the gates for God is with us, who hath shown his power in Israel."

"And it came to pass, when the men had heard your voice, that they called the ancients of the city. And all ran to meet you from the least to the greatest: for they had no hopes that you would come. And lighting up lights they all gathered round about you: and you went up to a higher place, and commanded silence to be made."

"And when all had held their peace, I said: Praise ye the Lord our God, who hath not forsaken them that hope in him. And by me his handmaid he hath fulfilled his mercy, which he promised to the house of Israel: and he hath killed the enemy of his people by my hand this night."

"Then you brought forth the head of Holofernes out of the wallet, and showed it to them."

"And Emmanuel the prince of the people of Israel, said to me: Blessed art thou, O daughter, the most-high God, above all women upon the earth. Blessed be God who made heaven and earth, who hath directed thee to the cutting off the head of the prince of our enemies."

The next day I moved a few of my things from home up to the office. Nothing too large or cumbersome that I could not carry with me onto the bus. But it left my apartment shockingly empty. I came home that night and did not feel comfortable. I did not feel that relaxation was possible. I sat on my counter. I poured myself a glass of water. I picked at my breakfast which I was too much in a rush that morning to finish. I walked outside and sat on the front stoop, hoping that I could relax like I had seen city residents in the movies do. But the stone stairs bruised my skinny body and too many people walked by wanting to talk and talking felt like work that night—and I was done with my work. I was ready to rest. Be quiet in my thoughts and retreat to comfort. For I hath remembered this life's duty.

16

A month after renting the office, late one night when Sue and Viktor were gone, I snuck my mattress up the staircase. No shower in the common bathroom, I joined the new Cheetah Gym a block over, once the apartment that the *Real World: Chicago* kids lived in, paying in advance $200 for 6 months, and when I needed a shower, I'd head over there, walk through the hard bodies and spandex, the swarm of eyes, cock, and clit stimulated and misguided towards the treadmill the lat-machine the elliptical, grab a towel, get what I needed from my locker, clean off, brush my teeth, deodorize, get dressed, put my hair in a pony tail, not worry about make-up, and head back out into the world. To meet Holofernes, to answer his questions—to meet Ursulines, to ask her my own.

During these weeks, I often walked the entire day, countless miles, and then stumbled into Cheetah Gym, and then as if waking, realize I had been staring at the pattern of institutional turquoise tiles for an undetermined amount of time as the water hit my shoulders and ran down my back. I was a vacant lot. I was still. Like a building abandoned, empty of other presences. Empty of story as well, but for the time I was content with that. In my office, I stared out the windows at the Blue Line platform filling up with commuters, the bands in Subterranean's third-floor green-room getting ready to play, at Tony the door guy at Estelle's, at the pawn shop, the dentist, the Mack trucks filled with rubble shaking the blacktop the traffic lights the El girders. I stared into the walls and entered into them. I became the city, surprised to find a person like me sitting there in a room of one of my buildings, staring at the world, wondering which direction the energies would flow, which neighborhood would turn. Ciudad Mujer was right—there were people fleeing. The very people we were interested to follow. And it was the city which knew what to do next. Time again I wandered into the city's consciousness and I knew what I would do after my next report on The Fortress of Bethulia.

I didn't bring much with me when I moved in, but I had a project in mind similar to the Wreck Wall at Miriam's. I would make a personal palimpsest blurring my authenticity. I had brought my archive of journals and notebooks to begin. All in one cardboard box. I remember pulling them out just to count them, to stack them on my desk and to see if I had done enough. Forty-seven. I had nothing to compare it to, but I told myself that was a lot, having began writing in my diary when I was in kindergarten. I recognized my first journal immediately when I saw it. Same for the journal I kept after fleeing my home in Denver.

Reading my past journals, I became curious about my childhood, about how I acted, what I thought and what drove me forward. Always thoughtful, filled with the desire to please, I read about returning home from school ready to tell my parents and brother what I had learned and who I had sat by and things my teacher said to me—things which would make them proud. Instead of the high-achieving Catholic school which my parents could have afforded, they chose to send me to the public school in the neighborhood. The education was poor, and there were many kids in my class who failed every test, missed every word on each in-class spelling bee, had no interest in multiplication tables. I can think of at least three who always refused to read aloud, did not attempt the early-readers, but nevertheless were passed on to the next grade. I realized that the other kids only accepted me when I failed along with them. There was no social value in being a good student. And the group at my school was a ragged bunch. This was before the notion of gangs spread its tendrils into the lower grades, but we knew that gangs were out there, and we listened to gangster rap. The boys imitated Easy E, Ice T, Too Short, The D.O.C. And I enjoyed doing what the boys did.

I did not know what a sociologist was; I only knew that was what my parents called themselves. Yes, they worried when I would come home bruised and scraped, but they did not ask me if I was scared or if I wanted to transfer to another school. They inquired into the names of the other kids in the fights, but not to file a report with the principal or, and often it was more suiting, with the police. They asked me what started the fights, what names I was called, what language I used to yell at my assailants or victims. What races were the kids; what did their families do—did they work, were they immigrants, where did they live; how did they fare in school, had they always been underperforming students or only recently; did they get free or reduced lunches; how often did their meals consist of sugar, salt, grease; had they suffered trauma as a child; were any other girls involved. They asked me so many questions that I could not help but feel that my daily life was important—that it had meaning. Although, I never knew what the meaning of it was, I trusted it was there—that a treasure was buried somewhere in my day, and if I could only think through it and move towards it, it would be mine.

When high school came around, I considered asking my parents to send me to the arts magnet school a neighborhood over. I specialized in music and performance arts, and my friend two grades above me, Howard, attended it. Howard saw the same treasure that I did, and we would get together to pursue it, directly, very seriously, with our instruments. I played the piano, the trumpet, and the violin. He played the drums with great skill but could pick up anything and work it out.

The day we attended the open house at the corresponding public high school, George Washington High, we were pulled aside by the principal and led into his office to talk. How brave I was, he kept saying. How important my position was in the school and how much good I could do for them. You will do such a fine job, he said. And I did not understand, but his words served to deepen the intrigue I held and the mystery I felt for my fate—that I would do more than my peers and be recognized for it, even celebrated by men like our Principal and other powerful fixtures of the community. Who they were I did not know, but of course, I thought, they are out there—out there looking for someone as courageous and artistic as me. And they are watching me. They are interested in what I do.

When I began using, my parents expressed more concern than I had witnessed in the past. They worried about me, I heard them say it. And they even had me begin sessions with a friend of theirs, Calvin Simpson, who was a psychiatrist and a man who had been over to our house many weekends for barbecues or nights on the front stoop.

This stopped me from going much further with heroin and crack, but it did not stop me from drinking and getting high, hanging out as much as I could with this group I had sacrificed so much to get in good with, and who my parents were so interested in. Everyday waiting for something. Some extraordinary task. An affirmation of my greatness and testament of my trials. All that happened was I skipped more and more school, drank Hennessy and tequila like a hardened old-timer, slept with boys who I did not care for and flirted with girls who did not know what to make of me, was known by my last name by the cops and was harassed and frequently brought in. Though always driven home as my friends took the brunt of the punishment, even several of them being sent away to Denver Juvenile, Marvin Foote, even Gilliam, though never drug rehab clinics which would have been more helpful. Many grew suspicious of this fact, and I would tell, like I believed, that the police let me go because they knew I was not fucking around with hard drugs. I also believed it was because I was white, but I didn't know how to say this. My closest friends, Shabazz and Proco, would say this for me, throwing accusations against me back on the system: they don't want to fuck with a white girl if they don't have to. You know 5-0 thinks every white kid's dad is a lawyer. A race thing. But more and more, my friends looked at me differently, quieted when I came into a room—that I was ratting on them and others was the only logical reason that I did not have a rap sheet.

They were right.

My older brother, Jean, worked construction in the mountains and he did not come home often. He did not fare as well as I did, never wishing to please the others in his class, instead working hard at school, only to find out that despite his straight A's, finishing second in his class, his teachers' admiration and accolades, when it came time for college, he was testing into remedial classes and would have to accomplish two semesters of pre-credit courses before any of his work would go towards a college degree. This embittered him to say the least, and he refused to go through with this, after all he had sacrificed and all the shit he took, he could not believe he had been failed by his school. A resentment built up like a tumor inside him—they should have known, he said. They had Master's degrees and should have known that he wasn't learning a goddamn thing in his classes. And he fled to the mountains, first to a town called Ward, small and troubled, fifty miles into the mountains, and then further to Gunnison on the western slope. Again, a misfit town where drug use got the best of many, and there was no more ambition than to get through a day's work and blur the nights at the bar.

One weekend he surprised us with a visit. I was out at Themada's playing video games and fucking around like I usually did early Friday nights. Smoking blunts and drinking Hennessy, we would stay there till we got bored and fucked-up enough to go begin looking for something to do. I remember the door being knocked upon forcefully and Frederico pulling his piece from behind his waist. When it opened, I was so convinced it was someone who wanted to fuck with us that when seeing Jean my first thought was how could that son-of-a-bitch be getting in our shit.

He came in and everyone loosened up, but I did not relax. He said his hellos, getting the same shit from my friends as we always gave him, and he sat down by me. We were playing *Street Fighter* and he said, "Stop playing that fucking game and come out with me. We've got to talk."

Conversations that began like this always ended up in fucked up news—Homie's been shot; Homie's been picked up; I need you to run a few things over to Homie's. And I was pissed that my brother had been fucking around with my shit, getting in with Homie.

I said sure, and we went out and got in his car, not speaking, pretending we were listening to the rain, until we were pulling into a bar on Laramie, and he said, "Don't worry, I'll get you in. I know you drink so don't pull any high-road shit like that."

We sat at the bar and Jean was friendly with about everyone in there. A guy came over and joked with him about some pool game from the weekend before. And so I asked, "You've been in town for a while?"

"Yeah, I have."

"What's up with that?"

"Been back a couple of weeks. Things I had to look into."

"And you don't come by home?"

"Here's the deal. I've got something to tell you and then I'm going to ask you a favor. I want you to hear me out, and I want you to agree to whatever it is I am going to ask because it is swear-to-god in your best interest. I've never lied to you; I've called you all sorts of shit, called your bitch-ass out on a lot, and you may not like that about me, but it was always the truth and you know it."

"Get to it."

As far as I knew this was it. My spine tingled up from my waist and I took a long draw from my MGD. Whatever it was that I was waiting for, this was the moment. My glory had come. My ruin. And my mind set off in a thousand different directions, barely hearing what he began to tell me.

"Mom and dad are fucked-up people. They've been lying to you since you were a child. They lied to me too but we're different; I never fed into any of it, not because I knew but just because we're different. I've been back a few weeks figuring things out. We could have gone to better schools. Better educations. But they didn't want that."

"That's what this is about? Jean—that's it? You are a psycho. Fucking get over it. Go to college if you want to, you can't blame all your shit on them."

"I'm over that, listen to me. I've been following them."

"What?"

"To find out what they do."

"You know what they do."

"I know they work at DU, I know they teach classes and all that shit, but what do they teach?"

"Sociology or some shit."

"And what the fuck is that?"

"I don't know."

"And I bet you don't know how someone gets a job at a university, do you?"

"Do I look like I'm on a job hunt?"

"You've got to have a reputation in your field. You've got to be published, writing articles for journals. You've got to be respected and you've got to have a focus."

"What's their focus?"

"Education."

"Jean, you're losing it. Go back to building shit houses and fucking bears in the mountains. I'm hitting it, don't worry about driving me."

And he shoved me back down on the stool. I shoved back but saw the bartender make a move towards me like he was going to break my arms if I fucked around in his bar.

"You've got some back-up."

"Phil's a gentleman—I'm sure he was coming to help out a lady in distress."

"This lady gets more pussy than you fuckos, so Phil can suck my ass."

"Lucky you."

"Spill it, just say what you have to say."

"They study the sociology of students at schools in poor communities. Schools like JFK and Montbello. I found a few of their articles, they write as a team, I'm thinking that's why Mom never took Dad's name. Yadda fucking yadda written by Kinzie and du Sable, right? Those articles they're writing are about you and me, mostly about you—the majority about you. They've been using you like a goddamn rat."

I breathed in the longest breath I've ever taken, spinning with confusion, not knowing what I would say or do when the exhale came, scared of what I would do or how I would react and breathing in deeper, longer not wanting to find out what was next.

"That's why we didn't go to better schools. That's why all the teachers and principals, all the goddamn pigs look out for you. That's the shit. Right there, that's it. Goddamn guinea pigs."

I was out of there before he could clamp me back down. I heard a car start up in the parking lot, but I ducked through the alleys and over fences into the Capital Hill neighborhood until I reached the park. I found a bench and I sat there surrounded by bums, fucking drugged-out sacks of shit, dudes who were looking to fuck with someone, but none of them, seeing them, knowing them, could stop the flood of tears and scrambled sobbing and pounding of my thighs and chest which erupted through me. I could not stop it. I did not know what it meant, to feel this way, to hear what I just heard. I did not know what was next or what had happened prior to now. I wailed and flipped the bench and pulled flowers and bushes up from the ground. No one would fuck with me if I raged and I raged and no one fucked with me. I fell to my knees beneath a tree in the dark and I pounded my head upon the wet ground until a white blur softened my thoughts, until my thoughts stopped altogether, and I was out.

Jean could not find me for two days; I found him. I slept at the park, wandered around downtown, slinking through the alleys and stealing bags of chips and powdered donuts and crap like that from convenience stores. I slept at the park. I did not shoot up but I watched others with their needles. I did not get raped but I witnessed a man pass out, skunked, only to wake up with his pants around his ankles. I did not engage with anyone and craziness hung naturally through my face. I would not go home, whether Jean was right or not, I would not go home. And so I went back to the bar, and asked the bartender if I could wait there until Jean showed up. It was midnight when he finally did.

"You alright?"

"Far from it."

"I checked with mom, she said she hadn't seen you."

"Was she upset."

"Somewhat."

"Somewhat, what the fuck is that?"

"I don't know. Little Sis, I'm sorry."

"I'll kill you if you're lying to me."

"I know."

"What's next?"

"You want to go back home?"

"I don't."

"I didn't think so."

"You want to check in with your homies?"

"I don't."

"Okay, here's what I've got worked out."

"Oh, so you got it worked out? This is all part of your plan? Fuck you, too, Jean. You're my older brother, you should have figured something out a long time ago. You spineless shit. If you weren't so goddamn worried about your academic standing, that's what you always said right, I remember your snot little voice."

"Fuck off, Judith."

"You just should have known. You're my big brother—I needed you to know."

"Don't give me this shit."

"Give you? I'm not giving you nothing, right—you

grab me out of Themada's and pull me here and tell me I've been an experiment, right? That's how I see it—I'm some fucking experiment that sociologists are reading about, right? I still don't get it. I don't get it."

"That's why they always asked you all those questions, see. That's why they were so interested. They were taking notes, don't you remember that? Parents don't take notes when they listen to their kids."

And I remembered the Steno pad, green lines against a beige page and a vertical red line down the middle—one of them talking to me, the other leaning against the kitchen counter, casually scribbling on the pad. I remembered it, and I never knew it was something that was worth remembering. But it was there, immediately in my mind.

"What did they want?"

"They wanted answers, from what I read."

"You read the shit?"

"Yes, I read it—you think I'd go that far and not figure out what they were saying, the details; otherwise none of this would mean shit. I read all of it, right here, Phil watched me from behind the bar. Cost me some money, too—they don't give out academic articles for fucking free."

"This guy knows about it?"

"Yeah."

"Jesus Christ. Jesus fucking Christ, Jean!"

"Here it is, this is what we'll do. We'll drive to Gunnison. It's a shit town but I know people there and it's far from Denver. I looked into the schools there and you can finish up high school."

"Fuck high school."

"Hear me out. You'd have to enroll as a sophomore, if that, but I think we can get them to agree to that."

"What?"

"It's fucked up, Judith, but this is it, this is the reality—here it is. I've been thinking through this for you because I know you are not in the mind to do it yourself. I'm your big brother now. Now I am."

And he was. He took me to his apartment after a four-hour drive of silence through the winding mountain roads. He put me in his bed and he slept on the couch for the first week. He took me to West Gunnison High and the principal already knew I would be coming and they had the paperwork figured out. I was in classes the Monday after that. Jean worked as much overtime as he could, and I was so lost in a fog I did not know how to apply the brakes to any of it, I did not know how to behave, I did not know what to say to other kids, and I kept quiet, avoiding any friendly greetings or smiles, and I failed many of my tests, got Ds and Fs on papers, but Jean helped me, even wrote a few papers for me, and I learned, and I got better, and I did not think about any of it, though Jean told me he'd been in touch with our parents and even threatened them by having his friend at the worksite call them pretending to be a lawyer. I turned eighteen the month I finished my sophomore year of West Gunny and I worked that summer and life moved on.

And there I was, filled with the first stories that I began writing senior year in Gunnison. At the age of twenty. I hung out with Jean and his friends from work at The Local and they were characters. Drunk mountain wild orators of a frontiersman type. They were good to me, although

I was quiet, maybe even rude at times, but I warmed up to them and I watched them, studied them, getting their manners down, critiquing and toiling them in my head, until they began to spill out in another form, as characters in stories. Wild stories of western towns. Stories which, I laughed rereading them, were poorly written, but stories which spawned a new world for me. A place to inhabit, even though only imagined and momentary, which told me that new life was possible. These stories were therapy and I got over the past, even though I occasionally ruminated on the parallel between me writing about them as my parents wrote about me. But more than therapy and energy for new life, these stories got me into college. Columbia College Chicago offered me a full ride and I took it, grateful to Jean but still wanting more than anything to move off that island he had taken me to. He was excited, maybe more than I was, but I could see his envy as well. When I arrived and fiction classes began, each story began to grow and a novel was written as if Jean was right there listening to me, as if I spoke those worlds directly to him. These worlds which sheltered me from the suffering of my youth. These stories, rereading them that day, consumed me again. And I headed out to find Holofernes, Ursulines, to find Miriam and Penelope, Gwynn, to find all of them in the city which had grown from my mind as much as from my wounds, and I told myself that I would not be a guinea pig again.

17

Dinner would be served at ten o'clock, but Holofernes wanted me to arrive early. He lived on Milwaukee Avenue, immediately south of Division, across the street from what many called the Polish Triangle. His building, four stories high, was wide and it obliquely elbowed at the corner of Milwaukee and Division. A crumbling and filthy intersection, it overlooked crack addicts and bum degenerates loitering around the fountain at the center of the triangle median. A Victorian-style facade, painted celery green with turquoise eyebrows above each window and a pristine caketop painted in purples and yellows. Somehow, he afforded an entire floor, twelve windows wide, angular at the elbow which centered the gigantic room of his apartment. Bookended by a large kitchen taking up the southeast wall, and two bedrooms down a hallway on the northwest end. I would describe his tastes as industrial country. More chic than shabby, but materials mixed in beautiful ways—cast iron and Toile de Joi fabrics, old growth wood and porcelain vases, marble end-tables with a copper base, an old oil drum cut in two, placed on coasters and topped with glass. The walls were papered above the chair rail with a sky blue background and orange floral designs. A soft complimentary brown beneath and accented with white trim. The couches and chairs were upholstered in various lime and apple green fabrics. The wall opposite the row of windows was a library from floor to ceiling, thirteen feet high, a ladder on wheels to reach the top shelves.

Our talks had been growing more in-depth, items

such as socks, use of silverware, even length of sideburn concerned him, not to mention the condition of parapets—were the bricks calcifying?—of alleys behind the buildings—were the cobblestones beginning to show through?—and the number of rookeries, if any, that had been burrowed into the residences by birds. The tremendous detail with which he asked me to perceive the world was overwhelming. And so he had taught me a trick.

Push pause.

One can do that?

When you are sauntering down a residential branch of Milwaukee, or wherever, push pause. When you have slumped against a building on California, push pause. Simply push pause, Judith.

And that is what I had began to do. The motion of history, of present bodies, the pull of the future—all of it ceased its mechanisms. I considered the gratitude I owed VCRs for introducing this technology, and I gathered as much detail as I could. The silhouette of a bird perched on a ledge against a blue sky, beak agape. The mercurous liquid in the alley. The affordable-housing compound viewed abstractly as a pattern of diminishing rectangles. The cotton grey hood resting on the oversized sunglasses. The one rusted stair of a fire escape. The whisker above the lip longer than the rest and rolling back into the biker's nostril.

Fine, yes. But remember I do not want a list—string these scenes together into story. Narrate them for me, Judith. I want you to push play again when you retell your observations.

And this is what I resisted, often, though giving in, at

times, to satiate his need. Isolated, I felt, these moments of observation were raw material. Objective data. They had a power to transform into many things, multiple existences, and contained the potential, which for me, I knew to be life. But when I said the biker stopped at the light on his fixed gear bike surrounded by rusting metal, affordable housing buildings, wearing a grey hoody with stylish sunglasses spying a bird on a ledge and taking out a pen to begin sketching it across his arm as if planning a tattoo—this was something altogether different. This was complicit. This complied. It was what Holofernes wanted.

I arrived and he had a glass of beer waiting for me.

"Wisconsin brewed."

"When were you up in Wisconsin, Holofernes?"

"I wasn't. I don't. Well, I have been, but I have friends who pick up certain items on my must-have list when they are up there. This is New Glarus. A lambic, made with Door County cherries. A little sparkle, a little bite, a lot of tart sour boldness. Fruity yet not filling. As perfect before a grand meal as for dessert."

"Hanging out with your crowd feels more and more like riding a carousel."

"I told you who's coming over. That is why you are here early. These are the men from downtown. These are the non-profit women, CEOs and CFOs. Creative Directors. Curators. These are the tastemakers. And Gwynn, of course."

"Gwynn, right."

"A very fun bunch is my guess. I have been relaying a few of your stories to them and they are fascinated. I think you might be the next Basquiat. Peggi Guggenheim's reincarnation will be here, if only in spirit."

"I miss the old crowds. Do you still talk with Penelope?"

"That ungrateful woman. Ten of her would not be worth one of these who are coming tonight."

"You should get out something stronger, then—it is a big night."

"Penelope did not care about success, about money, she loved her friends and drunken conversation more than a career would allow her. She was youth, I see it now, and I was form. And no other substance more than youth does form yearn to hold."

"Sleep with me once more."

"I will sleep with you whenever you ask."

"They like our ideas?"

"Which?"

"The Pickle Factory."

"Of course they do. And they have ideas of their own, too. Judith, be nice. We will further ingratiate them into our journey and we will, with their help, succeed. Here, have a cornichon."

"I thought these were gherkins."

"No, they are not. Do you like them? A purveyor on the north side, a tiny room almost hidden in a series of African clothing storefronts and groceries, he sells them there. They are fine. The gold of pickled fruits. He has many provisions you can only find in Paris or Rome—he does not quip about nationalities. Quality, Judith, is his only measure."

"I haven't told you about the Hungarian butcher on Loomis."

"No, you have not."

"The walls, I swear are splattered with blood. Not the walls surrounding the customer, but behind the counter. And his wrinkled heckling face. Quite rare to find a left-over like this."

"Who have you found shopping there?"

"He has a dozen different sausages. Despicable blends of innards and exxards. An old trembling woman hangs around, perusing. Mustachioed men—*dems ders dose*—the kind you forgot lived in this city. And occasionally, only every so often, a Rat or a Fox walks in. Wide-eyed, of course. Asking for a satchel of frozen meat. In response to the butcher, one said frozen so it would thaw in time for their future meal. And not too thick because they would be cooking it out over a fire."

"You will retell that tonight. But make sure to liven it up. String it all together so that all those people are there at once. And please, describe what all these animals are wearing. Do they have children? Yes, make sure one of them has a stroller. They can leave it outside if they want. Well, where did your clothes go?"

"Can you tell me what I was wearing?"

"I can see your chest is flush with a heat. I can see you have taken my advice on the Brazilian wax they give at Esther's."

"You didn't tell me they licked what they liked."

"You bad girl. I didn't tell you so many things."

And I grabbed one of the decanters he had readying for the party, pouring it into his mouth. "Get drunk with me Holofernes. We are almost there." And then pouring it down my chest before hopping up on the counter and dripping it across my hot cunt.

He had brought me a blanket and I laid across his kitchen counter to pretend to sleep. Holofernes drank. Danced around. And he started to sing a song, "We Built this City," but he didn't sing the chorus, just the verse: *"Say you don't know me, or recognize my face. Say you don't care who goes to that kind of place. Knee deep in the hoopla, sinking in your fight. Too many run-ways eating up the night."*

I perked my head up and sang: *"Marconi plays the mamba, listen to the radio. Don't you remember. We built this city, we built this city on rock and roll."*

He carried on: *"Someone's always playing corporation games. Who cares they're always changing corporation names. Who counts the money underneath the bar. Who writes the wrecking ball in two wild guitars."*

I sat up, threw off the blanket and in unison we belt out: *We built this city! We built this city on rock and roll!*

"What else you got?"

"How about 'Night Moves?' 'Don't Stop Believing?'"

"Those are no good." I laid back down.

Then, as he lit the stove and put on hot water for blanching the almonds, he began a song I did not know. *"I can see the older man looking at the younger woman. I can see the younger woman looking at the maid. Over there the maid is looking at the younger woman. I can see the younger woman looking at the man. Don't know it?"*

"Not yet."

"Cause every man sees in the younger woman the hope. And every woman sees in the maid the dream. Everybody lives the pride and dies the passion of the young. From the womb to the tomb we will remember what it means. Should I keep going?"

"I almost got it."

"*To celebrate youth—*"

"*—celebrate!* Rick Springfield, baby, I got it."

"*Those who have it—*"

"*— young ones!*"

"*Celebrate youth—celebrate —give them sight.*"

"That's ridiculous you know that, Holofernes."

He kept going: "*But everybody sees in the younger one the hope. And everybody sees in the younger one the dream. Everybody lives the pride and dies the passion of the young. From the womb to the tomb we will remember what it means.*"

"Alright, I'm up. What are you cooking?"

"Main course is a walleye dish I learned from Michel Comté, but I have a surprise, too. Hey, so guess what I did with The Fortress?"

"So it was you? Or us, I guess."

"It is the essence of what we've been talking about all this time."

"The grittiness, the disinterest, those indicators are 100% there."

"Think how many people want that, to see that, know that. It's an experience like no other."

"What do we do, charge admission?"

"Wouldn't that be something. No, we put a bid in on a few of the sites."

"The access points?"

"Actually, I bought those vacant lots you told me about a while back."

"Wait."

"I'm talking about the mothership."

"Slow down George Clinton. We've got some major

problems. The Fortress is underground. It stretches, I don't know, a mile in every direction, two in some—you can't purchase the entire area."

"We."

"I know my cut is coming, but right now, it's just you."

"Not after tonight. You'll get a kick out of them, Judith. Maybe most importantly is Ottavia Costa. His wealth will solidify our names in history."

"You want me here for this?"

"You're the reason I invited them. These purple potatoes were grown by Geoff."

"My friend, Geoff?"

"Yeah, Bucket Boy. He grows them in those pickle buckets on his roof. They're precious. I've got some chives and sea salt. Super simple meal we're having. Ursulines' asparagus crop came in last week. I'm not sure if you talked with her?"

"Where's my blanket?"

"I tossed it into the closet. These people coming over, we're going to tell them about The Fortress."

"You mean I am going to tell them."

"How about more wine?"

"Open a bottle of my favorite, Holofernes, I think I might herniate."

"That's gross."

"Suspiro! Suspiro! You are my fair hero!"

"Captain Beefheart?"

"The winemaker, Provo—metal. Writes songs and screams them at you."

"When did you meet him?"

"That night I went to Schwa with Ruben and Gwynn."

"Ruben and Gwynn are out too. They broke up; she moved to Seattle."

"Pour me a glass."

"He stepped away from the Office, a month ago, maybe. His vision transitioned to Armitage Avenue bullshit boutiques. Tonight we will entertain the upper echelon—I call them the Court."

18

Dinners begun at Holofernes' so fluidly that you didn't know food was served. Cocktail conversations migrated to the dinner table uninterrupted, as if a scent had been set in the air which set our feet to shuffle, our knees to bend and seats to sit, never looking away from each other's eyes, never not slightly smiling.

I didn't know when it would be my time to talk, if it was prearranged. The way the guests looked at me, I felt salty. Like my body had been brined. Typically, one would think this type of thing waits for dessert, for coffee. And maybe that was the plan, but as soon as I could inject, I did. Ready and willing, when the table talk veered towards violence, I poured my wine down my throat, feeling every drop of weighty red sizzle atop my stomach juices, set my attention behind my eyes as I had grown accustomed to in my clairvoyance, and waited for the visions to come.

"They do not share the same reality as we do, I am convinced."

"I agree, and a friend of mine on the police force, she said something similar—that it's a game to them. Shoot 'em up, like laser-fucking-tag."

"I know, though can you blame them?"

"I think so."

"Economically, there are no opportunities. Their parents eat Cheetos and nitrates."

"Don't bag on salami, Don."

"Phosphates, nitrates, sodium bicarbonates—all poisons."

"Well, they live in food deserts."

It was then that I saw her. La Ciudad Mujer. Standing there watching on.

"When parents don't work and watch daytime teevee what do you expect?"

"Daytime teevee is ghetto because the ghetto watches daytime teevee."

"Thanks Marshall McLuhan."

"Hey, *Annie Hall*—I watched it last weekend like you suggested."

"Yeah, and?"

"Thumbs down."

"Politicians have horrible taste."

"My guess is they prefer daytime teevee."

She had eased out from the kitchen, gently looking about and taking in the room.

"Their talk, it's crude. Their parenting, it's violent. Think of how they act in the classroom—and the mothers blame the teachers."

"Private school parents are the same."

"I can testify to that—they blame the teaching if their kid does not get an A."

"I always knew a spot in the education department called for you, Ottavia."

"Their world is hopeless. But they are human, and humans search for how they fit in to the world around them, this is how we find meaning."

Then I smelled it. Tamales. On the table, we each had a tamale in front of us. The steam rising.

"Alright, there you go—you've figured out the entire underclass."

"I think he was talking about black people."

"Black people in poor neighborhoods."

"Why do we even police those streets?"

"If the schools could be fixed, it all might be different for them."

I started to sing an Ella Fitzgerald song: *"Let's go slumming, take me slumming, on Park Avenue. We'll just hide behind a pair of fancy glasses, make faces when a member of the classes passes."* They all smiled politely.

"But think of the culture created in these places. Think of the beauty that emerges from their pain. The art—damnit, hip hop."

"I didn't know you liked hip-hop, Holofernes."

"I don't but you can't deny its vitality, how it's affected pop, rock—it's another American art form."

"So, let them suffer, if only to let the sublime in."

At this point, my legs had strolled twenty blocks into the brick and tar, glass and steel—the cement and meager trees.

"No, let them be, and know they make sense of their realities better than we ever could."

"That would be all fine if I did not fear for myself walking down the street."

But I looked again at Ciudad Mujer as she stood there staring at the window, eyes across the Polish Triangle, and I could not distinguish between this night we lived and the story she told me from her view atop the Northwest Tower.

"Where are you living now, Joseph?"

"Logan Square."

"Move to Lincoln Park—only thing to fear is rising property taxes."

"It's too homogenous for me."

"You are a walking silo of homogeneity."

"That's a tough word to say: homogeneity.

The words I spoke were not my words. They were everyone's. Eternally. And on this night they would be heard again. "About half the people I know have gotten mugged over the years."

"Is that so, Judith."

"In what neighborhoods?"

"I have been shot at."

"Really?"

"I have been beat."

"Was it serious?"

"I did not know what I was after, but I followed the river just the same."

"Which branch, Judith? I hear Pilsen and I hear Avondale, and I am torn."

"The river I follow is the Chicago River—the places I have seen will surprise you."

"Surprise then, I know I love a good story."

"As I have mentioned to you all," Holofernes began, "Judith has gained access to The Fortress."

"I knew it was more than just some legend developers spoke of when it seemed the streets were dry."

"We all did, Don—those who didn't, defected long ago."

"Where else would they be going? Otherwise, it doesn't make sense—all these artists, we each know several who are truly committed to the lifestyle and would never suburbanize."

"Bohemians, Ottavia—it makes more sense for us to

call them bohemians—the intellectuals, the artisans, the crafts people, the revolutionaries, the workers—let's just call them bohemians."

"Tell us, Judith, about The Fortress of Bethulia."

My eyes were glazed, but open, settled back into my walk forward, into the wilderness.

"The Forts are nothing compared to the Indians. I will tell you where they are. Follow me."

"We're leaving?"

"Are you kidding, Howard, these tamales are divine. Eat, drink, and listen to what Judith has witnessed."

"Tell us, Judith, about life there, in The Fortress."

My eyes opened involuntarily. I watched Ciudad Mujer push aside the curtains and step away from the window she had been preoccupied by. Though her eyes moved towards mine, I saw her begin to cut the curtain from its rungs.

"What is the chef doing to your curtains."

"Isn't she your landlord, Holofernes?"

"Are you ready, Judith?"

"*Listo.*"

Sue towered over me, pulled her cape slowly, lingering over me for what seemed like a minute but could have been only a second or two of darkness, just long enough to slide the cleaver into my hand, my fingers tightening their grip on the handle. She spun and faced the table of guests, mid-meal, and said to me:

"Be still. Be still, Judith, still be. That which began this was a fiddle in the frontier night. The nightengale's song which enveloped you and carried you. The tender fur of a bear. Be still. Still be. Your father built his home on the edge of the lake. Your mother knew less about Haiti than she did about the feeling of fur on her skin. The edge of the lake at the mouth of the river you walk right into the waters and you walk down to the bottom knowing you can breathe, knowing you can see. Submerge, beneath, the blue, cool, river. Feel how at ease you are here. The daughter of the first. How clearly you see, how peacefully you know. The father awaits. Settled inside, harmonious with the waters. Look. Look. What do you see? Feel the resistance of the waters slowing you down, your thighs strong and push against the water, your head's slow movements and the clarity of your visions. And you walk. And you notice others walking. Alongside. Past you. In the opposite direction. As if gum stuck to the bottom, your shoes feel slow to pick up. The daughter of the first. The father awaits. You are seeing their faces, you are seeing their clothing. You know where they are going and where they are coming from. Your father was the first to build a house at the edge of the lake where the river begins and your mother was the first to follow the river as you follow the river and see the buildings, see the storefronts, the apartments, the residents, the neighborhood. As you slip unknowingly into the chambers of The Fortress of Bethulia, as you exit the sewer line, as you wash the sludge from your skin and talk and listen, as you listen, you hear The Fortress and you tell us what you know. What the daughter of the first knows. What the father learns upon your return. Dearest daughter, excuse that we are eating. Please, begin with your outpost."

"Will this be cogent?"

"Nothing worth a speculator's while is."

I knew then that this was our story. A story cast by the mold of this world. A story that does not go away. Our story which we must rise to meet again and again each lifetime.

I tussled with Holofernes' thick curly brown locks with one hand, gripped the cleaver with the other, as he drank, far drunker than any of his guests might have imagined. And I spoke.

"I did not follow the realtor's guide, but instead the river as the natives did, knowing a different city would betray its dutiful concealment. I am Beatrice. I am Daniel Burnham. I am Hatshepsut. I am Cairo. I am Oglethorpe and I am Amenhotep. I am Empress Lü. I am Bangladesh. I am Santiago. I am the District. Red Light. The Alleyway. Gangway. I am the Sewers. Catacombs. Adulis. The Trombone. The Handkerchief. I am Natchez. I am Mohenjo Daro. Iron Ore. I am Sullivan's Zombie haunting Graceland. I am Total Night. Pagan Rome. Touch me before I go away."

And no one moved to put a stop to my threat of violence as I raised the cleaver above his neck.

"My outpost has been Ursulines' apartment. It is far down the river. Near a handful of entrances to The Fortress, you will find many Forts wandering around, alone in the mess of existence lived by the native population."

"The Northwest. Tell us about the Northwest."

"Doors and windows boarded up. Buildings seemingly abandoned but men and women standing in front of them, uncertain what they are protecting. First, she introduces me to Johnny. We meet in an alley, surprisingly decorated with blossoming trellises and a cactus garden.

When he arrives, we approach each other apprehensively. His fingers are bony, with nails like those of a man who has been felling trees in the city. His face very Indian, a few lone hairs on his chin, a woolen cap on his head. Here is my mother, he says, she and our ancestors have been at this for quite some time. His mother sitting there, using shards of glass to scrape oil paint off an old rocking chair. Striking teachers had locked themselves in the nearby church ten days prior and are ringing the bells. The students have nowhere to go but the streets. We walk through the masses unnoticed and at the market around the corner I eat a piece of grilled Monkey—it look like a naked Child."

As I clung to his brown curls and lifted his head, Holofernes interjected, "Everything that she says is not what she says. Remember that. We've developed a lexicon. Monkies are hipsters, or arts administrators. Indians are authentics. Chickens are yuppies, or the value of mainstream society. Children are innocent immigrants, floundering nobodies, fellaheen. Mothers are baristas. This is all slang."

He did not fight my grip, but spoke and listened from the block, his eyes on the tamales as his guests put them to their mouths.

"We were descending into The Fortress and I had not recognized the entrance, as if it was not physical. As if it were a simple turn of phrase to unlock the cellar door. In the streets, women delouse their children. Enormous fish across piles of gray ice. Barrels of fruit juices surrounded by swarms of flies, filth. Children playing marbles between the houses. I see a vulture spread its wings and remain in that statue-like position, presumably to cool off or to drive away itching mites. Cattle heads pass, skinned and bloody, on hand carts. In a bar, I see a man lying on the floor unconscious, dead drunk. An Indian steps outside into the sun and wrings a chicken's neck. Once underground the first sight I behold is a large pile of empty tortoise shells. Beyond aways, we walk under chickens tied by the legs to the ceiling, swinging in an empty-looking radius. To the right the cooking fires glow. Roast alligator is being served, and I recognize a few of Ursulines' friends sitting cross-legged with empty plates on their laps, laughing and waiting to be served. A few children crouch in a brownish water, doing laundry. When I arrive at my quarters, I see a room several steps wide by several long, consisting of a sturdy tree trunk into which treads have been sawn as the Natives do here, leading up to a platform that serves as a porch. There I have a crude table, roughly hewn from boards, two benches, a hammock, as well as wooden hooks where I hang my rain gear. Behind that a single room, which you enter through a swinging bamboo door. There are three windows, all fairly small. A bed with mosquito netting, the mattress stuffed with city grass and hard; it has peaks and valleys, into which one has to fit one's body carefully. A primitive wooden shelf for my journals, the two books I brought with me, my toiletries. Underneath them, hanging from a nail where I can find it always by feel, the flashlight. The toilet and washroom are in two-stall outhouses about fifteen meters behind my cabin; half the Forts use it, and usually there is a line."

"How far from the city's edge, Judith?"

"Yes, I'm not sure our locale."

"It's not as easy as that. Please, listen."

"Afterward, we go to have a brandy old-fashioned in one of the dives. The cardplayers are so loaded that they are playing in slow motion. When they have to pee, they do not even leave their stools but just swivel around and piss against the board walls. In the one where we are drinking, which is as small as a newspaper stand, the tavern keeper's wife and child are sleeping on the floor, without a mattress, blanket, or pillow. A scruffy, drunk old Chinese man shows us open scabs on his forearm. He approaches us several times, wanting us to take a good look. Through the window a view of the slaughterhouse on the river; what I see there bears no resemblance to proper killing. A cow escapes into the river and swims away. The foundry where many of the Natives work is a crucible in the ground like an iron volcano with a scalloped rim. Corrugated tin on poles forms a roof over the whole thing. In the midst of all this a pig is slaughtered, children are nursed. A dwarfish, crippled woman is sewing on a machine; she can hardly reach the pedal. In the background, palm trees, between them a decomposing pile of garbage in which hens peck around. Scrap iron, molds, a bench vise, a bellows. The whole things resembles a Bronze Age midden heap in which blacksmithing and pouring goes on."

"Tell us about the bars, Judith."

"In the discotheque, which someone pushed me into, it is so dark that the waiter collects the bill with a flashlight. The eyes of the girls you meet here are black on black, where the darkness is most intense. Shirt collars stand out as the most glaring ultra-white, and the writing on most pieces of paper is impossible to see. At the next table someone smashes his glass on purpose. The waiter brings me a beer and wants to know whether we also wanted *señoritas*. To hear that word *señoritas* felt so strange considering the population around me was made up of Laotians and Taiwanese. People spend their days watching the river. An archaic calm and composure in the mothers' gestures as they pick over the children's heads, searching for lice. They bite the lice in two with their front teeth. In the marketplace people are lying on the tables, sleeping. I decide to go deeper in, spend a few nights away from Ursulines in order to drum up a connection with a Fort."

"Did you spend any time on the river?"

"I took a river boat with several Natives. I spit into the water and a fish snaps it up. At night I buy meat, half of a wild boar, heavily salted to prevent spoilage. In the light of the moon, which is not even half full, my body casts a clear shadow, which obediently shrinks when I tell it to heel. Faces seated around a flickering lantern. Growing restless, I go outside to see whether the river is still there. At night, onions are lying on the table. Outside in the dark all that can be made out of the Indians are their fingers, with which they are holding onto the porch railing. For a long time I stare in the direction of the faces in the pitch dark, till the fingers gingerly let go of the railing and plunge into the night."

"Did you speak with anyone?"

"A fairly young, intelligent looking man with long hair asks me whether filming or being filmed could do harm, whether it could destroy a person. In my heart the answer is yes, but I said no. The people's gestures are unfamiliar, gentle and lovely: they move their hands like orchestral conductors in time with a soft, shy melody that emanates cautiously from the depths of the city, like wild creatures that emerge from the sheltering leaves now and then to go down the rivers."

"Tell us about any violence you witnessed."

"There is a strong Military presence."

"Military means banks. Or those in conflict with banks."

"And an Indian soldier, not more than seventeen, fires a shot at my window in Ursulines' apartment. It struck the fiberglass siding and the bullet lodged somewhere in the walls' insulation. We leave, feeling endangered, and the next night we sleep in an abandoned school."

"Surely, each of you has been briefed on the bus. Look for it in your inboxes."

"For the night I fix myself a bed by lying flexible sugarcanes on a half-collapsed frame. In the part of the school that serves as a storage area, there is hardly room to sit—no table just a few gasoline drums filled with stuff. Under my sleeping platform is a pile of hundreds of cheap sectioned plastic plates, the kinds used in prisons. These absurdly inappropriate gifts from the Department of Housing and Shelter's office are stamped with the Chicago flag and a handshake logo. Ursulines looks at me and says: 'This is The Fortress, too. You should know that. The abandoned schools are never what they seem.' In the morning I wake up feeling the silent eyes of children watching me at close range through the loose wall slats. I go with Ursulines to the wood shop, an impenetrable chaos of Trash, Chickens, Children, Open fires, and Pin-ups on the plank walls. Ducks and pigs wallow around in the dirt with the children. Among some in the crowd a brand of hostility springs up that I had encountered previously only in the reports of early seafarers, except that now the Natives are wearing "John Travolta Fever" and "Disneyland" t-shirts. I leave the school behind, doomed to certain demolition with its eroded riverbank crumbling into the water."

"Do you feel this is the next neighborhood to turn?"

"Since there is almost no work left at the pumping station, the neighborhood hardly receives new residents anymore. But the tavern keeper at the shabby bar in the wooden shack tells himself that a new boom will occur, and he is waiting for it, languidly, without lifting a finger. In a month at most the river will have claimed his shack, too. Space is getting tight. I have been quartered from the beginning in the little shed in back, next to the kitchen. It used to be the chicken coop, and the ceiling is so low and sags somewhat in the middle. So that my head hits it when I stand up straight. At night the Rat romp around above me, and when I am half asleep, it is as though they were riding their freak bikes right through my dreams. They are not committed like the Forts but they serve the cause nonetheless, loving its squalor. Such a peculiar sense of peace comes over me that I feel I am discovering something that has been missing from my life. Always on my tongue is to begin telling them the truth. But I never speak, desiring that their powers would surmount my illusion."

"Tell us about the far southwest."

"The buildings are occupied on a seasonal basis by

Polish lumbermen, put up four together in the fairly small rooms, and in a rather large lounge they play cards, huddled around a little woodstove, smoking, and cooking bacon directly on the stovetop, which sizzles with fat. They drink vodka and are drunk from nine in the morning on. The women among them, sturdy creatures in worn padded jackets from Siberia, join in the drinking. On a couch in their midst, one of the women has sex with one of the men, shortly after they returned from their day's work—the others in the room do not let themselves be distracted from what they were doing. During this operation the woodcutter keeps his jacket on and his rucksack on his back. Near the fermenting Narragansett garbage dump my bicycle has a flat."

"What bicycle?"

"Not mine but Johnny's, a Fort."

"The denim guy with the mustache?"

"Wait, I thought he was a Rat."

"Just listen, these details are barely worth mentioning—we're not police."

"Hundreds of Vultures poke around in the filth and some came hopping ponderously toward me, until a man with an overloaded pickup invited me to climb up on top of his crates of oranges. Later, Rats came and hauled the bicycle to a bar. The mechanic who is summoned first fetched his assistant, then both of them get drunk and sit around on the ground singing; actually it is more a chanting without melody, which soon dies away because both of them fell asleep. An hour later I wake the assistant, who seem less drunk, but he just stares at me, as if from a great distance, sings the end of a verse they had not finished, and slumped over again. A primeval Tortoise came crawling through the store, rocking its head and its body like it wants to have nothing to do with the world. Outside, Pigs are grunting. The tortoise gets stuck as it tries to squeeze under a plywood partition; its shell, which it cannot visualize, is too high, but it stubbornly works away, scrabbling with its claws in a futile attempt to move forward. The wooden floor is smeared with oil and smells of rancid grease. From the courtyard in the back, strewn with garbage, where dogs and pigs dig in the dirt, come the cries of an infant, and I go outside to check because the infants there never cry. The child is lying naked on a bundle of cloth on the ground, and the tortoise, which had somehow worked its way out after all, had been turned on its back by the mother, so it would not crawl over the child. It is lying there with its head and legs completely drawn into its shell. The mother, half-Indian, comes and picks up the baby, a girl, and shows me that she had just pierced her ears, but instead of earrings had pulled a piece of string through each hole and knotted the ends."

"Do you find the street food visually appealing?"

"Sweat, storm clouds overhead, sleeping dogs. There is a smell of stale urine. In my soup, ants and bugs are swimming among the globules of fat. My left leg grows inflamed from insect bites. How banal and humiliating to die like this, and I consider briefly whether I should sit down or be whisked away standing."

"Any signs of a scene, underground parties, tattoos? Those things are always there, somewhere—I can't imagine it being any different with these Forts you all are talking about."

"We travel a stretch up K-town to see Camarillo, the cook, where we are served fairly warm beer, and since I have already done some drinking at the fiesta, we go to the nearby waterfall and position ourselves under it. Lester and I let the water pound down on us; it feels like a herd of cattle trampling me, but afterward I am quite refreshed and also sober. A K-town woman with tattoos on her face and upper thighs speaks to me, gesticulating wildly and apparently asking to be taken along. She is very put out that I cannot speak Aguaruna—she found that unnatural. When she gets off, she does not go straight onto land but hikes up her skirt first and washes her legs. After a few hundred meters, however, she asks us to tie up again so she can get off, because on the bank she has spotted a woman with a baby whom she knows well. Cows roam among the huts, large and gentle and slow-witted. The bull, an animal of immense proportions and colossal strength, stands next to me for a long time under a roof, letting himself be fanned by the wind and flapping his ears. He looks at me quietly and sadly, and when he leaves, he is limping badly. A large thorn stuck in his front hoof. In the evening the place is completely dead. In one of the huts an elderman is sitting with a book by a kerosene lantern, reading out loud to himself. On the grocer's counter two scrawny boys are sleeping, their lanky limbs contorted, as if an explosion had hurtled them into a terrible, everlasting sleep. I gaze up at the starry sky, and it seems as alien to me as I do to myself."

"How secure is The Fortress?"

"At several intersections, paths open up unexpectedly into vast arched rooms. Surely, each of these clandestine colosseums would provide a useful stronghold for the concentration of forces in certain eventualities, just as the infinity of subterranean networks, with its thousand galleries running under every corner of Chicago, provides a ready-made sap from which to attack the city from below."

"Every city has a system of catacombs where the artists inhabit and utilize beautifully to their favor of freedom and movement and practice," Holofernes squealed. "The design an extension of the dreams."

"For months it snows enough to lead me to believe I am in the high mountains, Hindu Kushur the Himalayas, and at a great altitude I have to fight my way forward, sunk up to my chest in powder snow. When the snow falls on poverty, it purifies the stench, forgives the dereliction. The first building is a mostly-stone Goat shed. They always sit half beneath a staircase, leaning against a damp stone wall and getting drunk on stale beer. The painter working on the painting swishes his brush around in the dabs of paint on a mahogany board, and after I watch him for a while, I know that he is only pretending to be painting; in reality he would never paint, only mix colors, for all eternity. Across from the wretched Midway airport is a bar with a beautiful Monkey, black, with limbs that go on forever. He looks very intelligent and would make the ideal companion for any Mother. A drunk spits at the Monkey and almost hits him from behind. The Monkey inspected and sniffed with great interest at his globule from the depths of an unhealthy lung, as it lay on the ground, greenish yellow and steaming. It looks as though the Monkey wants to eat the spit, or at least taste it. I said silently to him, Leave it, leave it alone, and he let it be. He sits with his tail wrapped around his buttocks like a rope, his knees under his chin, and his arms around his knees. Chained to a tree limb. I realized I am sitting the same way, with my feet propped in the rungs of a second chair and my knees under my chin. In Beverly, which keeps exerting a pull on me for no reason, a woman is selling soup from a large tortoise shell. An older Chinese man is sitting nearby on a threshold and making frantic movements, as if he is drawing a thread out of the interior of his eye. He is engrossed with such extreme exclusivity in what he is doing that he draws not only my attention, but also that of all those who are eating the woman's soup. I have never seen anything resembling the intensity with which he is pulling that imaginary thread out of his eye, and later, when I pass him on my bicycle, he looks up slowly and stares at me so penetratingly and so insanely in the face that it scares me. On the way home, I stop by a hut where a dark crowd of people are clustered outside a window. From inside came the sound of two thin fiddles, a rattle, and a monotonous flute. Dancing. And when I cautiously push my way past the half-naked bodies to the window, I see that the people inside are dancing around a seated plaster Jesus wearing a halo. Above him is a canopy of mosquito netting, and around him are plastic flowers, stuck into the dirt floor. The dancers are holding handkerchiefs. I stared in through the window for a long time. No one realizes I am not invited, so I drink several of the cocktails being served. I sit down between a large fern in a terra-cotta pot and a column, so as to be undisturbed. Then an elegant young woman wants to discuss art with me; what kind of art, I bark, and she says something confused about my hostility to art per se. It is Ursulines. She tells me to leave. I am no longer safe. A little further upstream I shine a powerful flashlight on the opposite bank and make out alligators, their eyes glowing as if someone is smoking a cigarette over there. But they have been almost completely wiped out here, and are small. At night, I have first the feeling and then the certainty, that I am caught in a twilit prehistory, without speech or time. The river rolls along without a sound, a monster. Night falls very fast, with the last birds scolding the evening, as always at this hour. Rough cawing, malevolent sounds, punctuated by the even chirping of the first cicadas. My fingers are wrinkly, like those of the laundresses. I must have a hundred bites on my back from some insect I never did see; all of me is rotting with moisture. I would be grateful if it is only dreams tormenting me. Johnny comes out of the city, his hair matted and full of black flies. He is flailing at them, and we pick the nasty things out his wooly hair. A bat colony flutters off in confusion, along with swarms of wasps, birds, a cloud of small flying insects. Tiny, thin caterpillars flee, humping their midsection, then throwing their front section ahead, rushing along in a caterpillar gallop. The city is streaming now as if after a thousand years of rain."

"I think we have heard enough, Holofernes."

"The bakeries, she should tell you about the bakeries."

"With this we can map the coordinates and proceed."

"Extremely helpful. Extremely."

I pulled Holofernes' head to my lap. I petted his check and looked deeply past his absent grin into his heavy eyes. All these words I had offered him, no other gift could he be given to stir so much inebriated joy. I leapt off the couch, shoving his head to the seams and I ratcheted the cleaver. Again with more force. Again as she watched me from the curtain. As the patrons screamed. The thud of his headless body on the hardwoods, I held up my prize to take in every detail of the scene, kissed it's lips and wrapped it in the curtain she held out for me, before running through the door, down the stairs, and onto Division Street. Chicago night. Cold. Hushed, gray, inaccessible. Cement and brick. A spring in my step, she limped behind me as I hustled up Milwaukee through the bar-goers and degenerates, until we reached the Northwest Tower and she went in but I went on. As she watched from the thirteenth floor, as I walked the thirteen blocks.

19

I made my last walk, a midnight walk through Friday's havoc to Ursulines' bus. Blood dripping from the curtain. Milwaukee Avenue was lit bright, funneling commerce and cars into the Loop of skyscraping steel, accordion fences across the storefronts, a drunk mouth of syllables slumped in the entrance to the child-care facility. There was no tense muscle in my body, nothing in the shadows that I feared, so I decided to walk the way home, past the degradation of cafes. Along the road, stands had been set up, selling beer and grilled meat, and there was dancing. I played a game of chance and lost; the principle was like roulette, except that there were no balls but a live guinea pig under a small wooden crate, which was raised by a rope. Numbered Swiss chalets were set up in a circle, each with a dark entryway, and the guinea pig dashed around uncertainly for a while before quickly making up its mind and disappearing into one of the doors. The prizes were little bowls made of pink and light green plastic, and I kept on betting until I had no more money on me. No one in Bethulia mentioning the head.

Unable to be alone and therefore lost on these streets in these crowds picking their limbs and fabrics from my teeth. Young people in headdress, young people in hats, in scarves, young people in salvaged dresses and estate sale pants, young people in bow ties, in galoshes, in cor-sets, young people in cigarettes, beer bottles, in beards, bangs, in stained skin funneled into a building, into a warehouse, into a neon tube, red neon glowing within the veins of the narrow street, rugs laid out with wares, carts rolled with drinks, small market tents and arms waving everywhere language of purchase this deal this silver this dress this chair this pipe smoked through the gutters a rush of legs and in the pockets musicians singing, clarinets tipped to the rooftops, a moon reflected in the high polish of the violin, scraping across the strings, the power lines, the strands of hair the life of eyes, restaurants tucked everywhere, bars tending directly to the people in the streets, windows open in the residences above, doors flinging and shutting and cabs honking as everybody tries to get in, squeeze in, bodies, youth in hats, youth in headdress pumping spirits towards the center as the ends of the street do not end, only grow longer, spread out reconciling this onslaught.

I heard singing, strings. "Ursulines?"

"Baby, where else would I be?" she sang, sultry and bright.

I set his head outside in the weeds then pushed the folding door open and walked in.

She sat there at her makeshift desk, a blanket on, playing her ukulele.

"You didn't tell me you were coming over."

"I called your corporate cell phone but you didn't answer."

"You might be better off elsewhere. I'm working through this song and don't need to be soured."

"A big dinner at Holofernes's tonight."

"What's new."

"Different crowd than usual. A few alderman. That art collector, Ottavia Costa. Betsy Howard, do you know her? She owns a few music venues. Sally Pritzker, of course, Sue."

She sang. "Don't mean nothing to me. Don't mean nothing to me. Life is growing too damn wild for that city to be what I need."

"I told them our story. You would have loved it. Never has a group listened so attentively to me speak."

"You tell them about your parents, how they fucked you up real good."

"You're only really you when you hiss, Ursulines."

"Get out of here."

"They know about The Fortress."

"What are you talking about?"

"I told them everything."

She was silent.

"They are planning to buy up the property above all the access points, along each underground corridor."

"We're all leaving, you know, we've all left."

"Ursulines?"

"I'm the last one."

"Honey, don't give me that, I've been down there."

"Those were just a group of chimney sweeps. Gutter punks off the train."

"They're designers."

"Listen to yourself. You're so turned around."

"Fuck that, don't lie."

"Judith, we had to leave. You and Holofernes helped us. It takes some commotion to stir up a nest."

"Holofernes thinks they'll move on The Fortress before the fall. Chicago will be the most abundant city this side of Atlantis."

"Holofernes lied to you. About so many things."

"Holofernes is dead. It doesn't matter."

"But where is Nebuchadnezzar?"

"I don't even know, Ursulines, I don't know what I told them, but I know there was a line of color in the derelict brick. A vision, and I put it there for them, where they will follow it."

"Another yellow brick road is not a bad thing. Judith, it's just a big city. I'm just a bored girl."

The corona. An aurora. A street of bricks, printing press, pamphlets. Edicts on posters in the streets. Markets stirred with cosmos. Tenements strung along laundry lines drying gold and crimson and emerald silks. Trumpets in the window behind the windblown curtain. Porches laughing. A throng of intellectuals armed with guns. Graveyards, artists' graveyards, the bones in the soil of the parks and my feet dug beneath the grass running the souls through my body and I bloomed, Ursulines, a beautiful bloom and you did not see it. Standing there with me, but you did not see the flowers of my soul adorning my aurora. My headdress. An infinite rose. You will never know. Don't give up. Don't go home.

"The city returns to us," Ursulines said. "We don't return to the city."

I left her bus that night, saying nothing else. I left buzzing with a hum constant with the rubber tires across the expressway, the gathered electricity of millions, the pipe which sloshes in chorus becomes a tiger's stripes in the bamboo of buildings. A unison. A multitude. And it did not matter if I were one or all.

10: MOBY GRAPE

That Friday night in Santa Barbara cooled down more than I expected, and I had wandered further off State Street than I should have—not lost, but cold and concerned. Drinking Las Sangres, flirting with Ursulines, as if we had not learned our lesson the first time. These events set to repeat, and me, beset with their burden. The week I spent in Paris after Levi had fled was a turning point in my life. It brought to the surface of my personality everything society dispised: a disdain for the well being of others, a nihilistic pursuit of the pleasures awake at every moment, and an inability to process the moral value of one thing over another. Paris was a magnet up against my hard drive. Erased. And I though that meant freedom.

In the face of Ursulines, everything that had brought me to Santa Barbara faded into the background, and the many lives I led prior reared upon two legs. I felt like I was the finish line of a horse race, and my memories stomped my body to bits. That next week in Paris—what of it was a dream and what of it actually occurred I set my mind to parceling out, as if everything that was taking place now depended upon it. And I walked.

The palm trees, succulent growth and red flowers didn't fool me—once I had crossed beneath Highway 101, the little of Santa Barbara that I knew was no longer. Beauty has the power to do that—fool you into thinking that everything is under control, as it should be, that you are right where you need to be. But once you have experienced the danger beneath the illusion of beauty, the utter chaos it can mask, you know better than to whistle Dixie or daydream bananas—you know you should be ready to draw.

And I, one who thought he knew better, was without my gun.

With the first Blessed Virgin Mary lawn ornament I saw, I knew that crossing under the freeway was as cliché as crossing to the other side of the tracks. If only more city planners attended Iowa Writer's Workshop. I was now in the Mission District, overgrown with citrus trees, cacti in every crevice, gorgeous plant life vibrating beneath California stars. The colorful houses were smaller, much. The postage stamp lawns were landscaped, but a homegrown landscape mixed with lawn ornaments. Taquerias on the four corners of every sleepy mainstreet intersection I passed through. The alleys a red dust slowly building across my brown leather shoes.

Confidence from a drink is not confidence at all. It is simply a skewed perspective. The eyes that were on me, beating out from the dark veil of night, were no different in my mind than those on the summer steps of my neighborhood in Chicago. When two of them moved towards me, and two more followed close behind, I did not second guess grabbing the cloth across the chest and slamming the body against the palm tree. I did not doubt that action was the only answer, and yelling like a lunatic in Spanish would transform my hands into furious power. I doubted nothing about my instincts, and I doubted less about what I couldn't know. But my screams were met with silence, the weighty silence of a crowd of bodies. When the body of the one I aggressed did not tense in my grip or shout or push, no reaction to the fear I hoped to instill, I knew right then that I had mishandled the situation, and that silence was the most confident answer of all. That I had no handle, that the handle was there for the taking. That the bat across my back would leave my body upon the ground for the beating I deserved.

And they handled me until my mind was dark with succulent night, my thoughts absent by the cold ocean breeze.

Only then did she return to me. My Parisian mistress.

11: MOBY GRAPE

As I said, after the descent of events in Biarritz I could not go home. When you see the evil inside of you, you want it to grow—it is part of the masochism which evil latches onto in the first place. A desire to inflict pain on oneself in the most glorious of ways.

During our week prior to Biarritz, I had been friendly with the man at the Tabac stand beneath our pension. Herman. His hands stained yellow by the cigarettes, black by the newspaper ink. I'd lean against the stone wall, my feet rolling into different postures on the sidewalk, talking with Herman in a way I'd only seen old men do: not a constant conversation but interjections into the silence, hemming, hawing, commenting on the life passing by and the way it bubbled up the sours and fruits of our mind into words. I returned to his stall on Rue d'Assass. We picked up where we left off: the fickleness of market shoppers. How they turn a tomato over and over again, almost rousing the bruises to life, before putting it in their tote. We drank from the endless bottle of Chôtes du Rhône he kept at his side. In a long silence, as if I were asking who won the soccer match the night before, I said, Tell me where to find a woman. And a room, I said, for the week. He replied as nonchalantly It was only a few blocks away, and there were three spots in between for a girl. I paid fifty Francs for a five Franc bottle of vodka and when I turned the corner one block away, there she was, waiting for me.

Her name was Gwynn. The shrug of her posture made her seem shorter than I; she wore flats, a shawl draped over her shoulders, a skirt shorter than my lechery could handle. I grabbed her hand, walked a block, then pushed her up against a sidestreet building, vacant except for the eyes behind the open windows beneath the chimneys. Let me look at you, I said, and she opened her eyes. Her make-up hid everything I did not want to see. Her eyes circled with liner looked elsewhere. Take me to where your eyes hide, I said. She giggled. Show me the other world which entertains you. She said no, shaking slightly her head. I nodded, and reminded her with a twenty franc note the situation. Her eyes emblazoned with a presence not pre-viously there and her hands slid down my fly, between my thighs, unzipped, her body slid down, slithering to swallow, and then I did not see her eyes for some time. I lit a cigarette.

After a few puffs, I threw it aside and lifted her up. This is what I want, right now. She shook her head no, not here. She wore no underwear and my hand slid up her thigh, my fingers encountered no resistance, and my cock bucked and urged to burst. I spread her thighs with my knee, pulled her skirt to her waist. I have always wanted this, I said, entering her. Her chin lifted back and her eyes fluttered, I bit her trembling lip. My cock had never been so hard, throbbing and satiated by her wet, tight heat. I grabbed her ass and lifted her thighs around my waist and I rocked. If there were passersby, they did not interrupt us. Passionately and slowly, I melted inside her, my cum dripping down to the sidewalk on Rue Jules Chaplain.

She stayed with me through the afternoon, naked but for the shawl she threw around her as we smoked and drank from the bottle, looking out the window. What is it you see out there? she asked. A city. A postcard? she asked. I see cracks in the stucco, window ledges about to crumble. Who do you think these people are? These people you travel so far to be near. Parisians, they're nothing but cynics. Epicurean cynics. If you were a French man you would have fucked me in the ass several times by now. Is that what you want. I have grown to like it, but no, it is not. Am I paying you enough, is this alright? I asked. I am hungry, and a tad drunk. Let's stop watching this city—let's start being it. I am not as self-conscious as all of that. When I enter you, I enter Paris, you are my portal. So serious, all this desire, let's eat. I want to want, and I want to talk to you this way. There is something unfinished in my soul that you are completing. I will never complete your desire; only tend to the flame. And her mouth smiled, but her eyes descended into the shadows. There is a place I want you to take me. We can have dinner there.

The vodka gone, dressed, we were smoking cigarettes before we were down the five flights of stairs to the street. We passed the restaurants with seafood spilling from the front door, iced and unappetizing, heading deeper into the arrondissement than I had been before. I did very little questioning over the days, caught up in the power of money, what it gave me access to. Gwynn, a room, restaurants, booze, and whatever else came my way. That she had something particular in mind did not cause me any concern. I could have cared less once she had taken my hand a block into our walk and held it with a playful grip and swing, one reserved for new lovers not a client, and I caught myself having to remember we had not fallen in love. This was her game—she was good at it.

Turning onto a dark residential street, narrow and packed with five-story, crumbling mansard-roof buildings from the days before Haussmann codified the wildernesses of Paris, we stopped. There was no way to tell that the door we entered was a place that served food and drink to the public, no awning, no sign. As if anonymous rows of two-hundred year-old buildings wavered momentarily and she saw something that I did not. That I could not. Inside there were six tables, filled with patrons. A candle at each table dimly casting light on their faces and the space around them. A bar, two stools wide. A podium between the front of the house and the purple velvet curtains hiding the back. The floors were checkered white and black. The tables were black. No one knew her, no one said her name, but we sat down as the waiter walked through the curtain and a bottle of wine was set before us. The candlelit faces smiled. That night, on the streets as well as inside, women saw something in me, something they desired. I was nothing but loose thoughts and confidence. Relaxed into Paris as if it were my authentic home. The bill for my fantasy to be sent to Levi's brother, Gil.

Our food came from the curtain, and Gwynn did all the ordering. It was summer and the fare was light: escargot in a lemon butter, braised rabbit legs in a sauce of crushed tomatoes and herbs, a strawberry crepe. Before our dinner was over, a stranger had joined us. Another woman, who at first I had thought Gwynn had ordered, because she, like everything else, came from the back of the house through the purple curtain. We were drunk, loud, loving our hilarity. The tension of our urge to have one another building in our chest. Penelope was her name. She had the air of a high dollar call girl or a royalty who was slumming it. And there was nothing between the three of us going to bed together but the cab ride back to my room.

I paid with Gil's card. It was all handled quickly.

As we left, I looked back one last time amused by the charms of the little purple and black room and for one second thrilled with myself, that here it was, my authentic night in the substance of Paris behind the tourist surfaces. Then, from behind the curtain, I saw a man move forward. Levi. Unflinching as he took me in with his eyes. Before anything could be said or a drunken reaction could occur, the girls pulled me across the door's threshold and into the taxi where our trois began its ménage.

Pretending I had not been deserted in Biarritz on that cobblestone street, I let Gwynn play Ursulines' role. But it was Penelope who swooped in and pushed me into a sexual submission I could not shake the rest of my time in Paris.

Gwynn left the next morning before I had a chance to pay her in full. When I awoke and ran out to find her, Penelope stopped me. Sweet Penelope. There is no need, she said, she's been paid. I should have known then that her appetite for self-destruction was far greater than my own, but nothing could compare to that pit of a hangover and highly illicit sex. What do you want to do, she asked, today. Are you not leaving? Not unless you want me to. Be mine, Penny. She smiled. Is it Sunday? Do you want it to be Sunday? I don't, no. Well, it's Friday then. Friday. Take me to your favorite cafe. *Oui.* Your favorite park. *Oui.* Your favorite restaurant. *Oui,* Charles. I will take you everywhere.

No one called me Charles. I must have introduced myself as such. Or she misheard me as I slurred so eloquently the night before. But for the rest of our time together I was Charles. To her friends. To the servers and bartenders. The taxi drivers. Everywhere we went she seemed to know them, whoever they were. Maybe I knew them too, but could not remember. In bed, it was Charlie, more, Charlie, there, Charlie, yes, Charlie, Charlie, Charlie.

And to her family, she introduced me as Charlie, pinching my ass as she said it. We did not mean to meet them, her family, but one night, there they were. Guy and Marrick Toussaint. In the corner table at Chez Mexique. Our waiter brought us a bottle of wine before we had a chance to order, which I was growing accustomed to, and I did not mind—whatever the cost would be paid by someone other than me. So I thought at the time. When Penelope turned the bottle towards her and saw the label, her smile was erased by a stern searching around the room for the culprit. It was a bottle of Deux Mattheau from 1988, her father's wine. They waved us over, the corner table dancing with shadows from the candle light, and we joined them for dinner.

They knew their daughter well enough to have distaste for me. That I was an American tightened their tongues and soured their expressions further. A pucker only found in Paris.

It was late, maybe ten o'clock and we had awoke only hours before, having blown cocaine until sunrise at her friend's apartment with a few others who had followed us home from the basement bar where we had spent the night drinking cooled Côtes du Rhône and dancing to the sultry beats of the dreadlocked DJ. When dawn came, we greeted the sun with champagne and oysters in the 20th arrondissement overlooking the Seine. We laughed at the morning, all those sober in its presence, but I began to feel a fear inside, as if it were coating my bones. A delirium and I could not smile anymore. When one of the men put his arms around Penelope's waist and laughed, I do not know what at, but laughed and squeezed her hips, I threw him to the ground and kicked until I realized my neck was bleeding by Penelope's nails clawing at me to stop. The sleep I had that day was not sleep at all but reverberations of self through a stone sewer of the world's defecations, dread and regret.

Unprepared to let this rise to my consciousness, I pushed it back down by blowing more of the cocaine as soon as I shook free and climbed out of bed. Hair of an entirely different dog. A hellhound. And I continued to excuse myself to do more throughout dinner. I did not think much of her parents, I had met quite a few before. I did not know that I would see them again—although the circumstances had already been defined, they would only slowly be revealed to me. I spoke with abandon, laughing, coughing, telling stories about myself that I constructed at the time of telling—lies, yes, but more so stories that entertained me, amused my drugged energies. I did not touch the tomatillo soup, the spit-roasted chili goat they ordered for me, the lavender *poisson* custard. My mental state could not be trusted. After dessert I got up one more time, but Guy grabbed me by the arm and drilled his eyes into mine. His face softer than his voice and presence let on, his skin reddened and fair, brown eyes beaming hysterically, a full mustache extending beyond the ends of his mouth, his hair parted and long but combed down. He said to me, You are an imbecile. You will die. I pulled myself away, confused and turned the corner towards the restrooms, but quickly headed back for my drink. There, beneath the eye-line of the table, between Penelope and Guy, a doll was passed, no longer than a hand, no marks of real distinction. It was not a child's toy, but more like the product of a child toymaker: rough loose stitched fabric, slightly misshapen. Guy slipped it into his interior jackleg pocket, and I saw the x-ed out eyes. It was strange enough to stop me from approaching any closer. Enough to convince me to walk out the door of the restaurant and make my way back to the street where I was staying.

I slumped against the stone wall and slid to the ground. I had simply left, not saying anything, abuzz with cocaine, awash with wine. And there was Herman, in the window across the street from where I sat on the sidewalk. There was a throwback pinball machine in the cafe, Eight-Ball Deluxe, and he was playing it intensely focused, throwing his hips into the machine, watching the ball bang around the bumpers and be slapped by the flippers, up ramps and into holes, pausing for a minute and then shooting back out into the never-ending rebound of gravity's hold and Herman's control.

I saw he had a cup of wine and I got up, entering, approaching him as if he were simply at the Tabac stand, a waitress brought me a glass and a carafe, Herman paying my entrance into his night little attention, and again, like old men, nonplussed I watched him play pinball and made comments most of which he did not respond to, sipping wine until I found it in me to approach sleep. I left but Herman stayed behind, above that game, the same game he was playing when I entered, never once having let the ball fall through the flippers.

Two days of depression later, there she was again. Ready to take me to a party. More cocaine in hand and a dress that rose a devil's flame up my throat. Penelope. What were you doing to me? What world did you begin?

12: MOBY GRAPE

The room I woke up in was blurry at best. Hardly able to squeeze a sight with my eyes, I was drowning in a *thrump, thwack, thrump*. The source of the thrumping, the thwack melody I heard, and the fat baritone wheeze, a man surely thrice my size. Intended, I am sure, to be a soft peaceful croon, my head hurt and this song came upon me like a garage full of baboons drowning in liquid mice. Unsure if liquid mice did or did not exist, I breathed in deeply, yet not so deep as to notify my assailants that I was awake, and I fought through the thud and delirium to remember where I went wrong. The palm trees, the night, the kumquats I grabbed from that tree and ate, the eyes, my impotent gripping of a man whose face I couldn't see. Had I attacked them or had they attacked me? I recalled a paranoid hatred, and felt its remnants floating around in the acids of my stomach, but I could not pinpoint what had caused it. The sounds of the room came clearer to me and I recognized it to be the thrumping polka-style base of Mariachi music—I knew I must still be in the Mission District of Santa Barbara.

There was no one else in the room besides this musician, a hulk of a man, and needing to know how deep I was in, I took my chances on pulling some information out of this fella—sometimes the big guys are the sweetest.

So I said, "*Amigo, yo no sé lo que pasó. Juegas música bien*—can you tell me what happened, *por favor*?"

He grunted mid-pluck, pushed his giant guitar off his belly onto the couch, stepped over to me and thudded his fist across my head. Knocking me back into black.

13: MOBY GRAPE

It was a glamorous night, that last night with Penelope. She led me to a stunning mansion, a gala which I had no business being at, except I had impressed a young, rich Parisian with my ability to speak from the grave. Penelope had purchased a black suit for me that day—"like a gangster would wear," she told me. On our way I asked about Penelope's daddy, Guy Toussaint. He had grown powerful in the wine industry through selling France's ancient vines to California wineries—skyrocketing the fame of his wine and casting much influence across Napa, Calistoga, and Santa Barbara. Though many looked down upon him for his abuse of stalks authentic to French land and culture, he had no trouble filling a room. Monsieur Toussaint disguised his societal failings with the garb of aristocrats, statesmen, priests, movie producers, and sycophants.

Cocktailing on the veranda with all the beautiful artists and smokers, out of the corner of my eye, I saw a red dress being led through the door, back inside to the party. Blonde hair. Ursulines. My head spun and mid-sentence I exited the conversation. Excusing myself, I went first for Penelope. Kissed her, right in front of her father, and led her away. How could it not have been Ursulines, such grace, blonde curls, an exquisite figure outlined in red. We walked through the entrance hall and up the coiling marble staircase. Many turned to watch our spectacle. The venom that was in me then, if I only knew. Penelope saw it in my eyes and once we were in the bathroom she began undressing before I could spread the lines of cocaine. She took the vile from my hands, leaned back across the counter and sprinkled a pile on each of her breasts. I indulged, undid her bra, and gave a flick to each nipple with my tongue. She smiled viciously—her lips took control of her body and mine. As I pulled her panties down her soft thighs, she dabbled the cocaine into her nose with her fingernail and then pinched a mound atop the smooth skin above her clit. I licked it. She moaned. She did it again, my licks grew wetter and longer. To hear a French girl moan is to lose yourself in absolute pleasure and I would do anything that it asked of me. My heart beat loudly through my body.

Several times there was a knock on the door. Penelope did not quiet. After she came, before she could stop me, I drove my cock through her wet lips, eliciting cries which no doubt caused the butler to turn the volume up downstairs. The deep kiss she gave me as I came, her tongue wholly in my mouth, the only thing that kept me from shouting her name at the top of my lungs. As if she knew the name on my tongue would not be hers.

Returning to the party down the grand staircase, my arm around Penelope's waist, I squeezed her hip, trying hard to hold onto something other than my fantasy of Ursulines. Waiting for her to turn around, I heard my name—it was Penelope's father greeting us at the bottom of the staircase with the look of a man who has killed for less. He confronted me, and I felt her disappear from my side.

"Trash like you deserves a proper receptacle," no matter how much anger his words expressed, he spoke in a charming and aloof tone, a manner of intense detachment that only a Parisian can affect. As if we were caught up in a lifelong dispute that amused but no longer interested him.

"It is not my intention to insult you," wanting to be done with this nonsense quickly—my eyes still searching out her red dress.

"Class is not something your kind comes by naturally," Monsieur Toussaint continued. "But I will be happy to, as they say, school you."

"It is neither mine nor my kind's fault that you sexualize your daughters so fantastically, Monsieur." The wit of my coke-numb tongue unleashed. No matter how much it smart, he never left his post atop the totem.

"Is it too soon to ask if you can feel my thumbs digging into your temples?"

"If you mean your shit wine to be an extension of your thumbs, than no, my head already aches with every sip."

He raised his left arm, and simply snapped his fingers. A gesture which bespeaks a power I have desired my entire life. And with that sound came pain. Two giant claws—one at my neck and one around my wrist, bringing my arm against my back—squeezed. And I buckled. Only to be lifted by another, carried out into the streets of Montparnasse, beaten to a squid-like pile in a puddle of my own piss on Rue de Lapin. Bunny Street. Even then I laughed.

8: IN THE PENAL COLONY

In the alleys there are no street names, no numbers. I often became lost while searching for Brain Dead Fred and the Graffiti Girls. Surely that's what the riddle in the floss meant: the girls are not twins because they are triplets. As too were the Graffiti Girls.

The holes worn through my shoes I was not of the mind to repair. The seepage of alley liquids and muck—I could feel them entering my body through the bottoms of my feet. The cold and sweet corridors of my recently obliviated neural circuitry tasting across my tongue. Though I did not know how, nor where to, my old blood exited. A transfusion taking place as I walked along the cobbled stones, considered the weeds and vines sprouting in the cracks. A communion between my body and this maze. Maize. Minotaur. Twins. Dentists.

Many residents used ivy as a last layer of defense between their home life and the terrors of the city, as well as to ward off the freakish acrobats who had recently, from what I could tell, taken up residence in the canopy of trees which Wicker Park was known for. One stretch of alley, which grew larger by the day, had been covered by ivy in its entirety. The backs of the buildings and the garages, the telephone poles and the trash bins, all gorged by a thick wavering layer of green wilderness. You could watch it grow, stretch, engulf more and more. Four or five blocks long, with tentacles reaching out at different lengths down the intersecting alleys. Brain Dead Fred surely would emerge from this jungle.

High up in its vines one could see the petrified bodies the ivy had recently abducted. If one were to lean unknowingly, or sit upon a garbage bin, or squat while relieving oneself, then the ivy quickly slithered and swallowed one whole. Victims of the tension between sidewalk and alley, face and ass, social reason and nomadic fancy.

I knew Brain Dead Fred through some past research I had done into the power of color over the mind's ability to make rational decisions. It was for a series of riddles I was hard at work on—The Psychedelic Simple—where the goal was to confuse the participant through distractions when confronted with the simplest of questions. An example: *If Jack met Jill in the underworld and the underworld was one of their homes and Jack was homeless, then which of them came tumbling after?* Brain Dead Fred helped me develop the ritualistic color wheel which would spin in front of them, along with the purple backdrop—we found purple to be the most inhibiting color—which the interviewer draped over the ladder which he himself, or herself, stood upon when speaking the riddle.

Some say that Brain Dead Fred gathered up his crew in order to create a portal in between realms of being, but I knew for a fact that the Graffiti Girls searched out Fred and employed him as a shaman for deep spiritualistic, as well as symbolic, reasons. They needed him, almost as a sacrifice, to weight and balance the other side of sanity, so they could pursue their street art in mental peace.

They had set up in a garage somewhere in the alleys of Ukrainian Village, a subsection of the area the Wolf had laid out for the grounds of my riddle. I had stumbled upon them many times before, but never could I remember their exact location. After three hours of wondering through the maze of space behind the buildings, they finally made themselves known to me.

The alley I was walking intersected with another, and ahead of me at the nexus of the T which was formed, I saw a spectacle of color in every direction and in every dimension. As I came closer, a humming could be heard, growing louder and warmer until I stood in the middle of it. I could not see the sources of this chorus, but I began to distinguish the hissing and rattling of spray cans in harmony with the hum. All around me the work of the Graffiti Girls could be seen. Huge bubbling letters morphed into urban bodies of joy; streaks of line work revealed a marginalized sorrow. Battles between outrageous style and subdued subservience were depicted in the forms of electronic buildings bursting color at the windows, trains slithering through tunnels which began at the mouth of barbaric faces, bicycles leaping over canyons filled with severed limbs holding ghetto blasters and laptops. It was as if electrified sugar took shape and played the most artistic and savvy games across the garages and buildings' rear walls.

And then I began to see them. Not representations and caricatures of eyes, but real eyes—human eyes. Staring at me. Blinking. Beneath these eyes, I recognized the broad shoulders, the extension of muscular arms, the cup of stuffed bras, the Adam's apples. Suddenly, in unison, the shoulders jerked, and standing there only a step away from the majestic walls were the postured bodies of the three Graffiti Girls.

The humming morphed into harmony and beat. Their bodies bounced and struck elegant poses. Their tune became grittier and their postures reached for a more machismo perversion. Like sultry vultures, I thought at the time, they began circling nearer to where I stood in awe.

Whereas my body could not find rhythm, my mind danced eagerly along with them. In full bloom, music and body and the art they never ceased exploring upon these city walls.

In a bejeweled robe of Technicolor trash and decay, Brain Dead Fred spun into existence atop the nearest building's ledge.

The stark rhythmic movements of the Graffiti Girls ceased, and their sweet and precocious manner was unveiled. They sat down their spray cans and curtseyed as if in dresses. Their steps became classical and trained as if guided by piccolo and viola. They giggled to each other at the tricks of Brain Dead Fred, and made way to the nearest paint-covered dumpster.

Brain Dead Feed spun again, swirling out his cape and then disappeared from atop the building. The Graffiti Girls leaped in unison, then began to open the dumpsters. One at a time, they threw the lid open, then the next pair. This game went on as the playful nerves built up within them and a spring could be seen in their bounce, until all but one dumpster had been opened. They quickly gathered around it and the lid flew open. A huge billow of blue smoke spilled forth, green and gold sparkles shot out in every direction with a bang. Chairs, pillows, milk cartons, cigarette packets, blouses and pizza boxes flew out and rained upon us, but before striking our heads, disappeared with a poof. The music of the Graffiti Girls' giddiness crescendoed as a deep barreling laughter could be heard from within—arms outspread, robe removed, in the garb of a sophisticated hobo Brain Dead Fred levitated out from the garbage bin and landed in the midst of the Graffiti Girls. Brimmed hat, beard, tattered brown suit and leather shoes, curly dark hair down to his waist.

"My girls, my girls—it is wonderful to see you. Your youth, really it does, it pleases me how you show it off—ostentatious! But I know your old spirits spit upon the yachters and the yoke—I do I do."

One of the girls spoke up, "Fred. We need more orange."

"More orange?"

"For the wig."

And another, "Fred, we've gone too far up and need to compensate a little by going down."

"Go down, dimples, go down."

"Fred, the Germans called and want their *lederhosen* back."

"Fred, the city night sky is being colored by birds which we cannot rescue."

"Fred, the Ivy has grown proportionate to the day's length."

"Is it approaching our bunkers?"

In unison: "Yes."

"Do our colors run?"

"No."

"Well, we will prepare for battle. Race your gorgeous art towards the plaque of the spawning vines—when the graffiti meets the ivy, the battle will be to death or dimension."

In unison: "To death or dimension. Yeah!"

"Your Freddie-pie will take care of all the rest. Now excuse me, we have a visitor."

The Graffiti Girls shouldered and swayed back to their work.

"Manasses, Manasses, Manasses, Manasses, Manasses, Manasses, Manasses, Manasses."

"Yes, Fred."

"Manasses, Manasses, Manasses, Manasses, Manasses, Manasses."

"Fred, Fred, Fred, Fred, Fred."

"Manasses, Manasses, Manasses, Manasses, Manasses."

"Oh, Fred, Fred, Fred."

"Manasses, Manasses, Manasses."

"Fred."

"Manasses. Man—asses!"

"Yes."

"So nice of you to join us."

"I appreciate you making yourself available to me."

"I know you've been hard at work, Manasses. Don't think that I have forgotten."

"You haven't forgotten?"

"I forget nothing."

"Super. That helps me."

"Are you sure?"

"The thing is: I have forgotten."

"Forgotten what?"

"What it is you just said you have not said."

"Not what?"

"Not forgotten."

"I have forgotten nothing, Manasses."

"Good."

"And this is what you wish to discuss?"

"Yes, I believe it is."

"Good. Where should we begin?"

We strolled towards a couch which appeared shoved up against the building.

"At the beginning would help me most."

"Has any of it ended yet?"

"Ended? I do not think so."

They sat down.

"Then I must confess, Manasses, you amuse me. What of beginnings if there is no end?"

"Exactly."

"Is it yet to be determined then, the beginning, which is beneficial to you no doubt."

"Interesting."

"We shall begin at our own beginning and see what light sheds forth."

"Let me ask you, Fred. Are you here?"

"Here? Yes. No."

"There is nothing helpful here—only continuation."

"Don't worry about nothing, Manasses, because nothing is alright."

"All right. Really?"

"Yes. So you must worry about everything because everything is not."

"Then tell me everything."

"Such as?"

"What brought you here?"

"Have you forgotten my entrance—the smoke, the fireworks?"

"No."

"Well, then, what is it that you mean?"

"I mean to this location, to this city."

"A nice question to stir an afternoon chat. Let's sink in—relax, Manasses, for there is a beginning beginning and we do not want it to escape us."

"Yes, from the beginning."

"You know I was born to a mother in the grips of the 1960s. She fed me her milk, which was laced with the hallucinogens she consumed. So my first steps felt more like lift-offs, into the clouds, because I was very fond of clouds, and my first words were equivalent to the words of the biblical God. The one God. God, they called it. I said radish and yes there appeared a radish. I said blue and the vegetable was blue. I said there are three dozen eggs beneath my bottom and snap! What a mess. I was a heavy boy, though I do believe that life in the streets has treated me well around the waist.

"It was all in Montana. A small town by the name of Anaconda. My mother, let us call her Sunset, she raised me as if she were a pack of wolves incarnate. I was a feral child and the hills of that great vast land were my pillows, the rivers my teet. Many discussed the personhood of my father. I hoped I had been born by a divine intervention, a star and moon space child conception between my mother and Sun Ra. But no, the locals decreed I was the bastard child of fiction extraordinaire Richard Brautigan. With all this on my mind one day I went for a walk. A new home jumped out and scared me, for this was a walk I had often taken through the wilderness and no home was previously there. I peered around it and saw a cliff behind which fell into a gorgeous river. I raced home and prepared my fishing gear, all the while dreaming of the succulent spectacle of trout which must be that river. When I returned the next day, peering behind the new home in the wilderness, I realized that what I saw to be a river was now the long climb up a woman's green skirt. Wretched as this was, I looked up to what I had always known to be the vast wilderness of blue, blue sky and no, the sky I realized was not a sky but Richard Brautigan eyeing me as if I lived underwater, squinting and casting his fly, which I grabbed above my head and he reeled me up.

"Richard Brautigan held me tight and brought me up to his face. He said, 'Son.' I said, 'Yes.' He said, 'Swallow the fly.' I said, 'What about the line it is attached to?' He said, 'It will do you good.' I swallowed the fly to catch the chicken and swallowed the chicken to catch the kitten and swallowed the kitten to catch the moose but why did I swallow the fly?"

"I do not know why."

"I had a terrible time trying to enunciate my words with that fish line across my tongue but I said, 'Dad,'—here, I'll hold my tongue so you get the full effect—'Dad. Are you Sun Ra?' He did not answer, only twisted at his broad, twirling mustache and placed me in his wonderful woven Coleman brand nylon strapped basket with a bamboo trimmed lid. And he shut the lid.

"When the lid reopened, it had been some time. A

cloud carried me forth and set me on the ground. I did not know my age but looking at my environment I began to theorize that my age manifested not in my body but in the form of large rectangular blocks of heavy stone. I saw the various sizes of these blocks and knew I was not alone. Sure enough, millions of others were nearby, though none of them paid me any mind, nor offered me any of their fancy city clothes.

"Dressed in overalls, few welcomed my advances for friendship but one. Chicken Bill. Young and impressionable, I allowed him to take me under his wing. An elder if there ever was. He showed me the nonsensical thrills of food and shelter and he taught me the fantastic spectacle of pulling pranks on the unsuspecting populace.

"You know Carol and Kevin, right? Carol's the ambulance driver. Kevin's the bike guy with a spoke tattooed on his shlong. He's friends with Vicky the one who looks like a lesbian but is not. Chicken Bill was friends with all them and others before I even came around. He was known well around this neighborhood. He had a song that he would sing to tell his story:
'The day that I was born
My mother said to me
Be cute and be cuddly
And live far from the city
I took the world's advice
And the world took fine with me
It gave me all sorts of chickens
Which I cared for and kept pretty
Then the train came down the line
And I heard it cry for me

So I gathered up my chickens
And I hopped on towards the city
Once I arrived downtown
And began to walk the streets
I had the most curious thoughts
And met people who helped me see
My chickens pecked and gawked
And my friends gave me LSD
I tore up my ticket home
And I set my chickens free!'

"So Chicken Bill and I, we played our pranks and drank a lot and walked these streets and I began to disappear. Really, the strangest thing, I would be lying in the park at night, and I would wake up to Chicken Bill saying, Fred, Fred, where'd you go? Suddenly, I'd realize I was up in the tree. Above him. And I'd drop down and scare him.

"Other times we'd be walking in the alleys, and Bill would lose sight of me and sure enough I'd find myself walking above him on the rooftops. It began to become a riff between us when I'd reappear in people's apartments. They'd chase me out and I'd run to find Bill, but he would look at me disgusted for abandoning him.

"So I began to learn better the whys and whens of my disappearance and soon enough I could sense it coming on. When I finally got good enough at this, I decided I would see if I could make Bill disappear with me. On that historic day, Bill and I were sitting on a fire escape, lobbing eggs over the building so that they landed on the sidewalk people. I knew I was about to go and so I grabbed Bill's hand.

"We reappeared, no longer on the fire escape, but

impossible to distinguish where. I wondered if we were anywhere. Then Chicken Bill began to speak, softly and close to my ear:

'Fred, do you hear it? I know you hear it. Those squawks are my very own.

Where are we, Fred? My chickens, do you see them? They are coming this way. They

are flailing towards us. There's more than I remember, Fred. So many more. Get away!

Get! Scram, chickens. You stink. Your feathers, get them away from our faces. Leave

us be. Stop circling us, stop circling. All these chickens. Home to roost.'

"And then we were strapped down, their claws around our wrists and ankles. Suffocatingly comfortable in a soft, soft bed.

"And then we heard our names: Fred, Bill. Fred, Bill. It's me. It's Manasses. I have another one for you. It begins with an old blue tick hound. Fred. Bill. Do you want to hear it? It's me, Manasses. Okay. So how many raccoons does a blue tick hound tree if there are thirty in the county and six other blue tick hounds have treed sixteen and this blue tick hound has never treed more than ten in a night but has mistakenly been duped by three raccoons who jumped from the tree into the creek and double-backed so the hounds lost their scent and there is only three raccoons left besides the ones already caught?"

"I'll think about that, Manasses, while you take your turn."

"It's my turn?"

"Yes, you said Two-Players, right?"

"I said blue tick hounds."

"Ms. Pac Man."

Staring at the screen in the laundromat, the first intermission: "They Meet." But when they fled off the screen, a riddle pixelated in orange letters: *How do you make an egg roll?*

"Well, I'll think about that riddle while I play my turn."

"Alright, Fred." How could I both concentrate on this game and think through such a troubled tale?

"Just push it." Someone was talking to me.

"Look there—push it. Touch it. And push," said an elderly woman surrounded by fourteen Treasure duffel bags packed full of her personal items.

"Push it!" Someone yelled.

I looked around. I was on the bus. The driver stared me down in his rearview mirror and yelled again, "Just push the goddamned door!"

I pushed; the hydraulic door mechanically opened and before I stepped onto the sidewalk, I looked back toward the threshold and was reassured: there a knot held taut of the miles of floss I had woven in my search. I plucked it just in case, then feared I had alerted the spider who held court across this web.

"Step off the motherfucking bus!"

And I did.

14: MOBY GRAPE

It wasn't so intimate when I woke up again. No grating music—just the low chatter of Spanish and the smell of chorizo and eggs. I've never been able to stand the smell of chorizo—that churned up pig offal saturated with bold and zesty grease. Tied into a chair, albeit a cushy one, I jerked to heave up the contents of my stomach, but could not budge and bile spilled from my mouth down my shirt. Nobody moved, nobody yelled—I heard one high-pitched snicker, but that was the only reaction in the room. Woozy and winded, the room began to take shape before me. Six heads on the couches and chairs, two bodies back and forth between this room and the kitchen. No sunlight came in through the windows, and I was uncertain if it was still night or if day had broke. Something wasn't right. I had a lot to learn. Nobody was acknowledging my presence—no *good morning*, no *rise and shine*, no *coffee is on sweetheart*—so I decided to take up a little more space in that already small room. What did I have to lose.

"*Donde esta mi masacuata?! Dame mi masacuata! No quiero nada pero mi pene y mi corazon y mi esposa!*"

I heard that same snickering again—this little guy and I were already starting to hit it off. "*Tenemos un cabron.*"

"*Este puto no puedo soportar las drogas.*"

I yelled again this time in English: "Give me my donkey dick. I want my donkey dick and my wife. Did my wife cut off my dick?"

As I have said, I learned my Spanish in the kitchens of Chicago.

The talking stopped, but nobody got up, until a mustachioed, dark-eyed man wearing a white undershirt and a red apron walked slowly out from the kitchen grinning. It was Umberto.

"Very good, Senior Yeager. But we already knew you spoke Spanish like a five-year-old—you wouldn't keep quiet last night when we were fucking you in the *culo*."

At this the room erupted in laughter—punctuated by several Mexican yelps. Mexican men, I have found, live for gay humor.

"*Se duele su culo, Yeager? La masacuata de* Camarillo had you crying for mama."

So the big bass playing friend of mine's name was Camarillo. He sat there looking crazed, his head a large egg not even cracking a smile.

"You've come a long way, Umberto. Did you have a horse race scheduled?"

Another jumped on my shoulders and began bucking. "Remember my brother, Roberto? He'll ride you to the finish line." I was serving them lobs and they were spiking them down my throat.

"I tell you what, you stay quiet and enjoy yourself over there, and we will take you where you need to go. But if you keep acting like a shit, you might miss *Señor* Seeds' big party. Now he wouldn't want that, would he *amigos*?"

At this they erupted in Mexican yelps as if choreographed, lifted up their instruments—guitars, horns, tuba, and accordion—and broke into song. The only thing I can't stomach more than chorizo is Mariachi music. My head swelled until, again, I threw up. Blood-like bile—the juice from the grapes squeezed by the power and fortunes of Levi Seeds. I shut my eyes before Camarillo got up and shut them for me. And I wondered how I would survive this mess. These Mariachis knew *Señor* Seeds better than I did.

Umberto threw a black suit across my lap, and they all began to get dressed—no discretion, stripping to their underwear right in front of me. Such elaborate and effeminate costumes—the jewels of the rodeo. Silver thread, elaborately trimming every seem, tassels dangling limp, large hats as if it were the Derby—I wanted to deck each one of them and break their nose with my knee. They polished their brass instruments, tuned their misshapen guitars, and as I waited for them to untie me so I could dress, I realized how death can enter a room and sulk until it has its way.

I heard the snickering Mariachi behind me and felt the tension loosen from my wrists. Camarillo was quick to serve the function of the rope, interjecting his meaty limbs between my arms and chest.

15: MOBY GRAPE

As Camarillo held tight, they stripped me to my underwear, then dressed me in a black suit. I noticed a blood stain on the lapel—it was the same suit I wore with Penelope the night of her father's party. It was my blood. A quick retie of my wrists and I was thrown in the trunk of their Prius Hybrid. I did not expect that, chuckling to myself about my friend Levi and where he chose to express his Kabbalah ethics.

"Do not laugh," came a voice as it sat down in the backseat.

"Funny outfit you guys got. If I didn't know you were such man-handlers, I'd have no doubt you were *jotos* driving this car."

The trunk opened up. A leg came crashing down upon my gut.

"Monsieur Seeds wont appreciate a guest in a dirty suit."

"*Callate, puto.*"

I wondered if she missed me at El Prado Inn. I wondered if I she would charge me the regular rate. Surely, they'd understand how my weekends in Santa Barbara tended to unfold: drugged by a sexy woman from my past, a band of Mariachi's waiting to clean up her mess, abduct me and torture me with their nauseating music, humor and culinary skills. I could hear her sweet voice, "Mr. Yeager, of course, this isn't the first time such a turn of events kept you away from us for a night. Please come back and we will have your regular room ready."

I was getting giddy as we sped down Highway 101.

Past exhaustion, past confusion or regret—I felt that I was nearing a life-defining event, as if what was to come had been reaching back to me for so long, guiding me and tripping me upon its course. An inevitable future was sure to make itself known. And my carrier to this dramatic event was a clown car stuffed with Mariachis. Screw wisdom, screw cunning—there was no running away from what was about to play out. So I resigned myself to the occasion, and prayed for a bottle's worth of California wine, another pretty woman at my hip. Buckling myself in for the ride.

We were far from Santa Barbara when the car began to slow down. Sliding around in the hatchback trunk, I knew we were maneuvering switchbacks and I could hear the moment we went from asphalt to gravel beneath the tires. We finally straightened out, the roads got rougher, and we stopped. The whole ride, Michael Jackson's greatest hits blaring on the car stereo. I could have vomited, but that's the plus-side of an empty gut when one keeps company like this.

I heard another car pull up behind us as the band piled out. But they left me. And I waited. My normal self would have pounded and screamed, drawing attention to my predicament, hoping some innocent others would come to my rescue. But I did not want to be rescued; I was there for a show, and so patiently I waited. It wasn't long before the trunk opened. Just long enough for me to decide to kick the first face I saw. Or at least try—my leg nowhere near long enough to make contact, resulting instead in my body squeamishly rolling to the ground. That's when I knew I was right about being on gravel.

"Get up you schmuck." That was not the voice of a Mariachi. I looked over. A python stared me down. Placed decoratively at the tip of the black and silver, snake-skin boots. Black pants led my eyes to a black jacket, gold buttons, a white shirt, and a gold bolo around the neck, the threads decorated with turquoise beads. His face roughened as if he had stood in the desert winds for centuries, his eyes coal black, his lips like the eternal snake eating its tail, black hair greased down and gleaming in the sun. A jarring sight, to see a man native to the earth's myth, this land, as if his bloodline had no beginning—it only met with ends. My end, certainly. I could only guess: here was Ruben Rorick.

Down from the horizon he had been staring at, he looked at me, saying nothing. His eyes were not black at all, but a turquoise glowing fiercely like the stones around his neck. He struck a fear in me standing there, like a jaguar about to pounce, outlined by the utter blueness of wine country sky.

"You got my messages," Ruben said.

"They've brought me this far. I'm hoping you can tell me what I need to know, and send me back on my way."

"He needs your help. But he didn't want to ask you."

"I've got plenty of work—estranged hobos, heartless musicians, sex-crazed daughters—all with wealthy family. I don't usually take cases gratis."

"You read the book? Levi thought you would find it years ago."

"I found your card—was their more to it?"

"So much more to it. I go to the trouble of having my nephew—now dead nephew—deliver the book to your apartment and you do not read it. This won't unfold as we need it to."

"Can you give me the synopsis?"

"Life does not have short-cuts. We are here because so many are losing their lives, and your old friend, your dear old friend is losing his soul with every successful kill."

"What do you mean kill?"

"You didn't read the book. You will suffer its fate nonetheless. Go now, and see."

He handled me—picked me up and set me down. Dusted me off. Straightened my clothes. Then pointed with a grunt down a hill. Beneath a magnificent oak tree, the guests had gathered. White seats waiting to be filled, flowers laid in bunches across the grass, the Mariachi's were playing, stoic as ever. In every direction, long rolling hills striped with vines. I was standing in the middle of the most gorgeous setting I had ever seen. Las Sangres Vineyard.

Levi's wedding was about to start.

I walked the dirt road and cut through a row of grapes down to where everyone was waiting for the ceremony to begin. The vines were woven through six strings strung across wooden posts, fruit dangling in its infancy. The gnarly stalks knuckled at the many shoots which had been the source of past years vines. The utter care which these plants were handled—meticulous as if the farmer was under the illusion that his fingers handled god's gold, filigreed and adorning the earth. Only then did I notice that this was not earth that I was on—no rich soil. This was sand. I had traveled enough of Europe's vineyards to know that sand could not grow grapes as celebrated as

Las Sangres. But I too knew Levi—the one winemaker who would spit on Europe and plant his crop in thin air if only to prove a Frenchman wrong.

Ruben followed me as I walked. He shook his head and pointed again to the oak tree. Where did he think I would run off to? I had no idea where I was, marooned in the middle of these farmed hills. I gave myself five more steps to take in the beauty of this scene, and then I turned my attention to the troubles at hand, and began scanning the crowd for familiar faces. Facing the mid-afternoon sun, every face disguised by sunglasses—I would have to get closer. There was a bar set off to the side and so I stepped over for a drink, more just to suck on the ice, although the booze wouldn't hurt. I got a drink and took a spot in the crowd, feeling out of place for not having sunglasses, but laughed at how youthful I felt to be back in this black suit. Surely Levi had been at Monsieur Toussaint's house that night as well.

Someone to my left said, "Look," and the crowd turned in unison towards the top of the nearest hill where a red four-wheeler came flying down. It was the groom. He was followed by four others, cruising through the rows of grapes, descending upon the crowd who let out a collective awe. Bringing up the rear, a luxury golf cart, red and trimmed with rhinestones—surely they were not diamonds—with six seats for the bride and bridesmaids. A playful entrance, and I could feel the spirit of the crowd lift as they all laughed and remarked how impressive. Or maybe it was the first drops of booze in my veins, pulsing through my body. This was too much, and at that moment I knew every theory I had conceived so far was all wrong.

Though I could sense that Levi's blood ran cold, this wedding had nothing to do with me. I grabbed another drink before the ceremony and settled in.

At that moment I wanted to see the bride's face—to know how elaborate this prank was. I relished the chance that it would be Ursulines.

They parked the four-wheelers down the road a little, hidden by the vines. The crowd gathered upon the seats in the cool shade of the far-reaching oak, listening to the Mariachi's, smiling, chatting. It had been many years since I had kept company as debonair as this. I stood on the side in a small crowd with no one I recognized.

Levi and the groomsmen began making their way down the aisle. The first two I did not know, or at least did not remember—all of this, my friendship with Levi, had been another life for me—-then Ruben Rorick, my disgruntled suitor. I was startled to see the bridesmaids faces as they waited behind—each of them Mexican. Most likely not Ursulines' company. The Mariachi's switched to "Here Comes the Bride," and the Bride made her entrance. A veil down in front of her face, I could not see who it was, if I knew her. I badly wanted it to be Ursulines—it would make all my worries disappear, everything would be simpler, nothing besides a wedding renewing a couple's devotion and some strange violent coincidences would be taking place. Something I could later laugh about as I renewed my friendship with Levi. Just as badly as I wanted it to be her, I prayed that she was not in attendance if it wasn't—her presence would be her demise.

It took me a minute to recognize the officiant, and it hit hard when I did. Gil Seeds, Levi's brother. He dressed eccentrically: a beige, gray, and green plaid polyester suit, a light yellow button-up covered by a thickly double windsor purple and green paisley tie, a long face when he stared, yet exuberant when he smiled, diminutive metal-rimmed glasses, cordovan shoes and paisley socks matching his tie.

Bride and groom hand-in-hand, the music stopped and the ceremony commenced. As Gil waxed poetically about love, I studied Levi. The gentleman next to me was doing the same.

"He looks good." I looked over to see a very short man with freckles staring at me.

"Wish I kept my youth like he has," I replied.

"Though I'm not sure that's his natural hair color."

"It's obvious that he has put some money into lotioning his face."

"Who knows—maybe the California sun has been good to him."

"Better than Chicago has been to me."

"You live in Chicago?"

"I do."

"My wife is from Chicago. Small world."

"Right."

"My name is Chris Park, been friends with Levi for almost a decade."

"Chris, nice to meet you. Look, I don't think Levi has smiled yet."

"Not the face of a man in love—and I know, happily married for seven years. You?"

"Not even close."

"When he was young, Levi was a romantic."

"He looks terribly sober—has he turned to Buddhism?"

"Levi? Kabbalah is as far East as he goes."

"He seems very distant."

"Look beneath his eyes—like a hound dog."

The rhetoric of Gil's sermon raised, as if he knew there were some of us not listening. Not the typical vagaries about love and how it could save the soul. He spoke of the difficulties, the struggle of staying together. This was a man embittered.

"It is not simply said today. Love is something that falls apart on its surface as often as it comes together in beauty. That is why I say to you: Do not trust the surface. We must feed the depths. Do not diagnose the health, the strength of your love based on the surfaces it shows. Instead stay connected with the core of the earth and all the power that extends from there. Let your blood spill into the depths. Into the desires. Your passion for each other is the passion that the earth has for you. The depth. The desire.

"And we must remember the individuality of our souls. It is not that these two come together so that we can forget who they were—two become one and still that one needs to gratify the powers of the two, the separate. And to know that each of you will change, and your reasons for living will change. Like the tide greeting the shore, rise your hearts to meet the earth. The oak tree. The sand in the soil. The body in love."

I immediately looked over to Ruben who was looking inside of me. I knew now why I was here. This was a sacrifice, not a wedding. Levi Seeds gave new meaning to cult vineyards.

"You know many people here?" I asked Chris.

"No. I'm in accounting—rarely get out of the office."

"Neither do I. Maybe all this success has begun to take its toll on our friend here."

"The wine isn't the only red he's seeing."

"Really?"

"And looks like some Feds are setting up camp in Buellton."

I decided to play it as if I knew something. "Things like this always catch up with a man."

"I told him: let me come out and take care of your finances, but every time I offered he yelled at me, as if insulted."

I decided to bluff, "Well you know about the other thing, don't you?"

"Yes, I've always known, so it's not like he is hiding something from me."

"And now the Feds. Christ."

"Not for that, are you kidding? That would sooner stir a war than an investigation."

"Right—Levi would be hanging from this tree."

"Don't curse a man on his wedding day." And he nudged me, with a smile, in my side, winked and began to giggle.

I faked a chuckle and smiled knowingly as he said, "You've been to one of these before, right?"

"I used to attend quite a few."

His expression shifted quizzically. "One of Levi's weddings? Or do you mean the blood rituals?"

I was speechless. Chris carried on. "Don't you always wonder how great the sex is? To fuck right befor you die has go to be one of the greatest ecstasies a human has available."

I paused, trying to follow—trying not to let on that I had no idea what he was talking about. And then I said it—risked as much as I could think because his answer would change everything. "But Ursulines wouldn't go for that."

"She's no angel. I wouldn't be surprised to see La Sangre de Ursulines in a year or two." And my stomach retched, twisted and re-retched a hollow scream. Chris Park, you gossipy bastard, I almost vomited atop your freckled face.

The vows were read, the rings were exchanged, and Levi finally lifted the veil to kiss the bride. As they turned towards the congregation, I saw her smile: a Mexican girl no older than eighteen years. Looking around, I saw the only jaw that dropped was my own. The Mariachi's struck up. And the bride and groom exited, followed by the wedding party. It was announced that we should follow them down the road to the pond where the reception would be held. How many wives did Levi Seeds have?

9: IN THE PENAL COLONY

I stepped off and met a large crowd of bodies circling in a parking lot, coming in and out of China Dragon and Main Street Liquors. They milled around, mumbling, yelling at anybody near. I stared at their faces, muscles loosely in control of the expressions, the skin around their eyes wrinkled loose and hanging, lower jaws weighed low and flapping, exposing claw hammer teeth and swollen dark gums.

One man approached the edge of the parking lot where I stood, his body shaking and twisting as if it were numb from slamming into walls, his head did not budge as if it were being held in place as his limbs and abdomen flailed around trying to shake free of the grip. He lifted his arms about to grab me, yelling "Man, forty years. I can't do it. I can't do it." I stepped out of his path as he continued to approach what he had once seen. Across the parking lot, I walked towards a woman in loose, torn sweatpants stumbled, her t-shirt barely covering her breasts pounded thin, and whispered into my ear, "With a sucker, you give him nothing. A sucker is just a sucker. Sucker."

Voices drifted back and forth. I passed by a man with his hands fumbling deep into his pockets, pushing his pants down beneath his waist; a woman holding a newspaper in front of her face upside-down, laughing as another man reached around her, groping and shouting "Get up, get off your big fat nasty butt." I paid little attention, looked past the flock of bodies and decided the China Dragon held the most potential. If my calculations were correct, the answer to the Maze of the Minotaur's

Ornamentation was near. In front of the entrance to China Dragon, there was a frantic crowd pulsing with tics,
bouncing heads, limbs popping. Instead of going around
them, I cut straight through. No one seemed to notice my
body slide, duck, dodge through to the glass door, open
it and step in.

There was no menu to be found on the walls, but I
knew what I wanted. How do you make an egg roll? Just
push it. The man behind the counter wore a white paper
hat. My favorite. A blue name-tag read: Shove.

"I'll take the Sesame Chicken, Shove."

"No Sesame."

"Sesame Chicken."

"No Sesame."

"Open sesame."

"Don't be stupid!"

"Chicken Dumpling."

"No soup."

"Soup of the day."

"Why don't you try again, Detective."

"Orange chicken. Barbecue pork. Fried rice." I had my
back-ups.

"Next time bring your partner."

"Egg roll."

"Very wise. We have egg roll."

"I'll take it, Shove."

"Ten dollar."

"What?"

"Stick around any longer and it will cost you twenty."

"I can only pay in quarters. And dimes. A few nickels,
but mostly quarters."

"No change!"

"Here you go." And I pushed him. He fell, hitting his head on the shelve of idols behind him. Sometimes it's too easy, these streets, the little sense it takes to survive.

I grabbed the greasy wax paper bag off the counter and walked back out.

Immediately a crowd hovered:

"Let me get that egg roll."

"Taste man just a taste."

"The guy, see, standing over him, see, with a three-foot length of pipe I found in the bathroom. You see?"

"Egg roll? Shit, check out this egg roll."

"Don't crack it!"

I made mental notes, discerning what was relevant to the case at hand and what was bullshit. But the bullshit I was interested in, too—material for whatever might come next. And it was then that I knew my riddle writing days were not over. I'd come to write my best one yet.

A fat man, holding a beer, stepped in my path and nudged me off to the side with his belly

"I've been watching you. You might be the man I need for this set-up. Now listen: I got a couple questions I need to ask you. See where you stand." He wore a pork pie hat tipped low over his eyes. A skinny white tie, silk gray shirt, buttons popped showing the scraggily hairs of his dented and stretched belly, a purple suit encasing this sausage, white shoes to tie it off.

I grabbed the beer from his grasp if only to let him know I could dance. He looked up from his feet, staring directly into my eyes.

"It has happened many times—I see this is just your first. My name is Little Steve."

I took a sip of the beer and passed it back to him. "I have unwrapped quite a few egg rolls in my life."

"If an egg rolls and a jack hammer cracks it, then where does the chicken sit? Where does the chicken sleep? Which road is the chicken crossing now?"

"All interesting questions."

He passed the beer back. "Has it not already reached the other side?"

"It has already preached the brother's pride." I took a chug.

"Humpty Dumpty is no longer an egg once he has fallen from the wall. His shell is cracked and what will we do with the yoke? Give me that fucking beer."

"The egg rolls, but the cracked head smokes it."

"The remains of your disappearance, piles of rubble which others will sift through. It belongs to you but others use it more than you do. What is it?"

"My name."

"What can you hold without ever touching it?"

"My breath."

"Paul's height is six feet, his head size a 7, waste a 36. He is a butcher, and wears size 9 shoes. What does he weigh?"

"Meat."

"What invention let's you look through a wall?"

"A window."

"What building has more stories than any other?"

"In Chicago?" I grabbed the beer again.

"Ah-ah-ah."

"A library, Little Steve. No matter the city." I finished the beer and slammed it on the ground.

"Alright, player—see how you fair with the Ice Cream-iacs."

"You scream. I scream. We all scream," and I pushed by him, through the crowd, egg roll in hand, heading back north on Damen. At Kinzie I took a right and began to make my way through the abandoned warehouses, factories, manufacturing plants, and lumberyards situated along the train tracks, Chicago's diligent muscle overgrown. I slowed down to take it all in. But I noticed I was not alone.

On the pot-holed street between the meat packer and the steel-wool manufacturer, the filthy hobbling scavenger guided a grocery cart filled with aluminum cans, mostly Steel Reserve. I knew I was in the right place. From behind the mound, a laugh cracked, and the cart rattled past, revealing a face toothless, sun-burnt, wet with grease and garbage. Rising from the crackle of the man's laugh, a dozen more grocery carts could be heard, rattling across the wrecked streets. Everywhere filthy men limping along, collecting the rubble of rock, brick, stone, rebar, and metal which had slowly eroded off these abandoned buildings. Bodies emerged from the buildings, pallets piled high atop their heads. In the distance, a giant ball of steel wool rolled down the middle of the street, taller than the man who pushed it. Though I knew not from where it came, the slow song of an ice-cream truck could be heard: *Do your ears hang low/ do they wobble to and fro/ can you tie them in a knot/ can you tie them in a bow/ can you throw them over your shoulder like a continental soldier/ do your ears hang low.* Atop all this wreckage, silhouettes scaled the ruins, dislodging large hunks of the anonymous factories, shoving them over to the throng of bodies below, who carried the blasts of stone gnarled with twisted rebar away into the darkness of the shadowed streets. Then, one by one, they turned their attentions to me. These shadows drifting in my direction, moaning and hissing. The wind whipping through like the swallow of god's tongue. Again the song of the ice-cream truck, but the bodies sang along with it:

"Who escapes the escapees

once the escapee is fed

to the Minotaur's maze

is where what's purple, huge and lives

in the ocean looms a thread

bare of luxuries and walls

at the edge of what you hear

who escapes the escapees."

They descended upon me, a throng of shadows engulfing the light of day. One voice, shrill and with street bravado, yelled: "Before you, this was broken on horseback. Who are you, bitch?" They sprinted, attacking, arms waving.

As they overtook me, I yelled: "Chuck Yeager!"

Immediately they stopped.

I yelled again, this time ripping my larynx in two: "Chuck Yeager!"

Their sighs lit with kerosene burning at a pitch my ears had never experienced. As if I was on that jet with him. Chuck, that is, when he broke the sound barrier. That was the answer to the riddle. The Maze of the Minotaur's Ornamentation would lead me to him. Chuck Yeager lived in Wicker Park. He wandered the streets, disheveled. Bearded. Sunburnt, gathering the endless butts of his cigarette smoking life. Everyone knew his story, how he went mad. The terrors he suffered growing up in one gentrified neighborhood after another until finally he saw the eyes of Ciudad Mujer and never looked back. I went to find him immediately.

16: Moby Grape

The road stretched half a mile, up and down one hill and around a curve of vines. Fine sand kicked up on everyone's shoes. The wind rustled the green leaves. Something stirred here and there in the rows of grapes so cherished by wine drinkers around the world. A snake, a mole, a boar maybe devouring the buds of fruit before it was caught and slaughtered for a feast. Walking down there, I saw a man with a cigarette and remembered that I hadn't smoked since last night.

"Friend, can I bum one?"

"Bride or Groom?"

"Groom."

"Any friend of Levi's isn't worth the tar in this stick."

"Bride, then."

"Now that was just a joke. I saw you rushing in late. Glad you made it on time. How do you know the lovely couple?" The sarcasm in his voice stung. Who were these poor girls?

"Levi and I have quite a history."

"Is that right?"

"We grew up across the street from each other."

"And your name is?"

"Yeager. Chuck Yeager."

"I've never heard about you from Levi. That sounds ruder than I meant it—it's just that Levi and I have been worshipping together for quite some time now, and he speaks of his childhood in Montana often."

"Growing up in the hills, learning so much about farming and sustainable living. Did you fly fish like Levi?"

"You can't come to the breakfast table in Montana without a fish in hand."

"Makes me jealous."

"Well, it was what it was."

Before I could ask him more of this childhood Levi had concocted, I felt a hand on my shoulder and a nudge to my rib. Thinking it was Roberto or another Mariachi thug, I tensed and turned around.

"Is that you, Chuck? I didn't expect to ever see you at one of these!"

It was Chester Olive, the only good friend of Levi's from college that I had spent any time with. He was a crazy bastard, and I loved him for it. The nights we drank together were always debaucherous.

"Chester. I should have known I'd find you here."

"Quite a show, isn't it? Who would have ever thought that Seeds would become such a celebrity. And such a dirtbag."

"I could've guessed at one of those."

"The mayor of Santa Barbara was sitting behind me. And Onix Concepcion—I mean, random, but still an old baseball star. I guess Gil is quite the baseball fan."

"Jai Alai suits him better. Dying, esoteric."

"Kinda glum, buddy. My wife said she recognized some movie stars. Have you ever met Sally? I'll introduce you. What have you been up to?"

"You know me—drinking, fucking things up, scraping by."

"Aren't you a literature professor by now?"

"Not even close, thanks for asking. I'm in Chicago. Things have been alright. What about you?"

"Levi hasn't told you?"

"Nope."

"Hell, buddy. I'm the guy behind XO in Los Angeles. About as hot of spot that you can find these days. The other night I'm turning down Tom Hanks because Jessica Biel and J.T. took his table."

"Good for you, Chester. Are you pouring Las Sangres wine?"

"Of course, of course. Can't keep enough of it in stock— you know how it is with their limited productions."

"Well, let me buy you a drink."

"They're free, buddy."

"That's the thing of it."

"Clown. A little later; I gotta go back and check in with my wife."

"Let's talk later."

17: MOBY GRAPE

The road we followed wrapping around and veering through the blocks of grapes opened up revealing white linen tables, chefs cooking over huge stone pits, servers positioned throughout with appetizer trays, bars set up and bottles of wine on each table, a dance floor, the Mariachi band singing Mexican folk ballads. The bar was stocked with wine that Levi had made himself or bottles he had pulled from his collection. I recognized one bottle which he had purchased on our trip in Europe: El Troubadour from the region of Languedoc. If these weddings were a regular thing as Chris Park suggested, then they had to have a patron. Or Levi was delusional, in love and going broke ten times a year. The wine alone that was poured that night had to be upwards of $100,000. I walked across the dance floor, past the Mariachis, and I winked at my big friend Camarillo. His scowl tensed a little in unison with his fists tightening on the neck of his guitarron, but that was all he let on. I wondered where had Ruben Rorick gone—his black pythoned figure seared an unshakeable impression on the mind akin to a child first learning about death. I grabbed two extra glasses of wine, walked over to Chester Olive and his wife.

"Chester, for you, and for you, Mrs. Olive."

"Sally. Nice to meet you, Chuck—Chester just told me you were here."

"He's not the first husband to warn his wife about me."

"Maybe it's the mustache."

"Don't worry that isn't one of Levi's. It is a fine Bordeaux from 1982. I would guess $1,000 a glass, far more valuable than your husband's company—do you mind if I steal him away for just a minute."

"More than a fair trade. A sip alone is likely twice his value."

"You would know. Chester, one for you as well."

I walked him over to the side and tried to get all I could about who he knew was there, celebrity or hound. We sat down and looked at the dazzling view of California society's best, gracefully in evening's light surrounded by hills which gave life to the fruit of gods.

"How'd you manage to keep up with Levi? He dropped me years ago."

"We all know your history, Chuck—some version of it at least, far better from the truth I am sure."

"What's past is past."

"Not quite. The past resolves upon its own accord."

"Here's to resolution."

"Cheers. Yes, Levi and I have helped each other out in different ways."

"Do you share the same friends."

"Quite a few. But politicians and CEOs one never considers friends—they're just the type that are in the business of being known."

"Such a glamorous night."

"You should come to my restaurant—glamor is in the water here. I'll show you glitz."

"Who all is out there?"

"There's Mayor Winchester and his wife, Sarah. Lots of winemakers in the crowd. That guy, laughing like an idiot over there, he's the head winemaker at Pickle Barrel—a trendy affair for sure. The round one, with the mustache sitting down, he is in town from Australia. His wines go for hundreds. His wife, way less. See the slick guy with a bow tie next to the bar, standing with the red head—he runs distribution for a fruits and vegetables outfit which I can't remember the name of. But the crowd behind him— hell, there's five of the wealthiest individuals in Southern California—but the one who's closest with Levi is the black-haired fella, with the green tie, goatee, scarf in his pocket—I love his style—that's Gil Seeds. Do you know Levi's brother? His guardian angel. They're quite a pair when they're together. I'll introduce you to him."

"What about the old man, maneuvering through the crowd towards the band? He looks familiar."

"He, I will not introduce you to. A French prick you do not want to know. Owns half the old world and acts like it, now he's making a move on the new. His wines are as old as the earth—Toussaint is the family name."

Half of me—the jack-ass half—knuckled, while the other half choked on my tongue before it could speak.

"The wine world is a close family. You can't cut a grape without someone saying its time."

"Seeds was never the type to betroth the French."

"Levi Seeds is not the same man you grew up with."

Just when I thought I was invited to help. There was no way this could go well.

"Have you talked with Levi yet?"

"You know how it is—the bride and groom are always the hardest to approach. But don't worry who these people are—enjoy yourself. That's why we are here. And of course to give thanks."

My eyes did not let go of Toussaint even as Chester

continued to talk. He walked behind the tables and the cooks, along the edge of the pond, towards something that at first seemed childish and decorative, but adjusting my eyes and my understanding, it quickly entered into the realm of nightmares. As tall as the limbs of the surrounding trees, surrounded by a hundred candles of different sizes, flowers, and offerings of money and tequila, a figure stood before him: a smirking skeleton dressed in a red gown more beautiful than Levi's bride. She carried a soul-harvesting scythe in one hand, a magnum of Las Sangres wine in the other. Long tufts of hair hung from her gruesome skull. Ciudad Mujer, the Holy Angel of Death.

The music ended as Guy Toussaint approached the shrine. Everybody gathered in behind him. The guests, the wedding party, the Olives, even the waitstaff. Toussaint knelt before the shrine. "Play for her!" he ordered, and the mariachis began to play a song I have since come to know too well, "Reina de Arena." Queen of Sands. A narcocorrido praising the patron saints of death, drug dealers, smugglers, coyotes.

And there walking behind the idol away from the crowd back towards the ceremony was Ruben Rorick.

My experiences with Ciudad Mujer had been limited to the little Chicago grandmas who hired me. They would invite me to pray to an idol, almost like a Catholic at the feet of Mother Mary. Now, the same thing only twenty times larger and not one little old lady with a shot of patron and a cigarillo, but a mass of wealthy Californians offering drunken respect and notes and prayers. And somewhere, a knife was being prepared.

Gil Seeds spoke after the song was complete.

"Ciudad Mujer we pray to you, but it is Ruben Rorick that we honor tonight because it is his light and watchful eyes that keep harm out of ways, and if harm does befall us, he escorts us to heaven past the ugly guards, past the demanding demons who fight for our bodies arrival in hell. Ruben Rorick!"

"Ruben Rorick!" in unison.

Away he walked.

The spiritual dimension to madness terrified me the most.

"And of course, our patron, our vision. Grace, dignity, and power: Guy Toussaint."

The elder man rose from his knees, turned toward the crowd, and I knew then that this was not a joke. This was not another case, nor a wolf cry from an old friend. I knew what I had known all along but was too stubborn to admit: they wanted me dead.

"Cheers, to our good fortunes, our business, our network of friends."

"Cheers!"

Not to Levi and his lovely bride, not to the abundance of love or to soul mates, but to business. They cheersed to business. Surely, I was just another name in their ledger.

18: MOBY GRAPE

The evening moved on as weddings do. I spoke to a few strangers, avoided a few others. Drank the beautiful wines. After the long cocktail hour, we were finally seated for dinner. I was at a table seated with the Mariachis, obviously the last and least guest invited. But I did not feel sorry for myself. I was glad to see my old friends and congratulate them on their fine playing, their vast repertoire of songs singing Satan's praises. To my left was Camarillo. To my right, the chef, Umberto.

"We hope you aren't planning anything disruptive, Sr. Yeager."

"Really, I'm just happy to be invited."

"I see, yes. Are you drinking wine?"

"I'm not feeling very cannibalistic tonight, but thank you. But say, how did you bums get a seat? Don't the musicians usually eat backstage with the help."

"Very funny, yes, they usually do. That is true. And humorous."

"You all must be important. Wait, the bride must be one of your sisters. A shame to lose a pretty Mexican girl like that."

I felt Camarillo's meaty claw grip my thigh and squeeze. A cowbite.

"*Mi amor*, I thought you forgot about me. You know what, now that I look close—is that your daughter, Camarillo? Should be some wedding night."

My nose didn't break but it bent by the beast's head. My eyes shut on their own, as if they never wanted to see the world again. All I could do was smile to keep from falling out of my chair.

Umberto barked Camarillo back. Two others grabbed him. This is not what they wanted, and I knew that I wanted whatever it was they did not—against my body's best interest.

I needed to eat like a lion in a zoo needed prey—when the food finally came, I barely knew what to do with it. The *conejo* and *chivo* didn't swallow so nice. Was this Seeds' signature dish? I tried ruffling a few more feathers but nobody responded to anything I said. I was the child in their company they'd grown tired of.

The meal wrapped up. People began to get up from their seats and mingle, preparing for the bride and groom's first dance. I too sought better company, but before I could push back from my chair to stand up, Umberto pulled me back down.

"You are forgetting something."

"No, 'Bert, it was my plan to stick you with the bill."

"Under your seat, *amigo*. There is something that is yours."

I hesitated. Then reached for it, knowing exactly what my hand would feel. There, taped to the bottom of my chair was a gun. Not mine; somebody else's. Somebody in particular I was sure. I ripped it off, checked the clip, it was short two bullets. I sniffed the barrel. Somebody was dead and in my hands was the murder weapon. I gripped it harder, tucked it into my pants and did not look back.

The evening was orchestrated—it knew I was coming, how I would get there, who I would talk to and where I would sit. The evening dreamed me forward, and now it had provided me a gun. There was nothing good that could come of this, I thought, if I let it dictate my actions any further. But what I did not know was that even if I thought I was doing right, acting upon my will against that which led me here, and even if I shot who I thought was wrong, the evening would always know better and all would be according to the evening's plan. I had to talk to Levi Seeds.

10: IN THE PENAL COLONY

I made my way, until I encountered an entirely mysterious presence. One I knew well, if déjà-vu could be considered knowledge. Immediately I wondered why I had not come sooner, directly to this building. The Fortress of Bethulia. Its tenants forever searching for a path to exit this maze, as now was I.

Those who lived here had long ago been shunned by progress, civility, decency. Huddled into the corners of their existence, unaware that one day was different from the next—they housed the secrets of this city. They held no remorse for the extent of the evil they served; they desired odd avenues into the darkness and here they were allowed to entertain the full figure of mystery. Light creeping in from warped floorboards. Sitting in a chair at the center of the room staring ahead. Shifting postures if only to see better. Windows boarded up—this building, like so many others, a watermark of the tides history heeds upon our surfaces. As derelict and hopeless as the rest of us.

Plastic pulled taut across the windows, very few have ever seen past this grease and blur into this inhabitance. Like many Chicago afternoons in the fall, the northerly winds crossed these buildings in a way which transformed them, causing a wavering between the summer grace which they exited and the winter grey which has been etched into their memories. I stared at The Fortress of Bethulia, and it appeared to grimace. Its teeth crackled, hard calcium flakes scattering like confetti. I refocused my eyes, trying to find beauty in this scene. I sighed and tried to smile. Took deep breaths, hoping that occurrences unseen might shift the psychic balance.

It would be too hasty to say that those who lived here were men. Altogether inaccurate to claim they were women. The ones who lived here had long ago forgotten the performances particular to any one gender. And directly in front of me, in the window of the middle apartment on the first floor, a body appeared. A face. Pressed against the glass, peeling away the plastic. Peering out at me, a pale face with brunette freckles, wearing a long orange wig. One hand gently stroking their course strands. And then immediately they vanished.

As I watched the wind pick through the limbs, lofting off orange leaves with each swoop, remembering other autumns of fonder recollection, the creak of a screen door opening severed my reverie. And slammed shut. I turned to find they standing on the stoop. Watching me. Below the orange wig, a slender figure clothed in a floral moomoo, yellowed and moist from the body's processes.

Saying nothing, they motioned for me to come near. And I did; I walked to the stoop, and as I took my first step to ascend the stairs, they turned, opened the screen door and walked back inside, leaving the door propped open against a concrete block.

And I followed.

It is my belief that a building's soul is transmitted through the interior woodwork, and when I saw the splintering floors, the molded casing near to falling from its frame, the decrepit doors which led to dark bedrooms, the crown molding disintegrating with termites and crawled all over by cockroaches—at that point an obsession made itself known.

I stopped a step past the derailed pocket doors, standing there as vulnerable as a woodsman between two timbers being worked over by an ax. And they spoke:

"The password."

"You invited me."

"Into the foyer, but behind this no further. And without the password no backwards will there be."

"Can I offer this?"

"Offer only the password."

I lifted the grease-soaked, cold sack.

"What of the egg that goes unopened?"

I pulled it out, pushed my thumbs into the seem of the fried dough and unwrapped. Inside the riddle, an enigma. I spoke: "Conundrum."

"Your entry has been proven."

They turned, took me in with their deep eyes. Giving a flip to the orange wig, they stepped towards me and yanked the egg roll mess from my hold.

As we crossed the threshold of the foyer into the grand room, they stopped and removed their floral moo-moo. Immediately taken back, I crippled with nausea. A dower must, acrid and brown—the smell of their body rose above the putrid stagnancy which sat between these walls. Neither breasts nor genitals could be identified. As much a Lewis as they were a Carol. But hair and stretch, and growths and scabs, and crease and chaff.

Hands folded behind my back, an act of nonchalance, I began to mill around.

Beyond the disrepair and foulness, something mysterious and stunning could be seen. Something which sickens me, when I think back about it, to know that I was at first incapable of recognizing. That I was more concerned with cleanliness than the deep riches which that dirt disguised.

Spreading out across the walls of the grand room, a grotesque map had been drawn, spelling out the phantasmagorical existence of the city. First glance, it seemed to be an accurate depiction of Chicago. But one had only to stare a moment longer to notice the deformities which occurred regularly throughout. The incongruities between it and that reality outside were almost unspeakable. When I felt their presence behind my back, I had to ask: "When was the last time you left this building?"

"It has been some time since I have gone past the stoop. But there are more ways than one to exit a building."

It was as if the map had initially been accurate, and then corroded into this carnival of deformed imagination which I stared at now. Certain streets widened haphazardly, expanding to dominate their vicinity. Particular buildings were sketched in detail finer and more excruciating than the real; others had been bludgeoned by crayon or marker, paint or charcoal, corrupted at the seams, falling into the realm of cartoon, like the perverse realities of a child's coloring book. The bodies of weightless citizens in disrepair wavered in hordes. Near where I lived, chunks of a shattered curb, neon leaking from flashing bright signs. Certain neighborhoods had been banished by an amalgamation of supernova-like debris, blur, and light. Eraser rubbings littered the floor next to the decrepit crown molding. The lake waters, though obscure, struck horrific postures near the shore, yet further out they became tantalizingly gentle.

Lost in the details of the map, I came to with the sound of their lips smacking, chewing the egg roll nearly all of it devoured. Orange in my periphery. Between bites, they spoke, "You are not where you think you are."

"Is that so?"

"When you followed me inside, you passed an ancient threshold. I am never surprised that you don't recognize it. Entering a chamber such as this triggers the processes of transmigration. And for you more than anyone else."

"What is it you think you know about me?"

"Everything that the rest have told me. So much is shown to me by the map. Many others have guided you here."

I knew no other trick than to play along. "I've forgotten my way. You must accept my apology."

"Would you like to enter it?"

"Enter the map?"

"No. A walk along The Fortress of Bethulia. Beneath the stove in the kitchen, a trapdoor can be lifted to reveal a tunnel. That tunnel is dark and follows the maze of the map. I cannot emerge from its subterranean route, but it offers me access to the layers of earth beneath your walking life, your neighbor's dreams, the mumbling past as it squeezes towards the sky to sprout the most wretched vines and ivy growing across the facades of the walking city. There is a similar fate awaiting you. Go."

As he spoke, we had entered the kitchen. I opened the stove door and a gust overtook me, and I let go, slamming the iron back shut. Bracing myself, I opened the door again. I saw now the false bottom that awaited me.

I began to sweat just looking at the green glow of what

hid beneath. Lost in this daze, my energy sank, but I turned back towards the creature, one question still left unresolved.

"Is this my escape or my return."

"Go! Find out yourself, Manasses!"

A furious impatience peeled at my skin. "No offense but I don't want to end up looking like you."

They jumped at me snarling. "I've been fed, but I wouldn't turn down another meal." Drool oozing from their long sharp teeth.

My wit stopped mid-sentence when our eyes met again. It was as if they were empty; their body as if a sack of flesh. Halted in my rage, halted in my thoughts, my agency dropped out from underneath me. All I could say was, "Dr. Holofernes, where'd you get these instruments from again?"

"My brothers brought them to me." Somehow this puppet spoke, though as if their lips and face were numb with Novocain. "They left them around when they died. Most people do."

Right then I saw it. The grey fur. Dr. Holofernes' arm rose as if to wipe sweat from their brow with the towel they wore around their neck, but it fell from their grasp. The presence behind him flinched towards the towel but Dr. Holofernes did not. The snout sniffing, I could hear it; the canine dripping saliva down my cheeks as I lied there in the swivel chair. I could smell it. That breath, that padded paw sharply through the skin and tearing at the muscles from the inside.

"Roll me up a cigarette before you begin the fillings."

I knew this would cause great difficulty. they pulled the

pouch of tobacco from the cargo pockets of their shorts, and when they bowed their head, for a quick flash I saw the head of the Wolf. their arms stuffed into Holofernes' arms, performing a feat of puppetry and ventriloquism I never imagined possible.

I looked all around and saw the shimmering waters. Searched in vain for the signs of a nearby city or port. Nothing from my perspective but the intricate design of waterways. Passages which I had surely traveled and would surely do so again and again.

With this blast of recognition of my circumstances came an epiphany. I am no solipsist—surely someone stuffed their lungs, limbs, and voice inside the skin sack of me. Though with each sliding step I felt the tear of muscle and vein even more, I knew my body would be sacrificed to my master's amusements in this life or the next. There was no difference now.

And I dropped in.

I tumbled a ways before being able to steady my body's descent. Crawling became easier and soon enough I exited the tunnel and stood up. Everywhere I looked there stood the remnants of walls. From where I was, the only phenomenon which stopped my vision was a horizon in the far distance. Looking up revealed story upon story upon story ending only in a pencil point of light, which I feared was the lantern in the hand of the monster I had just escaped, staring down at me. I was standing at the epicenter of a phenomenon which my past experiences of physical being could not make sense of. My eyes were either the seat of delusion or the access points to a newfound proximity of distance, telescoping my presence deeper into an unfathomable well of minuscule solitude.

Fearful of the one holding the lantern above me, I walked straight, stepping over the foot-high remnant of plaster into a series of rooms stretching as far as I could see. Hallways branching off in every direction materialized with each step I took, forking infinitely towards doors graced by glowing brass knobs intricately cast in the shape of lion's heads. Behind these doors, waves of history transpired in the form of wooden tables, chairs, bookcases, armoires. Outlandish theories of existence surfaced across the upholstery of the chairs, the couches and the pillows. Scenes from another's life came to light across the wallpaper, shifting with each step forward.

Slowly, the hardwood floors gave way to a mosaic of tiles. I wondered if I was closer to the lake than I had reason to believe because the colors of the tiles were soft sea hues of blue, pink, teal and yellow. A pattern was emerging beneath my feet, but I understood my perspective was too immediate to see all of it. A sight only for the one who watched. Walking still, I looked up to see if there was a way to take in its entirety, and there, as if I had not moved an inch from the point where I started, tunneled the expanse of stories above me, and the pinpoint of light which I could only assume was the lantern in the hand of the monster I had just escaped. Stunned, I looked in every direction, to be sure that the orange wig was not near, the front door, the freckles, the map, the kitchen. Nothing. I walked on, looking up.

And the great height of floors followed me, as if the earth beneath my feet revolved but I and the sky above held our place. The tiles began to gradually grow up the walls and the places where they had been destroyed by sledge hammer to make my passage possible saddened me. I imagined families who once stared deeply across these intricate designs, whether it once was their kitchen or their sitting room or their bedroom, the walls had absorbed their familial energy and interior obsessions, but now were crumbled and dust to be swept.

Intent simply to walk, eventually I came across a quiet garden. Centered by a fountain and at the perimeter stone walls carved with lotus and curved shapes patterned into meanings beyond anything which I could decipher. In ruins and overgrown, I circled the fountain several times before I took a seat to rest on a large hunk of limestone. I replaced my thoughts with the motion of picking up small rocks, tossing them all around, listening to the sound they made against the damp ground, thick flora and stone. I spied a green rock, with an emerald shine, and grabbed it, deciding to throw it in the fountain. Through the air from my hand, just over the rim it flew. But I did not hear it strike the water, which I assumed to be there. Nor the sound of it landing upon anything else.

I stood up and looked over the rim. The water I expected to be pooling was not there, no earth nor stone neither. I could still see the emerald sparkle of the stone falling down, past the stories same as the ones I believed to be above me. Until at last it pinged my head as I heard it splash into the waters. I looked up and the pinpoint of light had grown as large as a moon, still distant but I had not climbed a step and knew not how I had ascended. I quickly carried on, nervous to walk off this scene which riddled me. The once ornate rooms had grown dingy, weathered and worn through. They were much smaller and the woods were either greasy or cracked. Ahead, I saw a portrait hanging on a wall. That of an old man sitting in a chair, dressed in plaid pants, an untucked shirt and a green fedora holding on his finger. In the next room another portrait, this of a boy curtsying in an elaborate hoop gown, smiling though it seemed begrudgingly. And then another, in the next room and the next, and I stared deeply at these faces, disguised, it seemed, in costumes of eras foreign to them. So entranced I was that when I fell to the floor I knew not that it was the sleeping body of a man which tripped me.

He awoke before I had the chance to pick myself up.

Dazed, he looked upon my face, his eyes swelled with a thousand years of sleep. Similar to the portraits hanging throughout this corridor of The Fortress, his attire looked awkward upon his frame—outfitted in an intricately embroidered tunic, dazzled with color and patterned arrangements which, like paintings on a cave wall, one might attempt to make sense of. His brown pants were a loose wool. He did not wear shoes.

His eyes gradually focused on mine, his expression lit up, and he sat up and spoke. "You've returned."

"Then I must have gotten turned around at the circular garden. But I admit, I did not see you when I passed through this room the first time." In reflecting upon my response, I see better how much my mind reaches to make sense of all that passes through it, adjusts the world around it to fit its expectations, never allowing the superseding of its limitations.

"Help me up. One would expect atrophy in the body

of an existence such as mine, but I forgo believing in atrophy, thus my ability to wait so long. Here, standing is too much—I will sit here on this bench, if you would join me."

Along the two intact walls of this passage, a bench had been built out of fine wood. Along the legs, animal faces had been carved—the boar, the hippopotamus, the wolf, the elephant, the bear. A cushion tapestried by hand, bands of orange silks alternating with lines of rough green burlap. A bizarre sight to see this man in his embroidered tunic lean back across these bright silks above the heads of great animals.

The patient man continued. "We should continue what we started."

"On who is it you are waiting? Possibly the people in the portraits?"

"You have been gone longer than it is desired. Who guided you back?"

"The one in the orange wig."

"Orange it is? Well, sounds better kempt than the millions of braids it one adorned."

"Where are we?"

"Didn't they explain? We are the paradox of The Fortress. It stretches just long enough for one to believe it stretches forever, and then, well, you know better than I. It seems you have just returned from that moment, the utter conviction that the line you walk is infinite. But I am here to tell you how one day prior to this, you escaped from me in search of the city which we conceived to exist outside these walls. I can see by the clothes you wear that something different than these ruins can be found. You look very strange."

I was wearing a green suit, tattering a bit but respectable; a pinstripe shirt loosened and light by the multiple wearings of the many who wore it before me; a scuffed belt and cordovan shoes to match, the soft leather almost worn through. A thin mustache atop my lip.

And in reflecting on what I wore, I began to remember. Though only a little at first: "Yes, my friend, as we projected—a city exists outside of here." And the excitement of remembering overtook me: "Multiple cities, more cities than one could count. But they are not lined up, nor are they chronological. There are cities buried in time, still told of and desired. Cities on the other side of the world which transform with every moment of our approach. Cities built atop of other cities. Cities which are ruins, though occupiable, left to the imagination to fill in the holes and patch back the rubble. The immediate city—the one outside this room where you wait—is known as Chicago. It is through a condemned building and with the help of a forgotten being that I have been able to return to you."

"Chicago. A truly devious sound. Tell me the names of others."

"There's Atlantis. Bangkok. Dubai. Paris. Troy. New Orleans. Tegucigalpa. Buenos Aires. Hawen Yore. Lagos. Berlin. Quito. Beruvj. Shanghai. Nalwat. Fictitious cities. Future cities. Cities of vast complexities and suffering."

"Incantations—you speak a spell over my heart. Tell me of this Chicago, your experience of it."

"It has frustrated me maniacally, yet gathered ecstasy around me depressively. I have felt my soul a toy within its grasp. And my body has stretched between its buildings like a canvas across poplar sticks. I've become buried by my knowledge of it, and then I walk another block up or down an alley and I see for the thousandth time a perspective which I've never seen before. The neighborhoods gather around train lines, and then gather on trains and disperse. It is filled with gorgeous residences, facades of sneering eyebrows which look down upon me as if my arch-rival, as if we were competing for the same flame. Its expanse triggers dreams which compound the reality of my days."

"Is there an upward expanse? One which the citizens climb without realizing? A vertical tunnel of stories which follows you and resets your mind according to its whims?"

"Many of the structures are built vertically, as tall as you can imagine, and the wealthiest citizens are subject to their powers, climbing up and down them daily. However, no upward expanse like the one we are subject to here exists. There are no vertical passions. No communion with the chaotic laddering of stories. It is a gray horizontal spread of bodies coughing and grinning and huddled in corners and filling again and again with the surface pleasures of linear and momentary past times. My friend, please, tell me you wish to see it?"

"If I were to go, would you wait here for me? Knowing it would be what felt like forever before I returned? Knowing there are phenomena such as atrophy, such as sanity, such as death, which you could no longer believe in?"

"But I am not very patient."

"That is what you said when I asked you once before."

"And who would show you the way? I can take you straight there if you come with me."

"To get there, I would need to search alone, as you did, for if not in my solitude, and if not lost in doubt and uncertainty, then no city would ever be built before me. Do you not remember this—our tenant of existence, our premise for the existence of worlds alternate to ours?"

"Still, what did you do here all this time? What would I do while you were gone?"

"I did what had to be done and I remained. I stayed, like a statue I did not budge. For if I did not anchor your journey, then there would have been no beginning, no reference, nothing to discover because everything would have seemed like the same nothing."

"But it is not nothing—it is something. There are wondrous somethings that I want to share with you."

"That, and I dreamt. I dreamt of cities, of citizens, of tall buildings, ruinous corridors, timeless stories, ferocious beasts, ageless pieces to newly formed puzzles. The one who remains, dreams the discoveries of the one who is lost."

"I cannot do that. There is more out there, more extravagant peoples to talk to, more structures, more powerful visions to be engulfed by, more awe-inspiring cities to submit my soul to. There is still too much more behind doors which I am just beginning to notice along the walls of my passage. I cannot remain here, my friend, my spirit would strangle my body and this room would be my coffin."

"Then I cannot know of the splendors you refer to. It is my patience, then, my acceptance which I must explore. This room for the uncountable time I must admire, the exquisiteness of boredoms which I must enjoy."

"I am sorry."

"Sorry? Do not feel sorry for me. I am transfixed by my interiors. I find an odd joy. I have even begun playing a game with the One Above who holds the lantern. If I whistle just the right melody, it whistles it back to me. And when that occurs, I feel effervescent, a sublimation of all this which weighs me down. And I tell myself stories about you. Stories which incite my imagination into fantastic worlds of delight and intricate situations of despair and fear. I am content, and I know you will return again, as you have before, for that is the pattern of The Fortress, the way we have conceived of it."

"Brick by brick."

"Morning each morning."

"All the unbuilt buildings are built anew."

"But one."

I hugged my friend, held onto him as if he was my own body, and then I left him.

"What will be saved, will be earned."

Beset with agony. The existence I cause him seems a hell to my tastes. Guiltily I wept with every step. A heartbeat rushed to the back of my eyes and I heard it amplify throughout this vast vacant space of metal and stone, plaster and stick. I took a step forward, coughed, and heard gravel shifting.

Finally, as if emerging from beneath the surface of the rubbled factory, Wicker Park began to appear. Every decadent inch of it. Each ornate flourish, each luxurious furnishing. Every lamp flickering, every curtain alive with an untraceable wind.

I did not need to move as the streets transitioned

around me. The city absorbed my every being, my every posture, my every thought. Swallowing me in its sinister grandeur—the lights went dim. It was him. No other presence could be spoken of. Arriving with each twisting churn of sensation. How many worlds are given a name?

"Chuck Yeager. Hush. There will be no harm."

He stood there, his skin burned by the winds, bearded, in red sweat pants, a white Kansas Jayhawks sweatshirt grayed by ash and browned by grime.

19: MOBY GRAPE

I had been watching him throughout dinner. Only a couple of tables over, though he never made eye-contact with me. His bride was smiling and laughing, enjoying herself with the rest of the wedding party at the table. Eating the beautiful rabbit legs, the artichokes, potato and vegetable medley, the chili-lime smoked goat, pouring from the endless bottles before them. While Levi sat there, seriously, disengaged, slowly eating, smiling every once in awhile when the table demanded him to acknowledge them with a joke or a gesture.

He was more handsome than I remembered. His dark brown eyes and his olive skin glowed. A dark radiance. His linen brown suit and matching brown tie Hong Kong-hugged his athletic stature. His hands though, were tied to a different tailor—calloused, rough, red splotches as if tattooed on his fingertips. His knuckles were mammoth and they flexed as if working blood clots from his veins. Who was he thinking of? Older, it was like he was a facsimile of his former self. As if a stranger. How many lives do we lead, how many bodies do we shed along the way?

His power and presence revealed itself in the wealth of people that came to his shoulder to speak into his ear. Each winemaker, one by one, brought over their most touted bottle of wine, which they brought with them for this occasion. They poured him a glass, discussed it with him from over his shoulder. He would turn to acknowledge, cheers and act pleased, and they would lean in, or sit down on their heels, and in private discuss whatever sentiment or business that was going on between them.

I felt that to know what they were discussing would be to know the meaning of all of this that had consumed me, that had drugged me, that had shot at me, that had kidnapped me, tied me up, and planted a gun beneath my chair for me to take and make a deadly mistake with. Then again, just to know he had this power over the fortune of others told of the power he had over me.

I was through waiting and watching. As sour as Levi looked, I did not hesitate. When he stepped out from the table and began to walk away, I, too, got up, slipped the gun between my waistline and my shirt, and met him face-to-face in line at the bar.

"I've never seen this much wine poured in my life."

"And yet you sound sober—are you not getting enough?"

"Certain situations sober me up at every turn—no matter how much I pour down my throat."

"It is strange to be standing here in front of you, Chuck."

"Did you forget that I had been invited?"

"I didn't think you'd come."

"But you reserved an honorary seat for me just in case?"

"I do not have time to bother with the details of planning a wedding."

"You just give the orders. Have others execute."

"When I imagined this moment, I saw two lost friends giving each other a hug. A few cracks between us and falling back into how it always was before. But here you are with your venom, a vintage I recognize from long ago."

"It doesn't feel how it used to feel. You don't seem to be

the same caliber—whereas before you had the bullet of a slap, now its semi-automatic."

"When did you get so hardened?" He looked around suspiciously and said, "Let's walk this way."

We stopped behind the caterer's tent. In these few steps, I had decided to let on to as little as possible; let him spill what he had and offer nothing to drink myself.

"Chuck, I need your help."

"Don't fuck around with me."

"You had to wonder why I invited you after all this time of not speaking. I haven't forgot you, not for a second, wishing we could erase those days in France. And when I got word that you were doing detective work in Chicago, I knew there was a deeper reason we had been such good friends, that we had grown up across the street from each other."

It pained me not to blurt out a wise crack about Montana, but Levi continued before I lost my restraint, "There's much more to all of this than you know. I apologize for the troubles it took, but you don't know how much I appreciate your presence."

"You've got to fill me in on what is going on here, Seeds. I do detective work, but as you can see from the bruises and cuts applied by your henchmen—I'm no bodyguard. How serious is this?"

Just then, the feedback of the microphone being turned on interrupted us. It was Gil Seeds, calling everybody's attention to give a speech and offer a toast to Levi and his bride.

"Meet me back by the oak tree after Gil speaks. Where Miriam and I got married."

"I'm surprised you know her name."

"No! Don't say that. After we cut the cake—I don't want any more interruptions. Meet me there, Chuck. Please."

And with that, the evening twisted towards a disaster that was invisible to me at the time. If only the future did not hover so close, calling to us, drawing us near like a guardian angel who had fallen from heaven long ago.

20: MOBY GRAPE

The wine ran tight across Gil's face. A deadly expression, but charming as he began to speak, as the wine began to dance and sparkle in his lips, his eyes. The sun was setting behind the hills, and the fading blue set the mood. "Good evening, everybody. On behalf of Levi and Miriam, welcome to the beauty of Santa Ynez Valley. It is deep, this beauty, is it not? I am Levi's brother, Gil. A few words, then, in honor of this celebration, in honor of little brother Levi. It is curious how an occasion arises for a toast and arises inevitably, even if one has despaired of it ever arising. Silly words like fate, or predestination, are used for this process. Maybe providence would be a better word. Maybe curse."

Why such a put-on when these weddings take place as often as has been suggested? I listened closer—more was being said, classified information all tied up in love's praise.

"Nearly ten years ago, I composed a very clever poem. I locked it in my mind, determined not to parade it until an occasion arose when it would be miraculously a propos. Do you follow me? I think you do.

"I have never been concerned whether I amassed an undeserved reputation for cruelty. That didn't bother me at all. I just wanted to clinch an issue, put my trump on somebody else's ace. Get me?

"Tonight, that poem is being recited in every action, every laughter, every loving smile and kiss. Tonight, every detail has been composed and is playing out right before your eyes. It is magical, isn't it? Do you believe in the mysteries of love? I think you do.

"To Miriam! To Levi! To Ciudad Mujer and Monsieur Toussaint. Cheers to making this night a case of aces."

All very touching, and I looked around to see what actions had been orchestrated by these words. The crowd seemed complacent, satisfied by the wine and the view, not too worried about the cartel rituals and obtuse speeches. But then I saw a movement, behind the faces of the crowd, a red dress, blond hair swiftly. Ursulines. She was running from something. Towards someone. Maybe it was Levi, but she did not get there in time, as he was pulled away by Umberto and a crying woman.

I gently stepped away, watching Roberto watch me, wondering what it meant that he let me go, and I followed behind Levi to hear what the trouble was. If he invited me as a detective more than a friend, then a detective I would be.

They were speaking in Spanish. *"Lo siento mucho, pero no hay tiempo para esperar. Su, el esposo de mi prima, el sueno del este tierra, y el alma de este fruta, yo tengo una pregunta para ti."*

Levi listened knowingly, expectantly—staring straight ahead.

Miriam's cousin carried on. *"Todavia tenemos una hijo, y todavia queremos que seas el Padrino de Umbertito. Tiene dos anos. El esta aqui. Por favor, Levi, necesitamos su ayuda. Por favor, no vamos a volver a preguntar. Va a ser el Padrino de nuestro hijo?"*

Levi responded, "Do not think that I do not know why. I have always known, and that is why I have always denied your request. Know that it is too much for me to bear. Everything that your family has asked of me is too much."

The husband interjected, "But it is not us. Don't you see? We are as squeezed by him as you are, if not more."

"*Callate!*" yelled his wife.

"Stop, Levi responded. Don't pretend to understand anything about my relationship with Toussaint. Not now, not ever. You pull me away while my brother stands up for me, speaking about our relationship, saying words he wants me to hear. I know who stands behind you. I know what power you must feel. But I will not be there for the baptism of your child. I will not take on responsibility for your troubles. I will not be Godfather to *su hijo*."

"So Miriam is the last?"

"I'm not even sure if it's Miriam. You might be drinking Las Sangres Levi tomorrow."

And he stood up. Slunk away towards the crowd as Gil finished his speech and announced that the bride and groom would cut the cake. The crowd gathered around; the photographer hovered uncomfortably close to the couple. The last light faded across the sky as the flash from the cameras sparkled all around Levi and Miriam. They smiled for all and kissed. As soon as they parted, Levi's eyes darted to his right—they looked furious and beaten. I looked over. There slithering in and out of the crowd, black suit, bolo tie, turquoise eyes. Ruben Rorick was on the move.

Miriam gently directed Levi to the cake, as if guiding a child into a funeral parlor to stand next to a corpse. As the knife they were both holding slid through the icing, a gunshot rang out in the distance. Quickly another.

The Mariachis began playing. A few people screamed. Ruben Rorick ran off and hopped on a four-wheeler, speeding down the road. Nobody knew what to do, standing there panicked waiting to be told none of it was true. Levi's face finally unfroze. Taking hold of Miriam tightly by the arm, he announced to the guests, "Do not worry. Do not panic. We are on a vineyard—there are gunshots that go off everyday. Surely the crew found a puma. Possibly a boar eating the early fruit on the vines. Please continue drinking, continue this celebration. The music has not stopped."

Somebody yelled, "But it was so close!"

"The grapes are growing all around you—this is the bow of the whaler's ship. Sounds play funny tricks in these privileged waters. We are close to the kill but we have nothing to fear."

Everybody shuffled around. There was nowhere to go—the bus which would take people back to the entrance of the vineyard was not there yet. Too far and too dark to walk, the only ones brave enough to try didn't care and kept getting drunk. Half the the guests grabbed drinks, retired to those that they knew and talked frantically amongst themselves. The other half did not think twice about the gunshot in the hills, continuing the celebration.

Levi and Miriam had disappeared without anyone noticing. When I had turned around they had fled. I grabbed a drink for the walk, in no hurry because the night which orchestrated my fate was everywhere always right in front of me. I headed towards the oak tree to meet Levi, wondering when Ursulines would meet me face-to-fac

11: In the Penal Colony

I had never paid Chuck Yeager much attention. Yet there he stood, elbows on the mailbox, mad with ancient nothings. He spent his days outdoors, watching everybody. Walking. A large head, brown prickly hairs, a rough-shaven face with patches of whiskers missed by the blade. His unbreakable stone blue eyes lewdly crossed the passersby, and his sweatpants revealed more than a blush.

Sitting outside Li'l Guy's Deli north of Armitage on Damen, enjoying the company of an acquaintance, a sandwich and a steady headache of sirens, Chuck Yeager came up to us and asked, "Trade you?"

"Trade me?" I responded.

"A smoke. Trade you for a joke."

"I like jokes," James said, the one who was with me, one of the workers from inside the deli, his red apron folded down and dusted with flour, taking his sixth cigarette break of the shift. I kept count. Chuck Yeager turned his attention to him, unblinking his eyes, and I noticed something shift between his legs. James did too and said, "I need a billy club as much as I need a toothpick."

He handed him a cigarette.

"What's purple and huge and swims in the ocean?" He took a drag staring at us as if these jokes were emerging from a machine. His eyes bounced back and forth between us as his grin grew.

I offered a guess, "Grape Jellyfish."

"Nope." Chuck Yeager took a long drag, coughed hard, enjoying this bizarre scene he had created. "Want me to tell ya?"

"Yes," James said. "We give up."

"Moby Grape." And he did not stop giggling, except to puff his cigarette. And occasionally to cough.

We laughed nervously along with him, then he bummed another smoke and walked away.

Chuck Yeager, I thought, yes—the answer is right before my eyes.

It had been confirmed by the deli employees that Chuck Yeager lived in an apartment nearby. A leftover from the days gone, no one could understand how he still afforded to live in a high rent neighborhood such as Bucktown. I'm sure they wondered similarly about me. I imagined his apartment windows blacked out. Despicable indolence smeared across every corner. A buzz of otherworldly activity. The glow of his eyes and his cigarette's red ember. I decided to follow him. Saying nothing to James, I stood up and began my walk.

Slowly he made his way through the Damen Avenue crowds. Never blinking—staring fiercely, stopping often to smoke, to lean against a newspaper stand, put his weight against a building. He kept to a set course. As if trapped; as if certain streets did not exist for him.

I kept a three-building distance behind him. I studied his movements, where he placed his attention, but nothing struck me as peculiar. Though everything was peculiar about him. Always. His posture erect, his shoulders bludgeoningly stacked into beastly dimensions. The sound, the snarling, the huff and scoot of his foot as he stopped to stare. His head, so large, his hair a wild burst of brown. I would not have been surprised if he dropped to all fours and charged.

We reached the north edge of Bucktown, the freeway ripped through this neighborhood at full speed, and the moment I thought we would we be walking along like this forever was the moment he turned. Left on Webster.

One block in: right on Hoyne. He stepped up to the door of a gorgeous yet decrepit four flat. He did not enter, instead just grabbed a handful of mail from the black cast-iron box on the exterior door frame. He turned around to walk back down the stoop and I panicked. All my body could do was collapse to the asphalt and hide behind a car, hoping he didn't see me. If he knew I was following him, then where would he lead me?

Unperturbed, he slid down the gangway. I scurried up, deciding to close the gap and follow him inside. A deep building, there was an entrance off the gangway to the back four units. What I believed to be four, I knew now to be eight units in this building. The floodlight released half his body from shadow, larger and more foul now I was up close. I stepped immediately behind him, just behind his back, entering the building along with him, hidden by what the light didn't reach. He reeked of nicotine, skin infection and sweat. Up the three flights of creaking stairs, I stepped in time with his footfall. His apartment door had been left wide-open. We entered.

He went straight for the bathroom, the light switch hit and the door shut behind him, leaving me to explore. I saw there were four small rooms in the shape of an *L*, seeming to take up only half of the available space. What I believed to be one, I knew now to be two. If the same layout held true, then that made sixteen units in this building. But I knew these Chicago four flats well enough to say with confidence that the front and back units on the first floor were once storefront and owner's residence, and I could presume were not divided into these workman quarters I was witnessing now. Making fourteen. Fourteen units inside this one building.

Before the details of the apartment's grotesque organization and ornamentation began to come to me clearly, my thoughts drifted towards the landlord. Who was it that created the logic of this building and maintained it for the residents? Who collected their rent checks and made up their lease? Who allowed such indolence and degeneration? I imagined a small bald man with a fat paunch speaking nothing but a grumbling Polish. Someone who never doubted that indeed this world held enough room for everyone. If only we learned to be content in our mess. I blessed this man of my imagination and at the same time I knew I feared him—a force content with the crammed suffering of the human form.

My reflections were interrupted by a heavy panting coming from the room Chuck Yeager had entered. He was not letting that bulge go to waste. I took a step and had a look around.

Before I went very far, I was overcome by the smell of rank tobacco. Cigarettes burnt to the butt littered the floors and windowsills of the otherwise vacant room. No ashtrays that I could see and no tables to set an astray on. There was no furniture at all. Only a glass sitting in the center of the room as if the artistic statement of a minimalist. Those minimalists—how incredulous they can be. But Chuck Yeager's sickness was a different breed. The second room I passed through possessed a stove and nothing more. A half-smoked cigarette lied atop a mound of butts on the space between the burners. I picked it up and lit it, hoping the fresh smoke would cover up the foulness. The stove was covered in yellow bile. Lung butter but no bread to speak of.

In the third room was a mattress, and on top of it a mangled blanket near a fuzzy wool cushion serving as a pillow. Everyone needs a pillow—even Chuck Yeager. In the fourth room around the corner, a giant refrigerator. I peered inside and found no food, only a half empty carton of cigarettes and a gallon of milk. I usually do not concern myself with brands, but I knew I would never buy a gallon of Dean's milk again.

There were no cabinets typical to a kitchen anywhere. No dishes, no books, no pens, no plates. Only a stove, a mattress, and a refrigerator. A couch cushion but no couch. A blanket but no sheets. No closets, just a change of clothes hanging from two nails in the front room. I returned to the glass sitting in the center of the first room. Finding as well that the panting had not subsided. That's the way, Chuck Yeager—you've got to beat it silly in order to last the night.

The glass was thick with grease marks and somehow the lip was stained yellow. Alone on the hardwoods. Against my better judgment, I picked it up, only to find something more: a string was tied around the base. From there it led through the hole in the ceiling where the light fixture should have been. I gave it a tug, braced myself for an anvil, yet nothing came of it but more slack.

Trying to get Chuck Yeager's exact routine down, as the clues so far logically instructed me to do, I walked with it back into the fourth room to the refrigerator, which I opened and grabbed the milk, pouring it into the glass. I grabbed a pack of cigarettes as well. I flopped on the mattress, rolled around a little, suppressed my vomit, and then went to the stove and lit a smoke off the front left burner.

Returning to the first room, there was nothing I could do but laugh in astonishment. A dozen yards of string had been laid out across the hardwoods exquisitely in the shape of a labyrinth. I dared not guess at how this occurred; instead, I chose to enter the path the string had opened up. Holding one end of that which walled me, I could only assume that leading the beginning of the string through these interiors would create a knot. And I hoped not a Minotaur. Not yet, I told myself.

One could imagine the delicacy and narrowness of such a labyrinth constructed of string across a hardwood floor—I had no choice but to tiptoe. Given the clarity of my perspective—I could obviously see the entirety of the paths—it did not take me long to reach the center, although there admittedly were several misjudgments and dead ends I had to backtrack out of.

There, waiting for me at the center, a bright copper penny. The answer to the riddle from The Fortress of Bethulia. A penny saved is a penny earned. Which we all know Benjamin Franklin never said. What he did say was this: A penny saved is two pence clear.

I picked it up, and I dropped it into the glass of milk, still in hand.

Immediately the liquid I took to be milk turned clear, fizzling, an unctuous smoke poured forth, rapidly filling the entirety of the once visible room.

My heartbeat quickening, I could no longer fathom how long I had been standing there. An ammonia-like burn disabled my sense of smell. For which I was grateful. The density of the fog-like substance impaired my sense of sound, refracting my orientation to the reverberation of walls and molecules. Noises reached me, unremarkable noises, noises which arrived as if they'd traveled across miles of unknown land, worn out and crumbling in my ear. A heat emanated from the glass, a pleasurable heat which slowly tingled through my veins up my arms, down my thighs and through my calves, up my neck, culminating in one large ridiculously pleasurable thought: *Fish fly through water; birds swim through sky.* At the time, it was gargantuan. Mind-blowing. Euphoric in its intellectual implications and clarity. Though now—I feel silly to repeat it.

I sensed motion in the pillows of smoke, shifts in the light, long lost reverberations of body and atmosphere. Densities seemed to gather and indiscernible forces began to interact with each other. Little plays undertaken by tiny outlines, tiny shapes, across tiny stages. I remember wishing them to be a little less abstract so I could make sense of it all. I do love making sense, finding meaning, even just a reason, a ration, a clear thought.

Finally, I acted on my long repressed urge to step. With one step, another. And again, each time a little smaller of a stride, careful not to collide with the wall. Dozens of steps later, I realized there was no way I could still be in the same room which I began. Unless I took account for fractal theory—how increasing detail through diminishing steps can cause a line to grow infinite not in length but in breadth. If each tiny step grew tinier at the proper rate, then not only might I be in the same room at Chuck Yeager's apartment, but I might be in the same room from my childhood home, or wherever else in my personal history these diminishingly detailed steps began. And along with this realization came a thousand tiny laughters.

Shapes swirling around me, the voices began to separate. And then they counted off: "One. Two. Three. Four! Five. Six. Seven! Eight. Nine! Ten. Eleven. Twelve. Thirteen! Four-teen."

And all at once: "Take a seat."

Out of the smoke appeared a chair.

As I went to sit, a breeze cleared the room, bright and I took a breath. Alone I stood. An ice cream cone in my hand. Melting down my forearm, as I stared though the window of Margie's Candies. At a family. A little boy held by my gaze, crying, scared by the intensity. His father getting up from the booth, soon out the door, shoving me down. The cracker crunch of the cone crushed by my weight against the sidewalk.

21: MOBY GRAPE

I saw his silhouette, standing there next to the trunk of the oak with his back to me. And I descended down the hill that I had leisurely just climbed hours before. I felt the bulge of the gun between my back and pants like an arrow pointing me in fate's direction. I listened to it, like a farmer listens to the leaves of his plants rustled by the wind. Only I listened in order to betray it. I was convinced that these plants should rot. Of course, I did not know what was right. The gun beneath my seat could have been planted by a friend, as caught up in this game as I was.

I know he could hear my footsteps, but Ruben Rorick did not turn around. As far as I could tell no one else was there.

"Revisiting the scene of the crime?" I said to break the silence.

"How's that, friend?" Ruben replied.

"It's a felony in every border state, not to mention marriage's affect on love—ain't a pretty sight."

"Of course, yes. Legal ease and an old joke. The shambles of marriage, our distrust. The crimes women play out against the sexualized male. Your humor precedes you."

As he said this he turned around: even in the dark I could see the sparkle of his green eyes next to his green bowtie. His black hair and black goatee. The green scarf in his pocket.

"I see you've thought these things through. Always helpful. To know what's coming, that is. It's easy to get scared of what's out there when we do not know what it is. Because of this we lose faith in whoever walks with us. They are the embodiment of all our insecurities."

"Me or my shadow? No doubt we are both in shambles."

"And there are so may illusions of oasis along the way. Have you ever stopped walking, Detective Yeager, and allowed yourself to live in paradise, what from the looks of it could only be paradise?"

"I've stopped many times, but never so lucky to find paradise. I stop when the Furies of hell are all that I can see."

"I'm sad to report that we speak of one and the same. Equally alluring in how it engulfs us. The paradises that I have been stalled by are cast by that same hellish light. Possibly you have just been more honest with what this world is made of."

"The way you speak, I'm not surprised the lovebirds asked you to marry them."

"Don't disgrace them with this smart-ass lovebirds shit. They were not in love—you're smarter than that, Detective Yeager."

"I'm dumb enough to come here in search of Levi only to find you. How about you give me a little hint."

"Don't you see the suffering in your childhood friend's eyes. The anguish across his face."

"All I see is a bunch of decadent winemakers playing footsie on a stage with their favorite bottles. It's all just show—some game to play so there's a reason to believe that they are chosen by paradise."

"It's far more severe than all that teenage angst, Detective Yeager. It's a question of reality—what is at the bottom of it? Who hides behind the curtain of illusions— these heavens and hells we have each succumbed to."

"You seem to have it all figured out. Why don't you just tell me. We can rope up the bad guys, get back to those fancy wines and find paradise with those sexy broads."

"I like you—I see why a personality like yours was good for our friend Levi to be around. But I don't think you really believe it all to be so simple. Not you. What happens, Detective Yeager, when you pull the curtain, and behind it you find a mirror? Well, I'll tell you. Do you know the story of San Juan Soldado? I see you do not. Listen to his story, it is very close to yours."

I stared at the oak tree and listened.

"Juan Castillo Morales was a soldier in the Mexican Army. In the year 1938 he was convicted for the rape and murder of a young girl in Tijuana. Not often practiced these days, though I enjoy the pageantry of it, is *La Le Fuga*—the Law of Flight. Juan Soldado was sentenced to face a military firing squad, but he was allowed to run. One thousand yards was his magic distance—if he could reach it without being killed, then he was a free man."

"Did he make it?"

"Many believers claim that Juan Soldado was an innocent man. That he had upset a general by falling in love with his daughter, a girl who the General himself enjoyed the pleasures of, and had no trouble killing her, and then accusing Juan of the deed."

"Did he get shot?"

"We pray to Juan Soldado," and he made a sign of the cross and kneeled on one knee beneath the hanging body.

"You're lost in head games, man. Cut this crap and tell

me something that makes sense to what's going on to-night, to the gunshots, to the beatings I've took, and the maze I've followed to get here."

"Look up, Mister Yeager. Just look up."

Draped across several limbs of the oak tree was her body. As if the red dress was melting from her skin, blood dripped behind Ruben's head. Was it Ursulines? The blond hair fell but the face had been cut away leaving only the skull. In that skull I saw Ciudad Mujer.

"Get her down!" I screamed. "Why have you been standing here beneath this?"

"It is too late. Her father saw to it long ago."

"Bullshit." I made a move towards the tree and Ruben stood up and shoved me back.

"Don't waste your time. We've got to find Levi before they get to him."

"They? Who the fuck are they?"

"Either bury this body, or help me stop others from dying. Your choice."

"Who is that? Hanging—who is this girl?"

"Pray with me! Do it now! Pray to Ciudad Mujer that you have light feet and find your thousand meters dis-tance. Like the daughter in the tree, you have both been dead ten years time."

As he said this, a four-wheeler was pulling up. Ruben jumped on, and they began to pull away. I felt the gun pulsing and almost shot him in the back as he pulled away, but I stopped myself. Was this what they wanted? Why did Levi tell me to meet him here? I had no one to trust, and I cast my anxieties out across everyone there tonight and the memories which led me here. I did not know how this would end, but embittered I would see it through. I took one last look at the blonde-haired skeleton in the red dress dripping with blood, then I ran towards the four-wheeler. Ruben yelled to the driver and it slowed down enough for me to hop on. Fuck it, I thought. Fuck it all. I'm just along for the ride.

22: MOBY GRAPE

When we got to the top of the hill, I could see that we were moving away from the party. I heard the joyous music and saw bodies dancing in the twilight. Everyone had forgotten about the gunshots and carried on with the night's celebration. They had to be wondering where the bride and groom had gone, right? Or did they know, too?

There I was in the darkness beyond, racing through the great expanse of vines and road, trees and boars with the knowledge of her death, Ursulines' and Penelope's. We pulled up to a double-wide home, tucked into the land at the far reaches of the vineyard. There were two other four-wheelers, a large van, and parked beside it was the Mariachis' Prius. Here's where the real party was taking place.

We hopped off and entered as if they were expecting us. There standing around the island in the kitchen was Levi, Gil, Guy Toussaint, and Miriam. Just like that, the worlds of my past collided. And they all turned to look at me. I hoped to god that they would not smile.

Levi spoke first. "Charlie, it has been too long, my friend. Wish I had the chance to give you more details earlier. How are you?"

"No one has called me Charlie since Ursulines, Levi."

"And Penelope."

"Sisters?"

"Yes, you flirted and fell in love with sisters. You weren't the first, of course. I mean their charms were wild, weren't they? I admit, it's hard to speak of Ursulines like this so soon, though. I apologize for the tears."

"Penelope is sad she could not make it tonight," Gil began. "She would have enjoyed your presence here. Did you know that Penelope and I, we were married. Madly in love, and married."

"She never said anything about you, Gil."

"When she bought your hookers, she paid with the same money you used to treat yourself to your days in Paris. You had fun, didn't you? Your sins were worth it, weren't they?"

"Gil, tell me you've been up to something more over the past ten years to distract you from that mishap."

"What you call a mishap, Penelope treasured. You ruined her, Charlie. You ruined her and she is gone now. Another dead woman in this game."

"I didn't kill her."

"Neither did I."

"How could you kill Ursulines, Levi? Does Miriam know she's next?"

"Enough discussion of my daughters!" Guy Toussaint could not keep quiet.

"Of course she knows. The ritual has already begun," Levi confessed. "This is an honor to her family. They nor their grandchildren's grandchildren will ever need to work again."

"Join us, Charlie, you will be amused," Gil said. "But in your line of work, a blood sacrifice probably only goes so far. Let me tell you, this tradition began with the pagan gods of Rome. All the marching, all the war destroyed many of the Roman's lands. To reinvigorate them, the people who once lived on those lands and who had now been conquered and enslaved, they were made to work the lands over. When they were ready for grapes, each year a sacrifice. You must know what it means to be on the right side of power, Chuck, you must one day understand how magnanimous it feels!"

I looked into Miriam's eyes and I saw the same look I saw every day in Wicker Park. The look in the faces of the poorer folks who each month were moving out unable to afford their rents, losing jobs, a slow alienation creping through their hearts—yes I knew this look. But then, it turned strange. Miriam smiled at me. She rubbed her hands up and down her body gripping her own flesh, high on her own physicality. She smiled and her eyes rolled in the back of her head. Why must those on bottom relish the predator's entry into the camp. Why must fear make our bodies heightened in a singular and engrossing way. A terror took over my every nerve and I knew I would never recover.

Gil and Levi lifted Miriam and she did not fight. They laid her body across the dining room table. She did not whimper. There were buckets, I now saw, beneath the table, a gentle slant towards the center.

I envisioned myself wandering the streets of Chicago looking again and again into the eyes of Hispanic women. I would always be lost in this moment, unable to reconcile how power plays out across our bodies.

"Three wines tonight?" is all I could ask.

Levi's earnest tone sent a shiver through my bones, "Just two." I told myself he did not believe what he was doing was wrong.

Gil continued, maddened to have Penelope's spirit in the air, "You never drank La Sangre de Penelope? I will share a bottle with you as a token of thanks—it will be in your room at El Prado when you return."

Guy spoke again, "Let me tell you a story, Yeager, as we prepare our sacrifice to these lands. I met Levi not long after you last saw him, if I understand your story correctly. And I do, don't I? He was wandering along the hills around my vineyard. He told me his troubles, that he had lost his friend. I offered him my assistance. If he would help me bury a few vines, I would help him find you."

"Don't listen to this, Charles," Ruben interjected. "Don't listen to his story. He is spilling tales to justify his revenge."

"Levi, did you not join my vineyard? Shortly after parting ways?"

"Yes, and I've done more than bury your vines, Toussaint."

"I miss the old name you gave me, in our high life, when your smile was so much larger. Call me San Sante."

Gil lifted his glass, "To San Sante. The Saint of Saints!"

Levi lifted his as well, "San Sante."

"Ursulines is dead," I yelled. "Levi, how could you let this happen."

"Did you know that Mister Seeds was there that night we first met. Do you know that it was him who filled me with an understanding of your despicable qualities. I understood that next day that I would kill you, that you would die. And it was ten years ago that Levi, Gil, and I devised this, everything you have experienced. All that you have been a part of. All that has led you here. Every minute orchestrated ten years ago. This is enough from me, Chuck. It is time for you to make your passage. Ten years is what I gave you. Your freedom awaits you if you can make it till sunrise tomorrow. I love a dramatic ending. So run you filthy louse. Your body will feel like bread breaking beneath my foot."

And I shot him. In the neck. A clean passage and out through the wall. His glass fell from his hands but his eyes did not change their expression.

Miriam screamed and fought the ropes around her wrists.

But then he tried to speak. And his blood began to spurt. A gurgle of malice.

"How did he get that gun?" shouted Gil. "Who the fuck gave him a gun?"

I knew it was the gun used to shoot Ursulines. I knew this in the same way I know things in my dreams. I was certain. Only later to think enough about it and remember that I had the gun when Ursulines was shot; and I was sitting at the table with the Mariachis. So it was not possible. But I knew it then and I knew San Sante, Saint of Saints had known this, known I would kill him with it as well. And that throughout the rolling hills of these vines, people would be looking for the blood to bubble up from the sand, and pronounce his glory and begin the telling of his story that would carry him to the mouth, minds, and hearts of our future smugglers, thieves, traffickers, bandits, and yes, winemakers. I knew the Mariachis had their ears to the ground, listening for their next narcocorrido.

It was then that I heard him laughing and saw his body rise. It was then that I saw Levi's face, every evil the world had ever known tightening across his face, intent on hating me, intent on my suffering. I was further into a world that I had always feared would swallow me, that I always feared would overtake me, that I always knew a mistake on my part, a mistake that crossed the wrong type of power would haunt me. And I didn't know what to think about this Toussaint rising to his feet, bullet hole through his neck. And this room of his worshippers. Above Miriam's screams, Gil's cackle rose alongside Monsieur Toussaint.

Sunrise it would be then. I did not want to but I ran. Tripping and stumbling, the gun in my right hand. There was no way of telling what direction was safety. Like Juan the Soldado, I remember myself thinking, through the unfathomable darkness my feet pounding the sand like my heartbeat through these hills.

But Levi caught me.

"Chuck, stop!" He tackled me in a full run. I heard the rip of my shirt, felt the rock against my cheek, but the gun did not move from my waistline. I stood up just as quickly and braced myself.

Levi was slower to get up. He grimaced before he looked at me, and I could tell his arm or ribs were broken.

"Chuck, son-of-a-bitch, this is not how I wanted it to end."

"What's all this talk about the past, Levi. I didn't come here to dig up any graves."

"Once turned over, a hundred times sifted through, Chuck. You don't understand. All this, the land, the grapes, all of this is ancient Chumash Indian land. It is sacred and there are customs that we have to follow, rites, Chuck, that have to be executed, or it would lose all that we have grown accustomed to it giving us."

"There is no soil here. You squeeze soul from sand you worthless devil-worshipper. For wine. That's it."

"Wine is only one part of this. Do you remember in Biarritz, that dream. The lobsters, do you remember or has your degenerate ways erased it all from your head."

"I've had time to recoup a few, Levi. I remember."

"Have you ever been dipped in boiling water? Felt your eyeballs begin to explode? Chuck! Have you? This is for the immigrants. The Mexicans—they need out of the water, Chuck. I am helping their people escape into this country."

"Levi, I need a car. I need to get out of here."

"You cannot escape. I could not escape, good friend, and I tried. Gil could not escape. Though I do not think he wanted to after Penelope died. You destroyed him, Chuck. And you about destroyed me, but San Sante was there. Gil had known him longer than I. The business worlds have a way of accumulating the worst at the top, and Penelope was Gil's prize for all he sacrificed."

"What has Ursulines been doing all these years? Living in the background? Married to you but at bay?"

"Don't worry about her! I have given so many shelter. So many good Mexican families. They are gathering power, security. Freedom, Chuck—you would escape, too. "

I was braced for him to hit me, eager to turn and run.

"She's dead, Levi. Her face cut away."

"You really don't have a clue. The power of these lands, I could tell you the stories, at first, of the goats, how we would hear them neighing in the night hours after feasting on their flesh, of the owls, the lamb, the pumas when it was too late to know they'd return. Ursulines is not gone. The others, and it is true, I have married dozens of others, they all return, these lands, Ciudad Mujer, Reina de Arena, has blessed us with this land and the way to access its magic."

He was crazed, drunk, and wounded. I eased my anger and played coy.

"Show it to me, Levi. I have not gotten a proper tour."

"If you can be forgiven by these lands, Chuck, then you will be forgiven by me. By Gil and Toussaint."

"Forgiveness sounds pretty good right now. If I would have known they were born again, I would not have interfered."

I did not know what to do, but I knew in a car, there would be options that my feet could not offer.

"All of them, before their lives of carrying drugs, immigrants, all these things the people of Mexico are forced to do—if they pass through these lands, then no harm will find them. No machete, no border guards, no dogs or vultures."

"I think I understand, Levi." This was madness. "And Toussaint found all this."

"He did. He brought me here. The wines are testament to the power of these hills. The power that coursed through the Chumash Indians' veins. We'll take my car. I'll show you. It's at the bottom of this hill."

"What ever came of that tribe?"

"They worked the land and then the lands worked them. They're scattered beneath our feet, Chuck. It all goes to feed the lands."

He struggled to walk, and spit blood off to the side before climbing into the front seat of the Ford Taurus. The sands rattled, absorbing the blood. A hiss.

"Are there snakes out at night, Levi?"

"Ruben has taken care of all the snakes, Chuck."

I got in on the other side. And there, two idols on his dashboard, a mustached young man with black hair wearing a white shirt. A noose around his neck. He was wearing a white cowboy hat. Juan de Soldado. Next to him, the same doll which passed between Penelope and Guy some ten years ago in Paris. The doll which I had forgotten but which I would never forget. Pins stuck into it. Tears, marks, a gun drawn recently on the back. Was this Vodou? I grabbed it from its perch on the dashboard, ignoring the other, and felt the immediate squeeze which had taken its toll on my last ten years now potently around my spirit. I dropped it, looked at Levi, his eyes alight with another presence, and I laughed. As one will do when one's curse runs the irrational rivers of men intent on power, a power intent on the lives of men. The powers of devils, demons, unknown uprisings in the minds and actions of men. I grabbed this doll again, though lightly, and I shot Levi Seeds, my childhood friend, shoved him out the car and heard a monstrous devouring. Shaking the hole where my soul once had been. I drove into the night, unsure of how to dispose of this hex in my hands. His blood, as sure as the others, spilling into the Chumash sands.

There was no way of knowing if Levi wanted me dead or if he was trying to help me. But I escaped. Never knowing into what I was escaping.

KEVIN KILROY is a writer and a teacher living in Kansas City. His stories have been published by Akashic, Dispatches, Fact-Simile, Masque & Spectacle, Hot Whiskey, Poets & Artists, Sherlock Holmes & Philosophy and others. Kevin co-founded Black Lodge Press. He is the author of *The Escapees* and *Dead Ends* (Spuyten Duyvil).